T

Gold in California! Its glittering yellow promise of instant wealth brings men by the thousands to pan the streams and dig the hills in an often vain search for the precious metal. But Mitchell Randolph, and a few others like him, find easier, surer ways to make their fortunes. Gifted with a handsome face, a quick eye for profit, and a friendly yet unmistakably commanding air, he relies on charm, foresight, and imagination in founding an express service that soon becomes one of the most successful enterprises in the West. But Randolph's meteoric rise to wealth will be a hollow victory if he cannot win the hand of the tempestuous woman who steals his heart.

TODHUNTER BALLARD

Todhunter Ballard is renowned for his bold sagas of the pioneers who tamed the West. The author of more than fifty novels, he is the winner of the Spur Award for Best Historical Novel.

TODHUNTER BALLARD

The Californian

LEISURE BOOKS NEW YORK CITY

A LEISURE BOOK®

September 1995

Published by special arrangement with Golden West Literary
Agency

Dorchester Publishing Co., Inc.
276 Fifth Avenue
New York, NY 10001

Printed in the United States of America.

The Californian

BOOK ONE

CHAPTER ONE

The first night I spent in California was bound to stay vivid in my memory. My father died at 6:30 that evening. That was the beginning of it.

The death had a special awe. I was thirteen years old, more than half a continent away from the latest place I had called home, and my father had been my last living relative.

I was not crying. Emotion and thought were both at a standstill against a wall. I sat near his head, on the bench the cook had dragged up, with the cook beside me, looking at the still body in the bunk.

The cook had been a frightening figure to me throughout the ninety-seven days it had taken the *Anne Marie* to beat her way up the rocky Pacific Coast from Panama, a big man in a limp shirt that always hung open, that was too small to button over his blue-black chest and stomach, a man with big features made ugly by a knife scar that puckered his left cheek from mouth to eyebrow. Adding to the fierce impression, the crew had said he was a runaway slave.

But it had been the cook who had come down into the hold where the temporary bunks had been built, after the other passengers had gone, and found me and my father's body. He had gone for candles, lighted them and anchored them in their own wax at the head of the bunk, had pulled up the bench and pressed me down on it. It had been his own idea. No one had ordered him. No one else had given us any attention. In the confusion of leaving the barque I doubt that anyone else had realized this latest loss among their number.

The light was dim, thrown from a single hanging oil lamp and from the candles. There was a hollow quiet down there. From abovedecks came the filtered shouts of the crew, the rattle of the lines as they lowered the topgallants and chewed up the canvas, the grating rumble of the anchor chain, emphasizing that the voyage was over.

I heard the shore boats bump against the wooden hull, heard the cries of the boatmen and the urgent hails of men in a hurry to leave the ship. Up there it was a celebration. Here ended the long, trouble-plagued trek, the final hard voyage of these men come to hunt for gold. This was the day we had all looked toward through the months since we had left our homes. It was the culmination of my father's dream, and he had not lived to be a part of it.

Neither was I a part of it. I had no thoughts about getting ashore. I was only aware of the rigid face of the man on the bunk. He was already a stranger. The face was losing color and cohesion. The reddish yellow mustache and sideburns were too big, no longer an integral part of the sinking features.

I suppose I should have been forewarned of these changes. I had watched my mother die only six weeks before in Acapulco. But I had never felt the close tie to her that I had to this man with whom I had shared my dreams.

Not until much later did I understand that my father had never wholly grown up. His reactions were nearer to mine than to a man of mature age. He had been a buoyant spirit and the two of us had lived not in drab present realities but in expected future glories.

My mother had been the practical head, concerned with the need for food, shelter, clothing, and I had been impatient with what I thought of as her obstructionist attitude. She had been against our move from Philadelphia where her roots were. She had hated the shacky river town of St. Louis where my father had insisted he could make our fortune. She had been appalled by the thought of the long, dangerous trip to the golden promise of the California mines. But she was a woman of her generation and I doubt it ever occurred to her to refuse to go with him, no matter how wild his flights of fancy.

She was dead, buried in the arid, unkind soil of the Mexican coast, a long way from her green and gentle home. And now my father was struck down by the same fever. It had also taken twenty-one other passengers on the three-month voyage.

I did not see it then but there was irony in Duncan Stuart being laid out on a wooden bunk in the stinking hold of a wind-battered hulk by the ship's cook, to whom he had not spoken a word. For

4

my father had been a snob. No matter how consistent his material failures, his sense of superiority, brought to these shores from Scotland, never faltered. He found no one in the new world who measured up to his ancestral line. His father and his grandfather before him had been officers in the King's Army and though he never spoke of it I have come to think that at least some of my father's restlessness could be blamed on the partly withered arm that kept him out of uniform.

It did not keep him out of trouble. Through that osmosis by which children learn what they are not supposed to know I had become aware that when he was a young man he had got himself into some scrape that had spurred his family to settle a quarterly payment on him with the proviso that he emigrate to America and not return to Scotland. Whatever shame was attached lay lightly on his conscience.

I recall these payments still coming when I was very young and the anxiety with which my mother waited for them. They stopped before I was seven. My mother, weeping, told me my grandfather had died and there would be no more money. Since she had never met any of the overseas family I do not believe she wept for the departed parent.

It was at that time that we moved west to St. Louis, my father excited over the prospect of becoming a buying agent for a Philadelphia fur dealer. But the project was not a success. He was rescued from that unpleasant fact by the discovery of gold on the Pacific Coast which he took as the opening of a doorway on a radiant opportunity.

His first immediate enthusiasm was to make the trip overland, but for the first time I had known her to do such a thing, my mother revolted. Another timely family death, her father's, left her a small inheritance. She offered it to finance our passage, down the river to New Orleans, by boat to Chagres, by mule across the festering Isthmus of Panama, by coastal ship to San Francisco.

Now it was all over and I was alone.

"You better cry, boy."

The cook's voice made me jump. I had forgotten him. The voice was soft, the words a gentle advice, making me look at him. His eyes were on me, big, brown, concerned. The idea that anyone except my father would show me concern worked through my numbness. Suddenly he did not seem as huge, as ugly.

"I don't want to," I said. "He wouldn't want me to cry."

Actually I didn't care what my father would want me to do. He was gone. He wasn't there. At the moment I cared more what this man thought of me.

The cook shook his long head. "Time come, boy, every man's got to cry. It's in you, hurting. It's got to come out."

I didn't understand him but I was very glad of the warm strength of his arm as he put it around me. I laid my head against his shoulder and for the first time since my father had taken sick I had a feeling of being secure.

The death watch was then a part of American life. I endured it without questioning. We continued to sit and gradually the sounds above us grew less, then quit. The ship's planking creaked, she swayed slowly, riding at anchor, rats began a scrabbling movement, but there was no sign of another human being aboard for a long while. Then a noise from the hatch took my attention up. I saw the captain coming down the ladder.

This was another fearsome personage to me, suspicious because he looked so unlike a ship's master. His dress was a rusty, dark suit so salt stained and dirt filled that its original color was lost. On his round head he always wore a hard bowler hat weathered to a mold green. Contrasted to the neat, gold-trimmed blue uniforms worn by the officers of the river packet that had brought us down from St. Louis to the gulf this captain was as seedy as a tramp. He had been remote, keeping himself apart on the afterdeck close to the wheelhouse and the helmsman, issuing orders that I never heard, consulting the compass, retiring in solitude to his cabin aft.

I had been close to him only once. When we first left Panama I had ventured to the wheelhouse pulled by a curiosity about navigation. The mate, standing with the captain, had promptly ordered me forward. The captain had not spoken.

The mate, Mr. Lord, was more ominous than the captain. I had watched him order and witness the whipping of a sailor until my mother had snatched me back into the hold, but I had associated the captain with the whipping too, for there were many stories of the brutality of officers at sea.

Now I was hypnotized by the short, square body coming down the ladder, the shiny trousers stretched taut over the big rump. He got his feet on the hold floor and came toward us, looking not at me but at the disturbed flames of the candles. He stopped at the foot of the bunk, took off his hat, bowed his head and his thick lips moved in silence. It surprised me that he should show this respect for death. Then he put the hat back on. His first words were:

"Better stitch him up and get him over the side."

I could not stop my sharp cry. Most of the fever victims had been buried at sea of necessity, but here we were in the harbor, the shore of the cove, the small wharf only a short row away.

"Please don't. I want to bury him in the ground."

The captain and the cook looked at each other. The quiet dragged out. Then the captain sighed.

"What do you think, Joe?" It was the first time I had heard the Negro called anything but cook.

The arm tightened around me, the brown eyes looked down at mine.

"Well, I guess I could. It ain't too much to do for the boy, seeing as he's all alone in the world."

"Oh, that's right." The captain had apparently forgotten. "He lost his mother too, didn't he?" He took off his hat again and looked into it. It was almost as if he got all of his ideas out of the hat. "Where are your relatives, boy?"

The lump rose in my throat spontaneously then. All I could manage to say was:

"Haven't got any."

He looked ludicrously disconcerted, his eyebrows shooting up like a clown's.

"Everybody's got people somewhere. Even I have."

I shook my head. "Not me. He was the last one."

There was another silent conference between the men, then the captain said uncertainly:

"Well . . . what do you figure to do?"

I hadn't thought that far and it must have showed in my face.

"He could be cabin boy," the cook said. "Save me having to cart your meals back to the stern."

"You're a lazy nigger." The captain spoke without rancor, still watching me.

"Yes, sir, I sure is. Almost as lazy as you is, and that's powerful lazy. You're about the laziest man I ever did see."

The cook was laughing, his red inner lips framing a set of strong white teeth. All at once he stopped, staring at my father's body in horror, as if by laughing in the presence of death he had committed an extreme sacrilege.

The mate arrived just then, came sliding down the ladder the way sailors do, as if it were a rope, a spidery, rat-faced man, small and quick. He stopped at the bottom and flicked a glance from my father to the captain.

"Another goner?"

He did not wait to be answered, but stepped into the cone of the hanging lamp, swept a hand under his coattail and brought up a pistol.

"Captain, darling, I'll trouble you for the key to your chest."

He was Irish and used an accent and idiom that sounded funny to me, and he was grinning. But it was not a generous grin. I realized with a shock that the man was making a deadly serious threat and was highly pleased with himself. He had caught Captain Barker completely off guard.

Barker, I knew, carried a pepperbox in his coat pocket. All of the officers had gone armed throughout the voyage. But he made no move to pull it. He was afraid the mate would shoot. I could sense it in the way he moved his head. He did try to bluster.

"Mr. Lord," he said pompously, "you are talking mutiny."

"Ah," said Mr. Lord, "would you call it that, Abner? Me and the crew now, we call it a fair division. You keep the ship, we'll take the chest. The key now, or I'll put a bit of lead in your liver."

Barker's eyes bulged and his voice was hoarse. "Now . . . now . . . let's talk this over . . . go to my cabin and talk over a ration of rum."

The mate's move was faster than anything I had ever seen. One instant he was standing five feet away, the next he was beside the captain, swinging the gun, bringing the barrel down to crush in the crown of the bowler. Barker fell like a tree, stiff. He fell forward, his head barely missing the bench. He did not move.

I was too stunned to make a sound but a growl like a threatening animal rolled in the cook's throat. The mate heard it and jumped back two steps like a dancing master, pointing the gun at us, especially the cook.

"Keep out of this, nigger."

"I don't got no part of it, sir."

Mr. Lord considered him, judging the danger he posed. He did not relax a muscle.

"Get that pepperbox from Barker and toss it here. Being careful how you move."

The cook rose with slow, deliberate gestures, knelt beside the captain, brought the gun from the pocket with his thumb and forefinger and slid it across the floor. Lord scooped it up and dropped it into his own pocket.

"Now the keys."

The cook searched for them, finally dug them out and tossed them so that the mate caught them in the air. Lord backed until he

8

felt the ladder with his heel, then he leveled the gun so that I thought he was surely going to shoot us both.

"You two," he said, "lie down on the floor, on your faces until I get up top. And if you stick your heads abovedecks in the next hour I'll blow them off."

We heard him go, leaping up the steep steps, and did not move until we heard his footfall fade toward the aft cabin. Then we sat up. The cook pushed his breath out in a gust.

"Land o' Goshen." He crawled over to Barker.

With death so much a presence in the hold I expected that the captain was murdered. I whispered:

"Did he kill him?"

"No, boy, no." Joe's tone was reassuring. "Can't kill the captain just hitting him on the head." He tugged the bowler off, poking at the broken crown. "But he won't like this, no, sir. He's right taken with this old hat."

The hat and the thick mat of hair had cushioned the blow. The skin was not broken, still, the captain was out cold. The big cook looked from Barker up at the open hatch, and from his face I thought he meant to climb the ladder. It gave me another fright.

"Don't." I hissed it. "He'll shoot you."

Joe straightened up and stood working his huge hands, clenching and unclenching them, then at last he spread them open and dropped his shoulders.

"Got no gun. Not so much as a knife. And there's the whole bunch of them. I'd ought to had better sense than to believe I'd get to share in that money."

"The captain's money? . . . Oh, you mean collect your pay."

"Lots more than pay." A wide grin spread up the puckered cheek. "There's all he got for selling the cargo of coal to Mr. Nelson in Panama, and for renting him the ship. Lot of money. Took me half a dozen trips to tote it from the rowboat to captain's cabin."

"But . . . but . . . doesn't it belong to the ship company? Didn't the coal belong to them?"

"Long time back I guess it did. It was going to New Bedford, before the captain decided we'd come to California instead."

I didn't know where New Bedford was, except that it was on the East Coast, and what I thought Joe was saying left me gasping.

"You mean Captain Barker stole this ship?"

"Well, it wasn't just him. He and Mr. Lord and the crew all talked it over when we heard about the gold in California being free to pick up. Everybody agreed we ought to borrow the ship for a year or so and come get some. So we turned the *Anne Marie* about and headed down around the Horn." His eyes lost their focus as he remembered. "That trip was real bad. I never thought the wind could blow like that, near took the tops out, it did."

I thought he must be yarning me and tried to catch him.

"But with a stolen ship how did you dare put in at Panama?"

"Had to. We needed water and grub bad."

A sudden burst of noise above drew my attention, the scamper of feet, shouts, then the rattle of a boat being lowered.

"There they go," Joe said. "There they go with all that money that was supposed to be divided up."

CHAPTER TWO

San Francisco's origin goes back to 1776, the same year in which, on the East Coast, the Declaration of Independence was being drawn. At that time the Franciscan padres built a mission about two miles south and west of Yerba Buena cove, and later in the same year the Mexicans established their Presidio above the Golden Gate. But it was not until 1835 that the first dwelling was put up, by Captain William Richardson, an American appointed harbor master by the Mexican Government.

It could hardly be called a house. It consisted of four redwood stakes driven into the ground, roofed with a tattered piece of foresail. Richardson opened a kind of store, very limited in stock, to supplement his salary which was small when it was paid at all. He gave the settlement the name Yerba Buena, after the fragrant mint from which he brewed his tea.

It was after the Americans had made their 1847 occupation that the community became San Francisco, and although it stood on the shore of one of the greatest of the world's harbors it had never amounted to much. An occasional whaling vessel used it as a port of call, but Spanish and later Mexican restrictions on trade kept its growth down. Even the Hudson's Bay Company, which had the faculty of taking a profit anywhere, had given up after a five-year struggle to make a post there pay.

Before the gold discovery the town had swelled to some seven hundred inhabitants, including Indians, Negroes, Sandwich Islanders, but on the morning we buried my father it had shrunk again to near a hundred. Almost everyone along the Coast had taken off to the mines.

I had not known that it had rained sometime during the long night but the surface soil of Yerba Buena Island was moist. Yet the dampness had not penetrated into the ground where Joe dug the grave, leaving it hard, caked, gritty. We put up a board we'd brought from the *Anne Marie*, then the cook rowed us back to the ship and we held what the captain called a council of war.

Captain Abner Barker was given to bombastic phrases and to posturing. He stood on the deck before the empty wheelhouse spread-legged, square, facing the giant cook and me as if he were facing down the whole crew. He had read a service over my father before we had lowered the body into the rowboat. Now he made a second ceremony, a pious thanksgiving for the successful completion of the voyage of the *Anne Marie*. Finished with that, he continued to stand, bowler in hand, and stared glumly down at the hole broken in its crown by the mate's gun.

In the hours since he had recovered consciousness I had made the discovery that he regretted the hat more than he did the chest. The money, come by so effortlessly, had never been a reality to him. The hat was. I don't know how long he had had it but it must have been a long spell, and in this distant place there was no assurance that he could get another like it.

"Damn Mr. Lord," he muttered, not speaking to either of us. "I'll keel-haul the bastard when I find him."

My awakening insight warned me that he would not keel-haul the mate or anyone else, that the captain was not a forceful man, and it occurred to me that the idea of pirating the *Anne Marie* had probably originated with Mr. Lord, not with Abner Barker.

Further, it was hard to picture the captain as a thief. My mother had brought me up on the premise that a thief was a very low form of life. A thief was almost as bad as a man who denied God. But both demanded a more positive attitude than I had seen here thus far.

I left him to his muttering and looked forward along the cluttered deck. The barque had been a trim ship flying up the coast. Now her three masts stood bare, the sails carelessly reefed, the gear flung in disorder about the deck by the crew in its haste to get away. She was square-rigged, too wide of beam to be classed with the clippers, yet with all her canvas set, her topgallants filled, she had been a remarkable sailor.

I had hated her throughout the trip for the hours I had been forced to spend in the foul-smelling hold and for the restrictions she put on a boy's activity, but she did not deserve to be seen as she was now, a lady shabbily abandoned by those she had served well.

She was not alone in her desolation. Over a hundred and twenty other vessels swung lifeless at their moorings, the morning tide having its way with them. They too had been deserted by their crews who had jumped ship to race for the gold fields. Many of them would never sail again, would rot in their chains and sink into the harbor mud.

Our captain, having paid his thanksgiving homage to the *Anne Marie*, issued his token sentence on his scurrilous mate, considered his duty done and now more eagerly joined his thoughts with those of captains and crews and passengers who had gone before him.

"The thing is," he said, clapping the bowler back on his head, "we've got to get up to them golden fields before the scum picks them clean. Question we got to figure out is how."

Joe, sitting against the wheelhouse, elbows on knees, his face buried in his hands, spoke without looking up.

"Which way is they, Captain?"

"Inland," was Barker's astute decision. "What we do first is load the dinghy with grub from the galley, then we'll go ashore and find out just where. You get the stuff in the boat. I've got to go below and fill out the log."

"Why?" said Joe. "Who's ever going to read it now?"

The captain did not deign to answer, but turned down the companionway to his cabin. The cook did not move.

"Seems like anyone mentions work, the captain's got to be somewheres else, fast."

"I'll help," I said. "I'm hungry."

"Yeah, I guess we all is that."

We ate first, then loaded the boat, principally with salt horse as sailors called the brined meat, with a keg of ship's biscuits and what was left of the last bag of coffee beans. Then Joe rowed us ashore.

We landed about where Clay and Sansome Streets now intersect, tying up to a clipper ship, the *Niantic*, that was already sunk in the shallow water of the cove. There was a sign on it reading NIANTIC HOTEL but there was no one on it to question.

The captain had brought what of his armaments the crew had not found, two pistols and a musket. He shoved one pistol under the front of his belt and left the other guns with Joe to guard the dinghy.

"Don't let anyone come near this boat," he warned. "There's probably thieves about."

All of us were thinking of Mr. Lord and the crew who might still be in the area and whom I for one did not want to meet again.

Barker and I followed a mud road along the edge of the bay. Later, when the tidal flats were filled in, it would become Montgomery Street. It took us into a plaza already renamed Portsmouth Square, after the sailors from the war sloop *Portsmouth* who had first raised the American flag over the borning city.

Here the tents and slab shanties and adobe huts that had rimmed the horseshoe cove were giving way to more substantial structures. Not any of them compared with the buildings I knew from Philadelphia or St. Louis or New Orleans, but they made up the emerging business center.

The square was still a deep quagmire from the rain and had to be waded except where makeshift sidewalks had been built, some of planks, some of abandoned goods. Most of the buildings were closed, their proprietors apparently having joined the general exodus. We did find one functioning establishment with a hand lettered sign over its door.

SELIGMAN

It stood just beyond the Tehama House which appeared to be one of the leading hotels, and although we had seen few people until now there was a group of men loosely gathered before the hotel porch, and several women who to my inexperienced eye still seemed overdressed for midday.

The captain stopped among the men, pulled off his hat and peered into it for a minute as though trying to recall why he was there. Then he asked them generally:

"What's the easiest way to the mines?"

They looked him over without interest, then a tall man in a slouch hat, hickory shirt, and scuffed half boots laughed.

"Just off a ship?"

Barker admitted it.

"There's two ways for you, mister. Shanks' mare or by boat. If you've got a boat."

"I've got a boat."

"Bully for you. Cross the bay and you can go up either the Sacramento or the San Joaquin River. The Sacramento will take you to Sutter's Fort. From there you walk to the Northern Mines. The San Joaquin goes up to Webber's Landing and you hike to the Southern Mines. You wouldn't have a drink on you?"

The captain shook his head and did not add that he had a jug of rum in the dinghy. The man wiped at his mustache with the back of his hand.

"Shame. They're getting thirty to forty dollars for a quart, and a man can't hardly stay alive in this rotten climate without a dram now and then."

From his breath he'd already had more than a dram, but finding Barker was not to be tapped he lost interest in us.

We moved on. Around the entrance of the Seligman Store was an untidy pile of picks, shovels, and what I was soon to learn were gold pans. The picks were plainly marked, forty-five dollars each. The captain bent down to make sure, and sighed.

"Beats all, boy, the prices they get in this town. If I'd known about it I'd have loaded the *Anne Marie* with hardware instead of coal."

Apparently his mind had already made a change in recent history, to a memory of a voyage carried through on an original course with a cargo that belonged to him. It was a new phenomenon to me, and I followed him into the store frowning over the puzzle.

The building was of brick, the first I had seen in San Francisco, but the room was not large. In it were two men, one I judged to be in his early twenties, the other thinner, younger, eighteen or nineteen. That one sat at one of the several counters, drawing a picture on a sheet of white paper. He did not even look up when we came in but the other hurried forward. He had a high forehead with arched brows and a face beginning to be fleshy.

"Yes, sir, what can I sell you?" The voice was possessive, guttural with what I recognized from my St. Louis days was a German background.

"About them picks," the captain said, jerking a thumb toward the pile. "Don't want to sell them bad, do you?"

The young man smiled and closed thick fingers in the sleeve of the captain's coat.

"Good picks, sir. Fine picks. The best picks money can buy, every point tempered so the rocks can't wear them down. They outlast any other pick made. Perfectly balanced. You swing one of these all day, it don't make you tired. Listen, sir, a secret. These are lucky picks, a certain property in them, it actually smells out the gold. Which one, sir? . . . Here, make your choice."

He was tugging on the sleeve, pulling Barker back toward the pile. The captain aimed a small, disparaging kick at them.

"Give you ten dollars, and that's too much."

I was horrified. The captain had no money at all. Every cent he had possessed had been in the stolen chest, and of course the cook had none. The money in Captain Barker's pocket was mine, the ninety-three dollars my father had left. Barker had taken it over, for safe keeping he said, to be returned to me when we got located.

The storekeeper was making a sham laugh, bobbing his head.

"Such a joker, sir. Yes, I like a good joker. For you I will knock off, say, five dollars . . . five and a half even. A bargain . . . which one . . . which one . . . ?"

I had caught the captain's other arm and hauled on it, saying in a loud whisper, "Let's go."

The storekeeper turned his heavy lidded eyes on me, blue and watery.

"Listen to somebody who knows, boy. You cannot get the gold without good tools, and if you go to buy them from Mr. Brannan at Sutter's Fort you will see that his price is much higher than ours. Much higher. It is a rule of our firm, the Seligman brothers will not be undersold."

He still held the captain's arm and was pressing a pick into his hand. Barker was hesitating. I yanked on the other arm and hissed:

"You can't buy it with my money."

The storekeeper could not help hearing and the captain wilted. Crestfallen, he let me lead him away.

That was my first meeting with Jesse Seligman. It would not be my last.

CHAPTER THREE

Two men who had much to do with the very early development of California were John Sutter and Samuel Brannan, and they were as different as two men could be.

Sutter, born in Germany and raised in Switzerland, had arrived in the great valley in 1839, become a Mexican citizen and been given an enormous tract of land around the juncture of the Sacramento and American Rivers. He had established a principality which he named New Helvetia and a fort for protection against the foothill Indians. It was one of his employees who first found gold in the American riverbed, and for a time he and Sutter tried to keep the discovery secret, but could not. And because of that Sutter lost almost all of his holdings.

Samuel Brannan was of a sharper breed. An early convert to the Mormon Church, he had been sent from New York with orders to found a colony on the Pacific Coast, away from the jurisdiction of the United States Government which had been harassing the Saints. But by the time his ship arrived Captain John Montgomery had already landed his sailors, and the Stars and Stripes were flying over the Presidio. Sam Brannan chose not to do as many of his followers did, working back eastward to the new church settlements in Utah. Perhaps he liked California or perhaps, as has been suggested by his enemies, he liked the church funds he had collected too much to share them with the distant Mormon elders.

He made a start in San Francisco and became very prominent in the early American development there, took an active interest in the town's affairs, published one of the first newspapers, played the real estate game with the sand lots that were being carved out along the rutted streets. With the discovery of gold and the torrent of immigrants flowing through the town he foresaw a greener pasture in the inland community.

When I first walked into his store built along the stockade wall of Sutter's Fort, Brannan was the leading merchant in California.

The fort was located back from the river, above the lowlands that flooded in the rainy season, but the town, called Sacramento as early as 1848, had sprung up willy-nilly on those flats, between the fort and the embarcadero at the river shore. When we arrived it was thriving, eclipsing its shrinking neighbor on the bay. Estimates of population ran as high as ten thousand people, but it was a rude sprawl of tents and slab shanties that were little protection against rain and cold.

It had taken us more than ten days to come up the river, time enough that the resilience of youth had pushed the loss of my family to the back of my mind, and I was in a sweat to get to that miraculous place where I could start picking up lumps of gold.

The evening when the cook finally pulled the dinghy against the bank was hot and humid. The whole trip had been hot and Joe, strong as he was, was exhausted.

Most of our food was gone and there was little else of value in the boat, but again we left Joe to protect it. Captain Barker and I climbed across the low dike that had been thrown up to keep the flood water in the channel and walked the level mud bank through the town toward the wooden stockade on the gentle rise.

Noise from Brannan's Store rolled out over us before we reached it. Through the door we could see the crowd, men in every type of clothing, all of it deeply stained from their mining. Most of them wore heavy beards, most were drunk in various degrees. It was a wild sight to me but one I later learned to understand.

Alcohol may have its faults, but these men were all far from home, far from their womenfolk. They worked in icy mountain water, sometimes to their waists, they slept on the open ground or in holes dug in it or in cabins that were more lairs than rooms. Their food could only be called primitive. For them whiskey was a temporary reprieve, a hiatus necessary to give them the strength to go on.

We pushed into the mob. The interior of the store was amazing, a greater clutter than Seligman's of piled tools, mountains of blankets with chains run through them and stapled to the floor, clothing also fastened down. Barker steered me toward a high counter where a whiskey keg sat. A pale-faced clerk behind it was busy filling tin cups that were attached to the counter by long chains. Brannan, it appeared, had little faith in his customers' honesty, but in a country where the most battered cup could bring five dollars it was pardonable.

The captain left me there to go ask the price of a pick and shovel. I had meant to stay close to him, but there was something else on the counter that fascinated me. It was the first time I had seen a set of gold scales, the shining seesaw balance bar hung with tiny pans at either end. Into one pan a clerk put a miniature weight, into the other a miner spilled flakes of gold from a pouch until both pans hung at the same level. That was my introduction to the fact that there was little coinage in Sacramento, less at the diggings. Gold dust was the medium of exchange even for those who had not been within miles of the mines. The reality of the gold, of watching it being used, held me rapt.

"Davie. Davie Stuart."

The voice was familiar. I swung around and found Mitchell Randolph standing over me. The *Anne Marie*, the long voyage, seemed so far behind me now that I was astonished to see him here.

He was a big young man, over six feet and magnificently built. He had wide shoulders and a strong neck, a large backhead over which thick black hair curled close to the skull. His features were large, bold, with a clean, rugged cut that made you look at him twice. His eyes were blue gray and intense. He was smiling down at me. I had never seen him when he was not smiling. There was a strong magnetic pull about him and I was very glad to see him, even though my father had warned me not to talk to him. I answered his smile without hesitation.

"Hello, Mitchell."

"You and your dad just getting here?"

"Not Dad. He died when the ship was coming into the harbor."

The smile went away. The eyes deepened. "I didn't know." He did not say he was sorry. He offered no sympathy. It was as if he knew I would take it for granted.

There was an intensity about his speech that demanded attention. It was what my father had marked about him, that and his appearance.

"He's European," my father had said after their first meeting on the deck of the *Anne Marie*. "But there's something peculiar about that person." He always referred to people he did not consider his equals as *persons*. "He's too pushy. I'd keep away from him."

It was an order and I knew it. So did my mother, but she found the voice to protest.

"He seems nice. So friendly. He took Davie's part this afternoon when the mate ordered him out of the rigging."

"Too friendly. A climber. A toady."

I had never heard the word and asked what it meant. He pulled at a corner of his mustache. "Someone who tries to weasel in where he doesn't belong. That name, Randolph . . . he's not English. Notice how he talks. English isn't his native tongue . . . he's translating in his mind."

My attention had jumped back to that conversation and I missed what Randolph said next, but I was saved from asking by the captain's arrival. He was shaking Randolph's hand as if he would pump it off.

"Mitchell . . . Mitchell . . . wonderful, running into you again. You going to the diggings?"

"Isn't everyone?" Mitchell sounded amused.

"Looks like it." The captain wagged his head in disapproval. "You haven't come across Mr. Lord and the crew, by any chance?"

"Your mate? No. Should I have?"

"Watch out if you do. All that money you got me for the charter and the coal . . . they stole it. Hit me over the head, knocked me out, or I'd never have let them get away with it."

Abner Barker had been terrified and would not have lifted a stubby finger to stop them, but I knew again that he was not intentionally lying. He had firmly convinced himself that this was the truth.

"That is too bad," said Mitchell.

The captain nodded, taking off his hat, staring into it. Then he stuck a finger through the hole.

"That's what Mr. Lord did to me."

He glared at Randolph as if daring him to laugh. Randolph was perfectly grave.

"But you've gotten safely here. Which camp are you going to? I understand there are several."

The captain put his hat back on, closing the subject of Lord. He was unable to follow more than one idea at a time.

"What's the best?"

Mitchell was smiling again. "I don't know that there is a best. Gold, they say, is where you find it. I've been talking to the men around the store all day, trying to get some kind of picture. They tell me it isn't too easy to find, not like we heard on the East Coast. For every miner who makes wages there are many who don't get enough to cover their bare needs, and as expensive as things are here, they are dearer at the mines."

Captain Barker reddened with a helpless indignation. "Dear they are. I was warned of it in San Francisco and I should have trusted my instinct there. Should have bought my tools. Now it looks like I'm up the river good." I judged he did not mean the Sacramento. "The ship's back in the harbor, but there's no crew and no money to outfit her to sail anywhere, even to the Sandwiches. We'll have to take our licking here, and go on and try our luck. Which way are you going?"

"I've been pondering on that," Mitchell said. "The way it shapes up to me, it's the storekeepers who make the most, and the liquor sellers. I've got a little capital . . . my commission on chartering the ship to Nelson . . . the coal deal . . ."

A new sharpness brightened the captain's eyes and he made one of his rare valid observations.

"But where would you get any goods to sell, without going all the way back to San Francisco?"

Mitchell's smile widened. "That is the problem. And I admit that I have a taste to give the mines a try."

"Fine, fine. Why don't we all go together? There's more safety in numbers, and I got Joe with me. He's not the best cook in the world but you give him a little to work with, he puts something on the table. Got a strong back too, hasn't he, boy?"

I nodded. "He rowed all the way up here."

"I spelled him some, but my back ain't what it was . . ." Barker had done very little rowing, but before I could comment on that Mitchell's interest had quickened.

"You have a boat with you?"

"Got the dinghy," the captain said.

"Well, yes," said Mitchell. "I think we could form a partnership. I'll see you in the morning. Where are you camped?"

As soon as Barker told him, Mitchell moved away from us, back into the store. I immediately felt his absence as a chill emptiness. There was in Mitchell Randolph a positiveness that I had never noticed in anyone else, a projected certainty that he knew what he was doing, that he would not make mistakes.

The captain muttered that he would wait to buy the tools until the partnership was spelled out, and we headed back toward the river. It was already dark, there were no street lamps and it was hard picking the way down the wandering trail.

It was also scary, with people often looming out of the shadows, on top of us before we really saw them. Not that we had anything they might want to rob us of, but they couldn't know that. Partly because I wanted the reassurance of voices and partly because a phrase in Barker's conversation with Mitchell had caught my curiosity, I said:

"What did you mean about the money Mr. Lord stole, that Mitchell got it for you?"

Captain Barker was now in a happier mood than I had yet seen him. His chuckle was rich with pleasure.

"You mean your long nose hasn't dug out the way I happened to charter the *Anne Marie* to Mr. Nelson? Well, it's a good story on me. We'd been at sea a few months and when I sailed into Panama I didn't know anything about those five thousand people stuck there, trying to get up here. I put in after water and grub, nothing more. I was meaning to sell my coal in San Francisco for the steamers.

"So we were taking the sail off her and before we could drop the hook here came a fishing boat with Mitchell standing up in the stern. They pulled alongside and he grabbed a line and scrambled aboard, and came straight at me, back by the wheel. I was some perturbed." He stopped, leaving a momentary silent pause, then went on:

"You know I took the ship? The cook told you?"

I admitted it.

"Well, I figured maybe he was from the owners, maybe they'd found out where I'd gone and sent him down across the isthmus to head me off. I jumped on him with both feet, ordered him off my ship, made quite a racket trying to get rid of him. But he just waited until I ran down, then he said he wanted to charter the *Anne Marie* to take some passengers to San Francisco.

"Like I told you, I didn't know about that mob stranded on the beach, so I argued that I had a cargo of about ninety ton of coal and no more room in the hold for an extra rat. It didn't faze him. He said he'd buy the coal, give me twelve dollars the ton, pay to have it lightered ashore and give me ten thousand for the charter.

"I didn't know what to think then. He looked pretty young. But he was talking a lot of money, more than the tub was worth, so I took him down to the cabin and we signed the paper.

"We no more than got back on deck before here came Mr. Nelson, the forwarding agent." The captain chuckled again at the memory. "Randolph stepped right up and said he'd sell Nelson the charter for eleven thousand and the coal at thirteen a ton.

"Nelson was hopping mad, but Randolph reminded him that the

people on shore had bought tickets from the agent and he had to come up with a boat, so they made the deal, and me standing there with my mouth hung open. Imagine that Randolph, comes on my boat without a cent in his pocket and fast talks himself into more than a thousand dollar profit.

"And if Nelson had come to me first I'd have settled for maybe half what Mitchell got for me. I hope he don't change his mind about going with us. I'd feel a lot better with a partner like that."

I held the same hope. I had as much confidence in Mitchell Randolph as Barker did, and in spite of my father's warning I liked him, trusted him instinctively.

It had been that way on the first morning I met him. I was heartily sick of Panama and despairing that my family would ever get out. There was no one near my age except the brown, near naked children whose language I did not know. I was bored past trying to find any occupation, loafing against the rough wall beside the gate of the old city, watching the desultory parade of two-wheeled donkey carts bringing fruits and vegetables from the back country. It was an endless line, trying to feed the growing back-up of migrants, with even more new arrivals swelling the flow of traffic.

Most of the gold seekers who crossed the isthmus rode the native mules as we had, from the landing at Gorgona to Panama, mules so small that even my short legs had nearly touched the ground.

Mitchell Randolph walked. His clothes were worn, mud-stained, tired. The bedroll on his shoulder was soggy from the sudden tropic rains that dumped on the land with monotonous frequency. Everyone in Panama was dirty and depressed. The town was a pest hole. But Randolph's head was high and his stride was steady as if he knew his purpose and that nothing in the world would bar his passage. He stood out from the crowd as he came swinging across the old, weed-choked moat and stopped before the Puerta del Tierra, the gateway to the earth, the entrance to old Panama.

He used his sleeve to wipe his forehead, leaving a streak of sweaty mud there. He was within feet of me, his blue eyes going over me with a quick appraisal, then he asked a question in Spanish.

"I don't understand," I said.

He switched to English. "Oh, you're American. That dark hair and sunburn . . . I took you for a native. Which way are the ships?"

I threw a frustrated kick at the crumbling wall. "There aren't any."

He stepped nearer, out of the way of travelers jostling past him.

"No ships? They told me in New York there'd be steamers."

23

I shrugged. "Sure, they told everybody that. But we've been waiting six weeks, my father and mother and me."

He looked at me closer, this time with the suspicion that I was a small boy telling a tall tale.

"And no boats have come?"

To defend my integrity I tried a fuller explanation. "The *California* came. She's the first around the Horn and she was supposed to have plenty of room, but she'd already picked up a lot of foreigners along the South American coast. She could only take four hundred from here, and there are thousands to go. There was a riot with them trying to get aboard and the captain armed his crew to drive them off. Some got hurt.

"Then a couple of square-riggers put in on their way to the Sandwich Islands and Mr. Nelson, that's the forwarding agent, chartered them and put a hundred passengers on each, but we were too far down the list. Now we're waiting for the *Oregon*, but she's way overdue and Mr. Nelson promised he'd get us on whatever boat comes next."

He looked along the wall, at the crowds around the native shops that huddled against it, looked through the gate, his eyes thoughtful, restless.

"Well, it sounds as if I'll have some time to kill."

I was pleased that he believed me now and I didn't want the conversation to end. Having someone to talk to was a relief from the dragging hours and since he was a newcomer here might be a chance to show off some of the things I had learned in my explorings, in which the people who had been here for any time were no longer interested.

"I could take you around," I offered. "Show you the ropes."

He considered at length, as if he debated getting further involved with me, while I hung on tenterhooks, then he smiled.

"I'd appreciate that. It could help me decide what to do."

I made it a full tour with accompanying lecture, leading him south to the Avenida Central, then west, and climbed to the top of the old granite wall and Las Bovedas Promenade from where we could look out over the distant harbor.

The city spreads over a rocky peninsula that juts into the gulf near the mouth of the Rio Grande. Across the harbor lies a string of sheltering islands, Perico and Flamenco the largest of them. The panorama is breath-catching in its color, shining blue water, red tile roofs and the dense green of the tropic forest.

Mitchell Randolph . . . we had exchanged names by then . . . looked at everything with alert interest.

"This is a very old town," he said.

"Not as old as the one the pirate Morgan burned in 1671. This is a new one that was built in '73."

"Where did you learn all this you've been telling me?"

"My father. He knows a lot . . . now, Sir Henry Morgan marched fourteen thousand pirates across the isthmus and sacked and burned the town that was down there, closer to the harbor . . ." I was pointing to the old location, absorbed in my picture of the howling massacre, the raging holocaust of that adventure.

"Yes . . ." Randolph looked at the angle of the sun. "I think it's time I began doing something about my own invasion of Panama. I'd better go talk to that forwarding agent about my chances. Do you want to show me the way?"

I surely did. I was having a wonderful time. We walked back through the winding, foul-smelling streets to the Zachrisson and Nelson office. The waiting room was as mobbed as usual with men crowding each other, trying to get their names as high as possible on the lengthening list for priority passage.

Reluctantly I left him there. I had already been gone longer than I had permission for, and I hurried to the palm-thatched shack we had in the community the unwilling visitors had erected outside the city walls, where it was hoped they could escape the pestilent fever. I had also ignored my mother's command not to go into the town for fear of getting the sickness, so I made no mention of Mitchell Randolph.

I looked for him every day but did not meet him again. Then, a week later, a runner from the shipping agents brought us word that a square-rigged barque, the *Anne Marie,* would sail for San Francisco the following Monday, and our turn had come at last.

I certainly did not expect to find Mitchell Randolph aboard her. With so many ahead of him it should have taken him months to get a ship. Yet there he was on deck when I went investigating the second day. He would not explain, saying only that a man with the will and the wit could usually find the way.

Not until Captain Barker told me how he had stolen a march on Nelson did I know how he had worked the miracle, and I did not understand the full significance of it for many months to come.

CHAPTER FOUR

His voice waked me early the next morning, calling from the levee top. Then he came sliding and jumping down the muddy bank to the dinghy, his bedroll over one shoulder, a heavy sack over the other.

He shook Joe's hand as if he were really glad to see him, pitched in to build a fire and start coffee while Joe warmed the salt horse and brought out the ship's biscuits, rapping each one on a stone to drive out the weevils. Then Mitchell unloaded the sack.

He had outfitted at Brannan's Store, bought two picks, two shovels, gold pans, a pair of heavy shoes for himself and a pair for me. I tried to thank him but he waved it aside. He had things to say.

"I asked some more questions up there last night. The gold was first found at a place called Coloma. It's on the American River and we can get there in your boat, Captain."

Abner Barker looked for wisdom in his hat. "You think that's the place to go?"

"It's somewhere to start and we won't have to tote our duffel. We can float more than we could carry, and it will be easier. Let's take stock and see what else we need."

We needed ammunition for the guns and a resupply of food. I went back to the fort with Mitchell for them, hoping there would be something other than salt meat and dry biscuit, but there was little else to be had.

We loaded up the boat and shoved off the bank with Joe and Mitchell each taking an oar, all of us in happy ignorance of what we headed into.

At Sacramento the American is a placid, ample stream twisting through a swampland of tule reeds taller than a man, giving the effect of a canyon. At noon we grounded on a bar of silt and ate a midday meal, and the day slid by without a problem.

The rest of the trip was not that easy. The season had been dry with little rain in the high mountains and as we progressed upriver the water grew increasingly shallow. Rocks broke the surface, then we reached a stretch of rapids that could not be rowed through.

Joe had an answer for that. He tied the bowline to the middle of a four-foot stick and with him and Mitchell each holding one end of the stick they towed the boat behind them. Barker and I walked on either side, holding to the gunnels, shoving one way and then another to keep off the thrusting rocks. Against the fast water it was hard going even with all four of us, hard keeping our footing with the current pulling at our legs.

It was sundown when we reached the top and turned to the shore to rest. I was cold, so tired I was shaking, and dropped gratefully on the warm sand, wet to my waist, barely seeing the others stretch out around me.

I dozed. Later I was conscious that someone was moving. I cared neither who it was nor what he was doing. Not until I heard the scrape of the shovel. I opened my eyes then.

Joe was filling a gold pan with sand. At camp the evening before Mitchell had showed us how a man at Brannan's had demonstrated its use. It had a flat bottom and sloped up at a shallow angle. After you filled it you dipped one edge under water and used your fingers to break up the gravel and loosen any mud or clay in the mix. Then you swiveled the pan around, counterclockwise, keeping enough water in it to flush over the rim. Gradually that washed away the lightweight materials. By repeating the action over and over you worked everything out except a streak of black sand, iron, in the bottom. As you continued swirling it, with only a little water now, if you were lucky you'd see a narrow fan of fine gold dust follow the edge of the iron. If your luck was really in you might find a nugget or two.

Joe carried his filled pan into the stream hip deep, where he could work it without bending down for the long job. Tired as I was I sat up and watched. He had an instinctive ease at getting the right motion, keeping the muddied water spilling out and a fresh flow coming in, reaching in now and then to throw away the larger stones. By the time he had it washed clear down Mitchell had gotten up and built a fire and gone to the shore to call.

"See anything in there?"

Joe disgustedly sunk the pan, rinsed it and waded out of the river. "Ain't no gold around here now. No, sir."

I scrambled to him, reaching. "Let me try it."

"You got the strength to waste, go ahead." He handed me the pan and stomped off to warm himself at the fire.

I chose a different place to take my sample, scraped away the surface mud and dug down to the rocky floor of the riverbed and put the last shovelful in the pan. It was heavy as I carried it into the stream but lighter when it rested in the water. Still, I was clumsier than Joe. It took me a long while to get the mud and bigger rocks out, then I began picking up the little stones and chips, rubbing them between my fingers under the water so that if any gold was stuck to one I would not throw it away. There were only a couple left when I washed off a chip not more than a quarter of an inch thick that tapered at the edge like an arrowhead. It was milk quartz, although I did not know it then.

There was nothing that looked like gold on one side and I almost tossed it after the others, almost didn't turn it over. But I did turn it, and saw a yellowish smudge that wouldn't wash off, an embedded spot the size of my smallest fingernail.

I closed my hand around it and floundered toward shore, dragging the pan, forgetting to work it on down, yelling my head off, yelling "Gold" over and over.

Joe ran, reaching me before the others did, grabbing at the pan and looking at the half-inch of silt still there.

"Ah . . . that's not gold, boy, that's . . ."

"Not there . . . here." I shoved the chip into his hand. It looked very small in the big palm.

He shook his head slowly, peering at the quartz. "Now, Davie . . ."

"Turn it over. Turn it over." I was hopping, still yelling.

He used a finger of his other hand to turn the chip, then brought his palm up closer to his face, looking at the smudge with deep suspicion.

Mitchell reached for the bit of rock, held it toward the fading light, then carried it back to the fire. He squatted there, took out his knife and used the point to try to pry under the smudge. A tissue-thin yellow edge lifted away from the stone. Mitchell held it toward me.

"Gold it is, Davie. The first for any of us."

Captain Barker let out a sharp breath. "Gold. Real gold. Davie, you've got luck, you'll likely wind up the richest of us all."

I slept restlessly, excited and impatient for daylight when I could dig further into the little bar. But in the morning Mitchell vetoed staying there. The men at Brannan's had told him gold washed down from somewhere above every time the rivers flooded. They said it came from a central place called the Mother Lode and that the closer you got to this lode the more gold you would find.

I was torn two ways, but we pushed on. In another five miles the river widened and the water ran only a couple of inches deep over the rocky bottom. We could take the boat no farther.

We divided the gear between us, as much as we could carry, and walked, following the river. We began to pass men working on both shores, each on a claim of approximately an acre. Mostly they were friendly, glad to stop for a short rest and talk to us, explain the contraptions they were using.

The miners in this area had already given up the pans as the sole method of retrieving gold, in favor of what they called the Long Tom. This was a narrow sluice box, varying in length according to what wood was available, the amount of water they could divert from the stream and the volume of gravel they thought they could handle. A simple, rude machine it was, but it miltiplied many times the product of a man's labors.

The box was built close to the shore, the ends and top left open. The upstream end ran under a slanting screen. From there a trough was built up to a point where the river level was high enough that gravity would pull water down the trough and through the sluice.

Working only the two feet of ground above the bedrock, the miners shoveled it onto the screen, which fended off the larger rocks and let the loose material fall through into the box. The flowing water carried this material along, washing it clean, while the gold-bearing black sand sank to the bottom. It was caught there by riffles, a series of wooden bars nailed crosswise of the sluice, or by burlap sacking anchored to the floor. When the riffles were filled the water was shut off and the black sand scraped out, to be finished in a pan. A lot of hard labor was saved and much more sand was handled in a day.

Before we reached Coloma we had learned that some three hundred men were working the bars and I had seen my first tailing piles, long low mounds of discarded topsoil and the barren, washed out rocks and sand, emptied of life and value.

The town, when we came to it, disappointed me. There were only half a dozen businesses, housed in canvas shelters with pole frames. The one general store was the meeting place and we sat on the unroofed porch listening to the gossip of the men as they drifted in after their day's work. What we heard was not encouraging. Either they were having thin luck or were lying. No one admitted to be making even a fair living. We camped for the night and held a pow-wow as to what to do.

Captain Barker was for going on, chasing his dream of picking nuggets off the top of the ground. Joe and I looked to Mitchell for his opinion, and he argued that since we were here we might as well give it a try. So in the morning we went upriver until about a mile above the store we found a claim that someone had begun working and then abandoned. It was the only place that was not in use.

The captain made a hard choice of labor, between digging and washing, and reluctantly picked up a shovel. He and Joe dug a hole to bedrock to test the bottom sand. Mitchell and I stood in the river, each washing a panful. Mine yielded one trace of gold along the swirling edge of black sand, so fine that I could only pick it up on the tip of a moistened finger. Mitchell found none.

We ate lunch and then moved along. We came on three men working in a different way, not on the sandy bank but in the stream proper. They called it pocket mining, probing with an iron spoon into the cracks between the underwater rocks. The way they explained it the river filled the cracks with sand that drifted down it and the cracks acted as natural concentrators. The heavier gold was forced deep into them and the sand washed away.

One man who said his name was Austin and that he had been a bookkeeper in New York, told us:

"Trouble is, once you've cleaned a section of river it's cleaned. Might take fifty or sixty years for those cracks to fill up again."

"How does it compare with working a ground claim?" Mitchell wanted to know.

"No better. I been here near six months and I haven't made wages. I'm just trying to save enough to get back home. You can have all of California."

One of his partners laughed. "Don't believe him. We haven't seen much color for a couple of weeks, but just let him hit a pocket worth a thousand dollars, say, and you couldn't drag him out of the hills with an ox team."

We left them and followed the river higher. The country had risen gradually from the flat valley plain into low rolling hills that were getting steeper. The river course was turning into a canyon. We had to walk in the water and the current was becoming too fast to go against. Finally Mitchell called a halt.

"There's nothing here for us," he said. "We'd better look at another camp."

We spent the night on a rocky point and the next day joined in the restless search that kept most of the new population in a continuing pilgrimage from place to place. We tried several localities, spent two weeks at Volcano, a month at Sutter's Creek, which took us into the fall. Then we turned south to Columbia.

Columbia had gold, there was no question of that, but it was short of water, and water was a necessity for washing the sand. We located on a hill above the valley bowl where the business section sat, took up a claim that had been abandoned for lack of water. We had to carry our sand a quarter of a mile to a small spring, and to conserve water we learned another method, an adaptation of the Long Tom, a rocker. It was built like a cradle. You dumped in sand and water, rocked it from side to side, then lifted one end and poured the water off into a bucket to be used again, sluicing it down the incline over and over to take off the barren grit.

We could not handle very much that way and we made only a dollar to three dollars a day between us. Few were doing any better and in the fall of 1850 the camp was dying, more and more men giving up on it.

Columbia would go on to be the greatest producer of the Southern Mines, perhaps of the whole gold rush era. Eventually it gave up a hundred million dollars accounted for, and no one knows how much more dust was carried away in men's pockets without being put through banks or express companies. But all that was far in the future.

We hung on, waiting with a diminishing number for the winter rains that we were told would swell the dry stream beds and give us water to properly work with.

They came at last, but they came in floods. It was the wettest winter of Mother Lode history, and the water was ice cold. The high hills above us were covered with snow and the wind blowing off them was bitter. Mitchell went down to the town one day and came back with the news that only Steve Bassett, who wasn't mining, was left there.

Captain Barker slammed his hat on the ground. "To hell with it. If I'm going to drown I'd rather it was in salt water. I'm getting out."

His clothes were torn, soggy, heavy with mud, his boots cracked. We had all been wet for days, with no way to either clean or dry what we had to wear. His face was no longer square but shrunken, wrinkled from too much work and too little food, covered with a scraggly beard that had a forlorn indecision of which way to grow.

Mitchell did not argue with him. He said, "I agree that we aren't making any headway here, but I'm not ready to quit mining yet. A lot of the boys have gone over to Sonora. I think I will too."

We went to Sonora, even the captain. It was only four miles away. With the migration from Columbia it had nearly five thousand people. Most of the claims stretched along Woods Creek. They were not as rich as at Columbia and the water was too fast, too cold to work now, but there would be enough of it through the summer months.

This time we built a cabin, taking the pattern from others along the creek, a combination of what lumber we could get and small logs that we cut ourselves. It wasn't much of a place, only one room with a crude stone fireplace for heat and cooking. When we had finished it there was little to do and time dragged.

My money was gone and Mitchell bought food for us all, sparingly, trying to make what he had last, but enough to keep us going. And never once did he mention that he was our sole support. In later years when I heard him cursed and accused of sharp business practices I always thought back to that winter of fifty.

Joe hunted and brought in an occasional deer. The captain whittled. He could make remarkable figures with a piece of wood and a knife, and Mitchell tried to sell them, but there was little market. The miners husbanded what money they had for necessities.

Mitchell and I spent most of our time in the town. There was no one else my age. Most of the miners were young, but they were past childhood. A woman was a novelty. One came through in a mule train from Webber's Landing, going to join her doctor husband in Angels Camp and the whole of Sonora lined the single street to watch her pass.

We knew everybody there. In the other camps we had been too busy to more than say hello to our neighbors, but here we had nothing to do. We had dances on Saturday nights, with the boys dancing together as partners and on Sunday everybody did his weekly washing. We talked, told tall stories, and those with too much energy going to waste played mischievous tricks.

Randolph picked up the nickname Mitch. He would sit for hours playing checkers in the rear of Gieger's Store, give a hand to anyone who needed it, bringing in wood for the stove, tending the whiskey barrel on the counter, generally helping out, and always with a smile. Men began seeking him out when they had a problem and his stature rose into a position of leadership.

It was natural then that they turned to him at the time of greatest excitement, the Indian scare, and bestowed on him the gratuitous title of major. That was a day.

I was loafing down at the bakery, Jopman's, whom everybody called Old Dutch for some reason I never knew. He was neither old nor Dutch, but I never heard him protest. I was hoping he would have an errand for me. Every time I ran one he gave me a loaf of stale bread, which was very welcome in our cabin because flour was bringing a hundred dollars a barrel when you could get it.

Pete Springdale burst through the door stuttering as he always did when he was excited.

"Indians," he yelled. "Indians . . . they murdered Steve Bassett, killed his cows . . . sc . . . sc . . . scalped . . ." He broke off for breath.

Old Dutch had just pulled a tray of bread out of his oven. He looked at Pete under his flabby arm.

"Scalped the cows?"

"No, y-y-you f-f-fool. Bassett. His body's lying out b-b-by the shed and the c-c-cows are gone."

Old Dutch dropped the tray on the table and slapped the flour dust from his hands on his pants, looking worried. Since we had left Columbia, Steve Bassett had been alone there. He had stayed because of the hay he had cut and stacked through the summer, while others were mining, as feed for his three cows. During the summer he had made good money selling milk, ladling it into the whiskey bottles his customers brought with them. He had put in a supply of food to last him through the winter, and when the population moved out he saved his cream, made it into butter, brought it to Gieger's Store in Sonora to sell twice a month.

And now the lone dairyman was killed, scalped.

Everybody knew about the Indians in the hills. At first they had hung around the gold camps, working occasionally, but they were natural thieves and after several of them had been whipped for pilfering from the isolated cabins they had withdrawn to the upper canyons. I had never seen one, but in such small, tight communities as ours where the work was hard and monotonous and where little happened to break the boredom, what stories there were were told and retold and magnified with each telling.

The Bassett massacre was a natural.

I jumped past Pete Springdale, still catching his breath, and raced down the street to spread the word. I was disappointingly late. Pete had done the job before he reached the bakery. Men were already running, gathering into groups. One of them grabbed my arm and swung me to a stop, shouting:

"Where's Mitch?"

"At Gieger's, maybe."

"No he ain't. We looked. Find him. Tell him."

I spun off to run down the path that wound toward our cabin, heard the ax before I came around the shoulder of the hill, guessed that Mitch was splitting wood and drowned out the sound with my yells.

"Indians . . . murdering Indians."

He was in mid-swing. He aborted it, nearly dropping the ax.

"Indians, where?"

I shouted Pete's news, bringing Joe and the captain tumbling from the cabin. Mitch listened, then leveled a finger at me.

"If you ever come howling at me like that again I'll split your fool head open. Joe, where's the guns?"

Joe doubled back, brought the musket and the two hand guns, then we all headed for Gieger's Store, half-running. The crowd in the mud of the street had grown, milling, too excited to realize that they were standing in a good three inches of water.

Mitch pushed in to where Ben Ives, who always sat at the head of our miners' meetings, was questioning Springdale. Ives was older, probably in his middle thirties. He had been a lawyer in Chicago and he fell back on quoting law whenever he got in an argument. He was a pompous man and overawed those who had less than his education. He was saying:

"So you didn't actually see Bassett dead?"

"No, sir." Springdale was subdued before this magisterial probing. "But I met a man on the trail, he'd just come from Columbia. He said he barely escaped with his hair and he was out of breath from running."

"Where is he now?"

Springdale looked around, confused. "Why, he came on into town with me. I don't rightly know where he's got to."

"What's his name?"

"I don't know, Counselor, and that's a fact. Seems like I've seen him around somewhere, but I can't recall what he's named."

The crowd was impatient with the delay, grumbling. There were shouts. "Let's get going. What are we stalling for?"

"Hold your horses." Ives raised his voice. "We got to have order, do this right." His eyes fell on Mitch. "You, Randolph, you're a sensible man. I hereby appoint you in command of this expedition."

No one thought to ask Ives by what authority he appointed anyone anything, but his choice was a good one. Mitch was by now one of the most popular men in camp. He accepted the charge with a bob of his head and turned to the crowd, ordering it to split, those with guns to move to the right, those without to the left.

They shifted without argument and he told the unarmed group, "You boys go get your guns. The rest of us will start for Columbia now. You stay in Sonora to guard the town in case the Indians circle around us to attack this place."

There was protest at that. Everybody wanted to march. Such a chance to break the doldrums of the wet winter did not come often, but Mitch cut them off with a wave of his hand.

"Ives, I'll leave you in command here as captain."

Ives snapped straight and saluted. It was not impressive, he was too stout, with a fleshy red face and eyes too small for his bulk. "Yes, Major."

No one thought to laugh. Everyone was deadly serious in spite of their eagerness for activity. A lot of the men had come West on the Overland Trail and been in brushes with the plains Indians. The fact that the native California variety had seldom shown hostility did not lessen their suspicion of all savages.

We marched. The line was uneven, straggling. I walked at Mitch's side. He carried the musket. I had no gun, of course, but no one made a point of that. And in the stress of the moment I hardly noted that Ives, in calling him major, had given Mitch a title that he would wear for the rest of his life.

Military titles were fashionable during the gold rush. Some were earned but many were simply appropriated or casually given. Mitch Randolph got his by general concurrence and never disavowed it even when the captain and Joe and I adopted it.

I marched in a stew with visions chasing through my head, of Steve Bassett's cabin burned and smoldering, of his log barn destroyed, of his scalped body sprawled in its bloody pool. But nothing I imagined proved true.

We came over the brow of a low hill and saw the barn first, still standing solid. Mitch stopped us and sent out scouts on both sides of the cabin so that Indians could not skulk up and strike us in surprise. But they saw nothing, and waved us on.

We went in closer and saw the cabin. The only smoke was coming out of its chimney. We eased on to the yard. Nothing moved there, but neither was there a corpse in sight.

Then the door opened and Steve Bassett stepped out and stood blinking at the grim, armed assemblage. He looked nervous.

"What the hell's going on? What are all you guys doing here?"

The column had stopped, every man gaping at the apparition. Mitch kept going, up to the little porch.

"Bassett," he said, "you're supposed to be dead and scalped by Indians."

Steve Bassett was a short man with a pot of a belly that jiggled when he was startled.

"Me? Who says?"

Mitch's grin broke wide. "All Sonora thinks so. That's why we came. But you're the healthiest looking ghost I ever saw."

Bassett shook his head vigorously. "No, I ain't. I mean I ain't no ghost." He ran his eyes again over the bristling multitude, a hundred or more miners now edging closer. "But all these boys turned out in the interest of avenging my hide? That damn Tobe Alcot."

"Who?" said Mitch.

"Lives down at Jamestown. Was up here yesterday. I was saying he was the only one who'd come around to see me, and he bet me I'd have visitors by the end of the week. Well, by God, I guess I sure got visitors. I thought you was maybe a hanging party. Well, come on, set a spell."

Dick Trimble called out: "You got anything to eat, Steve? We had a long hike on an empty gut."

Bassett waved an arm expansively. "Sure, fellows. There's a prime deer hanging out back in the shed."

The boys sent up a spontaneous happy yell and split into groups to divide the chores. One bunch dug a pit in the yard. Another fetched brush to fill it for a fire. Those who went for the deer set up a clamor of discovery. They had found Steve Bassett's whole winter's supplies also in the shed.

Bassett watched them carry out his barrel of flour and let out a howl. "Hey, take it easy. That's got to last me through to spring. Mitch . . . Mitch . . . stop them."

He might as well have shouted at the wind. There was a concerted rush for the shed. Mitch couldn't have stopped them with a cannon. He didn't even try. I had learned long ago that Mitch never argued with the inevitable. Instead he put a wry face on the raid.

"Why now, Steve, haven't you any gratitude to these brave men who marched all this way to fight an Indian attack?"

36

"There weren't no Indians, Mitch. It was just one of Tobe's jokes. He's the most miserable practical joker in all the Southern Mines."

"But we didn't know that. We were willing to risk our lives to avenge you. What kind of a sport are you, Bassett?"

Some of the boys paused to listen, then ran on to spread the words. Everybody was laughing and whooping. They hadn't had so much fun since the first rain, and they were dragging out every bit of food they could find, like an invasion of locusts.

Bassett picked up an ax and started wildly off the porch, but Mitch caught his arm and held him back, a crooked smile on his lips.

"No use to go against them, Steve, they've got to blow off their steam."

"But . . . they ain't got the right." Bassett cast about for someone to support him and his eyes fell on me. "Davie, you tell him, this ain't fair. All summer long it took me to buy that stuff. A lot of hard work."

As far as I had seen Bassett had never showed any interest in work, aside from milking his cows and cutting the wild mountain grass for feed. He did not mine. He had contented himself with the profit from his milk, selling it during the season at two dollars a quart.

I said weakly, "Mitch is the major. Whatever he says goes."

Mitch raised his voice to reach the men joyously preparing their feast.

"Armies always live off the country, Steve, and as officer of these volunteers I hereby commandeer these supplies to sustain them." In a lower tone he added: "You'll get it back, they'll all be your customers again next summer."

Bassett put his ax down, leaning it deliberately against the house wall.

"Well . . . hell . . . I guess I might as well go help with the biscuits . . ."

When it was over, the venison bones picked clean, the pan bread exhausted, not a remnant of Steve Bassett's winter stores was left. He sought out Mitch, massaging his own full stomach.

"Looks to me like I'll just have to go on back to Sonora with you, Major, and I'll ask you to pick out a delegation to lead my cows and to start hauling my hay. They can use my two-wheel cart."

The boys took that as a good turnabout on the fun they'd had and it was a hilarious army that pulled out and left Columbia totally empty.

And there was a dividend to the expedition. Sonora got its own milk supply and Steve Bassett again had a market.

"Best thing that ever happened to me," he told us after the excitement had settled down. "I was getting plumb tired of talking to nobody but them cows."

CHAPTER FIVE

Although the Indian scare put Bassett back in business, raised Tobe Alcot's reputation as a famous practical joker and gave Sonora a story to sustain her spirits through the rest of the winter, the memory of the feast did not sustain our bodies. That was the last meal of note I had for many weeks.

The deer had moved up onto the high hills, beyond reach of an increasing number of hunters and though Joe went out faithfully he could not find meat.

Those in camp who had saved enough dust from the previous summer continued to trade at Gieger's Store and Old Dutch's bakery, but Mitch, considering his dwindling fund, put us all on shorter rations. We could, he said, buy nothing except beans. No side meat, no flour, no coffee. On beans we could keep going until we could begin work again in the spring.

There was no way to make any money in the camp. We had all tried to find something, but no one was hiring help. We could not work sand in the torrent of the creek, but we did try, between the nearly incessant rains, to use the rocker from the Columbia claim. We all caught heavy colds and the captain nearly went into pneumonia. There was a lot of sickness among the other miners and some deaths where men weakened by too little food were prey to the exposure they could not avoid.

Few of the cabins gave adequate protection. Dampness and cold came through the walls and windows. There was no glass in Sonora. The frames were covered only with heavy paper coated with deer grease, which let in some light but could not be seen through.

Gieger's Store had fewer and fewer customers. He was not getting rich. His prices were higher than Sam Brannan's in Sacramento, but so were his expenses. Everything he handled had to be freighted in by wagon from Webber's Landing on the San Joaquin River and the road between was a quagmire.

Dell Gross was his teamster. Dell had driven his wagon overland from the Missouri frontier, with four oxen. How he had got it up the east side of the Sierras was his favorite story.

"Took it apart, yes, sir. Took it all apart and toted every stick over on my back."

No one believed it. Dell was a small man who did not look strong enough to swing a buggy whip. He was, in fact, not strong enough to survive in Sonora.

Mitch and I were in the store when the news came that Dell was down with pneumonia. I was sorry to hear it, but I was surprised too when Mitch immediately hauled me out and said we had to go pay the sick man a visit. So far he'd told us all to keep clear of anyone from whom we might catch an illness.

We found the freighter huddled under a pile of filthy blankets and pathetically glad to see us. He could hardly talk through fits of coughing, but he kept at it.

"Major," he said, "don't get too close, but listen. Listen. I ain't going to make it. I ain't going home. You write to my folks back in Illinois. Send them what's wrapped up in my duffel that's worth anything. There's some money, my Book, is about all. Will you?"

"Certainly, Dell." Mitch did not try to tell him the lie that he would pull through. There was no medicine in town that could cure him. "I'll take care of it. Now, about your oxen, do you want me to take care of them too?"

The freighter looked at him with outright love. He had a long coughing fit before he could speak again.

"Major . . . would you do that? They been good beasts, done a lot for me. I'd hate to see them just cut up and et."

"They won't be, Dell. I'll look out for them. But you'd better sign a paper giving me the right."

The man nodded, waving a hand weakly. "Make it out, I ain't got the strength."

Mitch found a tattered envelope that Gross must have carried in his pocket for months, and began writing. He held the pencil poised and said:

"Might as well add in the wagon, Dell, if they're to be any use."

"Sure, sure. You take it. I won't be needing it."

Mitch added the wagon, then held the paper so Dell could scrawl his name. After that he rummaged through the duffel and found the money and Bible and promised again to mail them.

"You better get along now," Dell said. "You stay around here you might get the sickness too."

We took his advice and went back to the cabin, Mitch warning me on the way not to mention the visit to Joe or the captain so as not to worry them.

That night Dell Gross died. Nobody knew just what time he left us. There was no one with him.

Mitch and I helped to bury him, then we went down to Gieger's Store. The storekeeper was less sentimental about losing a neighbor than he was worried at losing his teamster.

"Now how," he complained, "am I going to get my goods up here from Webber's Landing?"

Mitch already had the envelope in his hand and he held it out. Gieger read it over and visibly relaxed, then he looked at Mitch with suspicion.

"You can drive an ox team?"

"I can." Mitch never admitted in my hearing that there was anything he could not do.

"All right then. I need a trip made now. I'll give you fifty dollars to make it. Shouldn't take you more than a week."

"A hundred," Mitch said.

Gieger squirmed. He did not like to pay out more than was necessary. But he respected Mitch and trusted him where he would not have trusted some others in camp. We had citizens who were capable of taking the gold dust he had to send to Webber's Landing and keeping on going out of the country.

"All right. A hundred."

"And your buying price to me for a barrel of flour, a sack of beans, coffee, and some salt meat for myself."

The storekeeper grumbled, but after an argument more for appearance than because he thought he could avoid it, the deal was set. Nothing was ever bought or sold in the gold country on a fixed price. A certain amount of bargaining was a part of all trading.

Before we left, Mitch bought a piece of wrapping paper and bundled up Dell Gross's money and Bible and addressed it, saying that he might be able to find a freighter in Webber's Landing to take it on to San Francisco for mailing. Then we went down to the cabin.

Mitch poked his finger in Joe's chest, keeping time with his words.

"Did you ever drive a team of oxen?"

41

As with Randolph, I had never found anything that Joe could not do. He rolled his eyes upward.

"I sure can. I drove a plenty of them in Maryland."

"You'd better be good at it. You and I are taking off for Webber's Landing as soon as we can get my team hitched to my wagon. We should be back in a week."

They were not back in a week. They weren't back in two. Nor in three. With every passing day after the eighth Gieger looked more glum. Mitch had carried out over a thousand dollars in dust to pay for the supplies. His image in the town changed, the boys talked of nothing else. It was not only that Major Mitchell Randolph might have run out with the money. They were concerned that if the supply wagon did not return a lot of them would go without necessities.

Tempers began to run high. I hated to step into Gieger's Store, for whenever I did someone was sure to make a snide remark. We were about out of beans, but I did not dare ask for credit. The captain took the musket and went hunting, but nobody was finding any deer. I did manage to snare a couple of rabbits, but we would have starved if it had not been for Old Dutch.

The second week after Mitch and Joe had disappeared down the road I ventured into the bakery in desperate hope, asking if there were any errands to run. The smell of the place made my empty stomach cramp.

Dutch shook his head and I turned to the door, deep in misery. I had not eaten since the day before when we had finished the last of the beans for breakfast. I was pulling the latch open before he called.

"Wait, boy. Come back here."

I turned back quickly, supposing he had thought of some chore for me.

"You hungry?"

I nodded, not trusting myself to speak.

He reached to his shelf and took down a loaf of bread. It wasn't stale. It was still sweet and warm from the morning's baking. My eyes fastened on it, hypnotized.

"Take it," Old Dutch said. "You can pay me when the major gets back."

I ran all the way to the cabin. The bread was not wrapped. for paper was as scarce in camp as flour. Just as I turned in at the dooryard my foot slipped in the mud and I went headlong, the loaf rolling over and over in the red slime.

I picked it up and scrubbed at it with my sleeve. Not all the dirt came off, but neither I nor the captain cared. He brewed the herb tea. The whole camp was out of coffee. Nothing ever tasted better than that warm bread and hot, flavored water.

From then on I went to the bakery daily and every time Old Dutch gave me a fresh loaf, but at the end of the third week it was plain even he agreed with the rest of the town. Mitch Randolph was not coming back.

It was midway through the fourth week, late at night, that I heard the creaking outside the door. I did not know what it was and had a sudden panic that we were going to be run out of camp. There was the slosh of footsteps in the mud, then the door opened. Joe stood there, holding a lantern. Behind him I made out the canvas covered bows of the wagon.

I jumped up from the pile of boughs where I slept and threw myself at him with a yell. One big arm went around me and lifted me clear of the ground. I felt the wet roughness of his coat against my cheek and heard his deep chuckle.

"Why, boy, you appear real glad to see old Joe."

The captain came against us, shoving us out into the dark, stumping toward the wagon, hollering, "Mitch? Mitch?" as though he didn't believe it.

Mitch came around the tailgate, laughing. "What's the excitement? Anybody'd think we'd been gone forever."

"You have been." I ran toward him. "They thought you'd skipped the country."

"They did, huh? Old Gieger afraid I'd stolen his dust?"

I nodded, embarrassed that I had been wondering too.

Mitch laughed at my face. "You too, eh? Well, I'm here. Let's get something cooking. We're hungry."

"There isn't anything."

"There's everything." He rumpled my head. "Even half a dozen eggs."

Eggs were unheard of at the mines. In fact I had not tasted one since leaving St. Louis. The captain and I spoke together.

"Where did you get eggs?"

"From a man in San Francisco."

Captain Barker yelped. "You went to San Francisco?"

Mitch was unfastening the ropes, opening the canvas that bulged over barrels and boxes stacked inside, talking over his shoulder.

"We didn't have much choice. When we got to the Landing the supply boat hadn't come and they were on short rations there. We borrowed a dinghy and rowed on down."

Remembering our long, hard trip upriver I was awed at what they had done. Going down would not be bad, but rowing a boat back up, loaded with all that was in the wagon was beyond my belief. But I was only beginning to know Mitchell Randolph.

"Let's eat," he said, "then we'll go wake up Gieger and put the animals in Dell's shed."

It was not only Gieger we waked. The captain and I shouted at every cabin we passed. Miners spilled out of them, hopping, pulling on their boots. Some brought pitch torches, some ran ahead carrying the cry to the far side of town. The slow oxen came into the street to find it already full, and a yell went up that shook the hills.

In front of Gieger's Store there were a hundred willing hands to unload, a shouted demand that Mitch stay on the high seat and make a speech, tell them what had happened. Those who had been so sure he had defaulted now praised him as a hero. He had gone clear to San Francisco. He had brought back food. Sonora was alive again. Sonora would survive the winter.

He had also brought back something that was even more electrifying. He waited until the wagon was empty, then crawled back into the canvas shelter and held up a packet tied with a thong.

"Mail," he called. "I went to the post office and picked up mail for everybody I could think of."

From tumult there was sudden silence.

The gold camps of 1850 were as isolated as stars. Most of the men moved from camp to camp too often to have any permanent address, and those who stayed put were no better off. The postal department in California was a far cry from being a useful organization. It would be a matter of years before the official delivery of mail from the East Coast was more than a lucky accident.

It was not all the fault of the officials, although the men sent West to open offices showed a numbing inability to understand or cope with the problems.

The first move the government made in extending the postal laws to cover the growing population in California had come in 1848, when President James K. Polk recommended that Congress take action in the matter. But sending the recommendation to Capitol Hill and having anything effective come of it was not a simple transition.

True, subsidies and mail contracts were offered to encourage stage lines and later railroads, but in 1850 the post office itself was corrupt and inefficient, and both showed up starkly in the far tentacles of the department.

The first agent sent West was William Van Voorhies, charged by those in control in Washington with opening offices in the towns that the maps indicated were most important. San Diego, San Pedro, Santa Barbara, Monterey, San Luis Obispo, and San Francisco, where a local agent was already operating.

No one in the East took note that none of the locations were anywhere near the gold country where ninety percent of the new state's people were. That Van Voorhies was empowered to set up other outlets in the interior provided they would handle a volume of mail sufficient to pay their expenses was no help. The population shifted too often.

In the winter of 1850 no one in Sonora had received any communication from the East since he had come to the mining area.

They stood reverent before Mitch. There was no sound as he slipped the thong and read out the name on the top envelope. It had already laid in the San Francisco office unclaimed for months.

"James Tabor."

A man at the outside of the circle whooped and pushed through, his hand upstretched. Mitch passed the letter down and Tabor tore it open, jostling toward a man who held a torch, reading with a tense concentration as Mitch went on with his distribution.

I was close enough to Tabor to hear the small whimpering noises he made as he read. Then I saw that he was crying. I thought it wasn't fair that his first news should be bad, but suddenly he threw his arms in the air and shouted.

"A boy. A boy. I got a baby boy."

There was a murmuring, as if each lonely man felt the touch of a distant hand, heard a voice.

Tabor flailed to the wagon again, sat down in the mud, stuck his letter between his teeth and pulled off one boot. He felt down into the toe, found what he wanted, and climbed up over the high wheel. He grabbed Mitch's hand and pumped it, babbling in his gratitude, talking around the paper in his mouth.

"A boy, Major. I'm going to write to Mary, that's my wife's name, Mary. She's got brown hair and brown eyes. She's pretty . . . Thank you, Major. Nobody ever done anything like this for me. Here. I just wish it was more . . ."

There was a small bright wink in the torchlight as Tabor pressed a ten-dollar gold piece into Mitch's palm. It was something he must have brought with him, kept back for an extremity, for coinage was a rarity here. Then he jumped down and elbowed away with his precious letter.

Mitch held the coin between his thumb and forefinger, turning it so the light caught it, twisting it to make it wink. It took a minute for the idea to sink in. Some of the men who had got mail did not offer to pay for it, some did not have the dust to give. But others came up offering pouches.

Mitch had brought seventeen letters. When they were all given out we went into Gieger's Store to weigh what he had collected on the scales. It came to nearly a hundred and fifty dollars.

It was dazzling. Only that evening we had been without food. Captain Barker looked into the scales, breathless.

"What do you know? What do you know? What about that, Major? Joe? Davie?"

Joe's slow grin spread and he winked at me.

"Ain't he a something though? I didn't even know he had that mail with us."

Mitch poured the dust carefully into his pouch and tucked it inside his shirt. Then we went to put the wagon, the team in Dell Gross's shed, and from there back to the cabin. There were still some last ditchers celebrating in the store but Mitch strode past without a sideward glance as if pushed by some compulsion.

We were all by now tuned to each other, and Mitch projected an inner pressure that made going back to sleep unthinkable. We built up the fire, heated the coffee and sat around the slab table. We talked little, all of us seeming to wait for something. It was Joe who finally brought it out.

"A hundred and fifty dollars they just give you. It's a shame there weren't more letters."

Mitch's dark eyes had a burning in them, part laughter, part brooding. His smile was almost animal.

"Why shouldn't there be more letters?"

Joe gave him a look of blank surprise. "You mean you left some down there?"

"Maybe. I couldn't be sure I remembered all the names. I don't mean that. There are other camps. The boys in them must be as hungry for mail as these were."

"But you don't know their names," I said. "And you don't know who's where."

Mitch was pushed up from the chair by a restless energy.

"There's a way to solve that. We'll canvass the other camps, put up notices that we're going to San Francisco and will bring up mail for anybody who puts his name under the notice. Charge a dollar a name." He walked to the dark window and stood before it as if he were looking out, his hands hanging at his sides but closing and unclosing.

The captain grunted in skepticism. "A dollar a man wouldn't pay for the trip. You been gone a month on this one."

"That's right." Mitch turned back to us. "The dollar is just to sign up, to keep people who know they won't get any mail from cluttering up the list. Like you. Nobody even knows where you are. Those who put up the dollar agree to pay by the piece whatever we bring for them, an ounce for each letter. Does that sound better?"

I felt a belated wrench. "It would take a lot of time. We'd have to quit mining, and we're bound to find the Mother Lode if we keep hunting."

Mitch looked down at me with sincere sympathy and rumpled my hair.

"I know how you feel, Davie. Dreams die hard and there's a real excitement to mining, always the chance for the big strike. But that's the rub too. It's too chancy. We haven't made anything yet, and we haven't got goods to sell like Gieger. But you can sell an idea too. This one I can sell. This one will give us our start. This is where we all begin."

CHAPTER SIX

We all slept late, then ate a breakfast unlike anything I had had
since summer. Pancakes, fried meat with the grease poured over the
cakes, real coffee, hot and strong. I ate a dozen cakes and Joe was
still cooking more for Barker when I had to stop. Afterward I
walked with Mitch down to Gieger's Store.

He bought five dollars' worth of writing paper and borrowed a
pen, then sat at the counter making up his posters, printing them
in a bold, elaborate flourish.

NOTICE !!!

Major Mitchell Randolph is planning a return to San Francisco
for the purpose of collecting letters and parcels held in the Post
Office there for miners and traders of the Mother Lode.

If you want mail delivered please list your name and the location of your claim below. The fee for such listing is one dollar
payable at time of signing in either coin or dust.

Should a letter addressed to you be found it will be delivered
to your claim for an additional charge of one ounce.

> Major Mitchell Randolph
> c/o Gieger's Store
> Sonora, California

He pasted a blank sheet below the notice and sat back, studying
it with a critical eye.

"What do you think, Davie?"

"It ought to make everybody in camp sign up," I said. "I could help collect them if you'd take me with you."

He looked up at Gieger with a small smile. "The boy's a salesman. It's a hard trip, Davie."

"I'm strong. I can walk as far as a horse."

Mitch squinted at me. "A horse can't walk as far as a man, did you know that? A man leading a horse can walk him to death."

"You're funning me," I said.

"Nope. A horse can run faster, but he can't walk as far."

He was already working on another poster, this one addressed to the miners around Jamestown on Woods Creek. He made a third for the men at Murphy's and a fourth for Angels Camp. Every one of these centers had several satellite communities, so that we were reaching probably ten thousand men.

"I figure that's far enough away to go the first time," he said.

Gieger was pleased to let him tack the notice to the whiskey barrel when Mitch suggested that it ought to bring people into the store who hadn't been around for a while. Back at the cabin Mitch coached Joe and Barker on this approach, then sent Joe north across the Stanislaus River and the captain, protesting at the long walk through the muddy road, to Murphy's. He gave me the poster for Jamestown, only three miles down the canyon.

The trail ran down the gully following the rushing creek. Everything was so soaked that the sandy ground oozed water as if the whole place was a seep spring, and it started raining again before I was halfway there. Ike Eaton's Store was filled with men, keeping out of the wet, keeping close to the hot pot-bellied stove.

Eaton was a vain man with a trimmed and waxed mustache and suspicious eyes. When I pulled the roll of paper out of my sleeve where I had kept it dry and asked if I could put it up he took it gingerly, read every word, then read it again, and shook his head.

"No you can't."

"Why not?" For a moment I was so taken aback that I forgot Mitch's argument that it would draw customers, then when I did remember, I stammered it out.

Eaton sniffed, making his mustache wiggle.

"I already got everybody on the creek in here. And this looks to me like just a sneaky way to get a dollar for nothing. A man would be a fool to shell out a dollar to a stranger. Take it out of my store."

The thing that made me maddest was his slur against Mitch's honesty, and my voice went up. It was apt to crack unpredictably these days.

"There's nothing sneaky about it," I said, "and Major Randolph isn't any stranger. He's the man who led the volunteers to Columbia in the Indian scare."

Men looked around to see what the fuss was and a thin, green-eyed man with yellow tousled hair came over, saying:

"You're Randolph's boy, aren't you?"

Most of the people in Sonora called me by Randolph's name and I had never bothered to correct them. Some thought he was my older brother. I nodded.

"I'm Tobe Alcot," he said.

This was the one who had perpetrated the Indian hoax, and it was the first time I had seen him. His grin was infectious, with a small boy's love of play shining through the mask of an adult face. He held out his hand.

"What you got there?"

He took the notice from Eaton, who didn't want to let go of it, read it through, then fumbled through his pocket.

"Now that sounds mighty good to me."

He put a silver dollar into my hand, laid the paper on Eaton's counter and signed his name and location. The storekeeper's mustache twitched again.

"Tobe, this maybe another one of your tricks?"

Tobe raised his right hand in solemn disavowal. "No, it ain't, though I wish I'd thought of it. Give you my word."

Eaton sounded outraged. "Your word? That's a lot of good. I haven't forgotten when you hammered that watch chain into that piece of quartz and swore to me you found it in the creek."

The whole store laughed. Apparently it was an old joke, and the laughter worked to my advantage. They pushed forward, reading first in curiosity, then one after another signing the paper and giving me the money. Eaton looked on in disapproval, finally asking:

"How long is this trip supposed to take?"

"He was gone a month last time," I said, "but that was slow because he had an ox team part of the way. He brought seventeen letters for Sonora."

For the first time there was doubt in the storekeeper's antagonism, then, grudgingly, he signed his name.

"Well, I'll bite this once."

He went to his cash box for the dollar, but I had an idea.

"You don't need to pay," I said. "Just let me put up the notice in case somebody else comes in."

I thought getting his name included free might make him more cooperative, and it did, up to a point. Before I left he pulled me aside and said that he would act as a distributing point for mail for the area so the major wouldn't have to trail out to each claim. He would, he said, give the major half an ounce apiece and keep the other half for his trouble.

Mitch laughed his head off when I relayed that suggestion. A week later, when Joe and the captain had come in with their rosters, when we had started out with the ox team and stopped to pick up the list at Jamestown, Mitch talked Eaton down and they made a deal that Eaton would get two dollars a letter.

I was shocked that we would give away any of the fee, but Mitch only grinned.

"With dust worth twelve dollars the ounce at the mines I think we can afford a small commission. Take an honest profit, Davie, but don't be a hog. Keep him friendly and he'll work for us."

It was the first advice he had given me, a new thought after my mother's desperate penny-pinching and my father's philosophy that what was his was his, and barter beneath his dignity. I chewed on it as we wallowed toward Webber's Landing.

It had taken me all week to torment Mitch into letting me come. For all his gregariousness I had often been startled to find a wall of reserve isolating some part of himself from everyone, as if there were a different, lone being within the man I knew. I finally won because, I suspect, he read in me the wistful, lost, lack of family direction that had been crowding up through the monotony of the dismal winter. The hunger to be with him on this trip had brought it into sharp focus and it must have been apparent in my arguments.

Joe did not go with us. Mitch had learned to handle the oxen on the first foray and right away he began teaching me. It took us ten days to reach the Landing, and there we found the river in flood, the town seeming to sink into the ooze. In spite of its greater stature as a trade center the buildings were little better than those in Sonora, rough lumber with canvas tops that let in the cold and damp.

We made Bell's Store and looked forward to drying our soggy clothes, hovering around the big stove. It did not surprise me that Mitch had struck up a friendship with Bell when he had come here for Gieger's supplies. He had a total memory for names and faces and a flair for making the most casual acquaintance feel that he was genuinely interested. Bell shook hands with him heartily and looked down my gangling length.

"You look like a drowned rat." The tone was kindly, then he turned back to Mitch. "That camp of yours run out of grub already?"

"I'm starting a new business." Mitch told him about the project and pulled the lists out of the oilskin pouch.

Bell listened and looked, a shrewd man with thoughtful eyes and a quick speech.

"Don't know why I didn't think of that myself, or someone else before now. What this country needs more than anything else is an express company."

"What's an express company?" I wanted to know.

He didn't talk down to me. "Sort of a special delivery service," he said. "A conductor on one of the Boston trains thought up the idea six, seven years back. He'd carry packages for anybody along the railroad for a price. Then another Boston man, Adams, heard about it and went into business for himself. Now they've got routes all over the East anywhere a train or stage runs. Mitch, now, is going to start one here."

Mitch gave a short laugh. "Slowly, slowly. A thing like that takes capital. All I've got to begin with is what I can collect for picking up and delivering mail. Can I borrow that dinghy again when we dry out?"

"I'll rent it to you if you want to start your business now. Want to take a consignment down for me?"

"Be glad to. What is it?"

"Lot of gold stored up around here. I've been waiting for the weather to let up to take it down to Lord and Company in San Francisco. What will you charge to handle it?"

Mitch took this next step into his young enterprise without fluster. "Five percent."

Bell screwed up his mouth as if he had just eaten a quince, then he tipped his head to the side.

"Well, I guess I couldn't do it for less, what with having to hire help here while I'd be gone. Come on back here, I'll show you."

I trailed them into a back room where Bell bent to open a huge iron safe. The inside was nearly filled with boxes and leather pokes. It drew a whistle from Mitch.

"How much is in there?"

"About a hundred thousand dollars worth."

My mouth fell open. Bell sounded as casual as if he were talking about a hundred dollars.

"It's been piling up all winter and we've got a lot of supplies ordered from the East. Lord will need this to cover our vouchers."

Mitch's eyelids were half-lowered, his lips pursed. "What would you say it would weigh?"

"Around five hundred pounds."

I thought of the tiny single flakes of gold I had found in the bottom of my pan, of the backbreaking hours the miners around me had put in winnowing the rare trifles from their claims. It was hard to imagine five hundred pounds of them gathered in this one place. Mitchell, though, had a different concern.

"What could I haul it in? I can't just pack those pouches loose in the bottom of the boat."

Bell straightened, cast about the store room, discovered an empty butter keg, a wooden tub like a fat, squat bucket.

"How about that?"

Mitch's eyes measured the capacity of the vessel, the bulk in the safe.

"That ought to do it. We can take it down to the boat empty and load it there, first thing tomorrow. You got a place we can sleep?"

"Just the shed out back. There's some hay in it for the mule."

"What you doing with a mule?" Only I, knowing Mitch so well, recognized the lift of interest in his voice. His expression showed nothing more than amusement.

"Damned if I know." Bell laughed. "Miner came in here last fall, broke and needing tools. He'd ridden the beast clear from Missouri. I traded him, but I took the worst of the bargain. It's the meanest, blackest brute I ever saw."

"A black mule?" Mitch sounded surprised. "I didn't know they came that color. Let's take a look."

Bell led us across a muddy strip of ground and pushed open the shed door. The mule stood in a stall built into the far corner. I'd seen a lot of the animals around St. Louis, but this was the biggest and indeed the blackest. It stuck its muzzle through the bars as we came up, laid back its ears and pulled its lips back, showing big, yellowed teeth, trying to bite.

"I see what you mean," Mitch said. "You want to get rid of it?"

"It's sure no good to me. But I'd like to come out on the deal. I gave three hundred in trade for it."

Back in Missouri the best horse brought hardly forty, but Mitch did not even argue.

"All right, three hundred if you'll keep him until I get back from San Francisco. Or is it a her?"

"Name's Effie."

"Has she got a saddle?"

"I'll throw that in. Glad enough to get rid of her. Come on and wash up a little and I'll get us some supper."

We trailed him to the wash bench outside the single room at the right of the store, mopped off what mud we could, then went inside. Bell both slept and ate in the small space, but it was neatly kept and he was generous with his food.

Afterward we brought our blankets from the wagon and wrapped up on the hay in the shed. The mule was restless, noisy. It did not sound like either a horse or an ass, but as if it had something stuck in its throat. I would not have slept anyhow. That a man would so offhandedly turn over a hundred thousand dollars to a stranger he had met only once before was a conception outside all my early training. It gave me a feeling of unreality.

I had not yet the experience to realize the magnitude of the interdependency of the people in this just emerging society, nor to foresee the trust that the majority of people strung out through the foothills would place in the man who simply declared himself an expressman. But in the first couple of years of the new business there was almost a family faith in the express messengers. They were the lifeline of the remote individual miners, bringing out to them the materials needed to sustain them and taking back to the safety of vaults the gold they collected above the cost of their existence.

They would expend every effort to speed the messenger's comings and goings and woe to anyone who tried to interfere. It was several years before the appearance of the road agents.

It was in broad daylight the next morning that we took the butter keg and the dust to the boat, making several trips through well-trafficked streets.

The treasure nearly filled the keg. We nailed on the wooden top, Mitchell signed a receipt, Bell gave him a voucher ordering Lord and Company to pay him five percent of the value as express charge, and we shoved off.

The boat had no rudder and could be steered only by the oars. Mitchell rowed from the middle seat, I sat in the bow watching for floating logs, stumps, debris and shouting for him to pull one way or the other. The weight of the gold in the stern kept us balanced and we made good time. The river was high, the current strong and the riverbed wide and by keeping near the center of the stream we had room to maneuver.

It took us three days to reach the estuary. We anchored there and slept in the boat to rest for the hard pull across the choppy bay.

Mitchell zigzagged between the deserted ships, many more than when I had last seen the harbor, and more forlorn looking. I picked out the *Anne Marie* swinging logy on her rusted anchor chain, her sails hanging tattered like witch hair, and was glad that Captain Barker was not there to see. We passed close to her and pulled in against the wooden staging that had been built against the grounded *Niantic*.

Here we faced a problem. Mitchell did not want to open the keg and carry the gold uptown piecemeal even if I stayed in the boat to watch over it. There were men loafing on the wharf and the ship's deck. It was one thing to trust the miners in the foothill camps, but these people had the look of the hoodlums and rowdies who had flocked into the town like scavenging jackals.

We moored the boat tightly against the stage, our gunwale fortunately level with the dock. Our duffel lay just astern of the rowing seat. Mitchell walked the keg to it, tilted it up to the duffel roll then tipped it over onto the seat. He walked it to the end of the seat, making the boat list, but I sat on the far gunwale to help keep us on an even keel. My weight was not enough and for a moment I thought we would turn over and lose the whole keg in the bay.

Mitch must have worried too, the way he scrambled onto the dock, taking his own weight out of the boat, squatting and cupping his hands around the keg, lifting. It was enough to right the dinghy somewhat, but he could never raise the gold that way.

He shifted his footing, shifted his purchase to the upper rim of the keg. It looked remarkably clumsy of a man trying to move a tub of butter. Several of the men watched and sidled closer with mocking grins. They were all armed, some with pistols openly stuck in their belts, others carrying slingshots.

"Need some help there, mister?"

Mitchell did not look around. "No thanks, I'll manage."

He threw me a warning look and I sat very still, pressing down as hard as I could, hanging onto the gunwale, holding my breath.

His fingers whitened as he strained, tipping the keg, tilting it until the staves rested on the side of the boat, then he reached down to the bottom of the keg, dragging on it. The muscles of his shoulders and neck tightened, swelled. The boat listed further. The keg came up slowly, rolling onto the gunwale, then with a heave he tipped it across to rest against the dock and heaved again to upend it on the planks, clear of the boat. It teetered on the edge and again I thought it would fall into the water, but he kept his hold, pulled back, and it settled solidly onto the dock.

55

I had seen Mitch shoveling sand all day at the mines but I had never guessed at the strength he had showed here, handling that five hundred pounds, even, to a casual observer, making it look an easy job done clumsily. There remained, however, the problem of transporting the thing up through town to Lord and Company's office.

I came out of the boat and whispered to him, asking if he wanted me to go and find a wagon. He sat on the keg, resting, shaking his head. Then, after a time, he stood up, turned the tub on its side and rolled it on a wobbling course, up the incline ramp and onto the mud bank. We were followed only by a chorus of laughter from the loafers on the dock.

Rolling it through the deep, slippery mire of the road was a nearly impossible job. Mitch sunk in over his boot tops every time he pushed on the awkward keg. Several times he slipped and fell flat, and so did I when I tried to help.

It took a long time, most of it down the Montgomery path to the intersection. When we finally reached the wooden sidewalk that bordered the square the going was easier, but not much. The planks were not uniformly thick, making the way bumpy, and they creaked under the weight, but none broke.

San Francisco was a very different town than the one I had passed through the summer before. Then the streets had been empty, most of the buildings deserted. But the rain and winter cold at the diggings had driven many miners back and more were still spilling in from ships. The population was at its highest yet, some fifteen thousand souls. She was on her way to becoming a city and would never again sink to the low point of 1849.

We rolled our bucket through crowded streets, past new and re-opened stores, found the offices of Lord and Company and trundled through the narrow doorway.

Mitch's face was striped with mud and sluicing sweat, his beard was matted and his clothes hardly to be seen through the plastering accumulated in his falls, and I was just as caked. Three men inside gaped at us, caught rigid in astonishment. Then one, a clerk, rushed to block us, making shooing motions with his hands.

"You . . . you can't come in here like that . . . you can't bring that thing in here . . ."

Mitch didn't lose a step. He rolled the tub forward and the clerk jumped back tugging at his trousers like a woman lifting her skirts away from a filthy animal. At the side of the room one of the Lord partners climbed down from his high desk and came toward us with an officious strut. He was dressed elaborately, the first such clothes I had seen in California, with a ruffled shirt, an Ascot tie and a dark coat that reached his knees. His face was red, his sidewhiskers a bristling dull black, his eyes angry. He pulled up safely out of contact.

"Who are you? What do you mean, bringing that mess in here? What have you got there?"

Mitch straightened, easing his back, putting one foot on the barrel. He wiped his face with his muddy hand. His teeth flashed white in the black tangle of his beard.

"A hundred thousand dollars worth of gold dust."

"In that?" It was not the size of the container he was shocked at, but that the cradle of the world's most precious metal should be so rude.

Mitch stood the keg on end and broke in the top with his boot heel, then began pulling out the pokes and arranging them on the clerk's desk. The partner—his name turned out to be Joyce—watched, his mouth working like a fish out of water, and finally blurted:

"Who the hell are you?"

"Major Mitchell Randolph's Mule Express."

There was a joyous sound to the name. It was the first time I had heard the designation, Mule Express, but it was to become famous from end to end of the Mother Lode.

"The dust is from Bell's Store at Webber's Landing. You're his forwarding agents, aren't you?"

Joyce was beginning to settle down. "Well. Well. Yes." He nodded almost as an afterthought.

"Then if you'll get them weighed and give me a receipt and honor this draft for the express charges we will take our muddy feet out of your counting room."

Joyce signaled and another clerk came up to help the first carry the pokes back to the scales. The contents of each was emptied into the pan and balanced separately, the number of ounces noted before the next was weighed. I stood beside the scales fascinated by the piles of shining grains. There was an occasional nugget of fair size but the great bulk was in tiny particles of all shapes. Some were thin flakes, some round as peas, some twisted strands. But it was all gold, torn by the floods from the ancient river channels of the foothills.

To me it was clear evidence to support the belief held by most miners then that somewhere in the higher mountains was a huge hidden mass of solid gold which they called the Mother Lode. The bits I was looking at were supposed to be only a trickle, a fraction leached out and washed away by water action. The image made me shiver. The man who found the lode would be the richest in the world.

The weighing was finally finished, the receipt signed, and Mitchell was paid his express charges in slugs.

These were just coming into use, gold smelted and shaped and stamped in twenty- and fifty-dollar denominations. There was no mint west of the Mississippi and while dust was used as legal tender from Sacramento all through the mining districts it was becoming too cumbersome for daily business in San Francisco.

To solve the problem a number of citizens had gone into coining locally. It was illegal of course, no one except the Federal Government was empowered to mint coins, but the slugs were accepted without question. All a man needed to set himself up in the business was a supply of gold, some way to smelt it into blanks, and a coin press. The coiner usually kept five percent of the gold brought to him as his share, made up the coins and returned them to the supplier of the raw gold. The slugs were individualistic. Few were round. Some were hexagonal, some domino shaped, but in most of the establishments they were weighed on the same scales that had weighed the dust to assure they contained full value.

With the influx of miners from all over the world every kind of coin was circulating on the West Coast, American, English, French, German, plus money from the smaller countries of South America and the Orient. Still there was a shortage, especially in the lower valuations. The bit, worth twelve and a half cents, was the smallest I remember seeing and there were few of these since there was little they would buy. It was a time of carelessness with money. Goods were priced in dollars and few asked for change.

Mitch's express charges were given him as a bag of slugs weighing a little more than twenty-six pounds which he slung over his shoulder as we left Lord and Company. It was getting dark. The hotels and saloons were lighted and I lagged, gawking in at the bright interiors, the throngs of men, the blue smoke that made a veil over them. I was too interested in the sights to notice where we were going until we passed the Tehama House and Mitch turned in at the store where the captain had first tried to buy a pick.

It had not changed except that it was more crowded with both goods and customers and both of the brothers were working. Neither of them took any notice of us. Jesse Seligman was busy with two men and Mitch and I wandered around looking over the stock. Then Jesse made his sales, bowed his customers out of the store and hurried directly to us, both hands extended, calling ahead:

"My dear friend."

He switched at once to German, but from the flick of his eyes and Mitch's laughing gesture at our grimy condition I guessed that Seligman was commenting on that. However, he showed none of Joyce's distaste, dropped the subject immediately for a barrage of questions. I automatically assumed that this was another of Mitch's conquests, made on his earlier trip to the city. The only surprise was Mitch's speaking German, adding one more ability to the unending discoveries about him I kept making. Every time I began to think I knew him well he would turn up something else.

I balanced on one foot and then the other and Mitch, seeing that I felt left out, switched to English with an extravagant wave of his hand.

"Davie, I want you to meet Jesse Seligman, the smartest business-man in California."

Seligman made a puffing sound with his lips. "Mitchell with the big jokes again. I am just a poor peddler . . . David, my pleasure." He shook my hand while Mitchell chuckled.

"The prices you're asking, you won't be a poor anything for long."

Mitchell was much the bigger, more powerful man and they did not look alike, but there was something similar about the eyes that made me wonder if they could be related. Surely they were en-joying themselves enough that this might be a sort of reunion. Selig-man had hold of Mitchell's arm, tugging on it for emphasis.

"The prices, Mitchell . . . the prices are better here than you can find. Never will we be undersold. Show me goods like mine and I'll meet anybody's price. Now, clothes you need?"

"Some other things." Mitch dismissed clothes with a hand wave and brought out a list I had not known he had. He did not show it to Seligman but began maneuvering down the store toward the rear pausing to look at various articles, waiting as Seligman praised their virtues, then moving on without committing himself to anything.

At the back, behind a clutter of hardware, was a small safe. Mitch-ell nodded to it, arching an eyebrow.

"How do you use that thing, with all the stuff in front of it, dig it out every night?"

The storekeeper lifted his shoulders. "We don't use it. A saloon-keeper brought it around the Horn but when he heard he had to walk to the hills he thought it was a little too heavy to carry. So I bought it."

"What did you give for it?"

Jesse Seligman started to answer, then stopped. His heavy eyelids half-closed.

"You want it? There aren't many safes in California."

"Nor much use for them." Mitch's voice was idle and he turned away.

Seligman followed him. "But you have a use? You are interested?"

"I think not. Not for what you'd ask for it."

"Have I put a price on it, Mitchell?" He lapsed into German, pointing vehemently back at the safe, switched again to English. "Examine it, Mitchell. In this country a fire is the great danger. Back East I lost a store and the goods weren't covered by enough insurance. With this safe I would not have lost. It would have protected me."

Mitchell was skeptical. "It would have been an oven. Anything in it would have charred to a crisp."

"No, no." Seligman was intense. "Not this safe. This was made in England, by Tann, two boxes, one inside the other, both wrought iron, and in between them a cushion of alum and Austin's cement. That alone will stop the heat. Then there are tubes running through, filled with a salty liquid. They will break if the outside box gets hot and make a moist fire clay of the cushion. Nothing can char."

Mitchell was impressed, I knew it by his expression, but he laughed.

"Did you take it apart to learn all that?"

Jesse grinned widely. "Jokes all the time. The man I bought it from explained. And more. Come see." He was back at the hardware pile throwing things out of his way to reach the safe. "Look, this series of bolts that slide from the edge of the door into the frame—a single key will work them all." He twisted the key and the well-oiled bolts eased out, one on each of the four sides of the door. "A hundred and fifty dollars you can have it for. The iron alone is worth that if you melted it down."

Mitchell's eyes too were now half-closed. "If it's so good why aren't you using it here?"

Seligman straightened, weaving his wiry body, his hands clawing through his hair.

"Such questions, Mitchell. In San Francisco, with banks, who needs it? A hundred and fifty only, Mitchell."

"I'll give a hundred."

There were tears in Jesse Seligman's voice. "If you were my own brother I could not let this go for a hundred. I should have asked two."

"One twenty-five. I shouldn't be buying it at all. You admit it's too heavy to carry upcountry." Mitchell turned as if wrenching himself away from temptation but Jesse caught his arm and held him back.

"All right. All right. You will ruin me yet. One hundred twenty-five dollars. What else is on your list? Clothes you need, I can see."

Mitchell said nothing about clothes. He went through the store looking at a variety of tools, miners' tools, though if he were going to quit mining I did not see why he wanted them. He haggled over prices and quality and rejected one article after another. Finally Seligman shook an admonishing finger at him.

"Mitchell, you are playing games with me. You are not buying. I know why, trying to wear out my patience. It is clothes you need, be honest."

Clothes we did need, desperately. Everything we had was worn out, from hats to boots. I was in worse shape than any of the other three. I had grown four inches and though I was not yet filling out my trousers and shirt sleeves stopped halfway up my legs and arms, were darned and patched and still ragged.

And at last Mitchell admitted that he might be in the market for a pair of sturdy pants, and put me to watch the gold sack.

Seligman was off like a cat, dragging down from a high shelf the familiar butternut trousers, trousers of durable nankeen, trousers for the city, soaring off into a sales pitch in rapid German. Mitchell caught them up, yanked at the garments to test the seams, argued over each offering, he too using German.

It quickly turned into a shouting match. Mitchell bought pants for the four of us and turned to shirts, the heavy, bright-colored variety generally worn in the hills. And with every article he agreed to, the tempo of the argument went up. I thought they would attack each other. I backed away in hypnotized horror. When the other Seligman brother, Leopold, came up to me I knew that my eyes were round and popping.

He had a gentle, wistful smile and amusement in his face.

"Don't worry about them," he said. "Mr. Randolph understands. This is Jesse's greatest pleasure, and there are few people here who will bargain in the old ways."

Then he wandered off and left me to watch the raging performance. Mitchell piled up a stack of clothing on the counter, slamming piece on top of piece, socks, boots, even hats. From Seligman's scrambling search and a word I caught it appeared that Mitchell wanted a bowler. That would be for the captain, but of those the store was sold out. With apparent disgust Mitch settled for three slouch hats and a wool cap for me.

Both of them must have been exhausted when it was finished. I was, just from watching. Then Seligman totaled up the figures agreed on and with dire head-shaking presented his bill.

Mitch checked down the list, there was another flurry of name calling, then he came for the sack of gold slugs and hoisted it to the counter. Jesse's eyes bugged out when Mitch opened the mouth.

"So much gold, my friend. Did you find the Mother Lode?"

"I'm in the express business," Mitch said, and explained how he had brought mail down from the camps and would take back what had collected in San Francisco, how he had brought down Bell's consignment of dust.

"That's why the safe took my eye," he said. "Not that I trust your box, but it will impress my customers. I'd rather bury the dust in the ground and put Joe over it with the musket. People, though, think a coffer means security."

"A coffer?" I didn't know what he meant.

"An old word, Davie, the French still use it to mean a safe."

Did Mitchell Randolph know every language there was? By now if I had been told so I would have believed it beyond doubt.

Jesse Seligman's eyes were hooded again, his words soft now. "And you will also be buying gold at the mines. What will you do with all of that?"

"I haven't decided exactly, Jesse. At Lord's they told me the Adams Express people sent a man named Haskell out last fall to represent them on the coast. Theirs is a pretty big name."

As far as I knew the gold-buying idea had not entered Mitch's head until Seligman mentioned it, but you'd never know it from his manner.

Seligman made a spluttering, derisive noise. "He's been here since October, but he's not going to confine himself to this town. Adams is planning to establish branches all through the gold fields. If you use him as your shipping agent now, what will happen when he moves into your camps? I'll tell you. He'll force you out of business. Adams is the biggest express organization in the East, bigger than American. Mitchell, it is an old saying that big fish grow bigger by eating little ones."

"A chance I'll have to take, I guess. I'll need a correspondent on the East Coast if I go into anything more than handling mail."

Seligman put a gentle finger on Mitch's hand. "My dear friend, our family is headquartered on the East Coast. We are expanding. A good, solid house, Seligman's. Come with us, Mitchell."

They looked at each other like two wolves meeting over the carcass of a fresh-killed deer. Then they were talking again, but they were back in German and I couldn't follow. Leopold came from a rear room, listened awhile, then beckoned me and led me into their living quarters. He had a supper ready, enough for us all, but he served the two of us without waiting. We ate and talked.

Leopold told me that with the exploding population there was talk that California would soon be a state and admitted to the Union. That was exciting to me, but he sounded very depressed. He had not wanted to come West. He hated the grubby buildings, the rain, the mud. He was like a restless prisoner, complaining that Jesse treated him like a child, insisted that he observe every tenet of their religion, kept him isolated from people, hardly permitted him out of the store.

"He's so afraid," he said, "that I might get involved with what he calls gamblers and drifters and loose women. There's nothing for me to do here, no girls to talk to, no place to go. I was not meant to live like this."

He was not, I learned, nearly as interested in the business as he was in making pictures.

Still Mitch and Jesse did not come, and finally Leopold shrugged and took me into a bedroom where we went to sleep.

The other two talked all night. They were eating the supper for breakfast when I got up and Mitch did not go to bed at all. He left the things he had bought and took me on a morning errand.

The town looked more dreary and squalid in the foggy day than it had with the lights to brighten it, but the Bella Union and the rest of the gambling saloons were still open, the streets filled with people. After the winter in Sonora it seemed to me, contrary to Leopold, that there were unlimited opportunities for entertainment. I wanted to go in and look at at least one of the saloons but Mitch would not let me even stick my nose through a door. He swept me past them without a sideways glance, until he found the office of the *Alta*, the largest newspaper in town. There he asked for Mr. Moore.

I couldn't figure what he was up to now and Mitch, while he was not close-mouthed, never did give any advance explanations of what he was going to do. He did though tell me while we waited

63

that Moore had been a printer for the New York *Sun* before he came West, and the man who came toward us turned out to be short, with a pleasant smile and a genial manner.

Mitch introduced himself and Moore took us back to his desk and sat down, spreading out a sheet of paper Mitch had handed him. I went around behind him to see it over his shoulder.

At the top was a solid black silhouette picture of a mule with its ears tipped forward. It wasn't bad. Below it was a message in heavy block letters.

THE MULE EXPRESS

IS PREPARED TO OFFER REGULAR MONTHLY SERVICE BETWEEN SAN FRANCISCO AND THE SOUTHERN MINES FOR THE PURPOSE OF DELIVERING AND FORWARDING LETTERS, PACKAGES, MERCHANDISE AND GOLD DUST TO ALL SUBSCRIBERS.

THE EXPRESS HAS ARRANGED WITH CORRESPONDENTS ON THE EASTERN COAST AND WILL ISSUE LETTERS OF CREDIT AND ADVICE TO BE HONORED AT ANY POINT IN THE UNITED STATES.

THE EXPRESS WILL DEPART FROM GIEGER'S STORE IN SONORA ON THE FIRST MONDAY OF EACH MONTH AND WILL RETURN APPROXIMATELY THREE WEEKS LATER.

SUB-AGENCIES WILL BE ESTABLISHED IN JAMESTOWN, COLUMBIA, ANGELS AND MURPHY'S AND ALL OTHER CAMPS WHERE A VOLUME OF BUSINESS WARRANTS.

MAJOR MITCHELL RANDOLPH, PROP.

Mr. Moore finished reading and turned his attention back to the picture.

"Who did that for you, Leo Seligman?"

"No," said Mitchell. "I did it myself. Can you print it?"

"We'll have some trouble with it. It will need a wood block and I'm not certain we have anyone who can carve it."

"I will."

We were in the print shop most of the morning. Mitch's block was sharp and simple, an eye catcher when it was on the finished poster. He ordered fifty of the displays for which Moore charged him twenty dollars. Moore stayed with us while the copies were run off on the hand press. He had a more than professional interest in their content.

"Major Randolph," he said, "how do you go from here to Sonora?"

"Up through Webber's Landing."

"I meant, what is your equipment? Do you ever handle passengers?"

"Sometimes. I use a boat to the Landing, a wagon on to Sonora."

"There are sixteen men at the City Hotel. They came in yesterday on the *Antelope* from Panama. They're headed for the Southern Mines. Two of them are friends of mine. What would you charge?"

For once, I thought, Mitch was in over his head. Our boat would hardly hold six, let alone eighteen people, and I nearly gasped aloud when he said promptly:

"An ounce of gold apiece. They'll have to feed themselves and take their turns at the oars."

I couldn't imagine how he meant to solve this, but I didn't dare ask him here. I could only listen and puzzle.

Moore was saying, "They haven't any dust. Would fifteen dollars apiece do?"

Mitch allowed that it would, and when the posters were ready Mr. Moore got his hat and went with us down Clay Street to the City Hotel, so I still could not ask the questions that wanted to burst out.

We met the travelers in the low, dark lobby and none of them objected to the terms Mitch had set. Like all greenhorns just off a ship they were in a sweat to get to the gold fields. I knew exactly how they felt. Eight months ago I had been just as innocent and eager.

The bargain was struck. They would report to the *Niantic* landing at five-thirty the next morning. Mitchell limited them to twenty-five pounds of baggage each, and that drew a protest because they were loaded down with paraphernalia, but Mitch explained that they couldn't carry the excess beyond Sonora anyway. The restriction though did nothing to lessen my worry, and I could hardly wait until we left them and headed for the cove alone. Then I exploded.

"How do you think you can haul all those men? The dinghy will sink."

He lifted one eyebrow quizzically. "Who mentioned the dinghy?"

"But . . . but . . . It's the only boat we have."

"The bay is full of boats. Every abandoned barque and schooner had three or four."

"But they'll all have been stolen by now."

"Then we'll find one we can buy."

That stopped me and I was silent, trailing him down the muddy length of Montgomery. Then I remembered a question about the wording on the poster that I had wanted to ask until the problem of transporting sixteen men drove it out of my mind.

"Mitchell, are you going to use the Seligmans for New York correspondents?"

"Sure. It's a good firm, with several stores in the East and they're moving into banking."

"You must have known them pretty well back there."

He grinned down at me. "Never saw any of them until Joe and I came down here last month."

I found myself sputtering at that. "How do you know you can trust them? There's going to be a lot of money going through their hands. They're city people, not like the miners."

"How should they trust me?"

"Well, how?"

"We speak the same language."

"Oh sure, you both speak German, but what's that got to do with it?"

His face changed, turned brooding as if he were looking years into a past about which I knew nothing. "Not German, Davie. I meant the language of trading. They understand money."

I felt that I had to be content with that. The wall around his inner being had showed itself again.

It took us some hours to locate a boat that satisfied Mitchell, a whale boat twenty-seven feet long, built sharp at both ends, carrying a sail, and a rudder at the stern for a helmsman. It had been appropriated by some of the men who made a living meeting incoming ships and the bargaining was spirited. Mitch finally bought it for three hundred dollars and the dinghy, which of course belonged to Mr. Bell, but that did not seem to bother Mitch.

One thing did bother me. He had brought his sack of gold slugs from Seligmans' in the morning, had paid Moore from it and now he opened it to pay for the boat. Standing as I was I saw two of the boatmen exchange a look as Mitch counted out the gold. He gave them half at the time and promised the rest in the morning when they were to have the boat moored at the *Niantic* dock. After we left I mentioned them to Mitch.

"Yes," he said. "Thanks, Davie. It's good to be suspicious in a place like this."

We spent the rest of the day collecting mail and buying a stock of food for the trip, then took it all back to Seligmans' to stay another night there. Mitch napped until time for supper, then we had a quiet celebration with wine that he had brought, and again Mitch and Jesse sat up long after I had given out and gone to sleep.

Jesse had arranged with a drayman to haul the safe to the boat. Mitch locked the mail and his sack of slugs in it, saving out enough to pay the haulage and the boatmen. They loaded the box and the bundle of clothes into the open wagon bed, covered it with a tarpaulin, and we rode across the square and down to the hotel ship. Even in this deadest of hours noise rolled from the gambling houses into the dark fog.

The safe was heavier than the tub of gold had been and more awkward, but they had brought planks to make a bridge to the whale boat and Mitch and the drayman, a burly Welshman, wrestled it out of the wagon, across the planks and into the middle of the craft, tying it against a seat. Mitch paid the man with one slug, then we set about stowing the food and goods he had bought. Still the boatmen had not appeared to collect the rest of their money.

The drayman was gone, out of sight and sound, before we heard noise, saw a bobbing lantern and made out a group of men. They came toward us and at first I thought it was only the sellers of the boat. As they ran across the bridge I recognized the one in the lead, but now he was pulling a Navy revolver. I yelled a warning but it was too late. The gun was shoved into Mitch's face.

The next two aboard grabbed me and in horror I saw that they were a crewman from the *Anne Marie*'s last voyage and Barker's treacherous mate, Mr. Lord.

In the yellow lantern light his face was even more like a rat's than I remembered, and he recognized both of us immediately.

"The little lad Davie." He gave a high, ugly laugh. "And Mr. Randolph, bless me. Now it's a fine timely meeting for us old friends, especially with you owing us money." He left me in the grip of the crewman and raised his gun at Mitchell, who had not moved or spoken. "We wouldn't want to spoil the happy moment with any argument, now would we? My friends sold the boat too cheap, so we'll just relieve you of the sack, Mr. Randolph darling, and be on our way. No cause at all for anybody to get hurt, is there?"

I felt sick, remembering Barker's chest and the gold in Mitch's pocket. They would take that and take the key and open the safe. Then they would kill us and dump our bodies overboard to hide the murder. We could not stop it. There were four of them, all armed and ready to move in.

Mitch showed neither fear nor excitement. His voice was quiet and unhurried. "I'll pay what I owe, Mr. Lord, but the sack is back in town. Do you think I'm fool enough to bring it down here in the dead of night? Go ahead and shoot. But it won't get you the gold."

They had not expected that answer nor that Mitch would not be cowering under their guns. His coolness shook their confidence, seemed proof to them that he was telling the truth. They stood disconcerted, slack for the moment.

The man holding my arm was more intent on Mitch's words than on me. I wrenched free and spun away.

I had thought his grip was more solid. My force against the lack of resistance threw me against the rail and overboard. I went flailing into the cold water of the bay.

I could always swim, and in St. Louis the big Mississippi River was the main amusement for the kids. I went under, pulled down by the weight of my new boots, and after the first shock I wasn't frightened. I stayed down and struck out, swimming under water for as long as my breath held.

When I surfaced I was twenty feet from the boat on the side opposite the one I had fallen from and blessedly beyond the reach of the lantern's light. I rested there, treading water, filling my lungs, hearing the loud cursing and seeing the men peering over the far gunwale. Then I heard Lord say:

"He didn't come up. Brat probably drowned. Let's get on with it."

I watched his dark silhouette raise an arm and slap the gun against Mitchell's head, heard the rasping voice.

"Mr. Randolph darling, where is the money?"

I hated to leave Mitch but there was nothing I could do to help there. In a near panic of fear of what they would do to him I sunk again and swam toward shore, angling farther away. I hit the mud and crawled out and had to lie there a moment, panting. Then I scrambled up and ran along the path.

The only place I could think of where I might find help was the nearest saloon, and the idea was not reassuring. Leopold Seligman had told me hair-raising stories of the holdups and murders that were so common in San Francisco they went without notice, and how Jesse insisted the saloons were spawning grounds for such crimes. But there was nowhere else to go at this hour.

I had run perhaps a thousand yards when I saw a group of men turn the corner and walk toward me, one of them swinging a lantern. Whether they would help or join in the robbery I did not know, but they would be no more risk than a saloon crowd. I ran faster, not daring to yell but waving my arms wildly. They saw me and stopped and I came up to them gasping.

With a surge of hope I recognized them as our potential passengers and I fought to keep my voice from rising, carrying back to the boat, but my suspicion of everyone at the moment made me use a sly appeal.

"Please. Help. They're murdering Mitchell Randolph and if they kill him they'll take the boat and you can't get up the river."

The first man lifted the lantern, staring at my soaked clothes. "You're the boy with Randolph at the hotel yesterday?"

"Yes. Hurry. Hurry."

They hurried. They outran me and I stumbled behind. They were all armed. Almost no one landing in California from the East came unarmed.

A shot flashed from the boat, the heavy pistol making a shocking noise in the still morning, then the passengers were shooting back, dropping their twenty-five pound packs, scattering for position. I was afraid Mitch would be hit but there was no other way to attack Lord's foursome.

By the time we got to the dock the robbers were gone. I had a glimpse of a shadow vanishing into the dark along the *Niantic*'s deck and there was no more shooting. They had left their lantern on the safe and in the glow I saw Mitch sitting against the stern. His head was bowed forward and dark blood trickled from a deep cut above his ear. I thought he was dead.

Then as we jumped aboard he raised his head, saw who we were and smiled.

"Thanks, gentlemen. Are we ready to sail?"

That was Mitchell Randolph as I knew him in 1850. Whatever opportunity rose, he grabbed it. Whatever problem threatened, he solved it. Sometimes it seemed miraculous that he survived.

I wanted him to go back uptown and find a doctor. So did Mr. Franklin, the leader of our party, but Mitch would have none of it. He would only let them tie a clean handkerchief around his head. He even laughed that the money in his pocket had not been found.

We pulled the planks aboard and shoved off with the oars, then hoisted the small lanteen sail. Fortunately the wind was from the west, blowing in through the gate. None of us knew how to handle a sail nor much about boats. Our passengers had never touched an oar before. As we got acquainted I learned they were all from Scranton, Pennsylvania, where they had formed a company for the purpose of reaching and working the California mines.

There were any number of such companies initiated throughout the East, by men utterly ignorant of what it meant to mine or of the hardships involved. Most of them broke up soon after they reached the diggings, disillusioned and disgusted. This Pennsylvania company was one of the exceptions. They stayed together for three years, and our express company had the pleasure and profit of shipping one hundred and twenty thousand dollars out to the East for them.

Haphazard as our cruise was, we sailed north through San Pablo Bay and into the Carquinez Strait, on whose shore General Mariano Vallejo, Larkin, and Semple had once laid out a town they named Francisca, in honor of Vallejo's wife. Those early real estate promoters had believed their site would be of dominant importance because it lay so near the juncture of the Sacramento and San Joaquin Rivers, but the settlement growing up around Yerba Buena quickly outdistanced it, even stole its name. Alcalde Bartlett renamed the village by the cove San Francisco, after the mission there, and Vallejo had to rechristen his town Benicia to avoid confusion. At the time we passed it was a nearly forgotten community, most of its settlers gone off to the mines.

So long as we were in the bay the sail shoved the whale boat along at an easy clip, but once in the strait we had to use the oars. I say *we*, although neither Mitchell nor I rowed a stroke in the whole trip upriver. Mr. Franklin insisted that Mitchell, with his head wound, was in no shape and Mitch did not argue. For me these oars were simply too heavy.

They were almost too heavy for the company. When on the fifth day we reached Webber's Landing they were worn out, glad to climb into the big freight wagon and let the oxen pull them the rest of the way.

By the time we returned to Sonora the rains had stopped and the land was beginning to dry. Flowers that had only been waiting their chance sprang up in the patches of short grass and overnight it was spring.

With Captain Barker busy helping the company settle into an outdoor camp and while Joe took the team on to stable it I trailed Mitch into our cabin. The first thing he did was to dig out paper and a pencil and sit at the table figuring.

I did not interrupt, waiting until he looked up, his smile spreading wide. He had discarded the bandage only that morning. The cut was healing but was still red, angry. It would leave a scar, a white welt that he was always at pains to hide by combing his thick hair over it.

"We didn't do so badly." He tapped the paper. "We picked up a hundred and three letters. At an ounce apiece that represents about twelve hundred dollars."

I matched his grin. "With the five thousand you got for delivering Bell's dust that's over six thousand for about three weeks' work."

"Better than that." He was very pleased. "There's two hundred and forty for hauling the Franklin company. Then, I bought the whale boat for three hundred and the dinghy, sold it to Bell for five hundred and he forgot the dinghy. Two hundred profit there. Davie, I think we may just make a little more than most miners."

"It's a lot easier on the back, too. But you've got to be smart. And there's something you didn't count. You only paid the first half for the whale boat."

He laughed aloud, aiming a hand at me like a cocked gun. "You'll do, Davie. You'll do."

He was the happiest I had ever seen him, but not half so happy as I was next day.

Mitch and Joe, with plenty of help, unloaded the safe and got it placed in a rear corner of Gieger's Store where Mitch had made a deal to keep it. Included in the deal was a counter for the use of the express company, to run in front of the safe. While Joe and I were building that Mitch brought out a can of yellow paint and a brush he had bought from Seligman. It had been the only paint in the store and even Jesse did not know where it had come from. His stock was a conglomerate mess. He had brought twenty thousand dollars worth of goods with him across the isthmus, but even with what he had sold he had more than that now. He had bought anything any incoming shipmaster had to offer.

Mitch squatted in front of the safe, painting his mule insignia on the door face, kidding with his audience that its name was Effie, after the animal he had brought from Bell's. Then on the upper frame he printed in fine, flourishing letters the legend,

RANDOLPH'S MULE EXPRESS

When he had finished he moved back, letting the onlookers admire the work, and as the furor began to slack off he stepped beside me and raised his voice to cover the store.

"Gentlemen, I have a speech to make. Let me present our new general agent, manager of the Sonora office, Mr. David Stuart." He made me an elaborate bow. "Davie, you are it. Joe can't cipher, the captain is too careless and I have to tend to all the other camps.

From now on you are boss in this office. Don't let anyone put anything over on you."

There was an exuberant howl from the miners. They would howl for anything that was out of their routine. But I was too choked to make a sound.

I had never been so proud, never felt so important. I was the manager of Randolph's Mule Express, and it was my birthday. I was fourteen years old.

BOOK TWO

CHAPTER ONE

Ours was not the first express service on the West Coast. Even before the gold rush a man named Cady had tried carrying parcels and mail between San Francisco and Sutter's Fort, but at that time there were not enough settlers in the hills to make his venture profitable.

Now the situation was changed, and the way we prospered from the first showed that the potential for such a company had become enormous. The roads were few and bad. The country was extremely rough, cut by deep, twisting canyons with abrupt rock walls that made even foot travel dangerous. There was no system of supply. Every merchant moved his goods as best he could and although the camps were seldom more than three or four miles apart there was little communication between them.

We were filling a definite need and almost immediately we expanded. Mitchell opened branches at Angels Camp, where he put the captain in charge, at Jackson, where he made a deal with the storekeeper to manage it, and then others, one after another until we were operating in every camp of the Southern Mines.

Very early an even more urgent and lucrative, closely related necessity showed itself. There were no banks, no provisions for transporting the gold that was being torn out of the soil in rapidly increasing amounts. We soon outgrew the quarters in Gieger's Store and put up a four-room log building of our own with living space behind and an office in front. There we opened a bank, and extended it too to the network of settlements.

Other express companies sprang up, but some of them were unlucky, others downright dishonest, and few of the operators knew business management. Mitchell Randolph made no mistakes and he drummed into me and the other managers the importance of accurate accounting and efficient movement of our consignments.

His big figure mounted on the black mule became a symbol of security and his periodic arrival at the diggings was a cause for celebration. He brought them mail and papers and goods and took out their gold and held their trust.

Another express outfit was growing very fast. Adams Company were already big in the East, ranking with American and competing with it for the runs on the budding railroads, and they had sent Dan Haskell to California with plenty of money behind him. He had opened an office in San Francisco and begun buying up the struggling little lines in the Northern Mines, but he had not butted into our territory.

For two years all the southern business funneled through our Sonora headquarters, and to my inexperienced mind we were making a great amount of money. Then Mitchell came in from a long trip to San Francisco and dropped a bomb.

We were, he announced, moving to Stockton.

Sonora was home to me. All of the people I did business with were personal friends. There was almost a family feeling among us all. I knew their problems, how much dust I handled for each of them, how good or bad a credit risk every one of them was. For almost a year I had seen hardly anything of Mitch. Most of the time he was in San Francisco or somewhere else, and I had no idea what he was doing. He never bothered to tell me anything until it was necessary. If I went to Stockton I wouldn't know anyone at all.

"Why, Mitch?" I sounded shrill. "We're doing all right here, aren't we?"

"Better than all right, kid." He flashed his quick smile. "That's why we have to move. You know about the Adams Company?"

"Up north, yes. What have they got to do with us?"

"Haskell wants to buy us out."

I swallowed hard. "You're not going to sell?"

"Nope. Not at the price they're talking. But they are coming into Stockton and I don't want to let them get in a position where they can undercut us."

I began to worry. Our business was good but we were nowhere near big enough to challenge Adams and I said so.

"How would our moving to Stockton stop them?"

He smiled, very pleased with something that made his eyes light up. "In a way we'll join them. We'll still keep our own identity

76

though, and it will be good for both of us. We'll use a combined office. They'll agree not to open in any of our camps and in return they'll use our boat for their shipments to San Francisco and will handle our treasure for Panama, the East and Europe."

"Our boat?" All I could think of was the old whale boat, and I didn't understand. "We haven't got a boat. Don't you remember you sold it to Bell, two years ago?"

He laughed aloud. "We've got a steamer now. The best on the San Joaquin."

"Well, gee, you might have told me." I knew he was teasing me, but it made me mad. "Where did we get a steamer?"

"Bought it a month ago. I haven't seen you since. It's a ferry, really. A bunch of idiots sailed it around the Horn, believe it or not. I guess God takes care of fools at that. Well, let's get ready to move. We'll leave enough here to keep this office as an agency."

We took a single wagonload down. Mitchell was in fine spirits, catching me up on the news that he'd collected from trips around most of the state, and it was good to be with him again, and traveling. I had not been out of Sonora for a long while.

Stockton had changed a lot. Bell had a new store and several merchants had come in to give him competition, but there appeared business enough to go around. Their docks running out into the river were all busy. In spite of its swampy location the town's growth had been assured from the beginning of the rush because it was at the head of navigation on the San Joaquin Channel. Though this was not the main stream it had plenty of deep water for steamers, especially our converted ferryboat.

She was tied up at our own dock behind our combination office and warehouse across the river from Rough and Ready Island, and Mitchell showed her off to me like some great new toy. She was not large as steamers went, only a hundred and forty feet long, with a single track paddle wheel and a net tonnage of a hundred and twenty-five. She had been built in England for service between New York and some Jersey point, flat as a raft, and from what I remembered of the voyage in the *Anne Marie* I knew it was a miracle that this lubberly slab had beat through the big storms off the tip of South America. Maybe that was why Mitch was so proud of her.

He had renamed her the *Effie*, after the black mule, in a whimsical bow to superstition, and brought the captain down from Angels Camp to command her. Abner Barker was happy again. He had hated the gold fields, detested working in the mud, and had liked the finicky detail of the express agency little better. Now he had a bridge again and a new blue uniform with gold stripes up the cuffs, and he made a formidable figure supervising the hundreds of immigrants that rode under him on the biweekly trips up from the bay.

A single passage cost one ounce or twelve dollars, so she was a moneymaker as a passenger carrier but she was even more important to us for transporting gold. Mitchell had built a strong room in the middle of the lower deck, floored with iron plates and guarded by a heavy door.

Joe had been driving a delivery wagon through the camps but Mitchell had brought him down too and put him in charge of the strong room. The responsibility of safeguarding consignments that sometimes ran a hundred to a hundred and fifty thousand dollars worth of dust delighted him and gave him a swashbuckling swagger. He wore a Colt revolver and carried a cut-off shotgun in the crook of his arm, and I suspected that he rubbed some red cosmetic into the scar on his cheek to give it an angrier, more threatening look. He watched like a hawk while a shipment was loaded, then bolted himself inside the iron room and never opened the door until they docked in San Francisco and the Adams man there knocked on it with a code that was changed for every trip.

River pirates were making trouble for all boatmen, but thanks to Joe and the crew of men who would shoot at a hint of it, whom Barker had recruited from miners he had known, no attempt was ever made to board the *Effie.*

It was a good reunion, the four of us together again, my family intact, but it did not last. Mitch went back to San Francisco with them on the next trip and left me alone in the unfamiliar town. And when the *Effie* returned and clumsily bumped her nose in against the dock there was another change. Joe had brought a woman up with him.

As soon as the passengers were unloaded the captain came into the office to tell me about it.

"She's a looker," he said and sounded worried. "That Joe, she's got him not thinking straight. The damn fool meant to keep her on the boat with him. Can you fancy that? I put my foot down there. Them immigrants we haul would make it bad enough, but the crew seeing her around all the while, they'd make it dynamite. They'd figure a black girl as fair meat and Joe would blow somebody's head off with that forty-four. I told him she'd have to stay down in town or up here."

"Not up here, it's just as bad as the boat," I said. With all of the restless men in camp there was only a handful of women, Chilenos who hung around the cheaper saloons. "Tell him to take her back down."

"You tell him, maybe you can get somewhere with him."

I tried, when he brought her in and introduced her, but Joe put his arm around her and grinned at me. To Joe I was still the boy whose father he had buried, the kid he had taken upriver and nursed through the first winter at the mines. My stature as manager of the express office did not impress him.

"Davie," he said, "you take good care of Nora, hear. I'll fix up that little room out back of the house for us. She's a good gal. She can read and write and she's teaching me."

I tried to argue with him, that she could teach him on his lay-overs in San Francisco, but he scowled and shook his hard head.

"That won't work, Davie, on account of the man that brought her out from New Orleans is a mean old bastard and he's looking for her. I take her back there I'd have to kill him."

"You mean she's a runaway?"

He just looked at me. I gave up. I had never been able to think of Joe as a slave. Ugly as he was he had more dignity than many freeborn men. California was a free state and although some slave-owners had brought Negroes out with them no one ever bothered Joe. He was looked on as the major's boy and people did not want to tangle with Mitchell Randolph. Both at the mines and on the bay Mitch commanded respect. He was the Mule Express.

It turned out that Nora was my mainstay through that first year in Stockton. She was young, bright, pretty, laughing, and proud. She kept the office and the house clean and cooked for me and who-ever of us were there. She was a better cook than any of us, which I especially appreciated, and she was good company through what otherwise would have been empty, lonely evenings.

I was never happy in Stockton. I missed the daily camaraderie of the miners in Sonora. Here everything was business and a drudge. The three Adams clerks were city men. They neither knew nor liked the foothill country and they condescended to me because of my age. The fact that three quarters of the gold we shipped downriver came from the Mule Express agencies galled them and they constantly questioned my management.

I did not know then that friction is almost inevitable when two organizations try to operate under one roof and thought their ques-tioning was aimed at annoying me personally. We argued over the division of the rate we received on shipments to the East and Europe. We fought over how much commission was due them when Adams originated passengers and cargo for the *Effie*. They wanted the sailing schedule changed so that the steamer would make more stops at the river towns where they had agencies.

All in all '52 was a gloomy year for me. But the *Effie* plowed her monotonous way up and down the San Joaquin, San Francisco grew, Stockton grew, and the increasing treasure horde reflected in a rising balance in my ledgers. California was booming and we were booming with it. The Mule Express was becoming a very wealthy company, although the captain, Joe, and I were taking only a frugal living out of it. Mitchell kept a tight hold on the profits, building a fund, he said, for further development later.

I was particularly upset one Tuesday after another row with the Adams clerks, when Mitchell came breezing in off the ferry, bringing with him the sense of hurry and urgency that he always generated. At first I thought it was a routine call, but when we sat down over coffee in my office I knew there was something special behind it. He had not asked immediately to see the ledgers, which was unusual, and just as unusual, he seemed nervous.

"How's Joe Touney working out at Sonora?"

He knew how Touney was working out. A banker from Maine, he was doing a fine job, so the question had to be a way of getting at something.

"He's the best man we've got," I said, and waited for whatever was coming.

"Yes. Well, send for him by the next wagon. Tell him to put Morris in charge up there and come down to take over this office."

By that time I should have gotten used to Mitchell's surprises but I never wholly did. His mind was so constantly active, probing every situation for an opportunity, and I was still too young to see on my own the ramifications of the projects he kept taking us into. Never, though, did I doubt that they would succeed. Yet this announcement shook me up, and I laughed uncertainly.

"Does that mean I'm fired?"

"Of course not." The nervousness gave way to an intense effort to explain a changing picture to me. "Davie, the hardest thing in business is to find capable men and put them where they'll be the most effective. Right now our economy is growing faster than our population, and new banking firms are coming into San Francisco. At the rate things are moving, if the gold holds out, California will one day rate with London and New York as a financial center. We've got to keep up. It's time you learn the whole extent of our business.

I can't be every place at once, so I want you free to take over the supervision of our agencies. And I want you to spend time in San Francisco getting to know the business community, the men building wharfs and promoting industry and making fortunes in real estate. In other words I want you as an extra pair of eyes to watch the details I no longer have the time for."

The prospect of getting away from Stockton was better than a present, whatever it meant I was heading into.

"When do I start?"

"As soon as you can show Touney the ropes here. As fast as you can. There's another reason I need you down there. I'm getting married."

My reaction did not come at once. There was a time lag and then it came slowly, like the roar of an avalanche.

Growing up in the mining camps I had never thought of women as having any place in my world. Everyone around me was in effect a bachelor. Then as the whores came in and the madams began piling up sizable fortunes I did a good deal of business with them. Some of the men were marrying these girls, but even though Joe had brought Nora among us it had never entered my head that Mitchell Randolph would take a wife. The suddenness of his announcement jolted me like a threat. It must have showed in my face.

He was watching me, nervous again. "Well?"

"Well what?" I said numbly.

He gave me an embarrassed laugh. "You don't sound very interested."

It was suddenly important that I prove an interest and I said hurriedly, "Oh sure I am. Who is she?"

"Aurelia McLeod." He began talking faster than was normal for him. "Her father was a Scot sailor who landed out here twenty-some years ago and married one of the Lamas family. The Mexican governor gave him a grant, a ranch on the peninsula down toward San Jose. I saw her at a fiesta at Mariano Vallejo's when I went to Sonoma to see about locating an agency there. All these old Spanish families are related and she's some kind of kin to General Vallejo."

I had not had much contact with the Spanish Californians, the *Californios*. A few had tried to work some mining claims with *peón* labor but the Americans had insisted that every man must work his claim himself and they had been driven out of the diggings. They were a foreign race to me, and certainly they were not friendly to the Americans. Just as certainly I did not want Mitchell to marry one of them.

It was an instinctive feeling. I did not recognize it then as jealousy, but I strongly resented her. Mitchell was part father, part older brother to me. He had taken control of my life at a time when I was helpless. He had taught me all I knew beyond childhood, given me a sense of security and belonging. Now this unknown girl was shoving in between us, and some animal instinct was warning me that our relationship would never be the same again. I said warily:

"What's she like?"

"I don't know yet. I only saw her the once and I didn't speak to her."

I thought then that he had to be joking and relaxed a little. "Then how would you know if you'd want to marry her? Love at first sight?"

He ran nervous fingers over his face. "Love doesn't have to come first, Davie. Marriage is properly a business arrangement. In Europe it is a hardheaded, rational deal agreed to between fathers of children who are sometimes very young. It is a system for insuring the best available future for their sons and daughters. It works well."

"Maybe." I was skeptical. "But why do you want to bother getting married at all?"

He grinned then and slapped at my shoulder. "I guess you're a little young yet to know some of the reasons."

"Oh, I know that men go to bed with women, but why get married? There must be plenty of places in San Francisco . . ."

"For sex, yes. But I'm not marrying for that. I told you San Francisco is changing fast. The important men are bringing their wives out from the East and the women are going to dominate the society. When that happens a bachelor will be held in suspicion, kept at arm's length. I want to belong, Davie, to be inside. We're on a whole new trip out here and by God I am not going steerage."

There was a suggestion there that I did not understand. I didn't see why he didn't already belong since he was among the very first of the pack that was creating a solid business structure in the bay area. But I didn't pursue that. I was too concerned with this new individual who was looming like a storm cloud on my horizon, and I tried to fight against her.

"If she's Spanish . . . the Americans don't think much of them . . . I don't see how she could help you to belong in the city."

His smile turned ironic, even cynical, and he chuckled. "There's a funny thing about that, Davie. There aren't any titles in America but the people still feel that there's something special about an aristocracy. There's a class growing out here that's making a lot of money for the first time and they're not comfortable with it yet. They may not like the *Californios*, but when a house goes back several hundred years they can't help themselves from being impressed."

Oddly I had a swift picture of Mitch marrying some old woman, and I asked, "How old is she?"

"Fifteen. Same age her mother was when she married McLeod."

It was a losing battle for me. All I could do was find out how long before the sword would fall.

"When is it going to happen?"

Now his embarrassment really showed itself. "I don't know. Her family hasn't been approached yet. You see, the usual thing would be for my family to talk to hers, but I haven't got a family."

For a dreadful minute I thought he was going to want me to talk to them, then he went on.

"I'm going to have to do it myself. I've been waiting until I could get you down to the bay. I want you to go with me. I simply do not want to go alone."

There was small comfort in that. Only if he had tried to send me by myself could it have been worse.

It was ten days later that we drove down the peninsula. I had spent a week showing Joe Touney how to run the office, wavering between anticipation at leaving Stockton and dread of the onerous mission ahead. The two days in the new San Francisco would have been wonderfully exciting if I had not been so weighed down. I was uncomfortable with Mitchell and it was not until we were on the road and out of town that I began to feel a reviving interest.

Mitch talked all the way with an energy part genuine and part, I thought, to take his own mind off the purpose of the errand.

The road we followed south, he said, was the oldest highway in California. Few of the Americans who had come to the Coast had bothered with the history of the land, but that voracious mind of Mitchell's had soaked up information like a sponge. The Camino Real, as he told it, had been built to service the old string of missions that had a stranglehold on the country. The Church's power had held until 1833, when the Mexican Government took over the property and divided it between the old families from San Diego, Santa Barbara, and Monterey. Those grants had been huge and

Mitch named some of them as we passed, the de Haros, the Diazes, other families around the border of the bay.

"They had all of it, and what did they do with it?" He sounded contemptuous. "They're losing it, that's what. Every one of them is in trouble, and they don't even know why. Just look around you at what they're piddling away."

The land was beautiful, sand colored, gently rolling, gracious with clumps of live oaks and big, lone trees. A breeze from the Pacific moved the grass and made it pleasantly cooler here than in the upland valleys. Wild currant and gooseberries grew between bursts of chaparral, wild roses and manzanita with the shining dark green leaves and shining red bark warmed the picture with soft color. I thought of the seared brown weeds of the gold camps, the bare gravel tailing piles all along the streams, the raw ugliness left by the miners.

"It's sure a pretty place to live. Why are they losing it?"

He was irritated. "Because they don't know anything about money, business, and don't want to know. They've always known there was gold in the hills but they weren't even interested."

That was news to me. "I thought Jim Marshall found it first."

"That was the first time the Americans took notice, but the ships trading along this coast had been picking up bits of it brought down by the Indians for years. The ranchers were just too busy raising horses and cattle to think about gold. They didn't half do a job marketing the animals either. So the Americans are moving in and taking over."

At a dusty side trail he turned the team to the right and we climbed to the top of the ridge we had been paralleling. At the crest he hauled up and swept his arm across the view. We sat looking across a lovely, softly falling slope to a distant blue sea that stood vertical, its horizon hanging high in the sky.

"This is the ranch, Davie, La Playa de la Felicidad, the happy shore. It used to stretch for miles along the coast, McLeod ran eight thousand cattle and a thousand horses. Now there's under eight hundred acres around the house."

"He sold it off?"

"Not even that. The damn fool went in with a couple of sharpies from Boston to start a shipping line. I told you he was a sailor. He mortgaged the ranch for capital. Then the crews quit and went to the gold fields like everybody else and he lost one section after another. If he'd stayed in the cattle business and used a little imagination he'd have made millions. Remember what meat cost at

the mines that first year? Remember there wasn't any fruit, no vegetables? Remember the dried beans?"

I shuddered.

"He had it all here. All here. But no, the *Californios* didn't sell
their cows for food. They sold skins, and rendered the carcasses
out and sold tallow. And none of them could see what was under
their noses."

Angry at the waste of opportunity he slapped the reins on the
horses' rumps and trotted down the easy grade.

Much as I resented his daughter I felt sorry for McLeod. "Is he
going to lose the rest of the ranch?" I asked.

"He's dead, an accident in a cattle roundup about a year ago.
The mortgage on what's left is due in sixty days."

"Do you know who holds it?"

"I bought it from the bank a few weeks ago."

I turned to look at him but his eyes were on the track ahead. I
had pictured the McLeod family trapping him into a marriage because of his money. Now I was beginning to get another idea. I had
never known Mitchell to be cruel but I had seen him turn the mis-
fortunes of others to his advantage. He had taken over Dell Gross's
team when the man was dying, and without that team and wagon
we could not have started the express. Of course he had nothing to
do with the death, but he had been the only one in Sonora to see
the possibility, and had eased Gross's mind by rescuing the animals
from slaughter. The same pattern had worked in Panama when
without funds he had chartered Abner Barker's ship and resold the
charter to Nelson. He had done Barker a service, getting more
money for him than the captain would have dreamed of asking,
helped Nelson by showing him how to turn the coal holds into much
needed passenger space.

In Sacramento he had not suggested joining our floundering party
until he heard we had a boat to haul his duffel in. Who of us could
complain that an advantage had been taken of us?

CHAPTER TWO

The house was unlike any I had visited before. Located on a rise to overlook the Pacific, it was a long, two-story rectangle with a wing at either end turning back landward, embracing a garden. The garden, where these people did much of their living, was protected from the prevailing sea breeze. The architecture was Spanish except for a tower that rose out of the south wing and gave an unrestricted view of the sharp cliffs, the surf that broke against their base and the swell of the vast ocean as it stretched away toward the Orient.

All of the walls were of adobe brick, over three feet thick, laid up by Indian workmen in a mortar mixture of lime and small sea shells, coated with a sand plaster to protect them from winter rains, then whitewashed over. The beams that supported the heavy red roof tiles were tree trunks from the ridge that was the spine of the peninsula, hand hewn, tied in place with leather thongs that were knotted and then shrunk by wetting them. The floors were dark, square tiles, and at the far end of the main hall, thirty feet wide and forty long, a giant fireplace yawned, its throat large enough to accept huge, gnarled live oak logs cut on the slopes above.

The furnishings were plain. A long deal table made from a single slab of redwood, sat in the center of the hall. The chairs were boxlike, straight, with tapestry seats, some having arms, some not. I later learned that they had been bought from a Boston ship in trade for hides and tallow.

But this main room was in no sense a family gathering center. In good weather everything took place in the garden. Even the cooking was done outside the kitchen doors that also opened on the garden. The whole household ate at a huge table shaded by trees, everyone sitting down at the same board, the family at one end, the fieldhands, herders, and sheep handlers at the other.

After the rude cabins of the gold camps and Stockton, La Playa de la Felicidad was monumentally elegant that first time I saw it.

We drove into the square work yard to the north of the house. A stablehand came to tie our team to a post of the horse corral, then we walked along the seaward face of the building to the main entrance where we were admitted by a fat Indian woman. Mitchell announced himself in Spanish, asking to see Señora McLeod and she padded off, barefoot.

The wait was long. We had time to study the interior of the hall. The walls were ten feet high and the gable of the hip roof pitched up to twelve. There was a chill bareness to the space, certainly no clutter of furniture. Aside from the table, the straight-armed chairs and the smaller ladderbacks there were three chests that I was later told had come originally from Spain, then been hauled the rugged miles up over the mountains out of Mexico by one of the early Lamas. There was a highly polished steer horn above the center doorway. It must have spread for fifteen feet between the silvered tips and I could not visualize the animal big enough to carry it about. There was a bright bird that I did not recognize mounted on the fireplace mantel, two deer heads, both spiked bucks, very small, a dark little mirror, deep framed to the left of the door and a double row of pictures on either side of the chimney.

"Looks a little bare in here," I said. "Like they can't afford furniture."

"This room isn't designed to be lived in." He sounded glad of an excuse to talk, to talk about anything. "It's meant for dancing."

That made my brows go up. Dancing by whom? The lonely ranch, the silent Indian woman, the native who had taken our team . . . we had seen no one else. The place seemed deserted to me and I said so.

He wagged his head, looking over the great hall, telling me softly, "The California Spanish have the reputation of being happy, friendly, overhospitable. That's part of their trouble: they've spent so much time in pleasure they neglected their properties . . . The party up at Vallejo's . . . there were over a hundred guests and some of them had come from Monterey and Santa Barbara. Traveled three hundred miles to a party."

Then the Indian woman filled the doorway opposite the one by which we had come in, motioning us to follow her. Mitchell pulled his handkerchief and wiped it across his forehead. His nervousness was catching, but I trailed him as he went after the servant, and had my first view of the patio across his wide shoulders.

The place was breathtakingly lovely. It was close to noon and the sun was warm overhead but here under the trees and the trailing flowering vines it was cooler, restful, with the air scented by orange blossoms. Even the crash of the surf that rolled up the cliffs was dulled by the arms of the house.

The woman who stood up to receive us was tall, slim and graceful and though she was in her mid-thirties she could have passed for Mitchell's age. Her hair was not the Mexican black, but auburn, thick and fine and parted in the center, drawn back close around her head. Her eyes were dark and though there was no smile in them I felt that laughter could not be far behind them. I had expected to see a widow bent under her troubles, but there was nothing bowed about Concepción McLeod.

She greeted us with a serene coolness. Mitchell presented himself and somehow forgot to include me, going on in a long string of Spanish with gestures that I took to mean he was explaining why we were there. I caught the name, Aurelia. Señora McLeod answered in a low, unexcited voice, shaking her head slowly while she spoke.

Mitchell launched himself on a recital, checking off points on his fingers. The lady continued to shake her head. She said something that brought a flush up under his deep tan and I knew he was fighting temper, but he kept control and went on pressing his suit. There was a rapid exchange back and forth between them, then Mitchell acted and sounded like I had often seen him when he was making a final offer for something he wanted to buy. Señora McLeod raised a blue veined hand to stop him.

"Mama."

I at least did not know when the girl had come into the doorway. She was as tall as her mother but her hair was fair, her eyes a sea blue, and a spray of freckles bridged her short young nose. She had ripened early. She did not have her mother's classic beauty but she did have the poise.

She was wearing pants. I had never before seen a woman in pants. These were black, close fitting, the legs running down into soft riding boots. Above the pants she wore a soft draping white shirt with a smudge on one shoulder as if she had fallen or brushed against a fence. The hair was combed back and wound in a thick chignon under a flat-crowned, wide-brimmed hat from which a cord looped under her chin.

She came forward with the swinging stride of a boy, direct eyes on her mother, ignoring both Mitchell and me. The mother said something quickly and nodded toward the house but the girl did not turn back. She asked questions as cool as can be and when her mother waved them aside she turned on Mitchell.

Mitchell made another speech, very ceremonial, very courtly, and to my horror practically abject. Then to my further horror the girl walked around him, impudently inspecting him as if she were buying a horse, while he stood looking foolish. I wanted to wring her neck.

She went back to her mother, said something in no uncertain tones, had something equally certain to say to Mitchell, and that, I felt with a guilty relief, was the end of this marriage plan.

It was not at all the end. She came toward me and tugged at my wrist as if I were her pet dog and said in excellent English:

"Come along with me and give them a chance to do the formalities."

I looked to Mitchell for help but he winked and nodded me away. All I could do was let myself be towed off around the outside of the house and directed to climb the steep steps of the watchtower.

"There's a good view from up there," she said. "And if you're going to be my brother-in-law we'd better get acquainted."

The steps were narrow as well as steep. She was ahead of me and it would be humiliating to try to talk with my neck craned back to see her. I let the answer go until we came out on the open top. Then I had to follow her across to the waist-high wall before she stopped. When I finally had her cornered I said:

"I am not Mitchell's brother."

"Oh?" She looked me over more carefully. "Who are you?"

"A friend of his. David Stuart."

"And he brought you along as sponsor for him? But he didn't even introduce you. How odd."

Standing against the background of the moving sea, facing me with her shoulders rigidly squared and her cheeks burning she made me think of a bright bantam fighting cock. I said stiffly:

"I don't speak Spanish and Mitchell didn't want to embarrass your mother by talking English."

"My mother taught me English," she said. "I think he was just in such a hurry to make his deal that he forgot you."

My own color came up to match hers and I wanted to hit back.

"Then you are going to trade yourself for a cancellation of the mortgage?"

For an instant her lips tightened, then she changed completely. She giggled. Her eyes crinkled with mischief.

"Of course. It's a very good bargain. He says he's worth between seventy and eighty thousand dollars and he'll give me a generous allowance. He'll sign over the ranch to my mother and my brothers will inherit it. He'll put the boys through school and set them up in business if they want to leave the ranch. And he'll join the Church. I think that's a very high price for an ugly little country girl."

"You're not ugly." I could have bitten my tongue for saying that and I was getting madder at her every minute. "I wouldn't like the thought of selling myself for any price."

She opened her eyes wide, mocking me. "And why not? He's handsome, he's healthy, he's able. My friends will think he's quite a catch. Besides, the Americans aren't leaving my people much choice if we want to survive, are they?"

I countered lamely: "Mitchell isn't an American."

"If he were I couldn't marry him. From your name and your accent you aren't either. You're Scot. I'm half Scot myself. What is he, do you know?"

"He's European."

"So are my ancestors. They came over here with de Anza. Listen, Mister Self-righteous Stuart, in 1775 Captain Juan Bautista de Anza brought eighty men and a hundred and sixteen women and children north from Tubac, in Mexico. Our California families, the pure Castilians, the *sangre azul*, are descended from them. For over two hundred years every name in every family has been recorded by the Corte de Purismo de Sangre. That is a proud history. Now we are being overrun by barbarians, plunderers. My relatives are being cheated out of their homes, driven to begging charity from those who still have something. How long is it going to be before those too are run off?

"Well, the Lamas family is not going to be run off. Not while I can make a marriage that will keep our heads up."

Without any warning at all she butted her head against my chest and cried. Reflex made me put my arms around her, and then I would have been ashamed to take them away. I held her while the outburst shook through her, until she stepped back and brushed at her eyes.

"Thank you. I didn't intend to do that. It's just that I never imagined I would marry a total stranger." The wistfulness in the tone let the little girl show through for the first time, then it was hidden again. "I'm sorry I called you a name. You're his friend, will you tell me about him?"

I had come here abristle, angry about a girl I hadn't met because she represented a wedge driven between Mitchell and me, and here I was feeling sorry for her so much that I forgot the threat she posed. I told her all I knew, from the day we met in Panama, but I did leave out the things he had said today about the California Spanish. She began to relax, then to smile, finally to laugh. But when I finished she sobered and looked troubled.

"Before you knew him, what was he, where does he come from, who is his family?"

It startled me to realize I knew nothing about that except that he had worked in a London bank. When I told her and explained that he just didn't talk about himself she frowned.

"I wonder why."

"Come to think of it," I said, "none of us do. I don't know anything about Joe or the captain either. I guess we were all too busy trying to get along to look back, and then too busy looking ahead."

She looked up at me shrewd and thoughtful. "My mother says half the Americans out here are running away from their wives. Maybe he is too."

"Mitchell Randolph? Of course not." But I didn't know for sure.

She looked out at the sea as if it would give her an answer and when it did not she smoothed her forehead and shrugged.

"No matter. I will marry him anyway."

She went back to the stairs, beckoning me after her. I followed her, the doubt she had raised making a first small fissure in my mind. Then I saw that this was the beginning of the wedge and I shut it away, and resented her more than ever.

CHAPTER THREE

Mitchell Randolph's wedding at the old San Francisco Misión de Asis was one of the last publicly visible gatherings of the native *Californios* in the Bay City. They had withdrawn behind the walls of their ranches or fled south before the American invasion, but they all came out of hiding for this ceremony. From haciendas up the Coast and down, from Monterey and Santa Barbara and as far away as San Diego.

As symbols of a fading era they looked anything but pauperized. They carried themselves proudly even though many wore borrowed clothes and rode borrowed horses, and against the bridegroom's guests they made a glittering pageant.

Mitchell's business associates left their offices, their banks, their express companies, virtually closing down Montgomery Street for the day, and drove south across the sand hills. Newly rich from trading in goods and real estate, they were turned out in Prince Albert frock coats, starched pleated shirts, fancy vests, huge nugget watch chains looped across their middles. Contrasted against the red shirts and butternut pants of the mining camps they were impressive, yet they were a drab lot beside the bride's people.

The women wore tall silver and shell combs articulated with a hinge to bend over the backs of their heads and support the lace mantillas in a graceful drape above their hair. Full, bright, elaborately embroidered skirts, shockingly short by American standards. Soft, low-cut dancing slippers with high heels that flared top and bottom like the central section of an hourglass. Red heels. I hardly recognized the bride as the girl in pants I had met at the ranch.

On our ride home that day I had asked Mitchell about those

pants. He had told me they were the usual working costume of the ranchgirls and made my eyes bug when he said the girls worked the animals with their menfolk, that they rode before they could walk, used the braided lasso as well as their fathers and brothers, could kill a bullock with a single thrust of a thick bladed knife.

Today the men were as gala as the women, in velvet suits that glittered with silver lace, silver buttons, gold braid, bright red sashes tied around their waists.

If the people were spectacular, the horses were even more resplendent, the beautiful, cream pale palominos bred for ceremonial riding. The fine leather harness was silver studded, with long saddle cloths hanging heavy, covered with scrolls worked in silver, silver was braided into the manes and tails and silver bells tinkled.

All the *Californios* rode, even the bride and her older female relatives. The only other transportation the ranches had were clumsy two-wheeled carts in which they moved tallow and hides to the Coast for sale.

The Americans came on rented horses, in rented hacks, in an old French carryall that had once been used as a stagecoach between San Francisco and San Jose. In every way except money they were outclassed.

After the bare, unadorned Friends meeting houses of my childhood the interior of the mission dazzled me with its riches of silver vessels and candelabra, its red velvet and white laces, carved and painted statues, pictures painted on gold leaf.

The service was held in Spanish and Spanish was the language of the day. I was uncomfortably out of place and moodily out of sorts. Because I was Mitchell's best man I was a member of the wedding party and as we left the mission I learned that I was expected to ride a rigged-out palomino with the contingent that went with the bride and groom on the next leg of the ceremony. A party was being given by one of the Vallejos and only Mitch and I of the non-Californians were included.

I was wearing a new broadcloth suit. Mitch had had a Chinese tailor outfit us both and the two of us stood out like sore thumbs. The Americans were drawn aside, ill at ease, watching the show as if it were a theatrical performance, and I wished I could lose myself among them.

With much milling and sorting we got mounted, over a hundred of us, and lined out in a long parade down the sandy road, through the new town, across the square and on to the East Street Embarcadero, attracting as much attention as a New Orleans Mardi Gras.

Where the wooden sidewalks began they were lined deep with watchers all the way.

By Mitch's arrangement Captain Barker had the ferry *Effie* waiting for us. There was a hubbub of getting the horses aboard and secured on the lower deck, then the party trooped up the gangplank. Abner Barker stood at the top to welcome us aboard, freshly shaved and spruce in his blue uniform.

As Aurelia stepped up he took her shoulders in his big hands and kissed her roundly.

A hush fell, broken by gasps. Then the girl tossed her head back, laughing, and the people relaxed.

The top deck was festive with strings of Chinese lanterns that bounced and twirled in the stiff breeze. Some of the men had guitars slung at their backs and as we edged away from the shore they began to play and others to dance.

In the camps on Saturday nights the miners danced with each other to the tune of somebody's fiddle or harmonica, but the heavy clumping of their boots was nothing like the quick, light, intricate flashing of these feet. I had been delegated to escort the maid of honor and knew that I was expected to dance with her at least once, but even if I had wanted to I could not.

I stood awkward and baffled, then I backed off and quietly slipped down the stairs, more miserable by the minute. Worst of all, Mitchell seemed to be having a wonderful time. He was all over the deck, laughing, clowning, waving his arms, acting to my disgruntled eyes like one of the trained bears that sometimes entertained the gold camps.

On the lower deck I saw Joe. In a starched white coat he was busy directing a bunch of Sandwich Island boys hired to serve cakes and wine during the short passage. I hadn't known he was aboard. He saw me and came over, ogling my suit.

"Oh my," he said happily, "you're a real something. You look real grown up. Those pretty gals up top be setting their caps for you and that's a fact."

"Quit it," I grumbled. "Mitch can be a damn fool if he wants, but not me."

"You'll see," he cackled. "Juices start running in you pretty soon, then some gal going to reach out and snag you in."

He cuffed me playfully along the side of my head, grinning, seeming to enjoy the party more than anyone. "Don't you go calling the major a fool, you hear. This missy of his, she ain't no real beauty like some up there, but she's a lady. I see that in just one look at her."

I still did not like anything about the wedding. "She only married him for money," I fumed.

He was suddenly angry. Joe seldom lost his temper but when he did he was dangerous. "Where'd you get such a fool idea? Any woman would be proud to have the major."

"She told me," I said weakly.

"When?"

"The only time I met her, at the ranch when Mitchell went to talk to her mother."

The dark eyes lighted again and he chuckled. "Shucks, don't take no account of that, that's just nerves. You wait, they get in bed and everything will be just fine."

They did not get to bed for the next three nights. In Mitchell's own words they had no privacy at all.

The captain pushed the ferry right up through the slough of Sonoma Creek to the old landing. Sometimes it seemed that we were riding through a flat of tules without any water under us at all.

When we had disembarked and remounted the parade formed again for the ride to the Vallejo estate, Lachryma Montis, at the north end of the village. I had not been in Sonoma before and I found it different from anything I had yet seen in California. It was filled with buildings of historical interest. In a sense Sonoma was the first American capital of the state, for it was there that John C. Frémont and his ragtail band of American settlers had arrested Vallejo in 1844, seized the Sonoma barracks and raised the emblem of the short-lived Bear Flag Republic.

We crossed the plaza and passed the Misión San Francisco de Solano, which was the last and northernmost of the chain, established in 1824. It was no longer used as a church but as a warehouse by American settlers of the valley.

Then there was the Blue Wing Inn, built in 1840 and said to be the first hostelry north of San Francisco Bay. The whole place had been taken over for our visit and I was to be quartered there. Large as it was, the Vallejo house could not accommodate the entire wedding party and besides the inn two other homes had been pressed into service, those of the general's brother, Salvador Vallejo, and of his brother-in-law, Jacob Leese.

This Vallejo place was less than two years old, set deep in seventeen tree-shaded acres, and the wedding supper was waiting for us when our cavalcade reached the yard.

I had never seen such an outlay of food. A whole beef was barbecuing over an open pit. A sheep and a hog shared another blaze. I found myself eating many unfamiliar dishes. There were great pots of native beans, red chili peppers that burned my mouth and seared my throat. There were piles of mountain quail, plump and steaming, spaced down the long trencher table that stretched across the grass so that everyone could sit at the bride's board.

There were also abundant native wines and a great deal of native brandy. I had had little chance to develop a taste for drinking and had no head for alcohol, but I could not renege on the round after round of toasts as the good health and fair fortune of the bride and groom were drunk. Mitchell was too far away to rescue me, flanked by the general's wife and daughter, and from where I sat I could barely see Aurelia between the two Vallejos.

At the end of the feast I could hardly stand. Then more dancing began and there was nothing for it but that I must join in. Mitchell led a grand march with Aurelia on his arm. I struggled behind him with the maid of honor and the rest of the troop fell in by twos.

The first dance was an American one as an honor to Mitchell, and that I could follow, if clumsily. The second I must dance with the bride.

I found her at Mitchell's side and shook my head. "Mitch, I can't do it. I don't know how, and I'm too drunk. I'd just get us laughed at."

The girl was beaming, bubbling, already laughing at me. "Never mind," she said. "We'll do a slow promenade and nobody will notice, they're all having too good a time."

Mitch pushed us off together and she led me along the fringe of whirling skirts and flashing legs, as gay as if she had captured the man of her dreams. Only once she stopped and turned, looking all around her and said in a sad tone:

"This is the way it always was, Davie. Fiesta. On the saints' days, any excuse, there were parties like this. How is it going to be now for me?"

It was her wedding night and I didn't see any use in saying I thought it was a pretty silly way to spend your life. I told her that marriage didn't mean she would never see these people again and that there would be plenty of parties she could go to. Then her brother Duncan popped up and claimed her for a dance.

I slipped out into the dark trees, wishing my head would stop spinning, and before I realized where I was going I was back at the inn. I slept, and the next day I sulked in the room. I couldn't face going back to watch Mitchell being torn away from me.

He found me there on the afternoon of the third day. He sagged in the doorway, ruffled and exhausted, saying, "What's the matter? You sick?"

"Not now. I just didn't belong. I can't speak Spanish and I can't dance and I can't drink like that. I couldn't take it."

He crossed and dropped on the bed with a wry, tired smile. "I'll tell you something, Davie, I can't take any more of it either. Did you ever see such damn fools? They've gorged and swilled half the week and I don't think three quarters of them have had a wink of sleep. I haven't had one private second with my wife. Married three days and I've barely kissed her. Enough is enough. Tomorrow morning I'll take her to the hot springs. You line up the crowd and get them aboard the *Effie*. It's time she made her run up the river. We're not making a cent while she's tied up that creek."

I had been stewing about that myself. It was part of my resentment at the changing pattern.

"You take care of Concepción and the boys, rent the best rig in San Francisco and drive them down to the ranch, then get back on the job."

I chafed at that delay too, and it was no easy task to herd the *Californios* back on the ferry. They didn't want to stop the party and go back to reality, and tired as they must be they kept it going clear through the return trip across the bay.

I left them at the Embarcadero, getting their horses off the boat and putting their homebound parade together, and went up the street to the Carriage and Harness Depository, rented a barouche and hurried back for the family. The *Californios* were mounted and getting under way as my driver reached the dock. Some of them nodded but none of them spoke. I had been a member of the ceremony but that did not give me entrée to their circle.

Concepción, waiting with Captain Barker, was just as cool. Only thirteen-year-old Duncan and eleven-year-old José showed any friendliness. I had met them before the service, dressed as young *caballeros,* and they had kept close to me in the procession out of curiosity, probably because I was near their sister's age, and now they grinned at me shyly.

Their horses were tied on behind the barouche and the boys scrambled in, anxious to test the strange wagon. In the procession they had ridden haughtily, aloof from the new city and the staring crowds, but now curiosity kept their heads swiveling right and left until we passed the mission. From there on it was known territory and they pounced on me as the last available oddity. Duncan looked me over from hair to boots.

"Aurelia says your family comes down from the Kings of Scotland."

"Oh?" I was startled. "I guess she got the idea from my name."

His dark eyes were disappointed. "Then you don't?"

I had to smile. "I haven't any proof."

"Don't you know the records?"

We had a long ride ahead and talking with the boys might cover some of the uneasiness between Concepción and me.

"I know some history that may point that way. The Stuart Kings were descended from Walter, who married the daughter of Robert Bruce. Their son became King Robert Second of Scotland and started the line."

The boys nodded at each other and leaned forward, intent. Both looked more like their mother than Aurelia did, their hair auburn, their eyes a deep, soft brown, now fixed fast on me.

"And ours is a very old family, supposed to have come originally from Bretony where a man named Alan was the *steward* of Dol, and he took his title as a surname. The spelling got changed when they moved to Scotland."

"What's a steward?"

I was not too clear myself but I made a guess. "A person who takes care of a place or a territory for someone else."

Concepción's eyes were on the swaying floor of the carriage but I sensed she was listening and wondered if she would correct me. She didn't have the chance. Duncan pounced again.

"Our family comes down from a marquis."

"Hush." His mother did not lift her eyes.

"But . . . you told me . . ."

"It does not matter and stop bothering Mr. Stuart."

The boys groaned. I said, "It's no bother, it's fun, remembering stories my father told me."

It was fun, they were so eager. I went on, telling tales of the border wars, of the Hanover Kings driving out the Highlanders, of the feats of Robert Bruce and Wallace against the English. I found that I was hungry myself for talk like this. Since my father's death there had been no one to talk with. The captain wasn't interested in who I might be, who my family was. Neither was Joe, and Mitchell had discouraged any confidences by being so close-mouthed about himself. But Duncan and José were still children enough to be excited by wars, kings, knights, and we were all half Scot with a common interest in history.

We finished with what I knew of Scotland and the boys took over, cutting in on each other's adventures of the de Anza expedition, but before they got the explorers north of the Mexican border we turned in at the ranch drive.

Without unbending Concepción invited me to stay for a meal before starting the long drive back to town. I tried to plead the urgency of business but found that I would offend the tradition of hospitality. She shooed the Indian woman off to see that the coachman was also fed and led me into the shaded patio.

There was little conversation. The boys were too hungry to talk now, and there was a strained reserve between the mother and me. But when the boys were finished she sent them off, squared herself and looked at me directly.

"Mr. Stuart, thank you for your kindness to Duncan and José. As you saw, they are very interested in family history. It is an important part of our . . . my people's . . . ways of thinking." She stopped as if that were a preparation for something else she wanted to say but was reluctant to put into words.

I said, "Please, call me Davie. Everybody does."

There was an instant's hesitation and then a faint smile, the first one I had seen from her.

"All right, Davie." Saying the name seemed to ease her some. "I am embarrassed to pry, but I do need to know about my new son-in-law." She held up a hand to stop my interruption. "My friends at the wedding asked about him and I couldn't answer. Our people, Davie, are a tight-knit group. It is impossible to have a secret. Now my daughter has married a foreign stranger. She is not the first California girl to marry outside our race, I among them . . . Captain Richardson married Maria Martinez, John Read married Hilarita Sanchez, there have been many, but we knew about them. Mitchell Randolph . . ." Here she sounded exasperated. "Aurelia has been telling outrageous stories about him, different things to different people, and they cannot all be true. She says he was captain of a pirate ship, then that he is the youngest son of a ruling house who had to leave his country, a political refugee, or that he is an agent for a country that will try to take California away from the Americans, and other strange activities. I don't know why. Is there something wrong that she's hiding?"

I felt my mouth dropping open but there was such a depth of worry in her dark eyes that I could not laugh. As I had for Aurelia

99

I went over the whole history of my association with Mitchell and all he had done for me and others. Trying to give him some dimension I even drew on our old Columbia Indian massacre and our literally eating Steve Bassett out of his house.

To my relief that made her laugh, long, hearty, unrestrained. I hadn't thought of it, but as cramped as her means had lately been she would appreciate a locust horde of guests descending on her larder.

I caught onto that moment to finish quickly. "Aurelia's only fifteen and she's just saying anything that comes into her head to throw off questions until she finds the answers."

But on the ride back to town it nettled me that the girl would soon learn those answers and that I probably never would unless I asked Mitchell, and I'd be damned if I would do that.

CHAPTER FOUR

In 1853 the gold rush reached its peak. More than a hundred thousand people, mostly Americans, roamed the foothills and there was an explosion of new business in San Francisco. New express companies had started but there was room enough for everyone.

In the East in 1850 a group had formed under the name American Express to compete with the Adams Company back there, and in '52 many of the same men put together a separate company for the West with a capitalization of three hundred thousand dollars. Edwin Morgan was president and the board included Henry Wells and William Fargo. Samuel Carter and R. W. Washburn were sent to the coast as local agents, announcing their opening with a big ad in the *Alta*.

> Wells Fargo and Company's Atlantic and Pacific Express is now ready to undertake a general express forwarding agency and commission business for the purchase and sale of gold dust, bullion and bills of exchange: the payment and collection of notes, bills and accounts, the forwarding of gold dust, bullion and specie, also packages, parcels and freight of all descriptions, between the city of New York and the city of San Francisco and the principal towns of California.

They had established themselves in Sam Brannan's building, nearly across the street from the Adams Company, but had not been much competition. In '53, when at least sixty millions in dust was shipped East, Wells Fargo handled only about a sixth. The Adams

Company was much bigger and the Mule Express with Adams as an umbrella was growing strongly.

And I was running the Mule Express. It was a big job, and I was proud and happy.

No longer chained to the Stockton desk, I was able to travel through the Southern Mines, visit the remote agencies, get acquainted with our personnel and learn how to handle the reins Mitchell had passed to me.

I got over my jealousy of Aurelia because it turned out that I saw as much of Mitchell as I had for a long time and nothing was changed between us. I was even drawn into that other business life of his, in the city. At least once a month he called me into town for dinner at his house where I met the growing group of men he was involved with.

He had rented a square, nine-room house on Stockton Street which was still a fashionable section in the growing area, and he brought Nora and Joe in to run it, putting one of the captain's crew in charge of the strong room.

I didn't think Joe liked the change. He had been proud of the responsibility, of his guns and the respect he commanded, but he would never refuse Mitchell anything.

I grew seven inches that year, to be taller than Mitchell, but he stayed a good hundred pounds heavier. Aurelia grew too, with a pregnancy. As she swelled with the months I was more and more embarrassed to look at her and long before she went to the ranch to have her baby I quit going to the house. Mitchell never mentioned the pregnancy to me but when it became too obvious he quit giving the dinners and we had lunches with his business friends at some popular restaurant. Other than at those lunches, where the talk turned around the general financial climate, I did not pay much attention to what he was doing. I had my hands full with the Mule Express.

Then a letter from him tracked me down on a swing through the camps. He had a son. The baby was to be named after me and I was to come to stand as godfather at the christening.

I did not know what was expected of a godfather, but I turned around and headed for the ranch.

It was the first time I had seen it since the wedding and there was a different look and feel about it. Mitchell had brought in more Mexican labor. The rundown atmosphere was gone. Fences were mended, the house painted. Men raked hay in the fields. A new orchard had been planted to the south and young grape vines marched in even rows over the ridge. He might have signed the property over to Concepción but he was certainly managing it himself.

A new hand took my rented horse and Nora opened the door for me, whooped happily and dragged me inside, whispering against my ear before she let me go.

"We got a fine boy, Davie. He's gonna make folks sit up and take notice like his daddy."

I found Mitchell in the big room alone, at the table, energetically dealing through a sheaf of papers. He looked up and flashed his grin, came to me and did something he had not done in years, threw both arms around me and nearly squeezed the breath out of me.

Laughing as if there were some huge joke he turned to the brandy decanter on the table, poured two glasses, handed me one and lifted his above his head.

"A toast, Davie, to your namesake. A toast to the Randolph line. Drink up, boy, and come see him."

His cheeks were flushed and I gathered that he had already been celebrating more than usual. Mitchell had drunk moderately ever since I had met him. In the early camps everyone had drunk when there was whiskey to be had. The saloons were the only meeting places. The miners meetings were held in them and men driven out of their cabins by cold and loneliness gravitated to the bars.

I was still swallowing when he put a heavy hand in my back and shoved me loping down the hall and into a newly whitewashed and furnished nursery.

The baby was asleep with its tiny fists doubled, looking ready to do battle with a hostile world. My impression was of features too large, crowded into a misshapen skull that was capped with a sharply defined mat of tight black curls. At my side Mitchell was crowing softly, rocking on his feet, as proud as if this were the first baby ever born.

"My son." He said it reverently. "He's a handsome one, eh, Davie?"

I didn't dare tell him it looked more like a monkey to me. I just nodded. When we had stood in admiration long enough to suit him he took me into the hall again and pointed to another door.

"She wants to see you."

"How is she?" I asked it automatically.

His face clouded. "She had a rough time. The boy's head is so big, like they said mine was when I was born."

His tone alarmed me and I said quickly, "Is she all right?"

103

"The doctor and the midwife say yes, but she'll take time to heal. Go on in, they won't let more than one of us in there at a time."

The Spanish woman nursing her wanted to stay but Aurelia ordered her out. I stood at the side of the bed not knowing what to say, tongue-tied at being admitted into this intimacy. There was no color in her face and her voice was weak, but her eyes were sparkling the way they had on her wedding night and she reached for my hand, holding it.

"Davie, he's beautiful, just beautiful. Wait until you see him."

I told her Mitchell had already showed him to me. She didn't speak for a moment, then gave a small, odd laugh.

"Of course. He would."

I didn't know what it meant, and dismissed it as she immediately began bubbling again. At the monthly dinners I had attended she had been a reserved hostess, accepting me as part of the establishment but paying me no special attention. Now she was abandoned in her glorious happiness and wanted me to share it.

When the nurse put her head in and said I had stayed long enough I was glad to leave the room. I felt that I had had a look behind a veil, a glimpse of Aurelia Randolph that an outsider should not have been permitted.

Both she and Mitchell were embarrassingly extravagant in going on about the boy, with an enthusiasm that I thought all out of proportion. After a supper in the patio I went out to walk along the cliffs, to get away from it for a while. Even Concepción was purring like a smug grandmother. Only Duncan and José were less than ecstatic.

They were sitting dolefully on the corral fence as I came around the house and cornered me before I reached the path that led down to the rocks.

"Is Aurelia going to die?"

"Of course not. Where did you get that idea?"

"He won't let us see her."

"She's weak," I said. "It's hard on a woman to have a baby."

"I know." José sounded miffed, as if I were talking down to him. "My mare had a colt and nearly died. We watched."

I was put in my place. They were ranch raised and knew a lot more about the origin of life than I did.

"But we can't see Aurelia."

I tried to shear away from that subject. "Have you seen the baby?"

"It's ugly." They said it together, and Duncan added, "It looks like him."

104

I judged that him was Mitchell and that they held more against him than not being allowed to see their sister.

"Come on now. It doesn't look like anybody yet. And what's wrong with Mitchell? He's done a lot for the ranch."

"I hate him," Duncan said. "He makes us work, like *peóns,* and he whipped me because I rode my horse up the hill where he put some new grapes and some of them got pulled out."

The three of us were together in one thing, a resistance to the charms of the new baby. I got away to San Francisco, but only after the christening when the little brute wet through his wrappings and my clothes. Mitch wanted me to stay longer but I told him his letter had caught me on my way to Jamestown where I thought something was wrong and I wanted to find out quickly.

With the amount of gold our agencies handled daily I had to be alert for shortages, and by the time I got there our Jamestown man had helped himself to nearly ten thousand dollars and disappeared. I never heard of him again. It made for an expensive christening, but Mitch accepted it as an unfortunate part of the business.

During the months my godchild grew into a more human-looking being. His hair turned auburn and his features developed more like Duncan's than Mitchell's. The formal dinners at the house were resumed and Aurelia, a slender girl again, returned to her reserve. I was not aware how quiet she was becoming until one day when I took some papers to the house for Mitchell to sign and found he had gone to Marysville. She gave me tea but she was distracted about something and the visit was uncomfortable.

At the dinners I saw that Mitchell was becoming more and more involved with real estate as developments sprang up in all directions, but that was outside of my concerns.

Mining was in a falling cycle and our express revenues were sagging. We weren't really worried because it was another season of little rain.

Placer mining depends on the water available to wash out gold, and streams and springs were going dry all through the foothills. One after another miners were having to quit work until the water table was renewed, but it was not. We went into summer with many of the rivers only a trickle of their normal flow.

It pointed up sharply how tightly our economy was tied to gold, how dependent on it our business was particularly. Winter came again but still the rain did not. Our operation was cut to less than half. I had to make a choice between laying off employees and cutting wages, and chose to keep the men.

We were not alone in the squeeze. The pay scale dropped generally and many firms laid off most of their people. These men and frustrated miners in growing numbers moved out of the hills into Stockton, Sacramento, San Francisco, looking for jobs that were not to be had. Hunger spread and every day ragged men stopped you on the street, begging for the price of a meal. It was a hard depression, but the country would probably have been all right, without a panic. Some gold was still being produced along the larger streams and the rains had to come sometime.

Then a blow fell far back in St. Louis. It had nothing to do with mining but it would not have been so devastating if the placers had been in full production.

On February 18, 1855, the steamer *Oregon* churned through the Golden Gate and unloaded the news that the Bacon & Page bank of St. Louis had failed, and closed.

The original impact was slight. I first heard it when I stopped at noon in the Exchange Bar. Several men from the financial community were there, lined along the counter enjoying the free lunch with their beer.

Mitchell came in and as he joined me a group of bankers called to know if he had heard the news. He had. Ira Woods of the Adams Express office asked what effect he thought the failure would have on the local situation. Mitchell helped himself to a slice of turkey and accepted the schooner of beer before he answered.

"Shouldn't have much. From the information I've received they'd been speculating in Ohio and Mississippi rail stock. When the road went into bankruptcy last week it pulled the bank down. The branch of Bacon & Page here is all right, isn't it?"

Adams shared the Parrott Building with Bacon & Page, though they were separate firms.

Woods lowered his voice, sounding worried. "I think they are. We delivered a million in dust to them two weeks ago."

Through the afternoon the guesses floated along Montgomery Street, from bank to bank, from one brokerage to another. Mitchell had gone back to his office but I lingered in the bar, listening. Around three o'clock the rumor came down the street that Bacon & Page here had shipped a million dollars to the parent organization only three days ago. If that were true, the local bank was not all right. It was in trouble. I started for Mitchell's office to tell him and saw a line already forming in front of the Parrott Building.

Upstairs I found Mitchell at the window, a dead cigar clamped savagely between his teeth. I told him the rumor but he did not take his eyes off the growing line.

"Damn fools. They'll start a panic."

I looked over his shoulder and felt a tingle of dread run through me.

"You think they'll have to close?"

He pulled a watch from his vest pocket and snapped the lid open. "There's not much banking time left. Maybe by morning the crowd will calm down."

But by morning the crowd was even bigger. Many frightened depositors had spent the whole night before the doors to be among the first when Bacon & Page opened. Before noon there was a full-blown riot going on. I had never seen anything like it. Well-dressed businessmen, working men, gaudy women fought one another like wild animals to be first at the payoff counters.

And as the panic spread runs were started on the other banks along the street. After Bacon & Page, the Adams Company was the first to be hit, in a mindless association because they were in the same building. The mob ballooned and swept across to Wells Fargo's headquarters in Sam Brannan's building, and on to the Wright Company and the Robinson Savings Bank. The noise they made came up to us as a savage roar and we looked down on a scene of battle that filled the street as far as we could see.

I drew a long, thankful breath that we maintained no bank in the bay area, that our closest office was in Stockton.

"Won't they ever stop?"

Mitchell's answer was an angry growl. At one o'clock a messenger from Adams sneaked in the back way with an appeal. Would we furnish them any cash we had on hand?

Mitchell barely read it, and tossed it in the wastebasket. "Tell them there's nothing we can do to help."

I watched the messenger hurry away. "What did they want?"

"Money to pay their depositors."

It was a frightening thought. It would have been easier for me to believe that the mint was out of gold than that Adams could not meet their commitments.

"How can they be in trouble?"

He threw me a scornful look. "You know how. No bank keeps enough cash on hand to meet all claims at once. Money has to be out working to earn interest to pay on the deposits. You can't liquidate overnight."

Nor could anyone stop the frenzied demands that they do just that. At two o'clock the Adams Company forcibly closed its doors. The mob went even more mad. Bricks were thrown, windows smashed. Shouts rose from men wanting to drag the Adams partners out of their offices and hang them from the nearest poles.

There were nowhere near enough police to bring the wildness under control and those there were did not try. Before the banking day was done every financial house in the city had shut down. It was not safe to go into the streets, especially wearing the silk hat and swallowtail coat that was a banker's costume. But sometime after three o'clock Mitchell disappeared from the office. I was rooted at the window, hypnotized, and did not see him leave.

I waited where I was. Darkness came but I did not light the lamps. With night the noise and confusion grew worse. It seemed that while daylight lasted the mob held some hope of recovering its money, that darkness snuffed out hope. In despair and a recharged fury I thought they would tear the buildings down stone by stone.

Torches were lit and the flickering flames made the scene more horrible. I watched, powerless, wondering what the end would be and if the city could ever recover from such a devastating crash.

It was after midnight when I heard sound on the stairs. I did not know who was there. There had been looting farther down the street, stores broken into, windows shattered and goods thrown vengefully into the gutters. I got the revolver from Mitchell's table drawer and eased the door open, trying to see through the heavy dark of the hall. The scrape of footsteps came steadily upward.

"Who is it?" It took effort to keep my voice steady.

"Me."

It was Mitch's voice and I felt a rush of relief. I stepped back out of the doorway to let him in and in the wavering red reflection of the torches through the window he saw the gun in my hand, but he made no comment. His hat was gone, his coat torn and there was a raw bruise on his left cheek.

"How much gold have we on hand in Stockton and the foothill offices?"

Once I would have had the figure in my head but since I had begun working out of San Francisco the daily balances were left to others.

"I'd have to check. We aren't affected though."

He slumped into his chair. "Every bank in California is affected one way or another. A panic is like an epidemic contagion, and in people's minds we're too close to Adams. We'll have to move fast, before the news gets upstate and the run starts on us."

"I suppose so," I said. "The upper camps are all solvent. Only Stockton is drawn down, and the reserve will cover that."

I had always kept enough in the safes of the satellite agencies to cover full withdrawals, but periodically we made a major shipment from Stockton that temporarily left that office short of cash, to be replenished as more dust was brought down.

Now even in the dull, angry glow from the torches I saw the queer way he looked at me, then away.

"Don't count on the reserve, kid. You think I kept it in a box under my bed? It's invested in city real estate. Every damn dollar of it. And lucky it is. If it were in cash it would have been over with Adams and we'd be down in that street with the other jackasses howling for our money."

My stomach muscles tightened. "Are you saying Adams isn't going to be able to reopen?"

"How the hell do I know? You can't get anyone there to talk sense. What men I found are too scared to think. Most of them expect to wind up on the end of a rope before the night's over. Quit asking questions and listen. You'll have to find the captain. Pray God he's on the *Effie* and not out getting drunk in some whorehouse. Tell him to get up steam and be ready to cast off as soon as I'm there."

I hurried. I went out by the back way, but had to fight through the crowd to cross the street. They were still rampaging and now most of them were drunk. I hoped the Adams officials had got safely away from the stone building. I knew most of them and it was chilling to think what would happen to them if the mob got its hands on them.

The waterfront was quiet. The action was in the business section uptown. I was relieved that Barker was in his bunk and most of the crew aboard. Within five minutes the fires were lighted and by the time Mitchell came striding up the gangplank we had steam enough to shove off.

Mitchell wrapped himself in a blanket and went to sleep at once, but I lay awake a long while wondering what would happen when Stockton heard of the great panic on the bay. I was not too worried. A run might start, but I was sure Mitchell Randolph, the trusted Man on the Mule, could talk them out of it, explain that payment might be delayed a little while but would be met as funds became available.

When we routed Joe Touney out of bed just after daylight the

109

word had not yet reached the town, and I was fairly relaxed until Mitchell gave his order.

"Touney, get to the office and strip the safes. Start loading everything aboard the *Effie* and don't say anything. Not to anybody. I'll be there to help in a minute." While Touney struggled into his clothes and ran out, Mitch swung on me. "You, get a fast horse and start riding. Collect whatever there is in the camps and meet me in Sonora. I have to go to Sacramento."

He whirled out of the room and left me standing. I couldn't believe it. He had no idea of meeting any demands for withdrawal, either here or in the solvent agencies. I had a picture of the miners. Many of them I had known well for more than five years. They were having a hard enough time trying to survive through the depression. They needed whatever they had in our banks, especially now. And Mitchell wanted me to deliberately steal their gold.

I rode all right, and hard. But I meant to see that our depositors were paid, not robbed. I thought Mitchell must have suddenly gone crazy.

Our bank was closed when I reached Sonora but the express side of the office was open. I gathered the staff in the back room and told them what was to be done. I sent messengers on ahead to ride through the night to the agencies and have the gold there paid out.

We carried two types of accounts. The special deposits were the original pouches brought to us. They were ticketed with the names of the owners and could be picked up at any time. For that service we made a small monthly charge. The other type was the general account, where a man's gold was weighed, a slip of deposit was given him, and the dust added to our working fund.

I sent one agent out to buy every leather sack he could find and sat the crew down to fill them to match every name on the general account, change them over to special deposits. I spent the night altering the books.

We were still working when a man galloped in from Sacramento, spreading the news that the San Francisco disaster had struck the river town. The panic was creeping inland. By morning a queue was forming before our bank.

By opening time we were ready and I unlocked the door myself, smiling at the men as they filed in. Almost all of them were old personal friends, some still here from that first hard winter, but there was angry suspicion in their faces now. If I had done as Mitchell wanted there would have been violence, perhaps lynching, here.

The first in line was Tobe Alcot, the practical joker who had sent us off to rescue Steve Bassett with his story of the phony Indian attack. Tobe was a laughing man but his mouth was a tight line as he stopped in front of me with the challenge:

"I heard Adams has suspended payment, Davie. What about it?"

Others were crowding around us, rough men hardened by the years in the diggings. They had worked harder for their dust than they would have to make the same amount in wages, and they were in no mood to lose it. I kept smiling, saying:

"They did. We have not."

"You're mixed up with them, aren't you?"

I raised my voice to be heard across the room. "This bank is open. All depositors may withdraw their dust now. In fact I advise it, then you'll be sure of it."

They weren't fully convinced. They had trusted the Mule Express as they would their mothers but they swarmed against the counter nervously. As the clerks passed out the little leather bags the strain grew, men at the back afraid that the dust would run out before their turn came.

The distribution was agonizingly slow. We needed receipts for each poke and some of the men could barely write their names. It took most of the day to complete the payment, and at the end there was less than a thousand dollars in the safe.

Mitchell Randolph arrived an hour after the last man had gone with his poke in his hand.

He came in asking before the door was closed behind him, "How much have we got here?"

"Almost a thousand," I told him.

He thought I was joking. He started to smile, then it dawned on him that I meant it and he looked at me blankly.

"Where's the rest of it?"

"I paid it out."

He grabbed my shoulder and shook it. I winced and after a second he let the hand fall away, saying in a dangerously quiet voice:

"I told you to suspend. Close up."

"I couldn't," I said. "It was on special account, not in the general fund."

He knew I was lying but he spun and stalked back to the ledgers. Mitchell had not been in Sonora for nearly two years, so he could not know for sure that the books were changed. He took only a quick look, then slammed the cover shut.

"I trusted you, Davie."

"The miners trusted us. It was their gold."

"I suppose the other offices are stripped too?"

"I believe so. Mitch, for God's sake what's come over you?"

His dark eyes blazed at me for a long moment, then he dropped them and sank heavily into a chair.

"Do I have to spell it out for you?" His voice was shaking. "You knew Stockton was short of cash. We couldn't pay off in full right now. You knew the reserve was frozen in real estate. It's been a bad year and the land people were overextended. It was a time to buy cheap, when they needed quick money. I couldn't buy enough outright. I made down payments to be followed by monthly installments. I needed that gold to keep up the payments. Without it I can lose the property and the reserve I've put in. With it I could have kept afloat, kept control of the land, paid the depositors a little at a time to keep them off my neck until mining comes back, stayed in business." He stopped, crowded down his anger and said in a flat tone, "So that's that."

"You mean we're out of business?" It hit like a lightning bolt. I had been too absorbed in getting the miners paid to think that the company might founder.

"What do you think? How do you think we could go on? I can't get on a mule and start again the way we did. The time when that could be done is gone. It takes money to operate now. We haven't got it."

I felt confused, sick, and empty. I knew that I was morally right. If I had not given out the dust there would have been thousands more miners added to those who were already going hungry. But it was surely I who had wrecked the Mule Express. And just as surely I had lost Mitchell by my action. I was nearly nineteen, but I wanted to cry like a child.

"Somehow I've got to raise three hundred thousand dollars. God damn it." He shoved to his feet. "Well, put it behind. Forget it. Get up through the hills and close the agencies. Pick up the records, particularly every scrap of paper that involves the Adams Company. Take them to their Sacramento office since that's the one we worked through . . . I was too late there to collect anything from them . . . get us straightened out with them. There will be an investigation and I want to be damn sure we're in the clear. Then come on down to the bay and we'll see what we do next."

He went out without a good-bye. I did not need a good-bye. He had not cut me away from him. That was enough.

It took me a week, closing down, gathering records, paying off the clerks. Dismissing them made me feel worse than I already did. The continuing drought, the inability to mine had saturated the labor market and now the collapse of the financial houses was breaking the credit structure of the whole state.

Farmers and ranchers who had sold produce and cattle lost the money they had realized and deposited with Adams. When I reached Sacramento I heard a mounting tale of grief. The hill communities had suffered, but not in comparison to the cities. A number of men including two leading merchants had committed suicide. Another, after vainly hunting employment, offered to sell himself as a slave for five years to anyone who would feed his wife and children. There were no takers.

A miner who had worked on Woods Creek since the early days when we had first gone to Sonora was one of the first I saw in the river city. We had never been particularly friendly but he stopped me on the street like a long-lost brother. He just had to unburden himself and I was a familiar face. He had saved forty thousand dollars and come out of the hills on his way to rejoin the family in the East that he had not seen in six years. He had stopped at the Adams office to pick up his money. And found the office closed, the money lost. He had nothing and no hope that he would ever amass that much again. I gave him five dollars. I could soon be in the same straits but I could not walk away and leave him hungry.

Not all the stories that came out of that evil time ended as his did. A rancher named Remme who had been raising cattle up the valley drove his herd to Sacramento and sold it for twelve thousand dollars which he deposited in an Adams general account, taking a certificate of deposit. At breakfast the next morning he read in the *Union* that in San Francisco Adams had closed its doors. Alarmed, he jumped up and rushed to the local office, finding that already a line a block long was inching toward the counter and knew that he would never make the head of it before the funds ran out. He thought quickly of Marysville and the other nearby towns, but certainly word of the failure would reach those before he could.

There was one long chance in isolated Portland. There was a large Adams branch there and the telegraph had not yet been extended to the Oregon city. If he could reach Portland before a ship or rider brought the news he could cash his certificate there.

Remme was a French Canadian, a good horseman and a stubborn rider, but it was seven hundred miles to Portland. He checked the ship schedules at the City Hotel and saw that the *Columbia* was due to sail north from San Francisco the following day and knew that if he hoped to collect his money he must beat that ship.

His ride is still one of the classic stories of the early West. Buying fresh horses wherever he could, riding day and night over trails strange to him, sometimes barely passable, he covered the distance by noon of the sixth day. He was in the Adams office cashing his certificate when he heard the steamship whistle for the bar. An hour later he would have been too late. The branch closed forever.

The western Adams organization never reopened, although the parent firm continued to be very important in the East.

The Sacramento office was in chaos behind its barred doors. I spent three days making my figures balance with theirs, then I caught a steamer for San Francisco. The city was still rocking. Two hundred business firms had failed. Several Adams men had been arrested. Ira Woods, whom I had last seen in the Exchange Bar that fatal noon, had taken a ship for Australia, sneaked aboard dressed as a woman. Rumors and counterrumors kept the district boiling.

I went directly to Mitchell's small office on Montgomery Street and turned over the records and what remained of our cash and dust, a total of about eleven thousand dollars. A tenth of that in the winter of '50 would have made us rich but against the debts on the real estate it was pitiful. Mitchell had bought a great deal of vacant property and with everything on the bottom there was no market at all for unimproved land.

The Adams people owed us fifty thousand for charges in the towns where we had represented them and on gold dust we had shipped to San Francisco and which had not been paid for. I had listed that as an asset but as Mitchell went over the books he slashed a black line through the entry.

"It will be years before the claims are met, and we'll be lucky if they pay five cents on the dollar."

I said, "As big as they are I don't understand why they couldn't meet the run."

"Reason enough." He gave a harsh laugh. "It's beginning to come out. A lot of the partners were speculating in mining and real estate. With business squeezed the way it's been they were using company funds to cover their personal accounts."

He had been doing the same thing, I thought, and my reaction showed in my face.

He saw it and said, "Let's get this cleared up, Davie. Sit down."

I sat down uneasily.

114

"The reserve I used belonged to the express company, didn't it?"

"To cover the miners' deposits."

He waved this aside. "And the express company belonged to our partnership."

There were no papers to say that there was any partnership, and until this moment I had never thought of a need for them, but as soon as the thought came he made it sound unnecessary again.

"So the real estate belongs to the partnership. When its value comes back, and it will as soon as the placers are working again, we can sell enough to pay the Stockton debt and have plenty left to grow on."

"If we don't lose it," I said doubtfully. "Where are you going to get the three hundred thousand you said you need to hold it?"

"It's going to be ticklish all right. We'll have to scramble. But I've made a start. I sold the *Effie* yesterday. Alan McLane gave me thirty-six thousand for her. He's going to use her on the upper Sacramento where it's too shallow for his bigger ships."

Somehow that more than anything else rang a death knell for the Mule Express, for at the back of my mind I had been hoping against hope that we could yet get back into the express business. And there was a more personal casualty.

"What about the captain?"

Mitchell did not actually smile, but a corner of his mouth turned up a little.

"He elected to stay with the boat and his uniform. Said he didn't want to be in the real estate business and declared himself out of the partnership."

In spite of myself I laughed. So Abner Barker was not going to get away from the water again.

"Well," I said, "with the boat gone we might try to sell the agency buildings, although I don't know who would buy them right now."

"I've already done it." His mood was getting lighter by the minute. "Wells Fargo bought them."

"Does that mean they're reopened?"

"Not yet, but they only closed the San Francisco office. Bill Pardee says it was only to make sure they had enough specie on hand. They're going to expand into the Southern Mines now and I made a deal with them that I wouldn't start an express company in that area for five years if they would take over our buildings. They only gave twenty-four thousand for them and the furniture in them and in the rented agencies, which isn't much, but I'm in no position to dicker.

"And I have a buyer for the house, there are still a lot of people coming in here and they have to live somewhere. Also, I'm going to mortgage the ranch. Those deals and the Stockton money will keep us alive a little while."

It seemed to me that he had covered every possible angle and it was still far below what was needed to keep the real estate, but when I said so he had another card to play. He was going to try to float a loan. With California prostrate under the panic I could not see where he could do that.

"It will have to come from New York or Europe, and that will take time. Time's the enemy now."

"But the depositors in Stockton." They still worried me, but in a different way now. "Won't they sue? Attach the real estate?"

He shook his head. "We only hold the land under purchase agreement. And they won't sue because we'll make a token payment every month. When you owe money always let your creditor feel that you're paying something and will keep on paying, and that if he sues he'll risk losing whatever more he might collect. That's another reason I want the house sold, so there'll be nothing that can be levied against."

He had talked himself into a much better humor and it was always a marvel to me how he could keep working, squirming, maneuvering, finding solutions in the most impossible situations. For myself, I kept thinking how shaky we were, that one slip along the line would knock us over the edge into bankruptcy. The only thing that made the world look bright to me was that he did not seem to hold a grudge against me.

He stood up and reached for his hat, relaxed and confident.

"Come on, we'll go out to the house for dinner. You haven't seen your godchild in a while."

CHAPTER FIVE

I stood in the nursery with Nora and Aurelia watching the baby crawl across the floor after the ball I had brought him, and wondered about the impression I had had when Mitchell and I came in.

Aurelia looked different. Her dress was quiet and with her light hair piled in the new fashion she seemed older, but there was something more. A hint of resignation, even boredom in the quiet set of her mouth and her manner.

I had only seen her with Mitchell at their dinner parties, when she was the poised and formal hostess to be expected, but when she met us in the lower hall she was just as formal. She presented her cheek, he pecked at it. I felt an indifference between them. She took me immediately upstairs to see the boy.

I had gotten over resenting her long ago. I was not interested in any particular girl and without being consciously aware of it I had rather adopted her as partly mine. Now I had the uneasy sensation that something was not right.

When we returned downstairs Mitchell was in the front room with a brandy glass in his hand. There was another on the cherry table beside the legal papers for the house and ranch. He handed me the glass absently and handed Aurelia a pen, saying:

"I need your signature on this."

She took the pen and said without interest, "What is it?"

"I'm selling the house."

She was beginning to bend over the paper, but she straightened, obviously surprised. It was plain that this was the first she had heard of it.

"This house, Mitchell? Why?"

"Because I need the money." He did not elaborate. "This is a quit-claim deed. The other papers your mother will have to sign. I'm putting a mortgage on the ranch."

She did not move except to turn rigid and appear to grow taller. "Felicidad?"

Impatience crept into his voice. "What other ranch do we have?"

She stared at him, then turned to look at me, her eyes incredulous. She leaned over and signed the quitclaim deed, and backed away from the table.

"*We*," she said, "do not *have* Felicidad. The ranch belongs to my mother. Neither she nor I will allow it to be mortgaged again."

I would never have imagined that Aurelia could sound so cold nor look so bleak. From Mitchell's face he was as astonished as I. Then he smiled at her, but it was a queer, pained, accusatory smile.

"Aurelia, you must be aware that this town is going through a crippling financial crisis. Many businesses have been ruined, many fortunes have been lost. I must have all the cash I can raise, immediately, or we will lose everything we have. Think about your son. I am trying to protect his future."

"Oh. Now he is my son. Until now you have called him your son. He is only one member of my family and I am thinking of all of them. If you remember, you and I signed a bargain, when what little was left of Felicidad was all my mother had and we were losing it. What happens when you can't pay off this mortgage? Will you sell us for slaves?"

Mitchell swore aloud. "That's enough of your tongue. What happens when I can't buy food and clothes and a roof for you?"

She raised her eyebrows in a high, indifferent arch. "The *Californios* take care of each other. If you have lost your money we can all live at Felicidad. And live well, since you have made it prosper."

"I cannot live there and you know it. I'm an ogre there. I cannot run my business from there. I belong here and I need cash to keep control of the properties, only until I can get a loan from the East."

"What properties are those?"

"Land. Bayside lots. Business lots I am investing in. When this crisis passes and values are up where they belong again they'll be worth three to five times what I bought them for. Many times the value of La Playa de la Felicidad at its biggest."

"Why don't you mortgage them?"

He was finding it all but impossible to speak slowly. "Because I

118

do not own them. I hold them under purchase contract. I have to meet monthly payments on them. At this moment they are a liability, not an asset. The house I can sell because in spite of the panic people are coming into San Francisco by the shipload. And the ranch can be mortgaged because as you generously point out I have made it a paying operation."

"Sell the house. Sell everything you own. You do not own the ranch, as you do not own your lots. It cannot be mortgaged."

She walked away, as stiff as a doll, and stood facing the front window, her arms down against her sides with her hands closed into tight fists.

Mitchell looked after her in a dazed frustration. He looked back at me and I could see him frame both of us in his mind, his wife and his neophyte in a conspiracy against him. And I could not say a word.

Mechanically he picked up the house deed, folded it, creased it, settled it in his pocket, then he stalked across the room. A moment later we heard the outer door slam behind him.

Aurelia did not move until Mitchell was out of sight down the sidewalk. Then she turned around slowly and we looked at each other. Neither of us spoke, but there was a new bond between us. I had witnessed a furious family quarrel. I was no longer an outsider to the marriage. I was squarely in the middle of it, much as I wanted to cut and run. I had come here at least half-persuaded to Mitchell's course of action, but this girl in standing up to him had showed me again the question mark in his ethic. With his position so perilous was he entitled to put the security of other people in jeopardy?

After a strained silence she came toward me.

"Davie, tell me what this panic is all about."

"You don't know?" I had been living in the center of it for days and it was so all-pervasive that I did not see how anyone in the state could not be aware of it.

"I know what the papers say but they don't tell the whole story. I don't know enough about business to understand what is happening, from what I read."

She sat down on the sofa and I pulled up a chair. I told her what Mitchell had said about the officers of Adams using company funds and about the repercussions their failure was causing. I told what had happened with our express company. When I explained Mitchell's taking the Stockton money to protect the real estate she gave me a tight smile. She followed everything I said closely and asked intelligent questions. She comprehended all of it quickly. I found myself wanting to know her reaction to Mitchell's moves and motives and explained in detail what he was doing and why. She did not show any sign of disapproval. When I finished she said only:

"Mitchell should have told me."

It was like an echo of what I had often said to myself, and I felt even closer to her.

"You're not alone," I said. "He never tells me anything until he has to, nor anyone else."

"Well, that's worth knowing. I thought he didn't talk to me because I'm a woman." She drew a deep sigh. "I could never get anywhere close to him. He doesn't love me, I knew that when I married him, but I believed then that we'd build some kind of a life together."

Her hands were in her lap and she was looking down at them, picking at the lace edge of a handkerchief. Her voice had run down the scale to an open wistfulness.

"My family, my father and mother, always talked about everything they were doing, and the boys and I were included. We all had a share and a voice and everybody was interested, it made everything exciting. Here . . . it's just lonely."

I saw what the days must be in this house, the girl still in her teens, removed from her family and friends, starved for the pleasure of companionship and participation.

"The baby and running the house are not enough. Mitchell is so smart, I see it when people come to dinner, the men are all impressed, and I wanted to have a part in what he was doing . . ."

She talked on and on, unveiling to me a Mitchell I had a hard time recognizing but whom I had to believe existed, because her illustrations from a woman's viewpoint so often brought into credible focus one trait or another that I had noticed but had no cause to object to.

Admittedly he kept his own council, which had the effect of holding others from coming too close to him. He was a loner, dominating those who depended on him and expecting to be followed. He used people and events for his advantage but I had never seen him let himself be used. I had the underlying feeling that that would not be a pretty thing to watch.

Aurelia's Mitchell wanted her to take his guests' wives away after dinner and let the men continue at the table over brandy and cigars and talk. I had seen that much often enough. The women bored Aurelia with their chatter about children, dresses, servant problems. She was, as she said, raised on a horse, riding after cattle, roping, branding, interested in a man's interests.

He objected to her riding in the city in pants and astride, wanting her to use the long skirt and sidesaddle of American fashion. He was himself ritually conformist, fitting himself to the dress and customs of whatever society he inhabited at a time and presenting a deceptively inconspicuous figure.

He showed more pride of ownership than affection for his wife and son, never played with the boy, never let down his guard with her. She had heard rumors that he did relax with some women, actresses, in one or another of the French restaurants. And that I had seen too. She said she was not a prude, that her father and her mother's brother had both enjoyed women other than their wives, but the wives had always been given first consideration and more than equal attention. Aurelia too would have liked a gay evening at a French restaurant.

At last she ran down and looked at me shamefaced.

"I'm sorry to dump it all on you, Davie, but I needed that. I had to get it out and make room to think. Are you disgusted with me?"

"No." I smiled. "I wish I could help."

"You can. If you will. It will make Mitchell mad at you, but would you drive me down to the ranch tonight?"

"Tonight?"

"This house is sold. I'll have to move, and I can't stay with Mitchell after I refused him the mortgage."

"You're leaving him? Divorcing him?"

"My Church does not recognize divorce. But I am going to the ranch. If he wants to come and be with us there that's his privilege. If not . . . I am through with San Francisco."

CHAPTER SIX

Montgomery was a dismal, empty street when I got back to town late the next morning. Many buildings were shuttered, there was hardly any traffic and almost no businesses were open. I felt like I was going to a funeral. I was confused about Mitchell, dreaded having to face him, but unless I simply vanished there was nothing else to do.

He was working, making up a financial statement, and did not stop when I came in, only nodded to me. There was no sign of last night's stormy anger. He looked as he usually did, fresh, big, in brisk command, driving.

I had a hard time getting the words out to tell him I had driven Aurelia and the baby to the ranch, and he let me stumble all the way through it before he spoke, not even raising his head.

"Joe told me last night. It's a good thing. I can give possession of the house right away. Joe can take her things down there and you can put the rest in storage."

"Yas suh, boss suh."

His head came up then, snapped up as he heard my anger, and he sat back against the chair, looking me over.

"What's that supposed to mean? What's got you so riled up?"

"I'm tired of being treated like something on a leash," I said hotly. "And so is Aurelia. That's why she left. You've got a way of just firing out orders, telling people what to do, like you threw that mortgage at her last night without any explanation at all until she turned you down. Like you told me to go get the gold from the agencies but didn't tell me why. If you'd told me what was going on on the ferry that night we wouldn't be in this bind today. But you never tell anybody anything. She was interested in your business but you wouldn't talk to her about it, you never even told her about yourself. You never told me either, which is all right, but your wife . . . you just appear out of nowhere and marry her and then leave her hanging in the air . . . she doesn't know whether you're a bigamist or absconder or what the hell you left behind. You don't trust anybody with anything they don't absolutely have to know, and then not until the very last minute."

I wanted to go on and bring up Aurelia's other charges of neglect but I had run out of breath, and once I had stopped I couldn't find the way to start again. Their affairs were really none of my business. It was only in the area where her complaints overlapped with mine that I had any right to talk.

Mitchell sat listening, showing no emotional reaction, his eyes on mine, but gradually their focus went through me to settle on some thought of his own. He was very quiet for so long that I began to think he meant to ignore me completely, then his attention came back. He got up, rammed his hands into his pockets and walked around the room with a brooding prowl.

"Yes," he said finally. "I see what you mean. Davie, do you know what a ghetto is?"

I had never heard the word but the way he spat it out made it sound bad. I shook my head.

"I hope you never learn, and that my son does not." He was looking at me again and there was a ferocity in his eyes that made them blacker than I had ever seen them. "It's a district where the European Jews have to live, a walled place. No one can leave without a special pass."

"A prison?"

"Like a prison. And the people's minds are in strait jackets, chained in superstitions, smothered in suspicion. They make themselves slaves to a set of very old traditions that mark them as separate from other people, so they're rejected by the world. The people outside suspect them and are afraid of them and prey on them. And fear breeds fear. They're eaten up by fear. Nobody there talks about his business. If you have money you hide it. You don't even tell members of your own family. That's where I grew up."

I felt a cold shiver, as much at his tone as at what he said.

"Some of them escape," he went on. "Some have come to this country, but they don't change. In their minds they go on living in a ghetto, hanging onto the old ways and the old beliefs, keeping separate. I won't do that. I broke loose. It isn't easy, routing out all the old habits. It's hard not to be cautious of everyone." His strong lips turned up but it was more grimace than smile. "So you and Aurelia will have to make allowances. When I get another house and she comes back I'll try to tell her more.

"For you . . . let's talk about the loan I need. It will have to be made quicker now that I won't have the money from the ranch to carry over with."

I wanted him to tell me more about the strange people he came from, but he had plainly closed off the brief view he had given me. I would have to be content that he had trusted me this far and get my mind on business.

"Too bad we broke with the Seligmans," I said. "If we'd kept using them as correspondents they might help now."

He gave me an odd look. "They may still."

"I don't think so. Jesse was put out when you switched our shipments to Adams."

"Jesse and his brothers are never so put out that they'll let a chance to make a profit go by. As a matter of fact I'm having lunch with Jacob Pool. Come along and listen in."

Pool was an independent gold buyer and small private banker, not important in himself but he now represented the Seligmans locally, since Jesse Seligman had gone back to New York. All I knew about the Seligmans was that there were several brothers operating in various ventures but all tied together under the domination of Joseph, the oldest. On the walk to the restaurant Mitchell told me more, influenced, I thought, by our talk in the office. They sounded like a remarkable family. The boys had started out on foot, as peddlers in rural Pennsylvania, and had moved up in the circle of Jewish private bankers of which August Belmont, with the Rothschild money behind him, was the biggest. The shipping of California gold had contributed to the Seligmans' rise and as the Eastern agents for the Mule Express they had profited handsomely until we had switched to Adams.

It was on those profits that Mitchell played over the lunch with Pool in proposing that the Seligmans make a loan against his real estate, but it did not surprise me that Pool was doubtful.

"Joseph," he said, "was not pleased when you left them to work through another bank."

"Because we needed the outlets of an express agency that covered the East," Mitchell argued. "It was business, not a personal matter. This is business too. Jesse was out here, he knows that any commercial real estate close to the bay can't help doubling or tripling in value from what I paid for it when the mines come back. They'll never have a chance like this again. You know that as well as I do."

Pool was shaking his head. "Gold they understand, we understand. Real estate I do not think they will trust. They spent too many years in Europe where they couldn't buy land."

Mitchell made a disgusted sound. "It's not the same here, and it's time they got their heads out of the sand. You can ask, can't you? You can show them my financial situation, point out the opportunity I'm offering."

Pool kept us on tenterhooks, not committing himself until we had finished the coffee and were ready to leave, and then he was grudging, saying:

"I'll write to them. I don't know what they'll say. I don't see much hope for you."

Neither did I, and I said so when we were alone on the street, but Mitchell winked at me and chuckled.

"He was playing poker. He's good. But that credit statement I gave him hooked him. They'll make us sweat for it but don't worry, we've got our loan. He wouldn't have agreed to write if he really thought they wouldn't make it. It may take two or three months, which we can handle, so let's think about what we do while we wait."

Like a cork that cannot be kept under water, he already had another idea in his mind and we spent the afternoon talking it out. As crippled as we were and with our world still stunned under depression and panic it seemed like a far-fetched dream to me, but he was generating so much enthusiasm that once more I fell under the spell.

"I told you the other day that I couldn't get on a mule again and start another express company, but now I think I see a way we can do just about that."

"Without money? And you sold our territory to Wells Fargo, and they're already dug in in the Northern Mines." I couldn't see where anything was changed on that score.

"Not without money," he agreed. "We'll have to find that. As to territory, I've been hearing about two new strikes that are just opening up. One is down south on the Kern River and the other is way north, on the Trinity. They're both in about the same stage as the Mother Lode was when we went in there, no roads, just a lot of little fresh camps strung along the streams, but they'll grow just like the foothills. Wells Fargo won't be interested in them because they are geared to stagecoaches, and the wagons can't get back in there."

I said that even if he found money, when business picked up again I thought he'd be too busy with the real estate, and he agreed again.

"But," he said, "you've got to have something to do and I'm never going to make a promoter out of you, you don't think that way. You'll run the express and we'll feed the profit into land or whatever else turns up. We'll work it this way: while we wait for the Seligmans you go to the Trinity and make a survey. See what it looks like and listen to what they're saying. Learn everything you can. I'll stay here and look for money. When we get it you start the mule trains, take in supplies and bring out the gold the way we used to. When you're in operation I'll go to Wells Fargo and make a deal with them like we had with Adams. We'll make connections with their stages and let them ship from those points. They'll go for it because it won't cost them anything and they'll make a profit they wouldn't otherwise have. It works for everybody."

The more he said the better it sounded. It made sense, and by the time I could finish the survey money might be easier to come by. Finally, I liked the hills better than the city, which made it easier to convince myself that we could do it.

I took my time going north, finding out all I could on the way. As we had developed in the Southern Mines so other small outfits had spread a network above San Francisco, serving such camps as Downieville, North San Juan, Grass Valley, Nevada City. As the roads began to open John Whistman ran an old French omnibus between San Francisco and San Jose, then sold out to Warren Hall and Jared Crandall. Other independent, haphazard operations sprang up and were later gathered together by James Birch and Frank Stevens into the California Stage Company. Headquartered in the Oriental Hotel in Sacramento, they spread a system to cover the northern part of the state. The Adams Company had spotted agencies in the principal communities along that system and used their stages for transport.

But with the crash those agencies were closed. If Wells Fargo was in as good shape as Mitchell said they would probably move into those areas before we could. It was north of that territory, beyond a barrier of high, rugged mountains that the Trinity camps squatted in deep canyons. They could only be reached by pack train. That was what we would aim at.

I found it a beautiful country but much rougher than the Southern Mines. The camps were rich and there was plenty of water up there. And they needed our service badly.

I had been gone over two months when Mitchell wrote that the Seligman loan had come through and that he had found money for our new company, but he did not say from what source. He wanted me to bring down my report.

I turned back optimistically and as I rode south there was a feeling of revival everywhere. Late spring rains had finally come and the southern placers were working again. Unemployment was already dropping. The spirit of the new Californians, who after every ruinous fire in their camps began rebuilding before the ashes were cold, was surging up again.

In a newspaper some weeks old I read that Henry Naglee had been appointed temporary trustee for Wells Fargo and had issued a statement.

Wells Fargo and Company have completed a balance of their accounts this day and find to the credit of their house above every liability $389,106.23, and only ask their friends to be patient so that they may convert some of their assets and resume payment.

By the time I reached the city they had been among the first to reopen their doors and had emerged as the only major express company on the coast.

I expected to find Mitchell's enthusiasm at a peak. His handshake was vigorous enough, he poured us each a brandy and quizzed me about what I had seen while we drank it and seemed more than satisfied with what I told him, but when I asked him about the Seligman loan he gave me a sour laugh.

"They really put the screws on," he said. "Under their conditions it almost wasn't worth it, but I couldn't hold on any longer without them. The bastards knew it and they squeezed. Here."

He found the memorandum of agreement he had signed and sat watching me read it. A syndicate was formed, owned jointly by Mitchell and the Seligmans, to take over Mitchell's purchase contracts. Pool would manage it and have full say as to the time any or all of the real estate would be marketed. Seligmans would pay the monthly installments as they came due, but there was nothing said about the nearly two hundred thousand Mitchell had already put into the land. I asked about that and he swore.

"They wouldn't include that. It won't cost them more than fifty thousand a year to keep those payments up, and if they liquidate the property in less than four years they won't have as much invested as I do. I tried to argue with Pool but he wouldn't budge. He claims that if the depression lasts longer than the four years they'll have to put in more than I did. You know it's not going to drag on that long. It's raining again now and production is turning up. All I can do is hope that values skyrocket and that Pool holds the lots long enough to pull me out with something for profit." His mouth turned up at one corner. "I did get something out of them that will make you happy. They're putting up cash to pay off the Stockton debt. Which of course comes out of my hide, off the top of my share in any profit."

"Well, that's something," I said. "And for the rest, it could be worse. They could have refused to loan anything and you'd have lost the land entirely. As it is you've at least the chance of coming out even. Now what about the money for the Trinity Company?"

He lifted his shoulders in a heavy shrug. "That isn't going to be just the way we wanted it either. I had to take in some new people, three of the old Adams partners, Dexter Brigham and two friends of his. We each put in twenty-five thousand and incorporated the Pacific Express Company. It isn't much . . . Wells Fargo has increased their capitalization to six hundred thousand and there's a rumor they're going to a million soon . . . but it will get us started, and they agreed to let you manage it with a free hand. We'll use this place as the office. I'll get them over here tomorrow to meet you."

He had not yet mentioned Aurelia and I did not want to ask if she had come back, but I could ask where he was living, since he had still been in the house when I went north.

He shrugged again. "Hotel. The Cosmopolitan. We'll go over and get you a room there, then we'll go have dinner and celebrate. Davie, we're on the way again."

CHAPTER SEVEN

We did not tell the new partners in the Pacific Express Company of the plan to tie in with Wells Fargo later. It was too likely that with so many knowing about it advance word would leak out. Mitchell wanted our mule lines to be well established and making money so that when he approached the big organization he had a functioning, proven operation to point to in his argument that we would be valuable to them.

And since Wells Fargo had contracts with the California Stage Line that dominated transportation in the north wherever there were roads, giving them control of all shipments on the coaches, we could not use that route to take the Trinity gold out without making Wells Fargo aware of us too early.

I had to set up a temporary system, hauling over the mountain barrier to headquarters at Redding, Yreka, and Weaverville, then making a connection with the Independent Steamship Line to boat down the Sacramento. It would double our cost, but that would end when the agreement with Wells Fargo was made.

We had a big area to draw business from, small, scattered diggings like Happy Camp, Clear Creek, Scott's Bar, Burnt Ranch, French Gulch, and the rest. There were a couple of hundred of them in the northern part of California and another twenty-five or thirty in southern Oregon. Some of them could not even be called towns, merely collections of rude buildings along a creek. Others like Weaverville had two or three thousand people. Weaverville itself had a large Chinese settlement.

Wells Fargo could be expected to go into Weaverville and Yreka, and Jacksonville in Oregon, soon, but the mountain communities could only be served by pack train.

I located several of the packers who had worked for us on the Mother Lode, men experienced with donkeys and proven trustworthy. One string of animals worked out of each of our centers, made a swinging loop that sometimes took as long as a month before it returned to its base. Each of the three partners managed one of the central agencies. In the smaller camps I used the system we had found successful for the Mule Express, making our agent the local storekeeper, and we were welcomed with open arms. They were remote, their source of supplies a long way off across strenuous miles of twisting, rudimentary mountain trails, and our trains bringing their goods in regularly assured their cooperation.

With the partners established to receive and forward the gold we brought out and to fill the orders to be taken back in, my job was on the trail, seeing that deliveries kept up with our spreading network and opening a new branch as soon as a new strike was made. For the first four months after we began operating I never spent more than one night in any one place.

I loved it. The country was spectacular wherever I rode, the mountains much higher than the foothills of the Mother Lode, the canyons deeper, most of the trails so new they were no more than blazed paths. And from nearly every direction I could take a sight on the snow-covered head of Mount Shasta, rising alone out of its plain.

Before the end of the first year we were breaking even. The expense of opening offices, buying mules and hiring packers left us no profit, but these were non-recurring costs except as we would expand. There was not as much gold as in the Mother Lode, the placers were farther apart and the camps too small to demand too much in the way of goods, but the promise was there.

I wrote to Mitchell that I thought it was time to talk to Wells Fargo.

In less time than I thought a letter could make the round trip Mitchell himself rode in on me.

The news he brought was not good, but he was more perplexed than angry. Yet he was angry too as he always was with obtuseness in business.

"Pardee is gone," he told me. "He's been replaced by a man who was general treasurer, from the New York office, T. M. Ianes. And Ianes is an ass. I talked myself blue in the face and he didn't have the vaguest understanding of what I told him. A damned eastern ignoramous. I told him what we're doing, that there aren't any roads back in here that coaches can use and that we've got ten years experience in making mule trains pay. I tried to show him how our trains could meet their stages down below and how their taking over our shipments from there would mean found money for them in express charges without it costing them a dime, and extend their reach.

"The damn fool couldn't see it at all. Just sat there smirking and saying there wasn't enough in it to make the trouble worth their while. Davie, there are a lot of smart men in Wells Fargo. There have to be to make it grow like it's doing. How in hell can they put an idiot like Ianes in the General Agent's chair? He laughed me out of the office. You don't laugh at a man who offers you a good profit for nothing."

It was a hard blow to us. It meant that instead of being relieved of the higher cost in getting our gold out we would have to continue as we were. It meant that we could not grow financially as fast as we had expected. But it was not a fatal blow and if we watched the corners the Pacific Express could make a modest mark for itself. If bigger strikes were made we could hope for better than modest.

While he was up there Mitchell stayed long enough to make a swing with me and make his own estimate, and he went back to town satisfied but still muttering about Ianes and his stupidity.

By winter I was pushing our lines farther and farther north, taking a first train myself back to the most remote camp, loaded with an educated guess at what they might be needing, the food staples and miners' tools. Big Bar had just been opened, with about twenty men working and the signs indicating that it would develop well.

It turned out that I was especially welcome because a surprise heavy snow marooned the camp. For two months I could not get out. The passes were drifted too deep for the animals and the trails across the high mountains were obliterated. But the stores I had brought were enough to see us through, I bunked in with the only merchant, and the snow banked around his cabin helped to keep us warm. The men were good company and since the gravel was too frozen to work we spent the days yarning about other camps and playing poker. I worried that I should be back attending to business but otherwise I enjoyed the rest from so much traveling, enjoyed lazing with the kind of people I had known in Sonora.

It was March before I rode back into Happy Camp. I was in good spirits and in a hurry to find out what shape the agency there was in, so I made a shortcut over a hogback to come down at the rear of Elm's Store instead of following the main street that wound along the curve of the canyon bottom.

Elm was a short, thin wisp of a man with a mat of straw-like hair and light eyes that turned defensive as I came in. I was relieved to see that his counter was piled high with recently delivered goods, but I also had the uneasy feeling that something was wrong.

I said, "Trains came through all right?"

"Trains came through. One of yours and one of theirs."

"Who's they?"

He looked out of his front window, then back at me. "Where you been?"

"Snowed in at Big Bar. What's going on?"

For answer he nodded toward the window with a peculiar expression on his face. I did not stop with the window. I crossed the rough wood floor and pulled the door open.

Outside there was a narrow gallery with a makeshift roof that sagged from the weight of the snow. I saw that first and then as I went farther out I saw the new building across the muddy street. It was a solid log building and hanging from the gallery roof on that side was a sign, hand lettered but readable enough.

WELLS FARGO AND COMPANY
CALIFORNIA EXPRESS

For the barest instant I thought someone had gone to a lot of trouble to pull a joke on me. The boys in these isolated camps would go to great lengths to make a little amusement for themselves as a defense against the monotony and boredom. But even as the idea came I knew this was no hoax. I knew what it was and I knew what it meant.

I turned back into Elm's Store knowing that we were in trouble. The name of Wells Fargo was becoming monolithic. They had reopened when the Adams Company had not, and not one depositor had suffered a penny's loss. They commanded enormous resources and we had little behind us.

It took concentration for me to keep my voice steady. "When did they move in?"

"Agent showed up a month ago. He hired some of the boys to put up the store and move in his stuff. His first pack train came in last week."

I could not say anything more for a long moment. The muscles of my throat were too tight with the slow anger rising through me. There was barely enough business in Happy Camp for one express service, certainly not for both of us. Wells Fargo was not here for any innocent competition.

I finally managed to say casually, "Town's getting important. What's the new agent's name?"

Elm looked at me sidewise, disappointed that I was apparently not reacting enough to entertain him.

"Peter Ronson. He's a right pleasant spoken fellow and very obliging."

I had no doubt that he was obliging. That was what he was here for, to be so helpful that he would take enough business away from us that we could not operate. Mr. T. M. Ianes's eastern naïveté was as guileless as a cobra. He had listened to Mitchell and laughed, and sat back waiting until we were in so deep that we could not pull out without a big loss. Now he was deliberately coming in here to destroy the Pacific Express.

I could not blame Wells Fargo for going after all the profitable business it could find. That was what any business must do to grow. But this was hitting below the belt. There could not possibly be enough profit for two concerns in Happy Camp or any camp this size. There could be no ethical reason for this move.

I walked across the street. The door squeaked as I opened it. A cloth curtain divided the building. In the forward section was a chest-high counter on which sat the gold scales that were the mark of every bank and express company in the state.

At the sound of the door a young man pushed the curtain aside and came from the rear section, dark haired, with a quick, intense face and a wide smile.

"Hello there." He took in my sheep-lined coat, my cap and muddy boots and decided I was a miner. "Can I help you?"

"I doubt it." I managed a faint grin but there was no humor in it. "I'm David Stuart of the Pacific Express."

His eyes sharpened and I knew he had been told about me. If I had had any doubt that this was an intentional effort to wreck us it vanished with that knowledge.

"Oh, Stuart, yes. I guess we're competitors, you might say."

"You might," I said. "Just how much business are you supposed to originate a month?"

That brought a slight flush and a more defensive tone.

"There hasn't been any quota set."

"There wouldn't be, when your function is only to ruin another company. How many other offices are you people opening in this territory?"

He did not like it, but he had been well trained not to let himself be thrown off balance. He fixed his smile again and shrugged.

"I don't know exactly. A dozen, two dozen. They didn't tell me."

It was enough. Twelve offices would cripple us. Two dozen would deny us any chance of making a worthwhile profit.

There were two chairs behind the counter. I walked around the corner and sat down in one. Ronson hesitated for a moment, then sank uncomfortably onto the other.

"If it isn't a secret," I said, "how much are you charging to carry letters?"

His smile spread a trifle wider. "It's no secret. Six cents plus the government charge."

The government charge was demanded by the Federal post office on all mail, whoever carried it. Their service was so poor in comparison to that of the express companies that it was seldom used, so to get a bigger share of the postal revenues Congress passed a law. Any express messenger found handling mail that did not carry the government stamp was liable to a five-hundred-dollar fine. The miners still preferred the express companies, and most of us used our own franked envelopes with a government stamp added.

But six cents. We were charging ten.

"How much for treasure shipments?"

"Three percent."

It had been five since the beginning.

"I wish you luck."

I stood up and offered my hand. I did not wish him luck. I would gladly have cut his throat if it would have accomplished anything. But he was not to blame. The blame lay squarely on the men in the Parrott Building, where the big company had moved the fall before, and on those in the American Express Building all the way back in New York.

I rode out within the hour. I wrote letters to the three partners in the central agencies, warning them and asking them to meet me in San Francisco at a board meeting. I carried them out of the mountains with me until I could hire riders to deliver them, and made a fast tour through the camps to see just where Wells Fargo had moved in.

The partners beat me to town and had already talked to Mitchell, but my letters had not been detailed. When I got there we sent messengers to bring the men to the office and while we waited for them I told Mitchell all I had found out.

I was so mad I could hardly talk and he listened in a cold fury.

"Damn them. God damn the stinking bastards. It isn't only us they're after. They're buying up and stealing and running out everybody else. They've got the whole state in their pocket now but that's not enough for them. They want everything even the littlest man has. They're not businessmen, they're pirates."

The partners had been located together at the Exchange Bar and they came in in a group. I went over the story again for them with the extent of the invasion, the number of Wells Fargo offices I had seen in our territory, and what I thought it spelled for us.

"We're cooked," I told them. "They can afford to lose a hundred thousand dollars in those camps and still pay their regular dividends. We cannot."

Dexter Brigham had been made president of Pacific Express six months before and I thought he would explode. His hands in his lap clenched and unclenched in spasms and his jaw muscles worked. When I had finished he hammered a fist against the desk.

"We're not cooked. We'll outlast them. They're too damned greedy to take the loss for long. We'll fight their way, carry letters for five cents and treasure for two percent."

I choked. I knew that Brigham was a fighter, but this was too emotional a reaction. We were forced into an impossible corner and this action was suicidal. Mitchell joined me in trying to tell him but the other two partners, who had been with Brigham in the old Adams Company, sided with him. The meeting became a stormy argument but nothing we said changed his stubborn decision. The upshot was that a letter was made up to be sent to all of our offices.

Agents:
    As Wells Fargo and Co. have instructed their agents throughout the country to reduce rates of freight on treasure, etc. so as to obtain all the business . . . you are hereby authorized to do the same, regardless of former rates.

Brigham signed it as president, then the three took an angry leave.

"What a damn fool thing to do," I told Mitchell. "We'll last about ninety days with a rate war. That octopus can go on forever."

He was sunk deep in his chair with his head pulled down into his shoulders, the heavy eyelids hooded down, his body very still.

"Davie," he said it suddenly. "Did you ever hear me threaten anyone?"

I started, then shook my head.

"Listen now. I am going to get Wells Fargo. No matter how long it takes, no matter what it takes. I am going to break those bastards."

The words were spaced out, slow, even. They made my hair crawl. Not for what they might portend for Wells Fargo, but that it was Mitchell Randolph saying them. It was such a childish threat, and whatever faults Mitchell had he had never been childish. I could not believe that he really thought he could pit himself against this many-headed giant and make any dent at all in it. It was, I decided, only a way of venting himself of helpless, frustrating anger. Yet it hung in the air and I could not shake it off.

I wanted to get off the subject and when he didn't say anything more for an uncomfortable length of time I asked:

"What do you hear from Aurelia? How is David?"

As a distraction it worked, but the answer was not what I had hoped for. The target of his anger just shifted.

"I wrote her two months ago to come home. She didn't answer."

"Home?" I thought he was still in the hotel.

He smiled briefly. "I forgot you didn't know. Pool sold twelve acres below Market, to Gordon who owns the sugar mill, and he's opening up a new allotment with restricted housing. I bought one lot and put up a house."

"Does that mean real estate is starting to move again?"

He was interested now, in one of his quick changes of mood.

"It's booming. You wouldn't know that a year and a half ago they were crying that San Francisco was dead. Pool did a good job, got enough out of the sale that my share paid off the Seligman debt, bought the lot and built the house and left me some cash. We're splitting the rest of the holdings and dissolving the syndicate. With the mines working full time again conditions here are good, but there's trouble coming in the East. The Seligmans are selling out, turning their share into cash. I'm holding mine except what I have to sell for operating money."

He did not mention any possible share of mine and I did not ask. I wanted to know more about Aurelia.

I said, "Well, that at least is good news. Why don't you go out and see Aurelia?"

His anger came back. "I went. They wouldn't let me on the ranch."

"Who wouldn't?"

"It looked like every *Californio* on the coast is down there. Must be a hundred men. Armed. They stopped me at the boundary and said they'd shoot me if I didn't keep away."

It was ridiculous that she should have a guard that size, or any guard, unless something had happened that Mitchell hadn't told me, and it looked like the only way I would find out would be to go down myself.

"How about my trying to see her?"

He glanced at me speculatively, a look that should have warned me, and nodded.

"It's a good idea. You can take this to her." He rose and went to the safe and brought back a folded paper, handing it to me.

It was a court order, directing her to turn over David Randolph into his father's custody. I couldn't believe it. I looked up and found him watching me, challenging me.

"Mitchell," I said, "you've lost your mind. You serve her with this and she'll never speak to you again."

"She's not speaking to me now, and kid, between us I don't give a damn whether she does or not. She wouldn't stand with me when I needed her, and that's not the kind of a wife I need or want. But I do want the boy. I want him educated, trained to take over the estate I'm going to build. He's not going to grow up like that shiftless tribe."

"But to drag her into court, Mitchell . . . you'll only make her hate you. No court is going to take a five-year-old child away from its mother."

He laughed, a bitter, sarcastic bark. "Davie, the California courts are no better than the legislature, and you know what that is."

I knew what was said about it, that you couldn't find a more venal body, that any vote in Sacramento could be bought for five hundred dollars, and unhappily I admitted that it would follow that he was right about the courts. He probably could buy a judgment.

"I've been wondering how to get the writ served," he said. "A bailiff couldn't get on the place, but they might let you in."

I wanted to throw the paper away and tell him to go to hell. I didn't want Aurelia to think I was party to such an action. But I knew Mitchell. He wouldn't let it drop, he would find some way, if he had to buy an army of police. The service would come better from me and maybe in talking to her I could find some way out of the mess.

I rode down the peninsula, a country much changed since I had first seen it, and I found myself resenting the cutting up of the beautiful land. I turned in at the lane and climbed to the crest of the ridge where the ranch began, but there I was intercepted by two horsemen wearing guns. They were courteous but firm. I could not go farther. This was private property and strangers were not permitted. One of them seemed familiar, I could have seen him at the wedding, I was not certain, but I spoke to him, explaining that I was a friend, not a stranger, asking him to send word inside to Mrs. Randolph that Davie Stuart wanted to see her.

They talked it over in Spanish. Needled by the bilingual Lamas family and by Mitchell I had learned the language, but had not been able to use it often enough to be fluent, and this conversation was too fast for me to follow. Then the familiar man swung his horse and galloped over the hill. The second motioned me to dismount and when I was on the ground he too stepped down and we waited in an uneasy silence. Besides the gun in the holster on his hip he wore one of the heavy bladed skinning knives used by the vaqueros. He looked altogether fierce and warlike. I wondered if Aurelia did expect Mitchell to try to take the ranch by force.

And then she came racing over the ridge. She was dressed as she had been when I first saw her and she looked hardly a day older.

It was beautiful to watch her come. I had spent a lot of my life in the saddle but I had never become a part of the horse the way a natural rider does. She was flying. Even at the distance I could see her smile and she shouted before she reached us.

"Davie, Davie, how wonderful."

She dropped off the animal, running, and I put out my hands instinctively to catch her. She reached up, caught my shoulders and stretched to kiss me, hard.

"Davie."

I was surprised at the vigor of the welcome, then I laughed and kissed her back. "You look great," I told her, and meant it.

"So do you." She hugged me. "Oh, I am glad to see you. Why haven't you come before?"

"I've been working up near Oregon," I said, and started to tell her about that, but she cut me short.

"Come on, Mother will want to see you, and the boys . . . you won't recognize them, they've grown so."

She waved a gay hand at the guard and swung back to her saddle before I could offer help, and when I was up we rode on across the hill.

The house did not look changed, but the orchards and vineyards were established, larger, and the fields were full of men, working but all armed.

"Why all the guards?" I asked her.

"Squatters. They're causing a lot of trouble, haven't you heard?"

"There aren't many where I've been."

She said shortly, "There are here. Like locusts. They move onto anybody's land, hundreds of them. Then they dare you to throw them off. They claim the land is open, federally owned, and about half the time the courts back them up."

I knew that John Sutter had lost most of his grant, both at Sacramento and in the Feather River Valley, and that John Marsh who had been the first doctor in the state and had had a fifty-thousand acre ranch had been harried through the courts by such settlers. Marsh had been murdered the year before by two of his own vaqueros and his son was still fighting to keep the property from being chipped away.

"It's been a bad time, Davie. Two years ago in the depression the Californians were the first to lose their jobs and the last to be hired, so I began bringing them here. And lucky I did. We have no squatters on Felicidad."

We left the horses at the corral and the boys and Concepción came from the patio. Duncan had shot up into a tall young man and José was on his way. They ran to circle around me, pouring out questions. I shoved past them and took both of Concepción's hands. She squeezed mine and I knew that I was welcome.

In a strange sense I felt that I was coming home. I had never had a home in California and could hardly remember the places we had lived in the East, and the timeless serenity in spite of the armed guards here gathered me in along with Aurelia's dispossessed countrymen.

Then I saw the little boy hanging back at the patio corner, and remembered the writ in my pocket. David was a small edition of Duncan, with the auburn hair and chiseled features. I could see no resemblance to Mitchell Randolph. None of these people were going to give him up without some kind of fight.

I said to Aurelia, "May I talk to you alone?"

My voice gave me away. She motioned to her family.

"None of us have secrets when there's trouble, Davie. What is it?"

I pulled out the paper and held it. "I don't like this. I hope you will understand why I brought it rather than let it be delivered by an officer of the court. I think Mitchell is wrong, but . . ." I let the words die.

139

Aurelia looked at my hand as if I held a snake, then she reached for the writ, unfolded it and read it, and as she read her breath drew in, long, slow, filling her, choking her. Her head turned toward the little boy who still hung back shyly, then toward her mother, toward her brothers one at a time, and finally back to me, her pupils blazing dark.

"No." She exhaled rather than spoke.

Her mother reached for the paper but Duncan's hand was there first, trying to take it. Aurelia's fingers were so frozen around it that he had to pry them away. He read aloud. His voice had the bass tones of a man but it broke back to a high squeak as he got the meaning of the words. Then he ripped the paper into pieces.

"Damn him, damn him, damn him. He can't do that."

"He can if he can buy a judge," I said. "We'll have to think of some compromise."

"Never. We'll never let them on the ranch. We'll fight. The men will fight."

"Duncan, use your head. If you try that they'll send the militia and get a lot of you hurt." I appealed to Aurelia, trying to sidetrack Duncan. "Mitchell is mad because you wouldn't answer his letter and kept him out of here. If you would go and talk to him . . ."

Duncan's voice cut in with a wild, "I'll kill him."

He was as big as a man and there were a gun and a knife at his hip, and I hadn't any doubt that he would try to do just such a stupid thing.

"Stop it." I had to shout to get through to him. "Don't talk crazy. Supposing you did. You'd be hanged for murder. Then what would happen to your family?"

I saw the idea jolt him, but it didn't stop him, only swerved him, and he looked at me with a vicious, triumphant grin.

"A duel. I'll challenge the devil, and he can't refuse to meet me."

The idea of a sixteen-year-old challenging anyone should have made me laugh, but there was nothing funny about this boy's threat. He was big enough and he probably could shoot better than Mitchell, and dueling was common practice on the bay. Two or three of them took place every month.

"Duncan, that's not any better. You can still get yourself killed, and you're no good to anybody dead. Aurelia, if you won't talk to Mitchell let me find a lawyer for you, let him see Mitchell. All he wants is to educate David, and it is his son too. Maybe it can be worked out that he can spend some time with each of you."

Duncan was shaking his head so hard that I thought his neck would snap, then Concepción put a hand on his arm and took command.

"Thank you, Davie, you bring us to our senses. Yes, we must try that way, and there is a lawyer who will work for the *Californios*. Aurelia, you will ask him to help."

BOOK THREE

CHAPTER ONE

Vigorous, young, gay again as the depression passed and was put out of mind, San Francisco was a laughing city. Her theaters sparkled, her restaurants dazzled, and her people delighted in amusement. They took a deep civic pride in an assortment of characters whose odd behavior would have got them run out of a more staid society.

One speculator who had lost more than his fortune in the crash notified the newspapers that the legislature had appointed him Emperor of the United States. He decked himself out in royal regalia, paraded the streets bestowing benign greetings on his subjects, ate and drank at the best restaurants and saloons, and paid for nothing. San Francisco took him to its heart, solemnly made its obeisance, and picked up the checks.

It applauded a half-grown girl who embarrassed her family by racing after the engines whenever a fire brought them clanging through the streets. The volunteers on Engine 5 made her an honorary member of their company and she grew into the acknowledged if willful leader of the rollicking society.

It gloried in Dave Broderick, a New York saloonkeeper who brought Tammany Hall's methods West, plunged the city into a maze of debt and cynically sold a useless theater building to the city for three times what it was worth.

It made a hero of Baker, with his mesmerizing silver tongue, when that lawyer got himself into a difficult bind. He accepted thirty thousand dollars from the leading madam to defend her murderer lover and then, when public opinion frowned, tried to withdraw. An inveterate gambler, he had already lost the money, and in chagrin was forced by the madam's friends to continue the unpopular case. The people did not approve of the murderer but Baker was a great show.

In this climate Marion Boniface was not long making his mark. He had arrived as many men did, without explaining himself and hung out an attorney's shingle with an added line beneath his name, *Se habla español*. That brought him an immediate clientele from the *Californios* with court troubles. He worked on contingency for them and sometimes won a case, sometimes collected.

That was his early showcase, the springboard by which he leaped onto the legal scene. His particular forte was the theater of the courtroom. His dress was flashy, his personality electric, his wit sharp and his rhetoric and performance as exciting as could be found on any stage.

His enemies, as he made them, complained that he won his cases not by citing precedents but by either hypnotizing a jury or buying it. But in the half world of venal judges and ignorant advocates the complaints threw no cloud on his image.

His reputation spread quickly beyond the *Californio* sphere and his office thrived. Money flowed into and out of his narrow, supple hands. The newspapermen doted on him. He had a prodigious memory for names and cultivated the press assiduously. He became the toast of the French restaurants, the darling of actresses, the confidant of madams and robbers, equally at home in the Dupont Street dives and the best hotel dining rooms.

Aurelia Randolph went to Marion Boniface.

She had heard him praised by compatriots for whom he had been able to snatch something back from the Americans, but she was not prepared for what she found when she turned in through the door under his sign. A dim, narrow stairway of dirty, hard worn treads. She climbed them with increasing uneasiness. It was her first visit to any lawyer's office, and after the sturdy, polished doors of Mitchell's house the plain and scarred panel at the top of the steps was anything but reassuring.

She opened it apprehensively and stepped into a grimy room with a wooden fence across its middle. Beyond the fence were a table with a letter press and two high desks, a poorly dressed clerk working at each. On the customer's side of the fence a short man with heavy shoulders and disproportionately long arms, in shirt sleeves and galluses, stood looking out of a window so dirty it hardly let light through.

He turned at the sound she made and looked her over in a bold appraisal, removing neither his hard hat nor the chewed toothpick that bobbed in the corner of his thin mouth.

Aurelia stared back, trying to make this scene compare with what she had heard about her friends' champion, finally swallowed and said in a doubtful voice:

"Are you . . . Mr. Boniface?"

His mouth dropped open but the toothpick did not fall, then he laughed, a coarse bray. "Hell no, I'm Roper Duggan, of course."

He said it as if she must recognize the name, and indeed Duggan in his own way was as well known as Boniface. A ticket-of-leave man from the British penal colony on Van Dieman's Island, he had joined the rush of the Sidney Ducks from Australia for the gold fields. But Duggan had dug no gold. He preferred a slingshot or a knife to a shovel. He had never carried a gun, under the assumption that the explosion was apt to attract the attention of the police. The precaution had not been enough. When, as a bouncer in a Dupont deadfall, he had killed a customer, he was caught.

Boniface had found him in the old Pacific Street jail and got him freed by an impassioned plea and a liberal bribe, and from that moment Duggan had fastened himself to the lawyer like a lamprey to a fish. Boniface was seldom seen abroad without Duggan's square shadow trailing close behind. He was bodyguard, runner, procurer, utterly amoral, and he served no god except the attorney.

He saw that the name did not register on Aurelia, which placed her as a stranger to the lawyer's haunts, and from her youth and her fashionable clothes he made his guess at her errand here.

"You want to see him? I'll find out if he's busy."

He touched his hat but still did not take it off. Duggan was as bald as an egg and he resented it as a reflection on his virility. He wore the hat everywhere except in court. He went through the gate in the wooden fence and pushed open the door to Marion Boniface's private room.

"Something just blew in, counselor." Duggan drew a curvaceous female figure in the air, grinning. "Money . . . looks like another from a church to put the bite on you. And she's new . . . thought I was you."

"Very new, I'd say," Boniface said wryly. "No one in town a month would take a pug ugly like you for me. Let's have a look."

It was part of the office policy to contribute to any church that asked. As Boniface had explained it to Duggan, the ladies of the churches had husbands, some of whom served on juries, some of whom were judges or held other positions of power, and a favorable word from these ladies could sometimes be very helpful.

Duggan turned back and beckoned and Aurelia came in, hesitant, careful that her dress did not touch the dusty furniture. Everything about this den, the necessity of coming here and to have to ask anything of these people made her more bitter against Mitchell. The anger gave her face a flush and her carriage a determined rigidity, but the surprise of the inner office threw her off balance.

It was as rudely furnished as the outer room, but cleaner, and the man who rose from the chair at the desk looked nothing like she had imagined.

He was tall, very thin, clean shaven with hollow cheeks and deep-set eyes that burned with a dark spark, a strong, thin nose. He wore a black broadcloth suit, a ruffled, starched shirt, a wing collar and full black silk cravat pinned with a five carat diamond stud that threw back a bright wink. It was a costume that he had developed and always wore. Aurelia's impression was of a gaunt Shakespearean actor on the wrong stage, looming against the dirty window.

That was what his detractors called him, and jeered that he was always on stage, in a courtroom, at a gambling table, or holding forth at the bar of a waterfront saloon.

The eyes glowed on her with their own surprise. From Duggan's suggestion he had expected an older woman, one of the wives who were gradually coming West and setting out to reform the frontier town. What he saw was little more than a girl. She was not beautiful, but her high color was becoming and there was a freshness about her that he found charming after the jaded women he was used to.

He bowed as Duggan closed the door and left them and said in a rolling tone:

"At your service, miss. May I do something for you?"

Confusion made her nervous. She had pictured the lawyer as a full-blown man, gusty, overweight with too much food and drink like so many of the Americans she despised, and she sounded uncertain.

"If you are Marion Boniface. Alfonso Rodriguez said you are the best lawyer in San Francisco."

A hint of a smile crossed his thin lips and she knew the words pleased him and relaxed a little.

"And what would a child like you want of a lawyer, good or bad?"

She brought out the writ, patched together and wrinkled, and held it forward. He took it, handed her into the client's chair and sat down at the desk, read the paper, tossed it aside, folded his hands under his chin and leaned on his elbows, studying her.

"So you are Major Randolph's wife. I wouldn't have thought he had the taste."

"You know him?" She was further flustered. That had not occurred to her.

"I know everyone." The smile passed again. "Why did he think he needed this writ? Have you left him?"

She nodded, not able to answer, and he led her out.

"You want me to get you a divorce?"

She shook her head quickly then. "My Church doesn't permit divorce. But I can't live with him either."

He said gently, "If I'm to be able to help you I have to know why."

At first it was hard, her story halting, but as he kept questioning her, showing her sympathy, she found it easier to talk. He got the whole history of the marriage and a full portrait of the girl, to him an unusual girl in her frustration that Randolph would not let her into his personal or business life. It was her insistence on having a part in his business world that interested Boniface, her urge to be more than a wife. She amused and excited him. Not physically, he was too self-centered to be interested in any one woman. And he was like Randolph in that he sheltered himself behind a screen that allowed no one through, and manipulated people. He worked like a puppeteer, creating façades for his clients to present to judges and juries. He looked for a key to Aurelia, probing for what forces were within her that could be turned to the advantage of the case.

He drew out of her her concern for the ranch, her fiery anger at the American invasion, her movement to gather in the *Californio* victims, and decided that there was a very strong will here. It gave him a private pleasure that the arrogant Major Mitchell Randolph had this dominance to contend with.

When he had emptied her of everything she thought she had to tell he said casually, "Do you know exactly what you want?"

"To keep my child. I won't have him raised by servants. I won't have him left alone while his father chases business up and down the state. Can the court really take him away from me?"

"They can. Unfortunately women in this country haven't many rights. The laws, you know, are written by men."

"Then I'll take him and run away. I'll go to Santa Barbara and hide. If necessary I'll go to Mexico."

Boniface hid his smile at the desperation, the small clenched fists.

"That may not be necessary. Let's look for another way. Divorce is out, but is there someone else, another woman?"

"I told you, I don't know anything about him."

"I don't think so, I haven't heard any rumors of one. Now, would you agree to go back, not to live as his wife but merely as his hostess, to be in the house? I judge that all he really wants is the boy's presence. If you will do that the writ would be satisfied."

She fought against it. "Isn't there another way? The ranch is a better life for a child, and I am needed there to help the people."

"I'm helping the same people from here. Couldn't you help from San Francisco? Randolph is a moneymaker. Has he ever stinted you?"

"No," she said slowly. "Only when he wanted to mortgage the ranch."

"Would that have been an emergency?"

"Yes, I suppose so. But the way he demanded it. If he'd bothered to explain, told me what was happening the way Davie did."

Boniface's eyebrows arched. "Davie? Someone important to you?"

She told him about Davie Stuart and added, "He's the only friend I have among the Americans."

"No more than that? I have to know. I don't want any little surprises tripping me up if we have to go to court."

She flushed at the new idea but looked at him steadily. "No more than a good friend. He's Mitchell's partner but he doesn't always approve of what Mitchell does. It was Davie who advised me to see a lawyer."

He held his eyes on hers for a long moment, but she met the stare without wavering and at last he was satisfied.

"All right, Mrs. Randolph. Let me think about all this. Can you come back here tomorrow at the same time?"

She nodded and rose and he saw her to the door. When she had gone Duggan followed him back into the private office.

"How much did she want?"

For answer Boniface handed him the writ. Duggan read it and looked sheepish.

"I guessed wrong, huh? Seems funny, somebody with her class having this kind of trouble. You going to bother with it?"

"I am," Boniface said pleasantly. "If for no other reason than that I don't like Mitchell Randolph and his kind."

Duggan squinted at him. "What you got against the major?"

"I can respect an honest thief. I can respect a murderer if he doesn't pretend to be something he's not. But a hypocrite turns my stomach, with his scramble after social position. Yes, I'm going to cut him down some. Take this note to his office. I want him here at five-thirty this afternoon."

Duggan looked doubtful. "You think he'll come here?"

"He'll come. These respectability boys are afraid of me. They know I haven't any reputation to protect and they don't know what I might do to them."

Mitchell Randolph was flabbergasted at the summons. He had not thought of the possibility that Aurelia would ask the help of an attorney. He had used the writ in the belief that it would frighten her into returning home. And that she had chosen Marion Boniface was intolerable. The men with whom he associated looked down on Boniface as a part of the unsavory underworld focused on the police courts, a disgraceful parasite that fed off the stable business community.

His impulse was to dismiss the note and bodily throw the ruffian who had brought it down the stairs. But he knew Roper Duggan's reputation and the likelihood that in retaliation the man would waylay him with his leather-covered slingshot on some dark street. In the end he walked around the corner to the Market Street office and went into the waiting room at exactly five-thirty.

The clerks had gone and Duggan perched on one of their stools staring at nothing. Without getting up he aimed a thumb at the inner door and swiveled his head to watch Mitchell cross and go through it.

Boniface was in his chair reading a transcript, his long legs stretched before him, crossed at the ankles. He rose courteously and extended his hand.

"So good of you to come, Major."

Mitchell could not ignore the hand. He took it, noticing how thin it was and that there was no return pressure. He might have held a small bundle of bones.

Boniface was saying, "I thought it might be less painful for you to discuss the matter of your writ privately rather than in the atmosphere of an open court. Won't you sit down?"

Mitchell sat down. He had seen Boniface many times, in the French restaurants, in some of the better-class houses and saloons, but he had never spoken to him, had only ignored him. The lawyer's quiet courtliness came as a surprise, the warm voice, sympathetic, the suggestion of concern for Mitchell's sensitivity to public exposure.

"I suppose so," he said. "None of this would have been necessary if my wife had been willing to talk to me."

"I presumed that. We both know that women are sometimes unreasonable, and as I understand it your only intent is to have the boy brought home to live. Is that true?"

"That's all I want."

"Then a solution should be simple. Mrs. Randolph said frankly that yours was a marriage of convenience?"

Mitchell nodded.

"You would not mind if she came back with the boy? You would not object to a few conditions?"

"That would depend. I'll tell you bluntly, counselor, I will not be dominated by a woman. I saw enough of that in my childhood."

"Certainly not." Boniface used a little rueful laugh. "I wouldn't want that myself. On the other hand your wife is entitled to be an individual herself. She was raised on a ranch where she took an active part in its operation."

"If you're suggesting that she take an active part in my business . . ."

"Heaven forbid." Boniface held up one protesting hand. "That's the last thing I had in mind. And my client understands the impossibility of her doing so. No. She needs her own field of interests. I've outlined the conditions here." He indicated a paper on the desk. "First, she will no longer share your bed."

Mitchell reddened but the lawyer appeared not to notice.

"Second, you will give her an allowance sufficient not only to manage the house but to support her own activities."

"What activities?" Mitchell was suspicious.

"She wants to help her people. The last condition is that you will not interfere with her life as you require her not to interfere in yours. It seems to me reasonably fair."

"They're a bunch of lazy bastards. What could she do for them?"

Boniface laughed lightly. "I've had some dealings with them, I can appreciate your point of view. But she's in another position and she feels very strongly about them.

"If you will make those concessions she will make these: she'll bring your son home, be your hostess, attend such functions with you as you choose. Perhaps you should read the agreement I've drawn."

He handed the paper to Mitchell and went to stand looking out of the window, giving him time to read and absorb it. He did not turn until Mitchell said cautiously:

"I guess it's all right, except that I want one stipulation. I am to have full say about the boy's education. I won't have him growing up an ignorant, provincial ranchhand. He'll have to go to college and be prepared to take over the business I plan to leave him."

Boniface came back to the desk saying, "No one should object to that." He sat down and added the paragraph in his own hand and watched Mitchell sign it. "It's a pleasure doing business with you, Major. If everybody was as reasonable as you we lawyers would have to go to work for a living."

Mitchell grunted, stood up and left. When Duggan came inside Boniface winked at him.

"That takes care of that. Now we will enjoy watching our Mrs. Randolph drive her complacent ass of a husband slowly crazy."

"Oh?" Duggan widened his eyes. "How's she going to do that?"

"She has several ways already in mind, and if they aren't enough I'll think of something more."

When Aurelia came in the next morning Boniface silently handed her the agreement and watched for her reactions.

She read carefully and finally looked up with wonder in her eyes. "So quickly."

He did not have to ask if she would accept the settlement.

"There was no real difficulty," he told her modestly. "Major Randolph saw that your differences were better settled out of court and I felt certain you would not object to the clause about the boy's education."

She found a mischievous smile. "I've always taken that for granted anyway." She sobered. "I want him to learn all he can about this new way of living. Not knowing is at the base of my people's troubles. Not understanding the language well, or legal procedures or what rights are really theirs under the new laws.

"And now, Mr. Boniface, another question. How do you get to be a lawyer? How did you?"

Marion Boniface looked startled, then his thin smile came. "Somebody been telling you I got my ticket from a diploma mill?"

"No, and I don't know what that is. I have a reason for asking, it isn't just curiosity."

He watched her closely, wondering at the sudden switch from worried client to an intense, flatteringly interested questioner. He had never before even considered telling anyone on the coast, but he had nothing to do this morning and it might be amusing to see what she made of it.

"Well, why not? It's a roundabout story, if you have the time."

She bobbed her head in impatience, her blue eyes fastened on his.

"My father was an actor, in Europe they're called traveling players, and my mother was a Spanish dancer. I learned that language from her. We moved to New Orleans when I was pretty young and as I grew up they took me into their act, we worked the river boats and the theaters until there was a cholera epidemic and they died. Some friends had a show boat and they took me in, but acting didn't make me much of a living and I switched to running one of the gambling games aboard. Then at a card table I killed a man."

He stopped to watch her face. There was no revulsion in it, only an open eagerness for him to go on. If nothing else, she was the best audience he could ask for.

"I was arrested and they got me a lawyer. The man I killed had attacked me and I shot him in self-defense. I only meant to wing him, so it was actually an accident, but when we got to court my lawyer was so drunk he got his argument all balled up, so I jumped in and asked the judge to let me defend myself. I didn't know any law but I did know that unless I got my story across I was going to hang. I was scared and I talked hard, and maybe because I could act or because I was young, they believed me. The jury voted me not guilty."

He broke off again, smiling at the memory of the boy's desperation and at the way this girl followed every word as if she were eating them, but with something going on in her head besides listening.

Aurelia was listening, and thinking, When I came in here yesterday I was afraid. Now I'm not afraid. I feel that I've known him for a long time.

"You must have done a good job," she said, "but is that all it took to make you a lawyer?"

"Not quite." He laughed aloud. It was a long time since he had opened himself this much to anyone and he was surprised to find himself enjoying it so much.

"It did make an impression on the judge and he called me into his chambers and asked how I would like to read law in his office."

"What is reading law?"

"An apprenticeship. You go to work in a lawyer's office, read the books in his library, learn how to draw up writs and complaints and contracts. Then you act as a clerk, start drawing up briefs and looking up precedents. I did all that plus sweeping out the office and delivering summonses and sleeping on a couch in the back room because it didn't pay enough that I could afford a room. Finally I was admitted to practice on my own."

"And that's how it's done . . ."

"Not always. There are law schools. But most of the men practicing out here got their training like I did. The advantage is that when you are admitted you usually become a member of the same office and inherit a part of the clientele to get you started. My luck didn't hold that long. The judge was going to take me into partnership but he died just after I was admitted and I discovered that an outsider with no family or connections didn't get the cases. So when I heard about the gold discovery I came out here."

"I think that was a very lucky move, you've been so successful."

"It wasn't quite that easy. Every shirttail lawyer starving in the East rushed out too. And a lot of men who aren't lawyers are practicing here. I had an edge in speaking Spanish, but there wasn't too much money to be made from the *Californios,* if you'll pardon me, and it took time to work up into a wider field.

"So, that is how I became an attorney." He straightened suddenly, puzzled with himself. "Sorry if I bored you. I've never run on like this before. I don't know why I did now."

"I'm anything but bored. Mr. Boniface, would you let me read law in your office? I'd even clean it, and it could use a cleaning."

Marion Boniface blinked. This was a most unusual day. He began to laugh.

"You know, I'm tempted. It would brighten things up just to have you around. But not to clean up. The dirt is part of the act. It's the stage setting. Most of my clients wouldn't be easy in a place where they could see out of the window. Why in the world though would you want to read law?"

She sat forward on the edge of the chair and leaned toward him with quick eagerness.

"Ever since yesterday I've been thinking. I wasn't raised to sit around and do nothing." She began counting off her points on her fingers, holding her hands out to him for greater emphasis. "I want to help my people. You said I could do it in San Francisco. They're being pushed out because they don't know how to defend themselves. I can't tell them what they can or cannot do unless I know myself. If I read law I could explain to them. Please, Mr. Boniface. Or are you another one who thinks a woman isn't bright enough to learn anything?"

Marion Boniface felt the glow rising inside him, the fire that always kindled when inspiration was on its way. He had a flair for novelty and a shrewd regard for its usefulness, and now his eyes reflected the glow.

"You're smart enough." He moved toward the idea cautiously, sniffing at it for pitfalls. "You're smarter than half the practicing attorneys in California. There is nothing in the legal code here to deny admittance to practice to a woman because of her sex, but the courts are controlled by men. I'm sure many lawyers would find reasons for not wanting you competing with them . . ."

She raised a finger. "It doesn't matter whether I am admitted. All I need is to know what the law is. If a case has to go to trial you are obviously the one who should handle it."

He nodded slowly. "Yes . . . that could work . . ."

"Then you'll take me?" The little girl that still lingered in her burst out in excitement. "You will? When can I start?"

"Whoa, whoa. There are other questions to look at."

The child still showed in her disappointment. "You mean you're afraid of what other lawyers would say about you if I were here?"

"My dear," he was grinning, "I don't give a damn what anybody says about me, especially other lawyers. They hate me now. I was thinking about you, and believe me that is a compliment, I'm not often considerate of others. I have a wide and well-earned reputation as a philanderer and if you associate yourself with me your good name won't be worth a tinker's damn. Your husband would have both our scalps."

"Oh." She matched his grin. "But under the agreement he signed can he stop me? I'm allowed to help my people."

"Nooo . . . but he might ask me for satisfaction."

She thought about that at some length and finally shook her head slowly.

"I'd bet against that. He'll raise Cain, yes, but he's too smart to get himself involved in a duel over me that would surely cause a scandal and bring everything out in the open. He's too secretive about himself to want that."

"And you, how do you feel about people's opinions of you?"

She lifted her chin with a fierce smile. "I am Aurelia Maria Isabella, born Lamas, McLeod . . . Randolph. Like you, Mr. Boniface, I do not give one small damn what anyone thinks or says."

Ceremoniously Boniface reached for her hand and shook it to bind the deal. Not that he expected her to last very long as a student of the law's intricacies, but this was a golden opportunity dropped in his lap, to further embarrass Mitchell Randolph. Cynical as he was, what galled the lawyer was the pretentiousness of that rising group of men growing rich and powerful through practices as opportunistic, as conniving and dishonest as his own, who presumed a superiority over him. It was their hypocrisy that he delighted in puncturing, and the shock value of having Aurelia Randolph in this office daily would more than make up for the inconvenience to him.

CHAPTER TWO

The San Francisco Aurelia agreed to return to was hardly recognizable as the rude town of four years before. Where the merchants of budding Montgomery Street had ridden to the mission for her wedding over dusty, meandering paths there was now a grid of paved streets with lamp standards at their corners.

The Parrott Building out of which Wells Fargo continued to extend its tenacles still dominated the financial district, but other firms were challenging and the physical core of the city was hardening. The topography itself was being reshaped. The ships that had once been moored hull against hull with their bowsprits thrust in above the wharf street, Sansome, were gone. Their rotting hulks had clogged the cove, fill had been brought in to bury them and now new streets ran through on top of them.

More ships still came, to a new wharf, from Europe and the East and the Orient, bringing more immigrants. Forty thousand people clustered along the shore and spread back up the hills.

The area was changing in other ways. It was no longer entirely dependent on placer gold. Much of the Spanish grant lands was in the hands of Americans, being cut into farms. Miners disillusioned by the droughts and failing placers and the general uncertainty of that life were settling the valleys, planting grapes, raising grain and building new cattle herds.

San Francisco was the future, the beating heart of an economy with a second wind, peopled by men who had run from the narrow strictures of the settled East. It was a young city of young men with young ideas, a gambling city, where fortunes were risked less on the whirl of a wheel or the turn of a card than on the general conviction that one day California would be the center of the universe.

The periodic fires that had razed her year after year had been a blessing in disguise, wiping away the half-canvas, half-board jerry-built shacks of the first comers and the subsequent hasty false starts. Now along Montgomery, around the old plaza and down Market Street which was growing in importance the building was mostly of brick, and whole forests had been ferried across the bay from Richardson's Sausalito Ranch, from Mill Valley and Mount Tamalpais for the dwellings rapidly climbing the steeply graded back streets.

Yet it had not outgrown its frontier character. The men who had led the Vigilante committees to get rid of the predatory gangs, the Hounds and Regulators and Sidney Ducks remained influential but the streets were still not safe and men who ventured out at night went armed.

Before she met Boniface, Aurelia had dreaded the idea of coming back, but with the prospect of working in his office an excitement rode her, a hope such as she had not known since her wedding night. She felt free and strong and there was nothing she could not do, and she was in a hurry to make of herself a force in defense of the Californians.

Her first meeting with Mitchell under the new agreement, on the evening she moved with her son into the new house, began well enough. They were carefully, pointedly polite. Mitchell inquired about the trip up from the ranch, about her mother and brothers, she asked after Davie Stuart. The little boy had his dinner with them and eased the long pauses with his chatter. Mitchell, talking to him as he would to an adult, asked him to speak English at home for the practice, made a joke of it to ease the order, then kissed him good night when Nora came to take him away to bed.

Mitchell asked Aurelia if she liked the house. She admitted that it pleased her and spoke particularly of the open platform on the roof, from which there was a sweeping view of the new docks, the broad bay with the toy cities on the eastern shore, and in the opposite direction the solid buildings crowding up the unleveled sand hills.

"It's a beautiful home," she said, "and the city looks exciting."

She saw that he was pleased. He poured a brandy for himself and relaxed, making the effort to use his easy charm.

"I think you and I can really make a life for ourselves here now. When you get acquainted with the neighboring ladies you'll find that San Francisco can be very satisfying. There will be parties, which I know you like, and dinners and the theater and . . ."

Her voice was quiet. "But I won't have time for all that, at least not for a while. There is the baby to raise, and then, I'll be reading law with Marion Boniface."

Mitchell had been lifting the brandy glass to his lips. He set it down slowly, with care, saying as if he had not heard her:

"You what?"

She had been nervous, waiting for this moment, knowing that she had to tell him at once and dreading the argument she knew would come, but now that it was said she was calm.

"When I agreed to bring little David here you agreed that I could help my people. The best way I can see to do that is to understand American law."

He slashed the words aside with a cut of his hand. "With Boniface, no. Absolutely not. The man's notorious, a gambler, a lecher, a disreputable shyster. No law office is a fit place for a young girl, but his is impossible. He consorts with the most depraved people in the city. His bodyguard is a murderer from Australia . . ."

Aurelia had a wayward urge to tell Mitchell that Boniface himself had killed, but she did not. This was no time to aggravate him further than necessary, for she needed his acceptance of her plan if there was to be any peace in this house.

She said steadily, "I have been in his office for two whole mornings and his conduct was impeccable. He helped me when no one else would." She stared at him directly as she said it and his face flushed with embarrassment.

"All right, all right. You're saying that if I hadn't served you with the court order you would never have gone to him. But damn it, Aurelia, it's just not possible. He could be a white knight with you but the moment you are associated with him in any way you will be tarred with slander."

"He warned me of that himself. I had to beg him to let me read with him. I had to tell him that it isn't important what is said about me."

"Isn't important?" He roared, rising to stand over her and for a moment she thought he would hit her. "Isn't important if your name is dragged through the gutters? You are my wife, my son's mother. I won't have them talking about you."

"What them?"

"Any of them. Mrs. Gordon, Mrs. Tevis, Mrs. Gwin, the doctor . . ."

"Poof." She stood up to face him. "Let that bunch of cackling hens say what they want to. What do you care what they say? You're smarter than all of their husbands put together. Let them gossip. Just you keep your head up and your armor on and nothing they can say can hurt either of us."

The blaze of his anger gradually died and his expression changed, softened with a quickening amusement.

"You're still quite a spitfire, that's certain."

"Whatever I am I'm proud to be, and it's all I have left. It's about all the Americans have left to any of my people. And as long as I have the breath and wits to fight I mean to do just that. I am Aurelia Randolph. I refuse to be dragged down by fear of an inane mob opinion. I will make my own rules of conduct. I will fight in my own way, and Mitchell Randolph, I am going to win."

His amusement changed to concern and his voice was more compassionate than she had ever heard him.

"They'll wreck you. Society always tries to tear down anyone who dares to be different."

"That's not true in San Francisco, Mitchell. Read the papers. This town loves the non-conformers. Look at Emperor Norton. Look at little Lillie Hitchcock who runs after the fire wagons, look at Boniface himself. He does exactly as he pleases and ignores all the cluck-clucking over him. You just may find that Aurelia Randolph will turn into a new personality. And you'll discover that people will listen to me."

He was silent, studying her with a fresh, genuine speculation, then suddenly, with a volition all its own, a huge laugh rolled out of him.

"By God . . . By God . . . I want to watch this, Aurelia girl. I want to sit back and watch you just beat the whole bunch to a fare-you-well."

CHAPTER THREE

As predicted, the tongues wagged at both ends. First it was the lawyers. Within a week every attorney in San Francisco knew that a woman was reading in Marion Boniface's office and it was the wry concensus of opinion that whether or not he was sleeping with her Boniface had pulled another calculated and successful publicity stunt.

The first weeks were brutal for Aurelia. The temptation to quit hung over her day after day, but after making all of her grand boasts to Mitchell she did not dare give up.

A table for her was crowded into the anteroom, she was introduced to the staff and given the privilege of the library, then Boniface left her deliberately alone. If she stayed a week she would have served her purpose to him, and if by chance she really meant to stick it out, if she could make it at all, he knew, she would need the strength to survive on her own. The place to learn whether she was a dilettante with a whim was here, at the beginning.

No one spoke to her. No one even said good morning. Roper Duggan took his cue from Boniface and ignored her. The two clerks openly resented her. Both were middle aged and soured. Both had been admitted to the bar years ago but neither had had the flair to succeed in courtroom practice.

Ezra Horton was a Southerner, dried up and frail, with a hacking cough that made it harder for Aurelia to concentrate. Having been a failure in his home state he had come West for a new start, and failed again on the flamboyant California legal stage. Boniface had picked him up because he did have a vast knowledge of law. He could quote statute from memory and Boniface stopped at his desk again and again to outline a situation and ask for a ruling that could be used as precedent. It was discouraging to Aurelia how the man could reel off a date, a case, and the name of the ruling judge.

James Eaton had been a judge in a little Missouri town but whiskey had driven him off the bench. He still went on a periodic drunk, but he was valuable in choosing juries. He seemed to have a sixth sense in ferreting out the prejudices and weaknesses of men called for jury duty.

Aurelia sat in her corner and read and eavesdropped. She was astonished to discover that law was not a rigid discipline, that it grew by court decisions into statutes, that every point had to be interpreted by a human being, that each was haggled over and that there were as many interpretations as there were attorneys.

She was fascinated to find that an individual without an attorney could go before the court and represent himself *in propria persona*, then she was deflated by the obvious answer to why so few laymen availed themselves of the opportunity, that they do not know the rules of evidence or understand what a court is looking for in testimony.

She focused on the California code, trying without help to comprehend the land laws that were her special interest, trying to make sense of the briefs drawn up by the clerks.

The first relief to her frustration came after Ezra Horton nearly died of pneumonia. When he did not come to work one morning Duggan was sent to find out why. Boniface had left for court by the time Duggan got back with the report that Horton was delirious with a fever. Aurelia badgered Duggan into taking her to the clerk's cheerless room, then sent him for a doctor who said Horton's only chance was in a hospital. She was told that the army hospital would not admit him and appealed to Dr. Hitchcock, head of the Federal medical service on the Pacific Coast, whom she had met at South Park parties.

Hitchcock got Horton taken care of and two weeks later he was back at the office, white and thinner than ever. He came to Aurelia with embarrassed thanks, and from that day on he coached her, guided her reading, taught her the realities that were not written in the books, discussed the briefs that the office was working on, explaining what they were trying to prove, what evidence might damage the client and so must be neutralized.

The day after he came back from his illness Aurelia brought a teapot and a kettle to boil water, and served him a hot cup morning and afternoon. James Eaton thawed and joined them and after a time of grumbling even Duggan broke down, suspicious at first of the bland drink but soon brewing it himself.

She was fitting in. She had stuck it out for six months and Boniface had relaxed the austere trial. In the early days he had been puzzled and disappointed that he heard no rumors of a furious and chagrined Mitchell Randolph. Then as Aurelia continued coming in, working hard, he forgot the major, became convinced that she had the fiber to go ahead and pitched in to help.

Her first appearance in court exploded on the legal fraternity and blasted it into confusion. Every attorney in town had been speculating about the girl in Boniface's office, and when she walked into the room she caught the instant attention of the city. The fact of her sitting with Marion Boniface at his counsel table started a shock wave of scandalous conjecture spreading out beyond the law community. The detail that she had not been admitted to practice went unnoticed.

And the appearance was all but unplanned.

Boniface was representing a miner who had made a substantial strike in Placer County, come to San Francisco to celebrate and gotten mixed up with a woman. She was now suing him for breach of promise and for being the father of her child, asking heavy damages.

Boniface was talking it over with Horton when Aurelia came in that morning.

"The hell of it is," he said, "there are still so few women in this town. The men have set even the worst of them up on a pedestal and that jury is going to be damned sore at me for daring to cross-examine her."

Horton bowed a greeting to Aurelia and said in his dry voice:

"Shame Mrs. Randolph can't practice yet. One woman cross-examining another wouldn't have that problem, especially such an innocent-looking lady as Aurelia."

Aurelia started to giggle, but Boniface turned around and looked at her. He said suddenly:

"Go home and put on the simplest dress you own. Duggan, go with her, then bring her to the courthouse. Fetch her to the counsel table looking like a schoolgirl."

She took a step back. "You expect me to cross-examine her?"

"Of course not." He was impatient. "You don't know how. You're going to sit with me and take the jury's attention off her. You're prettier than she is and against you she won't look nearly so good to them."

It worked that way. It was Aurelia's first visit to a courthouse. Boniface had told her to keep away from them until he decided on the right time to expose her. When Duggan led her down the aisle between the crowded spectator seats she thought the dingy place was a poor house for a government arm that held so much power over people's lives.

There was a raised dais with a desk for the judge at the front. Below it on one side was a railed space with two benches for a jury box, and another railing set off an area between the dais and the spectators, enclosing two tables with chairs facing the bench. Marion Boniface sat at one of these beside the defendant and Aurelia caught a glimpse of the plaintiff and her attorney at the other.

Roper Duggan hurried Aurelia through the railing and Boniface made a ceremony of rising, holding the chair on his right for her. She sat down, demure, trying to be inconspicuous, but every man in the jury box turned his eyes from the plaintiff and held them on her, questioning. A noise of muffled comment rose behind her and the judge, a slight, sharp-eyed man, glared at her as he used his gavel to quiet the disturbance. She felt his disapproval but he said nothing. Aurelia kept her eyes lowered on the table and listened to the trial.

When she had first heard of the case she had instinctively sympathized with the woman, but this accuser was neither young nor good looking, her clothes were tawdry and in poor taste. Her voice was hard and as her story came out on direct testimony Aurelia's sympathy went to the defendant.

He was a square, blocky man, with big work-worn hands, a slow, stubborn man. His defense was that he had indeed written the letters presented in evidence against him, he had been willing to marry the woman but she had insisted on staying in San Francisco and refused to go with him back to the diggings.

When the direct testimony was finished Boniface rose to cross-examine. He bent over Aurelia and whispered against her ear:

"Every five minutes scribble a note on this pad and pass it to me. I want the jury to get the idea that you are directing me."

She looked up at him, rattled for the moment. "What will I write?"

"It's a nice day. You had scrambled eggs for breakfast. If you spot a lie point it out, show me how good your ear is. Nobody except you and I will see the notes."

165

She had to raise her head then to watch the proceedings. All attention shifted to Boniface. The room was intent on his performance, and she followed it with a keen sense of glory. She listened to the voice, warm, understanding, respectful, sounding as if he had more regard for the plaintiff than for his own client.

He stalked her gently but firmly back over the courtship. Where had she met the defendant?

On the street when she had dropped her purse and he had picked it up for her.

Was she in the habit of dropping her purse on the street?

She denied it.

How much money was she carrying in the purse?

She shrugged, then answered when the judge prompted her. It was very little.

Aurelia wrote on the pad, *How does she make her living?* She folded the note and held it up for Boniface to see. He crossed without hurry from the witness stand, took the paper, read it, crumpled it and stuffed it into his pocket and returned to the plaintiff.

The jury's attention swiveled to Aurelia. The judge watched her. She could almost see the question mark hanging over her head. The plaintiff glared at her.

Boniface continued the cross-examination in an increasing division of attentiveness. He won the case. The jury ruled for the defendant ten to two.

Boniface threw her a hidden wink, then came to whisper that he had to see the judge, telling her to go back to the office.

She stood up and followed the crowd that was filing out of the benches toward the exit. A group of men waited inside the door and as she came up they waylaid her, blocked her passage. She had a moment of fright before Duggan's voice growled behind her:

"Just reporters. You can handle them."

So Boniface had deliberately sent her out uncoached to face the press alone.

A tall man directly in front of her said, "Aren't you Mrs. Mitchell Randolph? I met you at a theater opening."

She smiled at him. She did not remember him but it was a relief to have someone there who knew her.

"What are you doing in court? Are you a friend of the miner?"

"No. I never saw him before."

"Why were you at the counsel table? Why were you passing notes to Boniface?"

She smiled again. "I'm reading law in his office. He brought me today to give me some experience."

"Oh boy . . ." It was a general chorus and they pushed in closer. From the back of the group a voice called. "Are you the Mrs. Randolph who rides the horse out by the Seal Rocks?"

She nodded in the man's direction and he called again, higher: "In pants, like I hear?"

She laughed at him. "Would you rather I rode without them, like the Englishwoman . . . what was her name?"

"Godiva."

There was a whoop of professional joy around her and a jostling against her as those at the back shoved for better position. For a moment she feared they would tear off her dress, but suddenly Roper Duggan was in front of her, blocking them back.

"Okay, Mac, that's all for now. Move out. Let the lady by."

"Ah, Roper," the tall man protested, "give us a chance. This is one hell of a story."

Duggan's slingshot was in his hand swinging suggestively. "Cut out the swearing you, and clear the way."

They did not give ground. Duggan caught her wrist and bulled into the bodies, forcing a path and towing her behind. By the time they got to the street she felt that she had been run over by a six-horse team, and when she caught her breath she told him:

"Roper, I'd never have made it without you. How do I thank you?"

The henchman grinned at her. "Ah, it was a pleasure. I got no use for them bastards and their nosy questions. But the counselor says I got to go easy on them so they keep writing about him."

"As a way of advertising his name . . . I see . . . Well, I'm learning. Now may I ask a nosy question of you . . . Is Roper your real name?"

He chuckled down at her. "You still got a lot to learn, ma'am. It ain't a name, not a real one. You could say that's my bit of advertising, that I'm the best jury roper in town."

"That's something I haven't heard about. What does it mean?"

"Getting the boys to vote the way you want."

"How do you do that? You aren't an attorney . . ."

He was wary now, uncertain whether she was ready to learn these facts of the profession.

"Well, there's lots of ways. Sometimes I just sit in court and stare at one man. Sometimes he's in trouble and he'll think I know about it and he'd better vote for the counselor. Then sometimes maybe he needs a little scratch."

"You mean you make him itch?"

He guffawed. "Lady, what you don't know . . . money . . . a bribe . . . Or sometimes I go to his family . . ."

He decided he had said enough until he had further directions from Boniface, and he walked on toward the office in more haste.

Aurelia was glad to have the time to think about these new and ominous aspects of the law now surfacing before her. She had been dimly aware that there were dark areas, but thus far she had not wanted to look at them squarely. The idea of using such tactics revolted her. But if they were indeed being used against the people she had dedicated herself to protect, then she was going to have to learn to handle every tool the enemy had.

They had barely gotten back to the office when the outer door banged open and Boniface leaped through. He was beaming, charged with an energy that demanded a physical outlet. He jumped into the air, cracked his heels together, danced to Aurelia, caught both her hands and swung her in a circle at arm's length.

"Baby, oh baby." It was a high, crowing laugh. "Hey there, Ezra . . . Jim . . . Roper . . . have we ever got a find in this little doll baby. What a team . . . honey . . . honey . . . we're going to spin this town like a red striped top."

The ugly thoughts that had followed her into the room swept away. Aurelia laughed back at the lawyer, her eyes shining, and she danced as hard as he, over the railing, over and around the chairs outside, a Spanish step, an Irish jig, a high French kick, a stomping Indian file that Horton, then Eaton and then Duggan joined until they made the floor shake and the walls rattle.

Aurelia Randolph had arrived on Boniface's stage.

The next day she burst like a Roman candle over San Francisco.

Aurelia, the papers called her. Our Aurelia. In pants. In court. In the Poodle Dog, where Boniface wined and dined her that first night, at the most conspicuous table down on the main dining floor. That quite respectable position was overlooked, as her not being admitted to practice had been, by one delighted reporter who slyly repeated a town axiom that *No lady went up to the curtained booths on the balcony to say her prayers.*

The next morning Boniface called her into his private room and motioned her into the straight, hard chair he reserved for clients, a chair he counted on to make visitors too uncomfortable to linger there and waste his time.

"You've proved you can work," he told her. "You've proved you're smart, and yesterday you showed me you can act. That's all step one. Now comes step two. Our job now is to make you into the best-known woman in this state. We want your name in print every day. We're going to build an image of you as a challenger against hypocrisy, a new kind of woman who isn't afraid to stand up and fight. We're going to make it automatic that any Californian in trouble will immediately think of you to come to."

She was still caught up in the excitement of the day before, but this extravagant talk made her draw back in caution.

"Marion," she reminded him, "you know very well I don't know that much law yet."

"Doesn't matter . . . doesn't matter. Don't let it throw you. You'll get there. Half the bastards who call themselves attorneys don't know any law and couldn't practice it if they did. The important thing is to know and understand all the political tieups in this state, know who holds the power, what his price is and how to pay it."

"I don't know anything at all about politics."

"Of course you don't. Yet, but you're going to. American politics isn't hard to understand if you realize that it's a dog eat dog game . . . no more honor among politicians than there is among thieves. Here's lesson number one. Who do you think are the two most powerful men in California?"

She thought about it and said slowly, "Well, I suppose the governor would be one . . ."

"Wrong. They're a fine pair of rascals named David Broderick and Dr. William Gwin . . ."

"Gwin the senator?" she asked, and when Boniface nodded, said, "Where did he get the title *Doctor?*"

"I guess because he is. The story says he passed the bar in Tennessee, looked around and decided there were already too many prominent lawyers in the state, and went to medical school."

"I've heard some less admirable stories about him. Mitchell says he came out here for the express purpose of getting himself elected to the Senate."

"What's wrong with that? He made a bet with Steve Douglas that he'd be a senator eleven months after he landed. He is a very smart man is Mr. Billy Gwin."

"And a bald-faced thief. I know something about that. Pretending he was drawing up land laws to protect the Spanish people, then getting the commissions set up so the government simply automatically appeals every case that's decided in the Californians' favor. That's downright deceit."

Boniface regarded her with increasing respect. This ranch-bred girl with no background of American ways grasped ideas as if she captured them from the air.

"All part of politics, Aurelia. Gwin is a politician and a good one. From an American point of view it was Billy Gwin more than anyone else who hammered out the state constitution in forty-nine, forced it through the convention, got it ratified . . . and took California into the Union."

"I know about that too." She was caustic. "There were only seven Spanish-speaking representatives in the whole convention. Two of them were cousins of mine. They trusted Gwin. He forced the delegates to outlaw slavery, with all the Southerners standing against him, and he wanted the state split into two sections, North and South. My people were for that . . . if we could have controlled the southern part the miners could have had the North and welcome to it . . . but it didn't work."

"Gwin knew it wouldn't." Boniface grinned. "The Doc is very good at promising something to everyone, part of which he does deliver. He has the last word with the Land Commission. But Dave Broderick has taken the state away from him. Gwin is strong in Washington but Broderick runs San Francisco. And this is where you and I have to do business."

"And who is Broderick? I don't know him."

"Very few do. Politicians have an image as hale and hearty. Broderick is not, he keeps aloof. He was a saloonkeeper in New York and got his training in Tammany Hall. He's organized San Francisco politics in the same pattern only more so. Everything is for sale. He makes no bones about it. If you want to be a judge or a district attorney he'll quote you the exact price. Oh, David doesn't keep the money personally, he doesn't drink or smoke and he lives very simply. The swag goes to support his political machine. Do you begin to see the picture?"

Round-eyed, she shook her head. "Marion, why do people permit men like that to get into such powerful positions?"

He laughed at her anger. "Why, there's no corner on self-seeking. The people out here were too busy digging gold and making fortunes, building this city, to pay much attention to government. You might say Gwin and Broderick and the rest won by default. The point you must learn and accept is that the judges and commissioners we have to deal with are corrupt. These land scandals will drag on for years . . . because the judges and the lawyers want it that way. The longer they can keep a case in the courts the bigger the fees they can charge."

"The lawyers will deliberately drag a case out?"

"As long as a client has any property that can be mortgaged to pay costs, yes."

"Would you?"

"I have. When I first started to read law my old judge told me, *If you can get two neighbors quarreling over a line fence you can always pay your rent.*"

She made gasping sounds. "Like a bunch of wolves hamstringing a deer and eating him alive. No wonder my people are losing everything. Well . . . This I am going to learn to do something about."

"I know you are." He nodded. "That's why I'm teaching you, telling you. So you will realize what you're up against. If you want to operate in the California courts you'll have to pay off just like everyone else."

Aurelia took the rest of the day off, to try to absorb and to make some sense of this battlefield that she was entering. She felt that she had to talk to someone, to sort her sensations out in words. Mitchell would not do. He would only laugh and tell her that he had warned her a law office was no place for her.

If Davie Stuart were only in town. And then it occurred to her that she could write. She bought all the newspapers and clipped every story that mentioned her court appearance, her evening with the lawyer, and sent them with the letter.

She began with her first meeting with Boniface, and detailed the arrangement he had worked out with Mitchell, described how she and her husband now lived separate lives, meeting only for dinner with the baby or those evenings that were convenient for both. She wrote at length about the office and the odd people with whom she worked.

I can't completely make out Boniface. Sometimes he's like a little boy who has discovered an enormous cookie jar. He clowns with the clerks and Duggan and me. He seems to have adopted me, to be trying to protect me and scare me away at the same time. He has never by so much as a word or glance showed any interest in me as a woman. I suppose I should be insulted, but I'm not. I'm grateful. It is hard enough to swallow the fact that I have to associate with thieves and criminals to have any chance of defending the old families.

She told him about Duggan's disclosures and Boniface's introduction to politics, and as she finished she wrote in a bold, firm hand:

But Davie, if this is the way things are accomplished, then it is time I grow up and learn to beat the other guy at his own game. I can't remake the world, but by God I can fight a good chunk of it.

CHAPTER FOUR

Every time he read the letter Davie Stuart found a new interpretation in what she was telling. At first the idea of the girl reading law made him laugh, but in thinking it over later he saw it as an inevitable conclusion, an inescapable result of the situations and her own makeup. Better than anyone he sensed the overriding anger with which she had been futilely watching her homeland confiscated by the Americans. In another place and time he could picture her climbing on a horse and leading a charge against invaders.

But there were simply too many of the Americans to fight off that way. The only possibility of any of the Californians hanging onto anything was through the courts. And as Aurelia wrote, the only chance of their having a successful hearing was through someone with political muscle. She had been realist enough as a young girl to marry Mitchell for the purely practical reason of holding the ranch. She was entering this new venture with the same unabashed calculation. It was there in her handwriting, in the passage about Boniface's stories of Gwin and Broderick which ended with her own assessment. He did not know whether to smile or admit the chill that it gave him.

Boniface is from the South and I would have assumed he would be a friend and associate of Gwin. Instead, he has aligned himself with the New Yorker, Broderick. Because although the "chivalry," or southern wing of the Democratic party controls the state outside San Francisco, David Broderick runs the city like his fief, and Boniface tells me that all the judges before whom he practices are in Broderick's pocket. So, dear Davie, I will become the friend of Mr. Broderick. And of anyone else who can conceivably help me. I'd climb into bed with the Devil himself if it would win me one case against those hogs in the Land Commission.

The newspaper clippings she enclosed made him laugh. The reporters were having a field day with their new celebrity, and he wondered how Mitchell was coping with all of the publicity. Of one thing he was glad, that their differences were settled on what sounded like really friendly terms.

As for Boniface, Davie tried to overlook that aspect. Like everyone in San Francisco he had been amused time and again by the lawyer's antics and amors, but he found that he did not like the thought of Aurelia being close to him. In his return letter he ignored mention of Boniface, said that he did not know much about either Gwin or Broderick but that he would bet on her to handle them, and wished her all good luck.

He did not write about his own business, partly because of an odd feeling that he should not discuss Mitchell's affairs with her and partly because all his news was bad.

Under Dexter Brigham's management the Pacific Express had sunk deeper and deeper into trouble, losing money every month. It was only a matter of time until they would have to suspend. He waited daily for the order from Mitchell, but when Randolph's message came it was another surprise. Instead of liquidating, the firm was going to combine with Alta Express, another small outfit still operating in the central part of the state. Davie was directed to contact a Mr. Eubank in Sacramento and work with him. Davie already had a poor opinion of the Alta organization, but if he wanted to stay in business he saw no option to cooperation, discouraging as the prospect was. In Sacramento he argued that the new combination would only delay its death unless it closed down some of the offices that Wells Fargo was hurting worst, and was given a less than satisfactory answer.

"We'll not close a one," Eubank told him. "I can't tell you anything now but there's a reason for keeping them all open. You'll understand why in a few months."

Feeling not at all reassured Davie headed back North and soon found that he disliked working under the Alta people even more than he had under Pacific Express. At least he had had some authority there, and now he was pelted with directives from men who did not so much as answer his reports. Nine months later, with no forewarning at all, he was ordered to deliver all company records to the Wells Fargo office at Jacksonville. Alta Express had been sold to them.

Wells Fargo? Wells Fargo? With Mitchell Randolph on the Alta board of directors? Davie Stuart could not believe it. Mitchell would have fought hard against that, and if he had been outvoted he surely would have warned Davie, not let this blow fall in this callous way. Unless something underhanded was going on.

He wrote, telling Mitchell about the order, asking what it meant, asking Mitchell to answer with a letter to Jacksonville, to reach him before he made the delivery. He delayed as long as he dared to allow time for the answer to reach Jacksonville, then he packed and made the trip over the mountains to the Rogue Valley.

There was no mail for him at the Jacksonville hotel. He waited overnight and when there was still no word he could stall no longer. He had to take the records to the Wells Fargo agent. Turn them over to the company he had fought for nearly three years.

The fight had been rough but wholly impersonal, yet he could not feel impersonal about losing again to the same omnivorous organization. He made his delivery with a formal, cool efficiency.

He received a totally unexpected reception. The local agent told him Wells Fargo was guaranteeing a place for all of the Alta personnel. He was directed to San Francisco for reassignment.

He went to San Francisco, but not to see Wells Fargo. He went straight to Mitchell's office. He could see himself going to Wells Fargo with Mitchell across the street, hating them the way he did. He would not even mention their offer. His life as an express man was over. He would have to learn another business, like it or not. Mitchell might be able to fit him in somewhere in the skein of his real estate involvements.

He did not recognize the place when he walked in. The room had been divided, a high clerk's desk installed and a stranger sat at it, wearing a green eye shade and black sleeve protectors. Mitchell was not there. It crossed Davie's mind that it would be like Mitchell to have moved without telling him. The clerk came down off the stool, his brows raised in a question.

Davie said, "Isn't this Major Randolph's office?"

"Yes, sir. May I help you? The major is not in town."

"Oh? Where is he?"

The clerk coughed delicately. "May I ask what your interest is?"

"I'm Davie Stuart, his partner."

"Ah, Mr. Stuart, yes. Why, the major is in New York, or perhaps by now on his way to London."

"London? Why?" Davie's stomach sank.

The man smiled shyly. "He does not confide in me, Mr. Stuart. He only said he would be away indefinitely."

"When did he go?"

"Some eight weeks ago."

"Would you happen to know if he knew the Alta Express had been sold to Wells Fargo?"

"I couldn't say, sir. The first I heard of it was when your letter came."

"Why didn't you write to me?"

In perfect innocence the clerk told him, "I didn't know what to say."

And why hadn't Mitchell told him he was going to Europe? Mitchell was surely careless in not telling him much, but something this important . . . and then he had the answer. The Alta board had acted without letting Mitchell know. Mitchell expected him to keep on working in the North while he was gone.

But that was not excuse enough. He should have been told about the trip. Then the clerk's phrase hit him again. *He only said he would be gone indefinitely.*

Did that mean that Mitchell was in some big trouble? That he might be gone forever? Had something out of that unknown past caught up with him and pulled him back? Was he running away from something, or to something? There was only one person who might know.

He went to see Aurelia at Boniface's office.

Even though her letter had told him about the dirtiness and the reason for it he felt a resentment at seeing her in the shabby surroundings. But the warmth of her greeting and his pressing worry pushed everything else to the background. She looked so sparkling. She kissed him so fully. He was hardly aware of the introductions. He asked if she could get away from the office to talk to him and she said he could take her to lunch.

"At the Poodle Dog," Boniface interrupted. "Show him the town and parade your colors."

They took a hack from the line at the curb, Aurelia calling the driver by name, asking about his wife, the man grinning, saying, "Just fine, Aurelia, just fine."

When they were settled in the seat she took both Davie's hands and sat searching his face as if she were starved for sight of him.

"My good friend Davie. Oh, I wish you were here more often. There's so much bottled up in me, I need you to talk to. Marion is too blasé for a lot of what I want to say."

"I want to hear all about it, but before we get into that, why did Mitchell go to Europe?"

She gave him a caustic glance. "So he didn't tell you either? All he said to me was that he had to go."

"Not even for how long?"

"Not a thing. You know how he's always been, and we very carefully keep out of each other's business now."

"Well, damn him. He's put me in a fine position this time. Wells Fargo bought the Alta Express. I really think he didn't know about it, but it leaves me stranded without a job. And express is all I know."

"Oh, that's just fine, isn't it. But as big as they are and with all your experience there should be a place for you with them."

"There is. If I could take it. But Aurelia, they play a very dirty game. For instance, when we opened our operation on the Trinity three years ago they sat back waiting until we were in up to our necks, then they moved in on top of us, undercut our prices and drove us out of business. They've done the same thing with Alta."

She pursed her mouth, looking past him, her head tipping to one side.

"Davie, I'm learning that almost everything is dirty. The law is too. I don't think you can survive without compromise, and I'd say if you can't beat them, join them."

He said sourly, "I might be able to stomach it myself, but if Mitchell came back and found me over there I think he'd knock my head off. He was so mad about the Trinity deal that he swore he'd spend his life breaking them."

"Mitchell? Break the Fat Cat of Montgomery Street? Davie, you're not silly enough to believe that? He's good, but not that good."

"Well, never mind. If you're so set against them maybe I can do something. I know a lot of people now . . . you'll meet some of them at the Poodle . . . maybe we can find a place in another line."

He felt a hollowness at the idea. Not only would it mean learning another kind of work, it would probably force him to live in the city, and nothing here would ever generate the thrill that the mining camps were charged with. He might, he thought, go back to mining himself, but it was a brief consideration. He had been in the camps too long not to know the odds against making more than a subsistence, or not even that.

The restaurant was crowded with the noon rush and a cluster of people were waiting, but the steward made a path through them, beckoning.

"Your table is reserved, Mrs. Randolph. Come right on."

She smiled at him. "Thank you, Pierre. This is Mr. Stuart, my husband's partner and a particular friend."

"Mr. Stuart. Welcome. I will remember."

Davie had lunched here with Mitchell time and again but the maître d' discretely did not mention that. He escorted them to a prominent table, whisked the reserved sign from the white cloth and seated Aurelia with a solicitous flourish. A waiter took their order, a wine steward presented a bottle for Aurelia's approval, and as they ate Aurelia pointed out various people in the noisy room.

"David Terry there against the wall with the striking blonde. He's a Justice of the State Supreme Court, and beyond him is Colonel Baker the famous orator. Over here are Judge Austin and Dalton Rumyard, one of my poker cronies."

Davie started. "You play poker?"

"Every week. My father taught me and Marion has taught me more. I can hold my own even with him now and he's the best I know."

"Where do you play?"

"At the Continental Hotel. There's a private Thursday night game. Marion takes me when he's in town, or Judge Austin when he isn't."

When a demitasse was brought she pulled a silver case from her purse, took out a small, black Spanish cigar and held it for the waiter to light. Davie looked quickly over the room. No one showed any surprise or paid any attention.

He wanted to pinch himself. These masculine habits. This fashionably dressed, professionally groomed woman who still looked so fresh and young. Could this be the little ranch girl of the Playa de la Felicidad?

He was still gaping when Terry came by the table and stopped for a word, plainly a familiar to her. She introduced Davie to him and then to Colonel Baker and half a dozen others. All of them showed a marked respect for the girl. Then Judge Austin bent over the table and asked about a case that had been decided in New York ten years before.

She quoted what he wanted to know. When he had gone Davie sounded dazed.

"You're telling the law to a judge?"

She grinned at his expression. "Part of a lawyer's job. No judge could possibly know every case that's been tried, so the lawyer has to brief him beforehand on any precedent he intends to cite. A judge can't stop in the middle of a trial to look it up for himself."

On the ride back to her office Davie was quiet, thinking about this girl and the strange life she was making, so obviously effectively. He did not notice her silence too until she broke it as the hack stopped.

"About you, Davie. I just can't picture you being happy in this town. It isn't your element. You're a . . . a mountain man. And there's a new general agent at Wells Fargo. That twerp Ianes is gone. Louis McLane is running the western division now and I hear he's a good man. Why don't you give him the benefit of the doubt and talk to him? You can't pin your whole life on Mitchell any more than I could."

It took him a moment to make the switch in his thoughts, another to think over what she said, then he nodded slowly.

"I guess you're right. I'll have a look at least."

"Go this afternoon, then come to the house for dinner and tell me about it."

And so Davie Stuart, trying not to feel like a pup with its tail between its legs, went to the Parrott Building.

He knew something of the McLanes' history. Louis's father had been president of America's first railroad, the Baltimore & Ohio, his brother Alan president of the Pacific Mail Steamship Line, the giant steam transportation company whose ships dominated the run between the coastal ports and Panama.

As a young man directly out of college Louis had joined the Navy, then spent an interim period with Frémont when the so-called Pathfinder had tried to take California from the Mexicans and set up the brief Bear Flag Republic. After that he returned to the Navy and raised the American flag over the Monterey customshouse when Commodore Robert Stockton captured the port and proclaimed Alta California a possession of the United States.

In 1850 he had resigned his commission and settled in San Francisco. He had come early and well equipped, and while others hurried to the mines Louis McLane built a shipping line between San Francisco and Sacramento. It was to him that Mitchell had sold the *Effie,* and now his steamers had a monopoly that was added to Wells Fargo's increasing empire.

When Davie walked through the door he found a scene that stabbed him with envy. An army of messengers and clerks hurrying on errands behind the long counter. Lines of wagons drawn up beyond the row of delivery doors at the rear. Banks of the green mail boxes through which Wells Fargo handled twice as many letters as the government post office did.

This against what he and Mitchell had had in their best days. And this was only the head of the dragon. The impossibility of beating such a power came home to Davie much stronger than it ever had from outside this hall. Whatever Mitchell was doing, wherever he was, Wells Fargo was far above his reach.

Louis McLane received him in his upstairs office without surprise. He was expected in from Jacksonville.

On the surface McLane was a pleasant-looking man, bearded, his face relaxed and friendly. He did not rise from his desk but gestured with the pen in his hand toward an easy chair and said:

"Sit down. I'll be just a minute."

Davie sat and watched the pen scratch signatures on a small sheaf of papers. He sat on the edge of the chair, knowing that he should at least disguise his tension but not able to.

The man finished, tossed the pen aside and leaned toward Davie, projecting a dynamic energy.

"How much have you heard about the silver strike in the Washoe Mountains?"

The abruptness caught Davie off guard. He said cautiously, "Why . . . a little . . . I've been north for several years."

"I know where you've been." A smile came and went quickly. "I know more about you than maybe you do yourself. We keep track of our opposition. We don't like to leave things to chance."

Davie found nothing to say, his mind foolishly frozen on the contrast between McLane's easygoing, polished appearance and the drive that came through it. McLane did not wait for a comment.

"Major Randolph brought you up and kept you close to him. But he's out of the picture now. I know his opinion of us. What about you? Does he do all your thinking for you or are you your own man?"

Davie flushed in anger and shook off his uncertainty. "I'm my own man all right, and I still don't like your tactics in the Trinity."

"Can't blame you for that." McLane showed no offense. "But it had to be done, though I would rather Ianes had bought you for a fair price. I wasn't here then. Now think about our position. The West Coast will be better served by a single express company than by a lot of little ones, fighting with each other. You've got the experience to see that. And we are *the* company. There are not going to be any others out here. What I want to know is whether you're so mad at us that you'll get out of the business entirely rather than work for us."

Davie got hold of his temper enough to dredge up a thin smile. "I'm here, aren't I?"

"Good. Now . . ."

"Just a minute, Mr. McLane. I want to know something too. Admitting that you're aware how close I've been to Mitchell you must realize that I owe him some loyalty. With him hating your guts so, why would you trust me in your organization? Why would you want me?"

The quick smile flashed.

"You're young, strong, unmarried, yet you've had years in handling express. We'll talk about trust in awhile. Before we go into it I want to tell you something about the new country we're opening up, the territory they're calling Nevada. You said you aren't familiar with it?"

"I've heard a little. I haven't been there."

"Then I'd better start at the beginning." He sat back, suggesting that the story was long, and Davie gingerly eased himself. "It all used to be considered part of Utah, and some people from Salt Lake made a first settlement, Mormon Station, in the Carson Valley, started some hay ranches, built a second town, Carson City. Later Brigham Young for reasons of his own called his flock back to Salt Lake and the valley pretty well emptied.

"Northeast of Carson City is Sun Mountain, the Emigrant Trail came down along the Carson River, around the base of the mountain, crossed the valley and climbed to Lake Tahoe, then on to Placerville."

"I know that end of the trail."

McLane nodded. "On the eastern face of Sun Mountain there's a ravine where a handful of men have been mining since the early fifties. Found a little gold, enough to keep them in food but not much more. Last year they made a couple of strikes farther up the gulch and over the divide and a camp started up there. They called it Virginia City, but it didn't look like anything big. The new placers paid better than the ground down the hill, but the gold was mixed in something they called 'blue stuff' that was hard to wash out. They didn't identify it until somebody named Harrison took some samples of the blue rock across to Grass Valley and Judge Walsh had it assayed." McLane looked toward his window, looked at the ceiling, looked at Davie, spoke softly, casually.

"The assay ran four thousand and ninety-one dollars to the ton."

Davie felt that each individual hair on his head was rising on end. His mouth was open. He closed it, swallowing.

"Yes," McLane went on. "The blue rock is almost pure silver. What isn't silver is gold. And there is a lot of it. It looks like that mountain will be a bigger producer than the whole Mother Lode has been."

The old excitement pushed at Davie, the thrill that news of a big strike always gave him, and this assay was bigger than any he had ever heard of. It must be a fabulous, an unbelievable lode, and he knew that however he did it, on his own or with Wells Fargo, he had to climb that mountain and see the rich "blue stuff" for himself.

McLane sat watching his face, letting the impact dig itself deep in the young man, then continuing in a quiet, even tone:

"We have two men over there now investigating. My brother Charles has already started a stage line between Placerville and Sun Mountain. I'd like to send you to Virginia City as our general agent there."

Davie blew a low whistle, spending the breath that had built up in him. The offer was a dazzling plum. If Virginia came on as Mc-Lane predicted that office would be second in importance only to San Francisco. But even as it tempted him it puzzled him more and he said suspiciously:

"I ask you again, why me?"

The hardness that made McLane top Wells Fargo man on the Coast showed plainly now, and he watched Davie closely.

"Your friend Major Randolph is trying to raise money to start another express line, between Virginia and California. Bluntly, we are not going to let him do it. He hasn't got a chance, not with my brother owning the stage run. But he'd try, counting on you to handle the Nevada end. He's too smart to take the risk without you. Now, if you wait for him and go into such a competition we could do the same thing Ianes did to you in the North, but aside from the distastefulness of that method I don't want to be bothered. It's better to make it impossible for him to start. I want to buy you. For your own sake and for his and because I know it will be a good deal for us. Your reputation is my assurance of that.

"You may not think so right now, but you'd really be doing him a favor. Do you want tonight to think it over?"

Davie shook his head. "I don't have to think any further. He's overseas and he may not get back for months. By that time you'll be so entrenched that only an ass would believe he could buck you, and Mitchell is no ass. What he'll turn to I don't know, stay with real estate I imagine, and I'm not interested in that. In the meantime I have to make a living. And Mr. McLane, I want to see that hill. You've bought yourself a boy."

CHAPTER FIVE

"I ought to feel as guilty as hell, coming into this house tonight," Davie told Aurelia. "As though I were betraying Mitchell, but damn it, it's his own fault. And what I really feel is just like I did on my fourteenth birthday when Mitchell made me manager of the Sonora office."

She gave him a wide grin. "It's my house too, remember, so go ahead and crow, because I'm very glad McLane convinced you."

"It wasn't McLane." His fresh excitement was in his voice. "It was his story of how rich the new camp is. I guess I'm just a prospector at heart, have to see every new mountain that comes along."

"You're lucky." There was envy in her tone. "To be a man . . . I used to listen to my father's tales about all the places his ships had stopped at, all the adventures he'd had. I've never been farther away from home than Santa Barbara."

Little David broke up the conversation, pelting down the stairs in answer to the dinner call. He had grown a lot and developed a cockiness. He threw himself into his godfather's arms and tipped his head up, his eyes dancing, challenging.

"I can beat you at chess. I've got a dollar says I can. Are you game?"

Davie raised an eyebrow at Aurelia and spoke to the boy. "Isn't seven a little young to be gambling?"

David laughed up at him. "Not if I win. I'm starting to get rich."

Aurelia's lips twisted with mischief. "Better watch out for him, he beats his father three times out of five . . . and he's a better poker player too."

Davie doubted that. Mitchell had taught him both games during the long rainy winter of '50, and he had never seen Mitchell's equal. But after dinner when they set up the board the child proceeded to beat him in less than twenty moves, and he wryly put a dollar into the small grasping hand.

Nora took the reluctant boy off to bed and the two sat on in the parlor with coffee and brandy, Aurelia chuckling over Davie's discomfiture.

"You're not the first grownup he's put in his place. I thought I'd break up the first night he whipped Mitchell. It was so funny. Mitchell didn't know whether to be put out or proud of his son. He says David is a genius, and at times I'm afraid he really is."

Nettled that she sounded like any doting mother, he asked her, "Why afraid?"

Her laughter was gone. "Because it isn't going to be easy for him, being too precocious. His life won't be normal like my brothers'. Already he's reading everything he can get his hands on, even some of the legal books I bring home to study. I wish he'd get out and play more, but he doesn't get along well with the American children in the neighborhood, not as well as he does with Duncan and José and the *Californio* children down at the ranch, and he'd rather speak Spanish than English any day in the week."

"Do you use Spanish with him?"

"When Mitchell isn't here, yes. I get so hungry for it."

"I guess any child prefers his mother's tongue. Do you have much time to spend with him?"

"In a strange way, yes. I've got my work of course, and I go to some parties because Mitchell wants me to put in an appearance, but I get very lonely for, well, warmth, and David is a real comfort. We talk like a couple of adults and it's gotten so that I even discuss some of the problems that come into the office with him. Every once in awhile that sharp, fresh little mind spots something I've overlooked. And I'm a good attorney. I could have passed the bar long ago if I were a man."

He said dryly, "Maybe David could, and Boniface could take him into partnership. Are you making any headway with your Californians' cases?"

She laughed at his joke and came suddenly alive with his question. "Davie, last week we won three appeals and moved a lot of squatters off the Morely place. I'm getting really important . . . to the point that the squatters have formed an organization to fight for the lands they've grabbed . . . the word has gone out that unless I quit interfering with them I might get myself shot."

"You? A woman? In this country? You can't be serious." But in spite of himself he was worried, and it showed enough to make her reassure him.

"People talk." She shrugged off the danger. "But I go to the meetings well protected. There are always a dozen or so Californians, plus Roper Duggan and some of his hoodlum friends with their slingshots."

But the reassurance worried him further and he told her stuffily, "I don't like the idea of you mixing with Duggan's type, Aurelia, it's too risky. They can be treacherous . . ."

"Poof." She cut him off. "You're as bad as Mitchell, and I've found that a woman is safe with any type crowd as long as she watches her own conduct. No one in San Francisco will lay a hand on Aurelia Randolph . . . all the police look after me, and the hack drivers and longshoremen . . . it's amazing how many different kinds of people want to do favors for Marion Boniface. Even the Sidney Ducks and Broderick's firemen would charge in if they thought I was in trouble. And the newspaper boys think I'm their private property."

He knew that she was making fun of herself, but the words brought home to him again the tough fiber that was the one quality unchanged about the little ranchgirl that had been. No, not the one thing, there was her dedication to her people that had made her fight her husband to a draw and that even kept her from being any ordinary kind of mother to her son.

"Well, I hope you know what you're doing," he said, and managed to sound very like a male animal superior to any female. He recognized it and had the grace to duck and put up a defensive elbow. Then he looked at his watch and got to his feet. "I'd better go now, I told McLane I'd be in his office the first thing in the morning."

She rose and reached both hands up to his shoulders, sighing. "It seems to me that you're always going away, and I never really realize how much I miss having you around until you come back. You're still the one honest-to-God friend I have, the one person who knows what makes me tick. Write to me, Davie."

She held her face up for his kiss and he drew her against him, holding her close.

Long after he had left the house he could still feel the warmth of her body pressed against him. If it were not for Mitchell Randolph . . . but what was the use . . . resolutely he put any thought of having her away from his mind.

Aurelia had assumed that he would be leaving right away but McLane kept him in town for a week for an indoctrination into the big company. It was a week he enjoyed to the full, different from any he had ever spent. He and little David and Aurelia roamed the city from end to end, rode to the Cliff House, to the Seal Rocks, crossed the bay to visit Maria Martinez and her American husband Bill Richardson who owned the vast Sauselito Ranch and whose daughter Mariana was even more bitter against the Yankee invaders than Aurelia.

It was on the way home from that ranch that Davie got his first specific ideas of what Aurelia's legal tasks were and how she was going about them, and much of the information came from the little boy.

"The King of Spain gave the land to the ranchers in grants," he explained. "But like a dope he just said they could have so many thousand varas . . . that's a measurement . . . or maybe they could have as much ground as they could ride around in a certain time, but he didn't say just where the varas had to start from, or if the riders could only use one horse, careless things like that. There was so much land that he didn't think it mattered and anyway most of the ranchers were related to each other and it was all right if the boundaries overlapped. The same with the Mexican governors when they started giving land away. Then California turned into a state and like my father says the Americans figured that every acre that wasn't described in a deed was public land that they could take up, and about the whole state has to be surveyed.

"Old Senator Gwin, first he gets Washington to say they'll honor the old grants"—he presented one hand palm up—"then he turns around and helps start a Land Commission to rule on who owns what." He presented the other palm. "Now everybody has to go to court and try to prove his title or he loses his ranch. It's a mess."

"I can see that it is." Davie was barely able to keep the awe out of his voice and face.

"But Aurelia's fixing it," the smug little voice piped on. "At least for the families at our ranch."

"Just how is she fixing it?" Davie asked, and that at last stumped the boy, but he covered it blithely with a bored order to his mother. "You tell him, Aurelia."

As the lawyer talked Davie watched her son, the wide, innocent, vulnerable dark eyes through which shone the avid young mind. And she talked to him rather than to his godfather.

"Why, first I had to learn what the laws were, to know what to

187

fight, then I had to make friends of all the important legal people and politicians so they would do what I wanted done. Then Mr. Boniface and I sent a Californian down to Mexico City and he is sifting through all the records there for any information that will help us prove a grant is valid. We have other men searching the church records because often they list the extent of a family's holdings, and say where it is located. We take affidavits from former governors and former officials. Then when we have all the proof we can get we show it to the court. Sometimes we are able to prove the boundaries of a grant, sometimes when a squatter has laid claim to a ranch and it looks as if the Land Commission is going to rule in his favor we can make a compromise with the squatter, agree not to fight his claim if he will let the original owner keep a part of the property. And sometimes we can squeeze out a cash payment, make the squatter pay for what he has taken. It costs the squatters a lot of money to take a case through the courts and sometimes they will give up rather than pay."

David picked that up. "It costs the Californians to go to court too, doesn't it?"

Her eyes flicked proudly to Davie, to see if he was properly impressed. "This is a secret I'm going to tell you both. We are taking these cases for nothing. Mr. Boniface because I showed him how much good will he could build among our people, and I because I don't need the money. I am paid with the satisfaction I get when we win something back from the land grabbers."

Davie had not known this, that Mitchell was financing his wife's battles to rescue the Spanish contingent that he so despised, but he thought it must be worth it to him to have this son under his hand.

At the end of the week he was both reluctant and anxious to leave the city. A guilt was building in him, a fear that Mitchell would come home unexpectedly, keeping him on tenterhooks. It was, he thought, because he was going with Wells Fargo. But when he said his good-byes, promised to send David a lump of silver, kissed Aurelia again, he had the odd sensation that it was his own family he was leaving.

He carried with him on the trip a magnificent present from Louis McLane, a Sharps .59 model rifle, a breechloader that used linen cartridges so that the powder need not be poured separately, one of the most advanced guns to be had.

"From what I hear of the camp," McLane told him, "it's the rowdiest one yet. Just keep the rifle handy, you'll probably need it."

In Placerville he found a crowd of more than a hundred men

gathered around the station of Charles McLane's new Pioneer Stage Line, fighting for seats to ride over the divide, and only because he had a chit from Wells Fargo was he given the place beside the driver.

The early autumn morning was warm, with no snow yet except in the high passes, and the road was full of travelers. The trail over which the immigrant flood had tramped ten years before on its way to the California gold fields had been graded and widened into a roadway by the new stage company. Still the six-horse team made poor time because of the solid line of freight wagons moving eastward to the new diggings.

Davie wondered aloud at the heavy column of traffic and the driver told him there were more than six thousand miners already in the Washoe Hills, and everything used by the camp had to come over the ridge and up Sun Mountain.

Even with this intelligence he was not prepared for what he found when the coach finally stopped on C Street and he climbed down with the other passengers and stared around in bewilderment.

C Street had developed from the original trail that twisted up Gold Canyon from the Carson Valley to the northernmost mine, the Ophir. It more or less leveled off and ran along a ledge about fifteen hundred feet below the top of the nearly eight-thousand-foot-high peak. The slopes of Sun Mountain were stripped of growth, first by the early arrivals to throw up flimsy shacks and feed their cooking fires, then for timbering for the mines, and the exposed naked ground was solid rock sprinkled with a thin layer of blowing grit.

Some miners had found natural caves to call home and others had burrowed holes in the mountain flank like gophers, hunting any shelter from the blistering summer sun, the brutal cold of winter and the Washoe Zephyr, a wind that seldom stopped shrieking down off the crest.

Davie spent the first week looking, listening, asking questions, then he wrote to Aurelia:

This place is as near hell as anywhere I want to be. The town is built along the side of a mountain, with four streets running roughly parallel in a north-south direction. The founding fathers imaginatively named them A, B, C, D.

C is the main street not only for Virginia but for the two smaller camps, Gold Hill and Silver City, which hang against the mountain wall farther downcanyon. The water here is so foul that the only way to swallow it is to doctor it with whiskey. The mines are no more than open cuts, although they are starting a shaft on the Ophir property. Ophir is supposed to be the best potential on the mountain.

The ore is incredibly rich but there is no proper mining equipment and no way of milling it, therefore only the higrade is hauled out to the Coast and shipped to Wales for smelting. The rest is stacked to wait until local mills can be built.

Housing hardly exists. I spent the first nights on a hard bunk in a room with a hundred other men, but by now I have a two-room shack on A Street, an office in front and a rear room where my assistant and I live. The only heat we have is an occasional cooking fire, because the scrub brush that once grew up here has been burned up already and the only wood available is what little is brought in bundles by the nearby Indians.

Half the camp is sick from bad water, cold and poor food but nobody seems ready to give up, so I guess I'll give it a whirl, at least for a while . . .

Aurelia read the letter to David, who was put out that Davie had forgotten to send the promised lump of silver and he said acidly:

"Why is he being stupid enough to stay in a place like that?"

"He has to make a living, and he has a job there."

The little boy shrugged. "He could probably make more money here in San Francisco . . . Are you in love with Uncle Davie?"

Aurelia started. It took her a minute to collect herself and to bridge it she said, "Whatever gave you that idea?"

He was direct. "I heard Nora talking to Joe. She said you are. She said it's a crying shame you don't divorce Mitchell and marry Uncle Davie. Joe told her to hush her mouth. Joe was really mad."

"Joe was right. Nora talks too much."

"Then you do love him?"

She reached for his arm and pulled him gently in against her, unsmiling. "David, you are a very smart boy but you are still too young to understand some things. Just take this on trust for now. Your father and I are married and we are going to stay married. Nora is wrong, about what I should do. Certainly I love Davie, he's the best friend I ever had, but I do not have to choose between him and your father."

She saw by his expression that she had only opened the door to further questions and had the panicky thought, *What can I say? How do I explain a marriage of convenience . . . ? Should I really try?*

Then his restive mind explored the next possibility. "You love Mr. Boniface better than either of them?"

She laughed from sheer relief. "That's quite different. I work for Mr. Boniface . . ."

"Sure, but you're always going someplace with him, a lot more than you go with Mitchell."

"I've explained before why that is, we have to go to meetings, I have to know all the judges and state officials and Federal land commissioners and keep them aware of me."

"Well . . ." he passed his judgment, "I guess you have to if you're going to kick the Yankees off of our land . . ."

He went away to write a letter of his own, dunning Davie for the silver lump and she sat on, mulling over the question her son had raised, deliberately turning the train of her thoughts away from Davie and Mitchell, considering her alliance with Boniface.

As a team they were accomplishing a lot. So far they had been much more successful than the cynical attorney had believed possible. By now hundreds of Californians owed the fact that they still had any portion of their original holdings to the Boniface office, and for all this she felt a deep and loyal gratitude to the man. But it certainly was not love. Admiration, yes, and her own cynical amusement in watching him operate.

Half at least of Boniface's successes were due not to the legal positions he posited for his clients but to his facility in reaching the men with the powers of decision. His ability to ride all the horses at once, to keep working relationships with all the political factions was a constant wonder. He was equally friendly, for instance, with those arch rivals William Gwin who as U. S. Senator had led the Buchanan wing of the Democratic party, and with David Broderick, a man who while calling himself a Free-Soil Democrat was closer in his thinking to the new group calling itself the Republican party. She watched in delight as he played off one against the other, since she had no respect for either politician. She had done too much business with their appointees to trust any of them. And she had no interest in the causes over which they fought.

The battle between those two men had flared beyond California to the Senate chamber in Washington, where Gwin had supported the administration's stand on what Broderick called the Kansas-Lecompton fraud. Now they were both ranging up and down the state accusing each other of malfeasance in office, which struck Aurelia as bitterly funny.

The nation's growing division over the propriety of slavery was not important to her. Nothing that happened east of the Sierras had any reality. As she told Boniface she felt no loyalty to the United States. She was a Californian.

From Boniface her mind switched to Nora and she considered warning her to be more careful in what she said in the boy's hearing, then decided against it. Acknowledging the woman's gossip at all would only give it credence.

CHAPTER SIX

It was becoming generally accepted that Gwin and Broderick would soon wind up meeting on the field of honor. Many bets both casual and with stakes laid down had been made as to how long it would be in coming. But the news that did break electrified San Francisco. Broderick was challenged to a duel not by Gwin but by Judge David S. Terry.

Terry was at the time Chief Justice of the State Supreme Court. He was a Texan, an ex-Ranger, a hothead, a volatile figure who had been elected to his high post on the Know-Nothing ticket. Then that party had collapsed and he had tried for re-election among the Democrats.

Broderick had blocked his nomination there. Terry retaliated with a bitter statement before the convention, attacking the anti-Lecompton Democrats. Broderick, infuriated, told a friend in the dining room of the International Hotel that Terry was a damned miserable wretch whose neck he had saved earlier when the Texan was in trouble with the Vigilantes. The remark was overheard and repeated to Terry. The challenge followed.

Aurelia heard of it when Boniface came fuming up the stairs, waved her into the inner office with him and shoved the *Californian*'s news story into her hands.

"The damned fool." He dropped into his chair and sat chewing his lip, watching her read.

She scanned the column and looked up in dismay. Terry had been very useful to them, had been instrumental in seeing that their many appeals were reviewed by the higher court, and she had been furious when Terry did not get the Democratic nomination.

"How stupid of him," she exploded now.

Boniface nodded. "They'll probably kill each other."

"You think Broderick will accept? After he led the fight against dueling?"

"He can't refuse, not and stay politically alive. But to hell with him, it's Terry I'm worried about. I need Terry."

Aurelia shrugged. "For what? He was defeated . . . what good is he to us?"

"He's my ace for what's coming. Don't you realize how close this country is to civil war? The whole South is about ready to break away, and, young lady, it's time for you to pay attention. The West Coast is run by Southerners except for Broderick and a few others. It will go with the South, and that, Aurelia Randolph, will be the most important thing yet for your Californians."

Aurelia laid the paper aside, propped her chin on the steeple of her fingers, said quietly, "You'd better coach me," and listened in astonishment to the secret plans he told her.

Perhaps because his letter had come only the day before, occasioning the talk with her son, Aurelia ached to write to Davie about Boniface's revelations, but Marion warned her not to repeat them to anyone without his specific permission.

The duel took place on September 13. David Broderick died three days later.

The funeral was the greatest orgy ever held in the Bay City. A vast crowd filled Portsmouth Square to hear the oration delivered by Colonel Edward D. Baker, and the former Illinois congressman outdid himself. His rich voice trembling with emotion, Baker made famous the purported last words of the boss of San Francisco:

They have killed me because I opposed slavery and a corrupt administration.

Inured as she was Aurelia all but gagged at hearing the shrewd, scheming politician she had known, the man to whom everything was for sale and who had saddled San Francisco with a mountain of debt and a blanket of corruption that would last for years, eulogized as a fearless, humane hero who had given his life for the good of the people. She looked at the women weeping openly, at the men red-eyed and stony-faced and whispered to Boniface in disbelief:

"They are crying. Marion, they're crying for a man who raped them."

Boniface smiled. "The way martyrs are made, my dear. If he'd been the better shot these same idiots would be crying over Terry.

Instead, our good judge is going to have to make himself scarce around here for a while."

Terry was not the only one who thought it prudent to leave California for a time. Four days after Broderick died Senator Gwin and Congressman Scott departed for Washington. David Terry headed for Nevada, taking with him a nucleus of a hundred men sympathetic to the slave states.

Before he left he met with Boniface and Aurelia and invited her to join his growing clandestine group, the Knights of the Golden Circle, and work to promote his fantastic plot, the scheme Boniface had so recently told her about.

Looking at the widening breach between the slave and free states, this core of fanatic secessionists were developing their own answer to the problem. If the next election brought in a President hostile to slavery the southern states would split from the Union and create a new nation. At that time, the Knights' dream went, they would pull out Oregon, Nevada, and California, form the three into a Republic of the Pacific and join in a loose confederation with the new southern country. Cuba was to be wrested from Spain, Mexico was to be invaded and her northern provinces added to complete the golden circle of slave states from which the conspirators drew their name. The old Californians who used *peón* labor could be classed as slaveholders.

Terry assured Aurelia that if she would enlist them to be ready to rise in revolt when the time was right they would have their lands restored to them and be included in the new government. To Aurelia Randolph it sounded like the call of destiny. With stars in her eyes she saw him off for Nevada, urging him to look up Davie Stuart and sound him out as another possible candidate for enlistment in the Knights.

Terry did contact Davie, but after some cautious probing he found Davie not at all interested in politics but definitely anti-slavery and so kept his own counsel. Davie did not take warmly to Terry, who was too opinionated and flamboyant for his taste, but it was good to talk to someone who had seen Aurelia only a few days before.

He was more than a little amused at the camp's reaction to Terry's arrival. There was a good deal of loose talk in the bars over the slavery issue and the population was about equally divided, but there was little polarization. Now with the judge on the mountain the miners suddenly crystallized into two factions. Notoriety came with him. Terry had killed Broderick, whom Colonel Baker had said was the only man in the state strong enough to stand up to the southern wing of the party. Terry was a murderer to the abolitionist element, a hero to the Southerners.

Quietly the fiery conspirator set about building his cells of Knights in the Nevada towns in the valley and on the hill, and the rumble of friction grew. Even that autumn there might have been trouble if an early winter had not paralyzed the whole territory.

The San Francisco stockbrokers, already trading heavily in the Virginia mines, had prevailed on Colonel Bee to stretch a telegraph wire from the mountain over the Sierras to Placerville where it connected with the wire to the bay. But the service was still so sporadic that its greatest value to Virginia City was as a warning system. When it went dead it meant the line had come down in a storm. When it stayed dead for an extended time the camp knew there was heavy snow in the passes, the long string of freighters that was the lifeline quit moving and backed up west of Placerville.

This fall it went down the first of November. By mid-month the town had four feet of snow to hide the ugly shacks and make the streets impassable. The mines shut down and the camp was marooned.

When he was snowbound in the Trinity country Davie had had a lark. He had brought along enough food to keep the little community in comfort, and for variety there were deer and rabbits close around them. On the white slopes here there was nothing, no game, not even a bird. The sugar ran out, but then so did the coffee. Flour was quoted at eighty dollars a sack and almost none to be had.

One desperate group organized a train and wallowed through the drifts that blocked the canyon to the Carson River and followed that to its namesake city in the middle of the wide valley. There was no help there. Carson City had no food to spare. It was hungry itself.

Only the scattering of horses and jackasses on the mountain saved the miners there. A Washoe canary, as the little pack animals were called, made tough chewing, but the men were young, their teeth good, and it was meat.

January passed, and February. It was March before the Zephyr stopped howling and the first mule train bucked through the sixty-foot-high drifts in the California passes and trailed up Gold Canyon. The whole camp gathered along C Street to watch it come in. The welcoming shout began as the string appeared over the crest, and peculiarly died as it passed along the crowd.

Davie could not figure why until it came by him. The lead mule carried no beef, no food at all, but kegs of whiskey. The second animal was loaded with brandy. The third brought gin.

It was another week before a load of flour came through. Davie paid five dollars for a pound and carried the precious stuff to the office with more solicitation than he handled the same weight in silver. They had run out of the brush the Piute Indians had occasionally brought in and sold for firewood, but even mixed with snow the gummy paste was a delicacy.

As the freight began to move more regularly Virginia City roused out of its torpor. After food the men were most starved for news. When mail and papers that had lain for months in Placerville were brought over there was an orgy of reading. No matter how old a printed page was it passed from hand to hand until it fell apart.

There was a letter from Aurelia, dated in December, with the word that Mitchell was back from Europe and a long, angry passage in which she described Mitchell's furious reaction at learning that Davie was working for Wells Fargo. He had cursed him up and down, she said, and would not listen to a word of her explanation that Davie had had no choice, and had since then bitten her head off if she so much as mentioned his name.

Davie answered her and wrote a separate letter directly to Mitchell. Mitchell did not reply and another letter from Aurelia said he had burned the one from Davie without even opening it.

At any other time he would have caught the stage and gone down to face Mitchell and thrash the matter out, but he simply could not leave Virginia City that spring. As the camp dug out of the winter the mines reopened, the volume of ore shipped increased every day, and there was a resurgence of crime beyond the usual rowdiness. When everyone had been starving there had been little to steal, and when the snow had been too deep for travel men thought twice about robbery and mayhem because their escape was blocked. But now an epidemic of violence swept the mountain. Gangs of toughs prowled the saloons shooting, knifing, rolling the unwary, with no one to stop them. The Wells Fargo safe, filled with the payrolls of half a dozen mines, was a tempting target and Davie slept with McLane's rifle at his side and a six-gun under his pillow.

Since the territory had not been formally organized there was no authoritative law. A sheriff and local judges had been elected by popular vote but they were too weak a force to have any effective control. So ineffectual was the arm of justice that David Terry and his hundred well-armed Southerners had with impunity seized and occupied some of the mines, built stone forts at the entrances and their sentries patrolled the buildings day and night, Terry boasting openly now that he would take Nevada out of the Union and her silver would support the coming rebellion.

If they could so easily capture the mines Davie reasoned that they might take it into their heads to reach for the money in his safe. So he was tied to his job. Frustrated and resenting Mitchell's unwarranted censure, he recognized the irony that Wells Fargo, the cause of the contention between them, was also the tether that kept him from going to try to heal the breach. He could only stew and wait for a chance to go over the hills.

He was still waiting in mid-April when a new and exciting project involving Wells Fargo came to a head. The length of time required to transport mail between the East and Sun Mountain was so great that it virtually isolated Virginia City. Several experiments had been made to shorten it. In 1850 a service from Independence, Missouri, through Salt Lake to Sacramento had taken thirty days. Then John Birch, former president of the California Stage Company, had tried opening a route from San Antonio to San Diego, and next came a coach line known as the Butterfield Overland Mail.

While each of these was some improvement none caught the imagination or stirred the laughter that Russell, Majors, and Waddell did when they announced they would inaugurate a postal service across the center of the continent that would make deliveries between St. Joseph, Missouri, and the West Coast in nine days. They were going to use individual riders on fast horses, running in fifty-mile relays.

The distance was near fifteen hundred miles. Virginia City calculated and hooted and made extravagant bets that it could not be done. And on the announced date when the first Pony Express rider was supposed to pass by the foot of Sun Mountain most of the camp trekked down Gold Canyon to Stafford Hall Station on the Carson River to see if he would make it. With all of the Indian country the lone rider had to cross the odds were heavily against him.

As Wells Fargo agent Davie was required to be there to receive the mail . . . if it came through . . . and to forward letters on to the West. He was among the first down the canyon but a delegation from Carson City was already at the station.

Mitchell Randolph's blocky figure stood out among them.

Davie saw no one else. For a long moment they faced each other like two strange animals unexpectedly nearly colliding on a forest path, then with a whoop Davie dropped out of his saddle and loped across the space between them. Reacting without thought he wrapped his arms around the big body and heaved it clear of the ground, holding it against him, grinning, repeating in a foolish babble:

"Mitch . . . Mitch . . . Mitch . . ."

The older man grunted as the swift embrace crushed the air out of him. He hauled back an open palm and clouted the side of Davie's head.

"All right, all right. You going to kiss me?" The voice was strangled, mocking, and there was no anger in it. "Put me down, you stiff-necked bonehead."

Davie lowered him, released him and stepped back. He found questions crowding to his lips but with the audience giving the meeting its interested attention he kept the words back and said only:

"God, it's good to see you. What are you doing in Nevada?"

Mitchell said glibly, "I'm as interested in this historic occasion as anybody. It's a new breakthrough in communications. If it works. I was in the mail business once myself, if you recall."

But as well as he knew Mitchell, Davie felt certain that this was only part of an answer, and instinct told him he would hear the rest in Mitchell's own good time. They crossed the dusty road together to the station's single saloon and found a lone customer at a table inside taking shelter from the desert sun, and joined him.

Davie was not surprised that Mitchell already knew William Stewart. A towering, red-blond man, he had been Attorney General in California. Now the owners of the mines seized by Terry's crowd had brought him to Sun Mountain to fight for a return of the properties, and a bitter court battle was in process. Stewart was also opposed to Terry politically and in Virginia City was the strongest personality on the northern side.

"Hello Stuart . . . Randolph," he said. "Sit down. Mitch, you poking around over here with a notion of putting a steamboat on the Carson?"

Mitchell sat, lit a cigar, leaned back in the chair and lifted his brows speculatively.

"Why now, Bill, that might be an idea, though I hadn't thought of it. I just came over to see the Pony. He's going to change the thinking of a lot of transportation people. And I thought it was time I had a look at Washoe."

"Whenever you start looking at anything I want to button my pockets." Stewart laughed easily and Mitchell smiled.

"By the time you lawyer boys get through with Sun Mountain your pockets might be interesting. What do you think of the camp?"

"Great camp, miserable town. I keep my family down at Carson where you can drink the water . . . What's the Pony mean to you?"

The blandness of Mitchell's expression brought a tingle to Davie's scalp. He knew that look, and was suddenly certain that there was a more definite target behind this visit than pure curiosity. Mitch's behavior made him think of a shark quietly cruising over an unwary school of fishes who would be its dinner. Also it came to him that Stewart's crack about a steamboat was not the idle joke it sounded like, and he itched to know what was going on. But this was not the place to ask.

As to what the Pony Express meant to him, Mitch shrugged his thick shoulders and said lazily:

"I've got a few dollars up that say he'll make it. How about you?"

"He'd better make it." The lawyer sounded ominous. "This place has been cut off from the country long enough. There's a suspicion on the mountain that Washington has forgotten we're here. The miners are tired of waiting for an organized territory and a recognized government. Some of us tried to get the district annexed to California, but we got turned down."

"I hadn't heard that," Mitchell said. "It would make sense. Virginia City is just as dependent on San Francisco as Sacramento and the Mother Lode towns are."

"That's right, and something had better be done soon, get some courts and officers in here . . . right now nobody knows who owns what and where. If they keep on stalling the people are going to start listening to Terry and his talk about a separate Republic of the Pacific."

Mitchell's answer was a grunt of doubt and Stewart started a heated insistence, but a pair of Southerners came in and he dropped the subject. The conversation bogged down and the waiting dragged on. Outside in the growing heat the crowd turned restless. All morning they watched the rocky trail from the East. When, by noon, no smudge of dust rose off the plain, many of them shook their heads, gave up, and started back up the mountain.

Then through the open door Davie heard the sound, the murmur of voices that rose to a shout, and everyone inside ran for the street. Shading his eyes with his hand Davie squinted down the trail. Far away he made out a small tan swirl of dust on the sky at the edge of the desert. It could be a dust devil. It could be an Indian hunter or a traveler. They still had to wait.

Excitement grew as a dark speck became visible at the head of the dust plume. At least it was a rider. It came toward them, turning into a flying horse, and finally they made out the diminutive figure crouched on the animal's back.

They were watching a miracle. All the way from St. Joe the precious letters had come. Up the old Immigrant Trail. Along the Platte. Over the Rockies at South Park. On to Salt Lake. Across the wide desert. Each fifty mile section completed by a different rider racing on to the next station. In only a shade over one week.

Davie looked down at the packet in his hands. Six letters bound for San Francisco. He left Mitchell and Stewart and walked to where the handler was bringing up the next horse, where the next small, lightweight man stood with a loaded rifle in one hand, a water bag in the other, waiting to take over and be gone as soon as the mochila (the mail bag) was transferred from one animal to the other. The fresh horse was bred for racing, saddled with a jockey's pad, one tiny part of the Russell firm's great investment in this experiment.

Whether or not he had been coached the incoming Pony knew the ceremonial importance of this first arrival. He made it a grandstand play, driving hard up the dusty road between the banks of shouting, hat-waving men, pulled up at the station with a flourish and flung himself down. The horse stood lathered and heaving, trembling with tiredness.

While the rider accepted the jug of water from the station keeper, drank and scrubbed the rest over his sweating head, Davie yanked down the saddlebag. It was of light weight, divided into four pockets, all locked. Three could be opened only at the military posts the Pony passed. The fourth was for letters to be dropped or picked up along the way.

Davie opened this section with his key, hastily sorted out the letters for Sun Mountain and dropped his packet in. All the letters were written on tissue paper, for the mochila was limited to twenty pounds. He locked the bag, threw it over the saddle of the fresh horse and made a step of his hands to toss the new jockey aboard.

The next relay was off, galloping up the valley toward the Sierra ridge and California.

A new shout wished him well and died slowly as he diminished in the distance. For a while they watched after him in wondering silence, then in a concert the crowd rushed for their horses, each wanting to be the first to reach Virginia City with the news.

The Pony Express had come to Sun Mountain.

Mitchell had driven down from Carson in a hired rig. The three of them hung back to let the dust of the rush settle, then Davie and Stewart tied their horses on behind the buggy and climbed aboard.

"Well, the first boy got through . . . some others won't . . . the Indians . . ." Where Stewart had been grimly anxious for the rider to succeed for the sake of the community, now he was anxious about the safety of the later riders through the long, lonely stretches.

Mitchell's reaction took a different tack. "And it will lose money," he said, and Davie caught a hint of smugness in the tone.

Bill Stewart waved the comment aside. "The money isn't as important as the fact that it will keep reminding the people on this mountain that we are still a part of the United States, keep them from listening to that wild-eyed Terry."

Out of his political innocence Davie said, "What beats me is how Terry can keep talking armed rebellion and nobody makes a move to stop him. It sounds like treason to me, so why hasn't it been reported?"

Stewart snorted his disgust. "Reported to who? The southern senators have run the government ever since the Mexican War and the President has a ring in his nose. He's towed around by the Secretary of the Treasury, Howell Cobb, a Georgia man, and by Jacob Thompson. Thompson, for your information, supported the Lecompton Convention, which would have made Kansas a slave state and destroyed the Missouri Compromise. You think those people want Terry stopped? Or take the West Coast . . . Gwin's a Southerner, Governor Downey, General Johnson at the Presidio . . . Did you see any of them lift a hand when Terry murdered Broderick last fall?"

Mitchell only arched his eyebrows quizzically but Davie said in surprise, "I thought that was a duel?"

"Duel . . . Duel . . . Dave Broderick never fought a duel in his life and neither of his seconds had ever seen one. Broderick . . . a sick man . . . and they drag him out in a wet, cold fog . . . if he hadn't been shot he'd have died of exposure. It was deliberate, calculated murder. Terry wanted him out of his way."

Then as if ashamed of his vehemence Stewart lapsed into muttering, finally changed the subject and he and Mitchell talked about the legal tangle and the bizzare, comic-opera manipulations of trying to win clear titles to the mines. He was a good storyteller and, laughing with Mitchell, Davie felt that his world was back together again by the time they reached Virginia. Stewart dropped off at C

Street and Davie directed Mitchell up the steep hillside to the office on A. The door was locked, the assistant gone off somewhere. Davie used his key, ushered Mitchell in and watched the way he stood, critically looking over the shack.

Then, without so much as a may I, Mitchell walked behind the high counter and flipped open the ledgers. Those books were the property of Wells Fargo and no outsider had any right to look at them, no business reading how the express company was doing in its Virginia City agency.

Davie started a protest, but choked it off. What difference did it make whether Mitchell Randolph knew how much last week's receipts had been? In fact he felt a small-boy pride in how much had been handled. He turned his back and opened the packet of dispatches brought by the Pony Express rider.

One of them reported that Congress had finally passed a bill organizing the Mormon settlements around Salt Lake into a new Territory, and the same bill carried a rider covering Sun Mountain. Under it the Washoe district was detached from Utah and made into a Territory of its own, to be known by its colloquial name, Nevada. The bill further directed the President to appoint a governor and the proper territorial officials, including Federal judges.

Davie held it toward Mitchell, saying, "It looks like Bill Stewart is going to get the law he was hollering about. I wonder what this will do to Terry's plans."

Mitchell read over the flimsy and tossed it aside. "Doesn't matter to us. Davie, how long will it take you to resign and train a replacement? A week?"

Davie looked into the hooded eyes, his mouth dropping. He had known in the morning. He had seen that imaginary shark and at the back of his mind he had known he was the prey. But then on the drive up the hill, with the jokes and laughter, he had let his guard down, and now it made him mad to be surprised.

"Why the hell should I resign?"

"Because I've got more important things ahead for you."

Cautiously he said, "What kind of things?"

"Nothing I want to tell you about while you're still with Wells Fargo . . ."

Suddenly Davie was raging. He had been provoked with Mitchell before, many times. But he had never in the world felt this way. His fist doubled and cocked back, ready to smash into the heavy face.

"God damn you." He heaved himself to his feet, towering four inches over the other man. "Did I ever give you any reason to say a thing like that? Even if I am working for a company you've got a grudge against. What the hell's the matter with you?"

Mitchell stared at him in amazement. "Davie . . ."

"Shut up and listen to me. You run off to the East or Europe or wherever the hell without one word to me. You leave me to break my back and my heart trying to fight off the fools and try to hold the Alta operation together. And then when they dump the company to Wells Fargo and I take the only job open to me in the business you get sore at me because I didn't sit down and starve while I waited for you to whistle me to heel like a good dog . . . Now you say you don't trust me . . ."

"You didn't have to jump right into that job. I'd have given you money. You knew that."

"From New York? From Europe? Sure . . ."

"From Aurelia. The money she has is mine. We were partners, weren't we?"

Davie did not miss the past tense there but he was too intent on this point of Aurelia to switch direction, and he found himself shouting.

"You don't think I'd ask her for money?"

"Don't be a fool. She'd have been glad to help. She'd do anything in the world for you."

Davie gasped with the ferocity that flared inside him, yelling, "You leave her out of this. If she had any sense at all she'd have divorced you years ago. Those damned priests . . ."

"I wish she had." Mitchell's voice held a new dark rumble. "Since she's been with Boniface she's been costing me a fortune. To divorce me and marry you . . . that's what you want, isn't it?"

Davie's lips stiffened. It seemed impossible for him to shape another word, and it came out in a muddy slur. "You bastard."

In one of the abrupt changes that so often confounded people Mitchell's manner made a swift swing. He put up his palms, pushing at the air and said rapidly:

"No . . . no . . . no. Let's both stop this. You're right, I was insulting, intimating I couldn't talk business with you now . . . but if a whisper leaked out as to what I'm doing it could ruin it. Now cool down and listen to me."

"Don't bother. I'm not interested."

"You will be." Mitchell sank into a chair, leaned back and grinned as if the bitter words of a moment before had never been spoken.

He talked about transportation. Stagecoach lines, freight wagon lines, mail routes, telegraphs, and ponies. And gradually Davie Stuart began to listen.

Wells Fargo had its tight monopoly up and down the West Coast and as far inland as Washoe, but east of Sun Mountain they had no control. Their freight went by steamship, south and across the Isthmus of Panama.

John Butterfield was operating his Butterfield Overland Mail between San Diego and Texas, through Fort Yuma. As a friend of President James Buchanan and the head of the Post Office Department, he was kept alive by a mail contract with the government, but if the southern states seceded as they were threatening he would lose that contract and probably could not survive without it.

North of Butterfield, William Russell, Alexander Majors and a new partner, William Waddell, had a web headquartered in Atchison, covering the Midwest. Having swallowed the Leavenworth and Pikes Peak Express and the Hockaday operation and now initiated the Pony Express, they were the biggest transportation organization between the Mississippi and Denver.

But there was a challenger upcoming. Ben Holladay began by freighting supplies for the U. S. Army during the Mexican War. When that was over he wanted a freight line of his own but did not have the capital. Instead he opened a trading store in Missouri and gradually acquired a few wagons and oxen. Then he ran head-on into Russell-Majors who blocked him just as Wells Fargo had blocked Davie Stuart and Mitch Randolph. He was all but out of business when an idea came to him. Several years before, right after the war, the Mormons were in Clay County and being hounded by the settlers around them. The governor called out six thousand troops to treat them as enemies and annihilate them. Ben Holladay carried the order to Colonel Doniphan. Instead of obeying it, Holladay and Doniphan talked the Mormons into surrendering and then were mortified when the general in command ordered the Mormon leaders shot. Doniphan refused, pulled his troops out of camp and set the leaders free. Doniphan was a hero to the Mormons and so by extension was Ben Holladay.

In the intervening years the Mormons had moved on West and settled the Utah area into a thriving territory, but expectedly they were suspicious of outsiders. Still, they needed a supply line. Only Ben Holladay would be accepted as the link. Wangling financial backing from a George Warner he bought fifty new wagons, loaded them with seventy thousand dollars worth of goods and freighted them to Salt Lake and was welcomed with open arms. The next year he was back with double the wagons and load, but this time he traded his goods for Mormon cattle and drove them on West to the California gold camps, then started a slaughterhouse at Benecia. Tough, shrewd, able, Holladay and his freight line prospered and no one else could come into his territory.

Except that the new Pony Express was using that route. Davie had wondered how Russell-Majors had managed that.

He knew all of the background and he was bored and sulky until Mitchell said:

"The Pony Express is the key for us, Davie. It's going to lever the Russell crowd right into our hands, Ben Holladay's and mine, because Gwin and the Southerners want them out of the way before they get so strong that the government will have to give them the mail contract that Butterfield now holds. It was little Willie Gwin who conned Russell into this Pony Express stunt. Told him if he wanted the mail contract to do something spectacular to attract Washington's attention . . . the Pony Express will lose nine hundred thousand dollars a year and Gwin figures that will break Russell before too long."

Mitchell reached across and tapped Davie's knee with a stiff forefinger. "Now Ben Holladay is a barbarian and a pirate on his own, and he feels about Russell and Majors the way I feel about Wells Fargo. So we've been loaning them money . . . they're overextended . . . they owe him a hundred and eighty thousand now and they're still borrowing every month, gambling that they'll get the mail contract. When they're into him deep enough Ben will step in and take them over. Which will give him a direct, central route all the way from the Mississippi west to Washoe.

"And we will then be ready to push on with coaches . . . in competition with Wells Fargo. Now, do you want to come in and play?"

He was laughing aloud, looking more like that shark than ever. Davie had been falling under the spell. Being a part of the Holladay expansion was an exciting prospect. If Mitchell only had not brought up Wells Fargo as his target, surfaced with the old obsession that Davie believed distorted his thinking . . . Wells Fargo was simply too big, too strong, too rich . . . it could not be beaten on its own ground, not even by Ben Holladay. He felt his growing enthusiasm punctured like a balloon.

"I guess not," he said. "I guess I'll stay here. But I'll buy you a dinner, we've got a French restaurant down the street as good as any in San Francisco."

CHAPTER SEVEN

For weeks after Mitchell's disclosures Davie mulled them over. It seemed incredible that men as astute as Bill Russell and Alex Majors would be gullible enough to be taken in by Dr. Gwin's ploy. Already financially shaky, in debt to a man they had once slapped down, why would they go further into debt with the Pony Express, which was so patently unprofitable, so risky, so vulnerable to attack by hostile Indians? Why would they allow themselves to fall into a position where Mitchell and Ben Holladay could grab off their whole growing stagecoach empire? Only when he remembered the Adams partners' follies in '54 could he admit the possibility.

Then there was the revelation of Mitchell in cahoots with the unprincipled Ben Holladay. Yet why not? The men who were the real builders of the West were all fundamentally dishonest, but in their greed they were developing a whole new wealth, a new section of the country, from nothing. It was there before his eyes, in the raw town springing up on the mountainside around him. As Aurelia had said, if you wanted to win anything you had to beat them at their own game.

For himself, he would not betray Mitchell's plans to McLane even though Wells Fargo was in some degree involved with Russell-Majors, responsible for the Pony Express way stations. He would keep his head down, do his job, and see what happened.

One thing did happen soon. The local Piute Indians did attack the Pony Express station closest to Sun Mountain. The first alarm was brought by a very frightened rider. The three handlers had been killed and the buildings burned. The Pony found the place deserted and had to ride his tired horse the extra thirty miles and expected to be jumped every foot of the way.

He came into Stafford Hall exhausted and the news swept up through the canyon camps trailing terror in its wake. The words *Indian attack* brought memories of the horrors of gutted wagon trains to those who had crossed the plains, and fearful fantasies to those who had come by ship and heard of the atrocities later.

The threat hit harder because the community had been lulled into complacency, violent as the town was. The Piutes had stolen a few horses, begged at the kitchen doors of restaurants, but made no real trouble. They had even helped the camp to survive its snow-bound winter. It was a heavy shock to find them gone on the warpath.

In a hurried meeting William Stewart was automatically called for to take the lead. Stewart was not there. It was said that he had ridden down Gold Canyon early that morning, but no one knew where he was headed.

The editor Frank Pix took the chair and chose a committee of five men to prepare a defense in case the Indians swept up the mountain right away. Sentries were rushed to the heads of Six Mile and Seven Mile Canyons to guard them and bring warning if the Indians appeared. The only six women in town were herded into O'Reiley's unfinished hotel building. Henry Meredith was delegated to gather an expedition to go out. Young, handsome, not much older than Davie Stuart, Meredith was Stewart's law partner and heir to the respect given the older man.

Meredith chose Davie and two saloonkeepers to enroll a fighting force. The three set up a table at the Crystal Palace and as volunteers flocked in they made a list of who owned rifle, horse or mule, powder and ball.

Other men polled the merchants who would contribute provisions, packs were made up. Then Virginia settled in to watch through the night.

The miners did not report for their late work shifts. Restaurants and saloons stayed open as usual and were heavily patronized. Men wanted the companionship of others, wanted the stimulation of whiskey and the comfort of boasting what they would do to the savages when daylight came.

Caught up in the joking and laughter, Davie took a calm view of the prospect. His memory kept harking back to the only other Indian scare in his experience, the day when all Sonora marched to avenge Steve Bassett when they thought he was murdered and scalped in Columbia. But whatever was in store for tomorrow it included a long ride, and he left the saloon early to go to bed.

The bugle waked him. He dressed, belted on his gun, took his rifle, saddled a company horse and rode down to C Street.

In the dawn's gray light he saw Meredith and three committee members in a huddle. At least a thousand men had signed the volunteer lists last night but there were fewer than a hundred gathered in the road, and they made a miserable showing. Logy with liquor and sagging from lack of sleep, with not a uniform among them, the mounted miners and town toughs were anything but a reassuring army. Meredith was monotonously cursing the defectors and as Davie came up he raised an arm and signaled the advance.

Davie said, "Aren't you going to wait for the rest?"

Meredith swore again. "We do and we'll lose those we've got."

The ragged column moved out, urged on by an inept bugler, as uncomforting a force of defenders as Davie could imagine. But on the sidewalk Julia Bulette and her girls cheered and the troop reacted, laughing, shouting, promising to bring back scalps for everyone.

The spirit of a pleasure hunt grew as they rode toward the divide. Then, just before they reached it, William Stewart spurred over the crest toward them, slid his horse to a stop, took in the sense of what he saw and rode to his partner.

"Where in hell do you think you're going?"

"After the Piutes. They burned out Williams Station. We've got to stop them from coming here."

Stewart cut him off. "I heard about it coming through Carson, but let's not go off half-cocked. Let's find out what it means. Old Winnemucca's a smart chief and he's kept his tribe quiet so far."

"Let them get away with killing three white men? That's crazy. They'll be howling down on us any time. Turn around and take the lead, Bill."

Stewart's eyes ran again over the sorry line. "Nobody's going to lead that ragtail bunch of drunks anywhere. If the Indians are out in any force you'll get the lot slaughtered. Go on back and wait until I get hold of the chief."

A grumbling ran through the men. They had keyed themselves up to go Indian fighting and they did not want to be stopped. Meredith sat uncertain, turning in his saddle to look back at his command, looking again at his partner, stalled in doubt.

"You, Stuart," the older lawyer said, "you've got better sense than this, haven't you?"

Davie flushed. He would indeed prefer to turn back until an investigation could be made, but he had a problem.

"I'm not itching to fight Indians," he said, "but Williams Station is Wells Fargo's responsibility. There'll be another Pony coming through there, needing a horse. If the handlers are dead and the animals taken he's going to be a sitting duck for any Indians still hanging around. I have to go down."

Meredith nodded emphatically. "And he sure can't go alone, Bill. Are you coming or not?"

Stewart hesitated. He loved Meredith like a son. He did not want him to go on this harebrained mission. But he acknowledged that Williams Station had to be visited and restaffed, for there would be not one Pony but another and another riding in there without anyone to warn them.

"Go on then. Go as far as the station and find out what did happen, but don't get careless. I'll work from here to learn what I can."

They went over the divide with rising spirits, an individualistic, undisciplined mob, stopping at each of the chain of towns for a drink and to recruit more people. At Silver City they picked up R. G. Watkins, an old soldier who had earlier been with Walker on the ill-starred filibustering expedition to Mexico and had lost a leg there. Meredith tried to turn over the command to the military man but Watkins would not take it, mourning that:

"A one-legged man ain't good enough to lead. I'll just tag along."

At Dayton they found a small company come to join them under Major Ormsby. Ormsby had lived in the valley for years and was respected and again Meredith tried to surrender his leadership. Ormsby accepted it when Meredith agreed to be his lieutenant.

The troop now numbered a hundred and five and was in somewhat better shape, but it was still thirty rough miles to Williams Station. Because many of the mounts were poor it took them most of the day.

They kept an alert watch but saw no Indians. Still, they approached the last rise gingerly, half-expecting to find some there. When they did look down on the bare flat they saw no sign of life. Only the buildings, gutted by fire that smoldered in the charred logs of the walls and the caved-in roof. The relay ponies were gone from the corral and the three station tenders were quiet figures on the ground.

They rode down and spread into a half-circle around the bodies, already swollen and stinking from the day in the desert sun. This was no Steve Bassett joke. The heads were dark red, scalped. The bodies were naked, mutilated, emasculated, the faces frozen in contorted masks of torture. Davie Stuart felt his stomach roll.

The whole company was sobered for the moment, then anger came, and noisy argument. In particular the mountain toughs wanted to take up the chase immediately. Meredith, remembering Stewart's warning to take care, wanted to return and send for reinforcements from California. One man who had fought Indians before rode a wide circle around the scene, picked up tracks and came back shouting,

"There's only a handful. Let's go get them."

Ormsby himself insisted that unless they stopped the Piutes now the isolated ranchers scattered along the river would be wiped out.

Sam Brown, a rowdy who had already killed several men in Virginia, had the loudest voice. He was big, with whiskers so long that when he went into a fight he tied them under his chin to protect his throat from the knife that was the popular weapon among the saloon brawlers. He was drunk, brandishing his blade in one hand, a whiskey bottle in the other, shouting and threatening anyone who tried to turn back.

Meredith turned on Brown, a white circle of anger around his lips, and yelled: "Shut up."

Brown stopped in astonishment. It was rare that anyone dared stand against him. "Huh?"

"I am leader of this company and I said shut up."

Brown pulled his head down into his neck. "Ormsby's captain."

"Because I appointed him. I am still leader and I say we will vote on what we'll do."

Brown shoved his knife forward, the blade held level for a thrust, and took a step toward Meredith. Davie, at Meredith's side, was suddenly very afraid. His fingers twisted around the grip of his revolver and he held his breath. If Brown charged he knew that he must shoot the man.

The crowd was quiet, waiting. The toughs who followed Brown grinned, expecting his explosion. Meredith did not move. Then Brown grunted and turned away. The only man on the mountain who impressed Brown was William Stewart, who had disarmed him twice, backed him down. Meredith was Stewart's partner and drunk as he was Brown knew that if he killed Meredith, Stewart would kill him.

The letdown was slow. It took time to dawn on the men that Brown had been buffaloed after he had made his brag. But Meredith had only half a victory. The vote went against him two to one. They did agree to lay over there until morning.

When sentries were posted, the bodies buried, and the cold camp was settling down, Davie sought out Meredith.

"How about sending a rider back to town to tell Stewart we're going on?"

The young man smiled thinly. "I should have thought of that, shouldn't I? You go."

"I can't any more than you can. You're an elected leader, I represent Wells Fargo. I've got to maintain the company's reputation."

Meredith went to find another messenger and Davie rolled uncomfortably in his blanket. An oblique thought struck him. What would Mitchell Randolph have done today? Could he with his persuasiveness have sidetracked this expedition? Davie himself did not see how he could have avoided being drawn in.

They rode at first light, picking up the trail found last evening. It led them toward Pyramid Lake where the Piutes headquartered at this season, and they were still following it when night caught them again, short of the Truckee. Again they made a cold camp and again an uneasy one, for as dark came the mountains around them winked with signal fires. The Indians above knew where they were.

The same fires were seen in far-off Virginia City. Bill Stewart fumed, worrying over what Meredith was doing. He should have been back by now. And Meredith's messenger, worn out by a night of drinking and a long day of riding, had not reached the town. He had curled up beside the trail and gone to sleep, and next day had ridden on out of the country in the fear of what would be done to him when his dereliction was discovered.

Old Indian fighters on the mountain read in the signals that the column was being watched and a warning sent through the hills. The guards at the canyons were increased and telegrams were wired to California for help. Tension tightened in the towns.

On the third morning Ormsby led his party north across the Truckee and into a narrow defile that opened into a long, rocky valley bordering the shore of Pyramid Lake. He was at the head of the column with Meredith and Watkins when they spotted a small band of Indians on the side of a low hill. They were in a strong position, a cluster of rocks, but few as they were Ormsby ordered a charge and the volunteers were glad to break the boredom of the fruitless search. They drove up the hill in a rush.

Just behind the leaders, Davie was caught in the press of horses.

He kicked his animal ahead, pulled his revolver and fired toward the Indians.

A few shots, a few arrows came down against them, then the Indians faded over the ridge. When the volunteers reached the crest they saw the Indians running down another, deeper ravine toward the floor of a neighboring valley. With a whoop the column spurred after them, firing even though the range was too long. The shots and yelling drowned out Ormsby's cries of warning that he smelled a trap.

Trap it was. As they poured down the narrow throat a long line of Indians appeared on each rim and a fusillade of shots rained into the rank.

Davie had a confused view of the savages on top, then of the horses milling around him, and tried to turn his own. A bullet slammed into it as he swung. The animal staggered, did not fall, but instead of bolting it stopped dead with fright. An arrow hissed past Davie's head.

Instinct made him drop out of the saddle and jerk his rifle from the boot. The Sharps Louis McLane had given him was a much more effective piece than the muzzle-loaders carried by most of the troop. Until now it had never been fired in anger.

There was a big boulder within two jumps of where his horse still stood and Davie dived for it, threw himself down in its shelter out of the way of thrashing hoofs and flying bullets. Twisting, he watched a flood of Indians sweeping down both walls of the ravine, some charging in the open, some dodging from rock to rock, filling the gully with howls. Screaming horses and cursing men added to the bedlam and a cloud of powder smoke rose over all.

Another cloud, denser, of opaque dust, blotted his view up the ravine and Davie knew that more Indians were charging down the grade he had just ridden over. Escape back that way was cut off.

There was only one avenue left, one place to try to reach. Outside the mouth of the ravine, in the valley, was a clump of trees against the bank of the small river. If they could get into the trees they might be able to regroup and make a stand.

Davie rose, heard a voice shouting and looked toward it. Watkins, the one-legged man, was on the ground far up the ravine, supporting himself on a stick and firing steadily, a one-man rear guard yelling for the others to get away. Davie could not reach him before the Indians overran him.

A horse crazed with terror was swinging in hopeless circles. Davie grabbed for it, caught its bridle, then saw Meredith across the

214

ravine, down on his stomach with blood on his head and shoulder but still firing. Davie jumped for him, shouting:

"Henry, Henry, up. Here."

Meredith turned, white faced, and shook his head. "I'm done. Clear out." He turned back to fire again and a bullet caught him squarely. His body jerked up and an arrow drove into his chest.

Davie shot at and hit the Indian, then leaped on the horse and spurred it downhill. There were others ahead of him racing for the trees. He saw a mounted boy rein in beside Sam Brown, on his feet, dancing and bellowing, and reach a hand out to the badman. Brown flung up to the animal's rump. The boy dug in his heels and the horse jumped, but faltered under the double weight. Davie was right behind them when Brown swung his big arm against the boy and knocked him out of the saddle and spurred on without looking back.

Davie wheeled to a stop, stretched a hand down to the boy as he scrambled to his feet, but a bullet spun the boy away and dropped him. Shots were striking close around him now and Davie flattened himself against the horse's neck, beat his heels against it and pounded for the trees.

Within the woods he found a wild confusion. All of the leaders were gone. Brown and a bunch of his toughs were already through the clump and splashing across the creek. Over half the men left had lost their horses. Some crouched behind trees and fired back across the valley. Others walked around in a numb helplessness, their minds befuddled with the shock of the attack. One small handful huddled in a council of war and Davie rode to these. They were noisy, shouting that they had to get out, get away. One among them was trying to quiet them, repeating over and over:

"No, no. Stay here. It's getting dark. Wait for dark."

"The Indians," Davie said, "there are a lot of them and they can get here before dark."

The man bobbed his head. "But they won't. They've got bounty and scalps back there that'll keep them busy long enough. Rest and reload and settle down. Don't panic. We'll make it."

Some did not make it. As the darkness thickened they stole away by twos and threes. Some struggled back to safety even though they were wounded. Davie was among those.

As the time to move came near he had volunteered to ride to the edge of the timber to see if the way was clear. The arrow came out of the shadow ahead, suddenly, without warning as he turned back. It almost knocked him out of the saddle and did throw him to the side. He lost his grip on the reins and the horse, already spooked, lunged away, running toward the river.

He could not stop. He barely stayed in the saddle by hanging onto the high horn. By the time the animal had run itself into exhaustion he had lost contact with the other survivors.

He did not know where he was or where to head. Behind him somewhere the Indians had reached the trees and would be scouring them. He could not stay with the river. They would come searching there next. They would expect the fugitives to keep close to water, not to strike out across barren desert.

He did not know the country but in the light of a rising moon he could make out the rampart of the Washoe Hills they had crossed the day before. If he worked west to them and turned south he should come into the Carson Valley someplace above the Williams Station.

Both he and the horse needed rest. He stopped for half an hour, then started toward the hills.

The arrow burned like a shaft of fire driven into the heavy shoulder muscle. The arm was numb, useless, and every time he tried it the pain was worse.

Toward midnight he stopped again and swung down clumsily. He had no canteen. He had dropped his rifle when the arrow hit and somewhere his revolver had been jarred out of the holster. He knew now that he should have drunk before he left the river but water had been the last thing in his mind at the time. Now his mouth was hot and dry.

He started to sit down against a rock and leaned against the arrow sticking in his back. The sharp pain made him cry out and started sweat from his forehead. It ran into his eyes, stinging and blinding him. He wiped at them, then reached his good hand back to try to pull the arrow out. The stone barb was deep and held. The flood of pain dropped him to his knees. He stayed there, overwhelmed by weakness.

It came dully to him that he was going to die. He had heard of men lost in the desert, wandering in circles until they lost their minds. He had to get rid of the arrow. That became a pervading obsession. If he could get rid of it he would be all right. He reached for it again, held it and slammed back against the rock.

The shaft snapped but his senses reeled. He went forward into darkness on his face. He did not feel the sharp rocks he fell against.

He did not entirely lose consciousness but his mind wandered.

He heard a voice calling Mitchell's name, then realized that it was his own.

Mitchell had always been there to help, to make decisions and push aside difficulties. But Mitchell was not there now. He was alone in a wasteland without water. Unless he got up and found his way out while it was still night, before the sun turned the land into a furnace he would surely die.

He clung to thinking, fought the nausea and dizziness and gradually was able to get to his feet and climb to the saddle. The horse was too tired to protest, but it answered the rein and plodded on.

When morning came he saw the snow lying like clouds on the distant High Sierras. Then below them he found the dark green line that meant trees along a river. He turned toward them and kept them as a beacon. He came to a road and followed it, and finally the town of Dayton rose out of the sand.

The first fugitives to return, those unhurt and well mounted, straggled in through Dayton and up through the settlements of Gold Canyon spreading their harrowing tales of the massacre. The stories lost nothing in the telling.

Sam Brown was among the vanguard. He stood at the bar of the Crystal Palace surrounded by admiring toughs and declaimed loudly about the hundreds of howling Piutes who had swarmed down on the helpless white party.

"I must have killed twenty anyway." He reached for a fresh glass as if the ordeal had drained him of moisture. "Then I run out of ammunition, or I might have stopped them."

He was listened to. He was known as a liar and a braggart but no one questioned his fighting ability or fondness of a fight. Men listened and were afraid. The volunteers had ridden out carrying most of the town's arms. How now could the camp protect itself from such a savage horde?

Bill Stewart chaired another citizens' meeting, questioning the fugitives more closely, particularly about Meredith. One remembered seeing him fall, the others were not sure. Beside himself with worry over his partner, Stewart put that personal concern aside for the immediate problem of defense. They wired Governor Downey for help from California again. The guards were further increased. Tom Peasley's firemen, wearing their red uniforms, organized a headquarters at the firehouse. At the first report of Indians being sighted the fire bell was to be rung and every able-bodied man would go to the firehouse with whatever weapon he could find.

But many believed the town could not resist an attack and most of the population decamped overnight, heading down the canyon and taking the old Immigrant Trail up the Sierras to California and safety. Those with horses rode. Others paid triple fare to cling to the tops of jammed stages. The rest walked, long lines of terrified miners who suspected a Piute behind every bush they passed.

After that exodus Virginia City sat helpless. Those stern-fibered souls who stayed waited. The agonizing hours passed in slow procession. The Indians were taking their time. The signal fires burned bright night on succeeding night. And still they did not come.

CHAPTER EIGHT

Broderick's death, Terry's flight to Sun Mountain, and Aurelia's enchantment with the Knights of the Golden Circle fired some intoxicating dreams in Marion Boniface.

Broderick's passing left the so-called Free Democrats virtually without leaders. True, thirty thousand people had filled Union Square to mourn him, but there was not one among them, not even Colonel Baker, to carry the banner.

The southern faction was in no better shape. Gwin was in Washington and Terry, the militant, was gone. Into this beckoning vacuum Boniface saw himself surfacing as the heir to the coming Republic of the Pacific.

His cynicism kept him from committing himself to any political philosophy for its own sake, but he had gauged the temper of the territory and decided that the more aggressive Southerners stood every chance of success. The mines would be seized and the torrent of their wealth used to defeat the forces of the Union.

He knew that Terry expected to be President of the new republic. He knew there were others, including Gwin, who would be in the center of the struggle for power once the die was cast, but he felt certain that the man on the ground, the man who organized and controlled the local scene would be the man on top.

The thought amused him. Marion Boniface, mountebank, in line to become the most powerful figure in the western world. For he never doubted that if . . . when, the West Coast states had been wrenched away from the Union they would emerge as the trading center of a new Pacific empire. The southern states to the East had cotton, the northern states had the beginnings of a manufacturing monolith. But California, Oregon, Nevada had a mineral wealth unmatched by any nation in the world.

So he set about expanding the groups of southern sympathizers into lodges, each with a hundred men. There were a captain, a secretary, and a lieutenant for each ten men, and each lodge was responsible for its own cache of arms and its military training.

Boniface had played at being a lawyer for years. Now he played at being a conspirator. Each type of people he approached heard from him a different appeal. His nature told him that while men might fight for an ideal they would fight much harder if their own self-interest was at stake.

He went to the miners. Many of them were foreign born and had little interest in the political arguments. To them he pointed out that it was their labor which produced the gold and silver, yet most of the treasure was shipped away to fatten the pockets of bankers, freighters, and the express company. Under the Pacific Republic, he said, the mines would be nationalized. There would be no taxes. It would be Utopia. So convincing was he that he almost came to believe it himself.

He and Aurelia drove down the peninsula to the Playa de la Felicidad to talk with the refugee families she had gathered onto the ranch.

"There are not enough of you people to make an effective cause in Washington by yourselves," he lectured, "but once we take the coastal states out of the Union the Californians will represent a good proportion of the population. Aurelia will be chairman of a new Land Commission as soon as our government is seated in Sacramento."

The response was cautious, for even with Aurelia backing him up, Boniface was an American, and they had heard promises before. Duncan spoke the general question:

"What makes you think you've got a chance to win?"

"I'm glad you asked that," the lawyer said. "It is important that everyone understands how much is in our favor. Half of the men holding power in Washington now are sympathetic to the South, and out here the governor is. The head of the Army at the Presidio is. He won't lift a finger to stop us, and the Union Army in the East will be too busy there to even think about us. Over in Nevada, David Terry has control of the silver mines. John Newman of Virginia City and Dr. McMeans of Carson have organized lodges and are already drilling in one of the mines. When the time comes the whole Comstock will be seized. Have you any idea what that means? Millions and millions to finance our new country."

They still wanted time to think about it. Boniface guessed rightly that even though he had championed their causes through the courts they would not commit themselves until Aurelia came back alone, without an American at her side to influence her, and told them this was the right thing for them to do.

When she did that they took up the cause as their own. A few of the Californians, such as the Vallejos, had accepted the American rule even before the Stars and Stripes was raised at Monterey, and these they stayed away from, but elsewhere the new cells blossomed with Duncan and José in the vanguard of the proselyters. Behind the white adobe walls they drilled, at Monterey, at Santa Barbara, at San Diego, with branches in the lesser communities. It was not long until Boniface could report to Terry that they had a thousand men under arms in California alone.

And then the news of the Piute massacre threw everything into hiatus. There was hardly anyone in California, Northerner or Southerner, who did not have a relative, personal friend, or business associate in Nevada, and both sides were united in the fear of what had happened over there.

The clamor was for news and there was precious little. The first word to come over the single telegraph wire was a garbled, much exaggerated account, and a frantic appeal to the California governor for immediate help. The newspapers further embellished the story. Then the military commandeered the wire, the only means of communication, and no one could find out whether the mining town was still there or had been attacked and burned.

The frustration hit Marion Boniface particularly hard. He could get no word of Terry. He could not learn whether the Southerners had marched out against the Piutes. If Terry had been among those killed in the Indian trap the mechanics of taking over the silver lode could be dead with him. The chances of a successful Republic of the Pacific would be drastically impaired.

He told Aurelia: "I've talked to General Johnson at the Presidio and he says over a hundred volunteers went to Pyramid Lake and less than fifty came back. If I know Terry, he was one of those volunteers. If he's dead I will have to take command quickly, and the only way I can find out is to go over there."

So far Aurelia had discounted the more extravagant rumors. Virginia City was a town of over six thousand men and surely there were not enough Indians in the area to really threaten it, and the volunteer force had been a nameless, shadowy band not related to her. But if David Terry might have been one of them, so could Davie Stuart. She looked up at Boniface with sudden fear.

He thought the fear was for his own safety and smiled to reassure her.

"It's all right. Johnson is sending a company of infantry, Major Hungerford of the Sierra Battalion has ordered his company in there, and Jack Hays, who was sheriff here, has been appointed Commander in Chief."

"Good, good, but Marion, do you remember my friend who came to the office, Davie Stuart? He's over there as agent for Wells Fargo. Could he have been in that ambush?"

The dread in her tone took his attention off Terry for a moment, long enough to say:

"I have to go to the express office for my coach ticket. I'll ask McLane about him." Then he forgot the stricken face and what it might imply in the urgency of his own problems.

At the Parrott Building he waited half an hour in restless irritation before McLane could see him, and the general agent's half apology was harried, with no attempt to hide his annoyance at the interruption.

"It's a bad time, Boniface. What do you want?"

Boniface was long accustomed to people showing their dislike of him, his armor was tough, and his reaction now was to sit down leisurely, use more of the busy man's precious minutes than was necessary, deliberately slow his speech.

"Several things, Mr. McLane. Some information that I hope you will be able to give me, for one, and for another, a place on one of your coaches out of Placerville at the earliest time I can reach there . . ."

"Impossible," McLane cut in. "All transportation has been taken over by the military."

Boniface smiled, slowly drew a pass from his pocket and laid it on the desk without a word. It was signed by General Johnson. McLane raised his brows and glanced at the lawyer, wondering how he came by the pass. He scrawled a hurried signature under the general's and shoved the paper back.

"All right. Show it at the counter downstairs. They'll make the arrangements."

A messenger brought a handful of pages to McLane and the agent bent over them in a dismissal of the lawyer. Boniface continued sitting, saying to the top of the man's head:

"There is something else I would like. You have a man named Stuart in your office in Virginia. Can you tell me if he is all right?"

If he had asked anything else, McLane thought, he would have ignored the lawyer, but Davie Stuart was a special worry and he looked up with less resentment.

"He is not all right. He was in the Pyramid Lake fight and got a poisoned arrow through his shoulder. The last report we had said he was in bad condition."

"I'm sorry," Boniface said. "And thank you. Is there anything I can do for you while I am over there?"

"Yes. Run another telegraph line and tell me what the hell is going on. Now if you please . . ."

Boniface stood up, taking his time, nodding. "I'll do what I can."

With his passage taken care of he went back to the office and reported on Aurelia's friend. Aurelia came to her feet, drawn up by an invisible force.

"I'm going with you," she announced. "I've got to see that Davie is taken care of."

Noting the white rim around her lips and the tight set of her mouth Marion Boniface discovered that Davie Stuart meant more to Aurelia than he had thought. Through all of their association the lawyer had deliberately kept their relationship impersonal because of the problems he could foresee in trying to work with a jealous woman, and when no matter how closely he investigated he could turn up no affairs with any man he had concluded that this was a sexually frozen woman. Now, in delight, it flashed upon him that she and her husband's partner were lovers. He felt sure of it when, after he had explained that he could not get a military pass for a woman, she fled out of the office, calling over her shoulder that she had to tell Mitchell.

Aurelia had not been inside Randolph's office before and he gaped at her as she flew through the door, foreboding catching at him, confirmed when she gasped:

"Davie . . . the Piutes shot him with a poisoned arrow . . ."

Mitchell kicked his chair over coming to his feet and grabbed her shoulders hard enough to make her wince. "He's dead . . . ?"

She stood shaking her head, panting for breath before she could speak again, her words disconnected. "No . . . wounded . . . I don't know . . . McLane told Marion . . . he said wounded . . ."

At the name McLane, Mitchell spun away, snatched his hat, threw her a bleak look meant to be reassuring and ran down the splintered steps. He had not been in the Parrott Building since the interview

223

when Ianes had laughed at him, but nothing about Wells Fargo was in his mind now when he hurried to the desk and asked for McLane.

The clerk knew him by sight and sent a messenger upstairs to announce the visit and the general agent took the unusual courtesy of coming down himself. He did not offer his hand and Mitchell did not wait to make amenities, let a nod suffice, and said immediately:

"Tell me all you know about Davie Stuart being hurt."

"I'm sorry, Randolph." The man sounded genuinely so. "We don't know much. He was in the fight and was hit in the shoulder with a poisoned arrow. That's all we've heard. The military has taken over the telegraph and the coaches and no civilian word has come through since."

"Then get me a seat out of Placerville tomorrow morning," Mitchell said, asking the favor without hesitation.

As he had told Boniface, McLane said that Randolph would need an Army pass.

"Save me the seat," Mitchell insisted. "I'll get a pass if I have to go to the governor."

Then he was gone, almost bumping into Aurelia as he strode out. He stopped long enough to brief her on what little he had learned, to tell her he was going to Washoe, then he went on to find his pass. He got it without the governor's help, bribed it, then rode all night and was in time to catch the morning stage. The coach was crowded inside and on top with soldiers and there was one other civilian passenger, Marion Boniface.

Mitchell had never approved of the lawyer and had disliked him even more for knowing so much about his personal life, and while he was civil he did not initiate a conversation. Boniface though, putting Aurelia and Davie Stuart in bed together, took the opportunity to ask his barbed question:

"I suppose you're anxious to find out how your partner is?"

Mitchell understood the insinuation. The same thought had come to him once, but knowing Davie's code of ethics he had discounted the possibility. He had a quick impulse to slap the smiling face across from him, which he knew was just what the lawyer wanted. Instead he returned the smile, told the man, "Thank you for telling Aurelia." Then for the rest of the ride he gave his attention to the tales and speculation with which the Army boys passed the time.

When the coach hauled up on C Street in front of the International Hotel the soldiers went off in a group to find their headquarters and Marion Boniface went into the lobby to ask where Judge Terry could be found. Mitchell Randolph was right behind him, overheard the question and heard him directed to John Newman's stone house. Then as Boniface went out and Mitchell reached for the quill and registered for a room, Bill Stewart unfolded himself from a chair across the lobby and came toward Randolph. He greeted Mitchell, waited while a key was given him, then beckoned him out of the clerk's hearing and asked:

"Marion Boniface . . . what's he doing in Virginia City?"

Mitchell, not at all curious, shrugged. "Looking for Terry is all I know. Bill, what about Davie? Is he all right?"

"Out of danger now." There was pain in Stewart's voice. "But my boy Henry . . . he was killed. God damn it, Mitchell, I told him not to go beyond the station. Why didn't he listen? Why . . . ? Henry Meredith. He was like my son. Same as Davie is to you." The lawyer bowed his head and stood as though he waited for a spasm of physical agony to pass, then looked up, smoothing his face, forcing his mind away from the tragedy and ignoring Mitchell's low spoken sympathy. "Boniface and Terry, huh? Boniface and the Knights of the Golden Circle . . . I hadn't known he was involved." He was silent with thought, then his eyes sharpened on Randolph. "What about your wife? If Boniface is in it . . . ?"

"I hope she's got better sense." Mitchell hid his amusement at Stewart's grim suspicions. He was anxious to see Davie but Stewart was not ready to let him go. He had other worries to ask about.

He wanted to hear if Mitchell knew the extent of military help California was sending. Mitchell told him that the Sierra Battalion was on its way over the mountains from Downieville, that General Johnson had ordered out a company of infantry from the Presidio, which, he commented, ought to be enough, added to the miners already there.

Stewart snorted. Most of the camp, he said, had hi-tailed it for California right after the massacre and the men who stayed were unarmed and without ammunition. They had lost most of the guns from the mountain at Pyramid Lake, and while they were recruiting a militia, lead was so scarce that they were melting down silver bars and pouring bullets of the precious metal, racing against time. Though the Indians had not attacked the towns yet they were gathered in some strength and burning signal fires in a ring around the surrounding hills every night.

When he could finally get away, when Stewart had told him that Davie was in the stone hotel down by the Devil's Gate, which Eilley Orrum and Julia Bulette had appropriated for a hospital, Mitchell rented a horse and rode down the hill.

Stewart was right, the town was nearly deserted. There were no ore carts on the street, no supply wagons, and very few men on the sidewalks. From the corners as he passed them Mitchell looked up-hill at the blank eyes of dirty, uncurtained windows in a drab block of graceless buildings, and down on the ragged roofs of a formless shantytown below D Street, on the mean row of the six tiny identical cribs. For all the several hundred thousand dollars worth of silver produced here every month, precious little was spent on making living conditions better for the men who mined it, and it was particularly ugly now, so vulnerable and under siege. But a town must be judged by the quality of its people.

Eilley Orrum. The South Park society circle sniffed at mention of her and Mitchell had heard many ribald stories about her. She was reputed to have arrived in Washoe early, the imported Scot bride of a Mormon who brought her as far as Salt Lake. There she was said to have left him to come south with another man, and surfaced again in the valley camp of Johnstown running a boardinghouse. One of her boarders, unable to pay his bill, gave her his mining claim and moved on and Eilley, finding that the claim lay next to one owned by Sandy Bowers, married him. When their neighbors sold their mines cheaply, before the silver strike, the Bowers held theirs and were now making upward of a hundred thousand dollars a week. Yet it was Eilley who stayed out the siege to nurse those men wounded in the massacre.

And Julia Bulette. A lady of pleasure who had adopted the camp and mothered it through all its woes and now worked beside Eilley in their hospital.

Mitchell had never met either woman until he came into the empty lobby and hesitated, uncertain which way to turn. Then an upstairs door opened and the work-worn millionairess, in a gaudy purple dress, carrying a slop pail in either hand, bustled down the steps.

Mitchell took off his hat, made her a bow of gratitude and asked after Davie Stuart.

Without stopping she bobbed her head. "He's coming along now, dearie. Julia's taking care of him. Up the stairs you'll find him." She had reached the door to the rear quarters and now turned, bumped it open with a heavy buttock, went through and kicked it shut behind her.

Mitchell went up to the second floor, heading for the nearest door, but before he reached it another opened down the hall and the second woman appeared carrying a pan and trailed by a square-faced man. She was handsome, black haired, red mouthed, and warm eyed, and she answered his question with a moan of sympathy.

"My poor Davie, he so nearly died. You talk to Dr. Bryant here . . . I have my other boys to see to."

She swung on down the corridor with a light, provocative step, taking away her pan of blood-stained bandages.

Dr. Bryant chuckled, watching after her with open appreciation. "My poor Davie . . . every man in here is my poor somebody to Julia. They all belong to her."

Mitchell, too, watched the woman until she was out of sight, then he asked the doctor about Davie's condition.

"Well, he's alive." Bryant sounded skeptical of the fact. "I don't know how except he's young and has the constitution of an ox. Only thing that saved him was that the arrowhead didn't go very deep and in yanking at it he enlarged the wound, fortunately, made it bleed a lot, which washed out most of the venom."

"Venom?" Mitchell's mouth twisted with the ugliness of the idea as Bryant explained that the Piutes had a nasty habit of milking rattlesnakes and painting their arrowheads with the poison. "My God, can he survive that?"

"He has survived it. And he'll probably recover. You see"—the doctor paused and leaned against the door jamb, settling in for a clinical discussion interesting to him—"with snake bite the first few hours are the most critical. You get nausea, double vision, lightheadedness. If you're going to die it will normally be within the first twelve hours." Shaking his head in wonder Bryant said, "Stuart stayed on a horse, kept moving all that first night, rode into Dayton the next morning . . . Well . . . If you do live through the first shock to your nervous system your recovery is pretty fast. Stuart is out of the shock now and the only danger is his weakness from loss of blood, the chance that the wound might infect and he'd not have the resistance left to fight it."

Mitchell Randolph took a slow, deep breath. "Then I suppose I shouldn't see him?"

"Oh, I think it might do him good to see a friend, cheer him up. Just don't tire him out. He's in the corner room on the left." The doctor shoved away from the jamb and went whistling on his rounds.

Even forewarned, Mitchell stopped when he opened the door, not prepared for the pallor, the heavy limpness of the gaunt figure on the bed, then as Davie discovered him and stretched his mouth in a death's-head grin, he crossed the room, dropped on his knees and buried his face against the pale hand lying outside the cover, fighting his tears.

"Thanks for coming," Davie said, but it was more a sigh than words.

"Don't talk," Mitchell ordered him. "Save your strength to get well. My God, what an ordeal for you . . ."

Davie heard the choke in the voice and tried to offset it with a joke. "It wasn't quite like our going after Steve Bassett," he said. "I'm okay now, thanks to Julia . . . just weak. How's Aurelia?"

"All right. Worried as hell about you. I'll try to get word to her, if I can find somebody to take a message down." Then when Davie would have spoken again Mitchell cut him short. "Keep quiet, I said. I'll be in tomorrow." He shoved up onto his feet and left, obedient to the doctor.

He stood with William Stewart that night in his room at the International Hotel and watched the Indian signal fires wink, ringing the town. They had been talking about the debacle of the volunteers. Of the more than a hundred men who went out, less than fifty had returned, and it was eerie to look off at those pinpoints of light and know that at any time a howling horde of savages could come swarming in on the all but defenseless camp. Mitchell's mind was on Davie and how to protect him, but Stewart was less worried about Piutes than he was about Terry and his Knights.

There was no attack the next day or the next, and gradually the military force gathered, under the command of Colonel Jack Hays, a one-time sheriff of San Francisco. Mitchell visited Davie several times each day and on the second afternoon Davie, gaining strength and getting bored with bed rest, stopped him as he would again pop in and out of the room.

"Mitch, for Pete's sake relax, will you? Sit down. Talk to me. What's going on outside? Are the Indians still around?"

"They are." Mitchell sat down gingerly, ready to bolt if Davie showed weariness by so much as closing his eyes. "But I think the danger is past now, with the troops here. Bill Stewart isn't worried, except by that silly bunch of Southerners."

"Terry?" Davie sounded surprised. "Silly? Mitch, you don't know. He can make real trouble here, start a shooting war on C Street if nobody stops him."

Mitchell made a pained face. "That loud mouth? Davie, they're a bunch of kids playing games. Secret cells . . . secret handshakes . . . secret passwords . . . they're . . ."

But Davie, deeply influenced by Stewart for the past months, came up on one elbow, intent, challenging Mitchell's airy dismissal of the conspirators, and Mitchell waved him down in quick concern, saying:

"Never mind, never mind. Don't get excited. You're supposed to be resting. Lie down and we'll talk about something else, anything you like, just take it easy."

Davie dropped back, miffed that Mitchell was not taking the growing threat seriously, and in retaliation took advantage of the offer to choose a subject.

"You might," he said, "give me a rundown on what you're doing, how the Ben Holladay thing is working. If that isn't a secret."

"It's cooking slowly." Mitchell was plainly relieved that the wounded man was not going to press his argument, and offered, "But there's something else you might be interested in. That project I've been working on in Oregon . . . did I tell you about it?"

Davie only looked at him.

"Well . . . I haven't seen much of you lately . . . This is on the Columbia River. You know the Columbia?"

"I know there is one."

"Indeed there is, and it's even more important than the Sacramento. It runs clear up into the upper reaches of western Washington Territory, on up into Canada, and they're finding more and more gold and silver around there. The river is the transportation system for all the new camps."

"Steamboats." Davie snapped his fingers in sudden recollection and grinned. "You've got a steamboat line, which I should have guessed the day Bill Stewart asked if you were going to put one on the Carson."

Laughing at him, Mitchell hitched his chair closer to the bed. "No, but I've got a finger in one, and it's going to be a moneymaker."

"So tell me about it. What's your competition?" Davie lay back resting and listening as Mitchell spun out this latest product of his restless inquisitiveness.

There had, he said, been some boats on the Columbia for years, but the steamers got their real start there in 1850 when Berryman Jennings, who had run boats in California, and a partner, Lott Whitcomb, built one on the northern river. As captain they hired J. C. Ainsworth, who had come from the Mississippi River west to the Sacramento, where Mitchell knew him, before he went north.

Ainsworth was not paid his salary and claimed a participation in the ownership, and when it was sold in '54 he had a stake with which to build the *Jenny Clark*. In '58 he sold that boat and began building the *Carrie Ladd*, but ran short of money. Mitchell Randolph had loaned him enough to finish it, the finest stern-wheeler on the northern waters.

The loan had come about when Mitchell was up there investigating the gold rush to the Fraser River, and had turned his interest to the steamers. He had found that the water routes were interrupted by portages around shallow stretches. Several places between Portland and the Cascades, between there and The Dalles, and on the upper river the freight had to be shifted to little railroad lines, then shifted back to the boats. There were more than a dozen individual boat owners, in cutthroat competition, and the portage men gouged them so that everyone was losing money.

"What they needed was organization," Mitchell said. "So I went to Ruckle and Olmstead who had two of the portages, then Ainsworth and I went to the boatmen and we all put together the Union Transportation Company, and everybody can make something. We're capitalized at a hundred and seventy-two thousand, five hundred. Three hundred and fifty shares were issued and split among those who came in, and I took twenty shares for my part, untangling the mess."

"Beautiful." Davie felt the glow of pride in the magic of Mitchell's ability to bring men together. It was only Wells Fargo who had not fallen under his spell. He wanted to ask again about the Holladay developments, but between the thought and the words he dropped into sleep, and did not know when Mitchell went out softly, on the balls of his feet.

The next morning Mitchell came early and helped Davie up and into the chair at the front window to watch the soldiers head out in search of the Piutes. It was very unlike the ragged, drunken column of volunteers of which Davie had been a member. Jack Hays led them, riding his famous black horse and looking every inch the Texas Ranger he had been before he came to California. Behind him trooped his mixed command. Two hundred and fifty mounted militia, then Major Hungerford and his Sierra Battalion, next the company of regulars from the Presidio, and finally Captain Storey and his Virginia Rifles.

While Davie watched, impressed, Judge David Terry stood with John Newman and Marion Boniface and sneered. "Look at that Army. With that many men I could take San Francisco today, and they're going chasing a handful of half-starved savages . . . All those guns . . . if I had those guns the Comstock would be in our pocket."

Boniface looked, and whistled thoughtfully, his eyes on the figure of the colonel as he dropped out of sight over the crest of the divide.

"Maybe we can have them after a bit," he mused. "When Jack gets through with the Piutes he won't need them any more. And if I know Jack he won't be anxious to lug them all the way back over the mountains."

Terry snorted at him. "Did you ever know anybody to get anything away from the Army?"

The attorney's eyes were beginning to glow with his idea. "I knew Jack pretty well when he was sheriff. When he comes back I'll have a talk with him. Don't forget he's a Texan. I can point out that there are a bunch of Southerners here who would have gone after the Indians and saved him the trouble . . . if they had had the proper arms."

Terry was shaking his head, but with less and less certainty as Boniface went on:

"He knows you and he doesn't know most of the northern men. You were a judge, a responsible citizen. Why wouldn't he leave the guns in your care? Where else on the mountain could he store them? At least it's worth a try."

Still Terry was skeptical. As much faith as he had in Boniface's powers of argument he could not really believe the military could be persuaded to drop such a windfall into his lap. But he could almost taste those guns.

"Tell me something else, Judge. If these arms are added to what you have, how will your strength compare with the opposition?"

Terry chuckled. "There isn't any opposition . . . organized, that is . . . except a Tammany Hall type called Tom Peasley. He put together a volunteer fire department but there are only about sixty of them. They can't put up much of a fight."

Boniface was not satisfied. "But there are a lot of northern sympathizers. When the showdown comes what will they do?"

"Nothing." Terry was contemptuous. "Look, Marion, the key is in the difference between how the North and the South think. We know that if slavery is outlawed our economy will collapse. We know you can't grow cotton without slaves, and without cotton what have we got? So we're fighting for our lives . . . our way of living, yes, but for our actual survival. We'll shoot if we have to. The North is not threatened. They'll go on about their business whether or not the South withdraws, so they're indifferent, except for a small hard core of fanatic abolitionists. There'll be no real contest. And up here we have another advantage. Most of the miners are foreigners, immigrants or the sons of immigrants and they won't care who runs the mines as long as they get paid for working. Sure, the majority are probably against us, but they don't care enough to fight with the will we have."

With the possibility before him that Boniface might be able to pass a miracle and secure the guns that would give him a clear dominance over the mountain that was now largely stripped of arms, Terry was impatient while they waited for Hays's return.

He counted the lagging days until a single rider on an exhausted horse rode back. The Piutes had been cornered at Pyramid Point and a battle joined. Many Indians had been killed and the rest driven into the desert in a rout. But the fight had cost. Among the white men killed was the popular Captain Storey.

When Hays finally brought his troops in Boniface corralled him and took him to Newman's house, to celebrate with a drink, he said, and to relax after the campaign.

He made a good deal of how tiring all the travel as well as the fighting must have been, and how unnecessary. Over his glass he said as if it were a fresh idea:

"You know, Jack, if Terry here had had arms enough he could have done this job without your having to come rushing all the way across the mountains. This town is so remote . . . it takes so long to get help here . . . Suppose this kind of thing happened again and the Indians surprised Virginia City. If they had attacked this time right after they hit the scouting party everybody in these camps would have been dead before you got here.

"Now, instead of hauling all that weight back over that trail, if you could leave the guns here in Terry's care that kind of risk wouldn't arise again."

Hays knew Terry as well as he knew Boniface and respected him for his stand in the southern cause. He also knew that Terry's was the only disciplined organization on the mountain, and Boniface's argument made very good sense to him.

When he took his command back to California he went largely unencumbered. He left seven hundred guns and a heavy load of ammunition with David Terry.

With that bonanza they need now only wait for the election in the fall, when the nation would, on Tuesday, November 6, 1860, choose between a pro- and anti-slavery President. The Comstock was theirs for the taking. Terry went down to the bay with Boniface to press the work there.

CHAPTER NINE

William Stewart came thundering up the hospital stairs and barging into Davie's room raging. Davie was out of bed, spending his days in the chair by the window, kept from going out of his mind at his inactivity by Mitchell. Mitchell had opened himself as he never had before, talking about the widening range of his activities, and for the first time Davie understood how he had risen from the desperate days when Aurelia had refused to let him mortgage the ranch, when they had lost the Pacific Express and then the Alta, in six short years, to a position of apparent unlimited wealth.

The explanation came when Davie again asked about Ben Holladay. "What's your real connection with him?" he wanted to know. "Are you his partner or what?"

Mitchell raised a quizzical eyebrow. "You never did have a real handle on the way financing works, but it's basically simple. You see, there are two kinds of banking operations . . . one, the publicly owned institutions which take in deposits from their customers and loan the money out to business firms who need short-term loans. The way we did in Stockton. Then there are private individuals, in England they're called merchant bankers, who handle money the way a merchant handles goods. They use their own funds to supply capital for big projects—governments, states, cities. They'll buy a block of government bonds, at a discount, sell them to the public at full value, and the difference is their profit. Or they'll act as 'finders' . . . Someone with cash to invest will pay to be put in touch with someone who needs a loan and the one who needs the loan will pay to have the money found. The 'finder' collects at both ends.

"Ben Holladay, for instance, he's a perfect customer for a merchant banker, which is what I am. He's always going into something new, always short of cash . . . and we're doing very well together."

"All right, all right, I see that, but Mitch, where did you get all the money to loan? All your real estate deals can't have netted you that much."

"Of course not. I don't back Ben with my personal money, I only guarantee his credit. When I went to Europe I made connections that Ben doesn't have, and I borrow for him . . . from Belmont or the Rothschilds, the Seligmans, the Jecker brothers or one of the English houses like the Hambros. There's all kinds of money to be had if you know how to look for it."

The idea made Davie nervous and it told in his voice, in the shake of his head. "This guarantee . . . How do you know you can trust Holladay? From what I hear he's a pretty fast operator."

Mitchell nodded. "That he is, Davie, but he's also very shrewd, he knows that if he wants to keep expanding he'll always need fresh money, and that I'm the source of it. I'm the agent for all these foreign outfits. If he double-crosses me he's dead. Don't worry about . . ."

Both of them started as Bill Stewart stormed the room, without greeting, slammed his hat on the bed and yelled, "He got the guns. God damn Terry . . . God damn Hays . . . he gave him the guns . . . seven hundred guns . . . Damn him for a fool and a traitor . . . in command of Federal troops . . . in possession of Federal arms . . . He had no business turning those guns over to the damned Copperheads . . . The most dangerous thing that's happened to us yet . . . We've got to get hold of those guns . . ."

Mitchell Randolph was not impressed. Looking from Stewart to Davie, Davie with his mouth suddenly clamped tight, half-rising out of his chair, he said mildly:

"Do you expect the judge to start shooting today? Or tomorrow." *Tomorrow* was said on a falling note as if there were only the two choices, but instead of quieting them it drew an angry outburst from Davie, another from Stewart.

"No. Not today—not tomorrow. But there's big trouble coming in the East. You know that. And when it does, then you can look for David Terry to haul out his guns and grab for this mountain. And who is there to stop him? Tom Peasley and sixty firemen?"

He glared at Mitchell, challenging him to answer until Mitchell sighed and told him:

"I think if I felt that way I'd ask the Union Army to send over a counterforce."

"Ask the Army . . . You know what good that would do? With Johnson more southern than Terry and Governor Downey even worse? They're going to put anybody in Terry's way?"

"I wasn't thinking of San Francisco. I meant to ask Washington."

"Oh sure. Washington is crawling with Southerners, and the rest of the bastards are asleep. They don't know what Nevada means in a showdown. Don't even care. How do you get through to them, tell me that."

"Money usually manages to get listened to. Use a little leverage."

"And what does that mean?"

"Go through Wells Fargo. The last thing they want is California and Nevada splitting off from the country, breaking their connection with their eastern headquarters. Davie here could swing it, when he's better. Take his hat in his hand like a good little loyal errand boy and go tell McLane that Washoe is teetering on the edge of anarchy and that you need Federal troops in here if he doesn't want to see the mine quit making him money."

Stewart was cooling down, listening, but he said dubiously, "McLane is from Baltimore, I don't know which side he's on."

"He's on Wells Fargo's side. He'll tell his bosses in New York and they'll bear down on Washington and you'll have your own army in no time."

When Stewart had left, admitting that it was worth a try and saying he would get a letter ready for Davie to take to San Francisco, Davie barely waited until the door closed behind him before he jumped on Mitchell.

"With my hat in my hand like a good little errand boy. What are you trying to do, swiping at me like that? Why?"

"Because, by God, I want you with me. What do you think I've been doing all week . . . trying to get you excited like you used to be, to have some fun out of your life. You going to stay a lackey for that meat-grinder company forever?"

Davie did not know whether to stay mad, or laugh at Mitchell's confession. Always, always, Randolph was maneuvering people, and trying to fight back Davie knew he sounded stuffy and could not help it.

"I don't think being Wells Fargo's general agent for all of Washoe is being a lackey. And at least I know I won't suddenly turn around and find the ground cut out from under me."

Mitchell dropped the hoods of his eyes and sat for a long moment watching Davie, then he stood up quietly, put on his hat, said, "Maybe . . . I'll be by tomorrow," and left.

Davie spent a bad night with his conscience. Why, it asked, did they argue this way? Why did he fight Mitchell so? Yes, he had been tempted, more and more through the week as the skein of Mitchell's web was unrolled for him to see. Yes, it would be fun to have a real part, working with Mitchell, not for somebody. What if Mitchell did use him? He always had and it had always benefited both of them. The fluke of his not telling Davie when he was going to Europe was not a betrayal, for it was Mitchell himself who was betrayed by the Alta partners. So why had he flung it at Mitchell again, like a slap in the face? And what was there, really, pushing them apart?

He apologized the next day. Mitchell shrugged it off and said no more about Davie leaving Wells Fargo, and the day after they went over the mountains together, Davie carrying Bill Stewart's urgent argument and Mitchell turning off at Sacramento for another trip to Oregon.

Davie caught the night boat for the bay, still feeling weak enough that he slept through the trip and then through the following day at the Oriental Hotel. So it was the second morning before he walked into the Parrott Building and up to McLane's office.

The superintendent welcomed him, poured brandies and asked after his health, but his first interest was in news. Davie found that he had to get McLane's questions answered and out of the way before he could count on the man's attention to Stewart's letter.

When he reported that Williams Station had been rebuilt and staffed McLane wanted to know if anyone had found out why it had been attacked in the first place.

Davie told him, "The handlers' own fault. Williams was away and the hands caught three Piute women swimming in the river. They raped them, then shut them up in the harness shed. When the women didn't get back to camp one of the braves tracked them, talked to them through the locked door, but he couldn't break it open alone. He went back to Winnemucca for help but the old chief didn't want trouble with the whites and said that when Williams came back he would take it up with him. That didn't satisfy the husbands, so they stirred up Winnemucca's nephew and some feisty young braves to ride to the station, rescue the women and revenge them."

He had to stop and rest, tired by the return of anger at the handlers' stupidity that had cost so many lives. He sipped the brandy, then went on.

"I'm not proud of my part either. Bill Stewart told us not to go beyond the station. I should have been able to hold the party there until Bill heard from Winnemucca, but I let myself get talked into chasing off like a damned fool. So the Indian scouts saw us and called on the tribe, and we got ourselves ambushed for no good reason at all."

"Hindsight," McLane sighed. "A lot of our Indian troubles could have been avoided . . . but what made you go, against Stewart's advice?"

Davie had a stray wish that Mitchell could hear this question, hear McLane putting something other than Wells Fargo's interest first in importance.

"Williams Station was my responsibility," he said. "I had to see that the Pony didn't find himself in trouble."

McLane was pleased by the answer, but he still had questions, asking next if Washoe was generally back to normal. That gave Davie the opening he had been watching for.

"Most of the mines have reopened," he said, "but so many of the miners who ran out aren't back that production is still slow. And there is serious trouble coming between the Northerners and Southerners there. Bill Stewart sent you a letter about it."

He handed the letter across and sat back while McLane read it. McLane's eyebrows climbed as he followed the pages and when he finished he laid them on the desk as if they might explode, and looked at Davie squarely.

"Do you agree with this?"

"I most certainly do. Those guns in Terry's hands, with nothing to oppose him, are dynamite. I don't know why Hays gave them to him, but both he and General Johnson are southern and maybe he was told to do it over here. It doesn't matter. They're there and it's damned dangerous."

McLane poked a finger at the pages, shoving them farther from him without really knowing it. "Your friend Randolph was over there to see you. What does he say?"

Davie frowned. "He called the Knights a bunch of schoolboys playing games, but he's wrong there. Louis, *they are not harmless children.* Bill Stewart is no scarehead, you know that. You'd better believe him."

"Politics." McLane grimaced. "They're not my bent. But we certainly do not want the Comstock, the West Coast, taken out of the

237

Union. I'll do what I can. Tell Stewart that when you go back, but you'd better stay down here and rest for a while."

Davie left the express office much relieved. Mitch might laugh at Terry, but for himself, the threat was very real. Next, with business taken care of, he wanted to see Aurelia, thank her for worrying about him and reassure her that he was on the mend, but almost subconsciously he wanted to talk to her about Mitchell's strange blindness to the threat of the secessionists. He did not want to see her in the office, he wanted an evening with her, so he spent the day resting, had an early dinner, then walked across the extended Montgomery Street.

By the time he reached the corner of Bryant it was nearly dark and as he turned into the side street a hack drew up before the Randolph house. A man stepped out, helped a woman down, then a second man followed and the three of them moved up the steps onto the shallow porch. Davie stopped. The woman walked like Aurelia, although it was too dark to see her face. Then the door opened and the yellow light from inside showed her and her companions. The first man was Marion Boniface. The second one was Judge David Terry.

Boniface being there he could understand. But Terry . . . Davie had thought Terry was still on the mountain. It was surprise enough to see him in San Francisco but to find him going into the Randolph house was very upsetting.

He stood in the shadow, uncertain what to do. As he hesitated a second hack stopped before the house and then a third. It must be a party, he thought, but then as the arrivals went into the house he saw that they were all men. Aurelia was the only woman. Seven men and Aurelia. A poker game?

When the newcomers had been admitted and the empty hacks pulled away impulse made Davie go around the house and knock lightly on the kitchen door. He hoped Aurelia might answer it and he could arrange to see her after her guests were gone, but it was Nora who opened, and stared at him with startled eyes.

"Davie . . . where'd you come from? You just about back from the grave, the way I hear it."

"Come back to haunt you." He grinned at her and then as she backed inside he reached for her wrist and said in a low voice, "I know Aurelia has company and I don't want to meet them but . . ."

"You sure enough don't want to meet them." It was a whisper but strong with vehemence. "They're bad . . . real bad."

He said sharply, "Bad how, Nora?"

She looked over her shoulder, then moved close to him. "Bad as can be. Oh, Davie, you know what they're up to? They're fixing to steal California. That's right, take California and make it a new country. A slave country."

Davie drew a harsh breath. "Aurelia is mixed up in that?"

"Way over her head. That lawyer she works for, he's got her all twisted up with his evil eye."

"Nora, does Mitchell know about this?"

"I don't say he do, I don't say he don't. He's not around here much, and when he is I dasn't say anything to make more trouble between them. But Davie, maybe you can talk to her. You tell her to stop this crazy stuff before the sheriff and the soldiers come and take her away. She'll listen to you. She don't listen at all when I tell her."

"Go get her, bring her out here."

"She won't come now. She bites off my head if I go near that parlor when they're here. You go sit in the pantry until they leave. They won't stay long. They never do."

He took a chair into the pantry. Beyond the closed door he could hear the murmur of voices, not clear enough to make out many words but he did hear a loud toast to the Republic of the Pacific. He waited, sweating with nervous impatience and the hour they were there seemed like a whole night. Finally he heard the scrape of chairs being shoved back, a round of good nights, then the closing of the front door. Still he stayed where he was, wondering if Mitchell himself, for all his scoffing, was a party to the conspiracy, trying to frame his words to warn her, to make her withdraw from this adventure.

Then Nora's soft voice called to him. "It's all right now. She's by herself in there."

Aurelia was watching out of the front window when he came from the kitchen. She heard him and turned, and surprise held her for a moment. Then she ran to him, reaching for his hands, lifting her mouth for his kiss.

"My dear . . ." She laid her head against his chest. "Oh, it is good to see you walk in here. Mitchell sent a man to tell me you were going to be all right but . . ."

"What was Judge Terry doing in this house?" He had not meant to begin that way, nor in so tight a voice, and he groaned inwardly as the smile went out of her eyes and she bridled.

"Why shouldn't he be here?"

"Aurelia." Urgency softened his tone to pleading. "Don't you know what they've dragged you into? Don't you understand what this Pacific Republic plot means?"

"Oh." She smiled again. "So Nora's been scaring you."

"Not Nora. I accidentally saw Terry come in. I know all about his plan to take the West Coast out of the Union, break up the country. But whatever Mitchell says, you must not involve yourself in this."

Her eyes opened wide and she sounded genuinely shocked. "Why, Davie, I thought you approved of my working to help the Californians."

"Helping them, yes. But this other is something else again. This is treason, Aurelia. Terry is a traitor to his country and if you join with him you will be a traitor too."

She took a step back from him, flaring. "I am not a traitor to any country of mine. Nobody asked me if I wanted to be a citizen of the United States. No one asked any of the Californians. The gunboats and soldiers just came in and grabbed our land. Then the politicians came. And the squatters. I think I have the right to fight back. I think the South has the right to fight. When an oppressive government has a stranglehold on the people they have the right to revolt against it. Even the United States rebelled and broke off from the British, didn't it? Now we are going to do the same, and make a new country where we can all live under laws that are fair to everybody."

He looked at her helplessly, confused. She sounded as blind as Mitchell, but more dangerously so. "A slave country, Aurelia? Where men and women and children are owned, like horses and cows? Nora and Joe . . . Do you call it fair to everybody when somebody can own them, hold the power of life and death over them? Shouldn't they have rights too?"

She tossed her head. "Nora and Joe are unusual. Davie, you don't know anything about slaves . . . or *peóns*. I do. I grew up with them, and we took good care of them. We protected them. They can't survive by themselves, so we depend on each other and everybody is better off. Now, when this new country is born the Californians will have their ranches back. They'll be part of the government. They and the Southerners can work together for what's best for all."

"Oh, I'll bet on that." Davie was suddenly out of patience with her. "Sure. Half the government out here now is southern, and I haven't noticed that they've done so much for you people. They're making you a cat's paw, Aurelia. They're using you. And they'll get you into the kind of trouble that even you can't wiggle out of. Doesn't Mitchell see that?"

She laughed at him harshly, as put out as he. "When did you see me afraid of trouble? Mitchell, he just laughs at Terry, so I haven't bothered to tell him I'm working with them. Go ahead and tell him if you want to, and he'll laugh at you too. For myself, I know I am right and I am going to keep on doing everything I can for *my* new country."

Davie Stuart gave up. He could see no way to reach her now and if he kept trying they would be at each other's throats. He would have to go away and think it out when he was not so mad. He nodded, not daring to speak again, and stalked into the hall, toward the front door.

Behind him he heard her call, shrill and commanding. "Davie Stuart, you come back here."

He did not turn. He went out into the night and closed the door firmly after him.

CHAPTER TEN

Davie Stuart had come down with the intention McLane later suggested, of staying on the bay until his strength built up again, but lying wide-eyed in the dark hotel room that night he gradually changed his mind.

He was dreadfully worried about Aurelia. Why, as smart as she had proved herself to be, could she not see the immorality of a slave state? He made an effort to think it through, boiling it down until it distilled into the difference in their backgrounds. She had grown up in a class society which he supposed honestly believed that their *peóns* were of a lower mentality, that they must be taken care of by a more sophisticated master. He had his roots in a Quaker childhood, seeing his mother's quiet help to the Underground Railroad that spirited black shadows into the North. He had grown up knowing Joe as his equal.

Who was actually right? He personally loved the individual freedoms that had been taken for granted in the mountains. He even resented the regimentation it required to live in a city. He had been formed by Mitchell's credo of live and let live. But slavery was a very old institution. Why did he reject the idea so out of hand, of two nations, one slave and one free? Had Bill Stewart made a zealot out of him, instead of Terry being the zealot? Would Mitchell's tolerance extend to accepting two such nations as reasonable? He did not believe it. He believed that slavery must be as repugnant to the man who had come out of a European ghetto as it was to himself.

So what was he to do about Aurelia? To talk about secession was one thing, it was done openly, it was even fashionable to be a parlor rebel, but if the election went against the Southerners, if the Knights of the Golden Circle did try to take military action, would not the Union Government be obliged to move against them? One thing surely would be done. The leaders would be rounded up, arrested, imprisoned, if not shot as traitors. He wondered if a letter to Mitchell saying this might help. But even as he thought it he knew that he could not put Aurelia's name on paper in connection with Terry, supply written proof of her involvement. It could fall into the wrong hands. Nor could he ask Bill Stewart's advice without risking that he would implicate her if Terry moved.

By morning he knew that he could not solve the quandry alone and he could think of only one place to turn. He went back to Sun Mountain.

Still he hesitated for two days, not trying to work, spending the time in the saloons listening to the talk. Virginia City was still largely empty, the miners not yet all returned and the mines working only part time. The Pony Express, disrupted by the Piute trouble, was not yet running again and the telegraph line was down. Cut off from the world the town was more restless and the saloons crowded, the arguments louder.

The national election was coming closer. Most of the men on the mountain were Democrats although the party was split into northern and southern factions and the Republicans, the new group that had risen from the wreckage of the Whigs, seemed not to have a chance of winning. The main topic of the talk was whether the Democratic nominee for President would be for or against slavery.

Every time Davie heard a Southerner with a few whiskeys in him ranting about the northern oppression he thought of Aurelia, and on the second night he jammed on his hat, left the saloon and tramped down to Julia Bulette's house.

Julia, the *Territorial Enterprise* claimed, was the only civilizing influence in Virginia City, a person apart. She and her girls were not only respected, Julia held a place of honor in every parade, at every celebration. She rode as a queen in the carriage that led the marching men of the fire department. Her house was the best furnished on the mountain and none of the toughs were allowed inside. She served only the best wines and brandies and permitted neither argument nor profanity.

Davie was no stranger there, but in the time he had spent in her hospital they had become good personal friends. Her warm brown eyes looked him over critically and she said in disapproval:

"You're still too peaked to be back here and you promised me you'd go down there and rest until you were strong again. You don't keep your word very well, do you?"

But she presented her cheek for his kiss and squeezed his arm to take the sting out of her scolding.

"I meant to," he told her, "but I found something going on down there that I don't know what to do about. I came running back to you for help."

"Oh, that's different. Well, come along and tell Julia about it over some coffee."

She led him into her private sitting room, shoved him down on the horsehair sofa and went on to the kitchen. She brought back a tray, a silver coffee urn, a setting of her treasured Canton cups and a bottle of brandy, put the load on a mahogany sideboard, laced the coffee with brandy and brought the cups, settling down beside him.

"Now, honey, what's troubling my boy?"

Now that he was here he did not know where to start. He took a long pull of the drink, grateful that it warmed his tense insides, and said tentatively:

"I don't know what your politics are."

She gave him a quizzical glance. "In my business a girl isn't supposed to have any, but as a matter of fact, while I come from New Orleans I don't like slavery and I don't like this secession talk. I guess Tom Peasley is responsible for that. Is that what's bothering you? You can't make up your mind?"

He shook his head. "No. I think your way, but I have a friend in San Francisco who doesn't, and she's letting herself in for trouble, bad trouble."

At the word *she* Julia listened more closely, not prompting him when he stalled, waiting quietly until he fumbled his way on.

He made several false starts before he could tell her about Aurelia, then he told a great deal more than he intended. In doing so he told a lot about himself and his relationship with her and with Mitchell.

"When I found out how deep she is in with Terry I tried to make her see where he's wrong, the danger she's in. I couldn't get through to her. Julia, what am I going to do about her?"

Julia went back to the sideboard before she answered, filled his cup again, this time with more brandy, brought it to him, then sat down in a chair where she could watch him directly.

"Do you mind if I pry, Davie?"

"If it will help figure this out, go ahead."

"How long have you been in love with her?"

He began to laugh, then stopped and said with a strained tone, "What makes you ask that?"

"The warm way you talk about her, your concern, your taking her as your responsibility. Davie, you may be the best express man in the country but my business is understanding men. You'd be surprised how many come in here to talk about their wives and sweethearts. This mountain can be a terribly lonely place."

He said nothing for a long while, drinking from the cup, not looking at her, and finally lifted and dropped his shoulders.

"I told you, she's Mitchell Randolph's wife . . . the man who spent all that time with me in your hospital . . . Anyhow, what can I do to get her away from Terry?"

She said softly, "I don't see that you can do anything. From what you say she is strong minded and her heart is with the Californians. There's no denying that they've had their land stolen out from under them, with the government's acquiescence. I'm pretty cynical about their chance of doing any better under another American rule, but the judge can be a convincing persuader, and nobody suggests he isn't dedicated."

"But . . ."

She held up a hand. "I know. You're a man, and consciously or unconsciously men believe they understand major questions better than women. I'll grant we're apt to be more emotional, but we do think, and do come up with answers. She has come up with hers. Let it alone, Davie. Forget it if you can, for there is nothing else you can do."

The bell over the front door tinkled and with a little show of annoyance she left him to go into the main parlor to see that the new guest found a partner to his liking.

Davie was glad to break off the talk at that point. Julia had no magic formula to solve the problem that had brought him here, and indeed she had made matters worse by showing him still another alley that he did not know how to get out of.

He pushed to his feet and headed for the door, wanting to take his troubles away and walk alone with them through the dark bluster of the night.

Julia came back before he had crossed the room, with a big man looming behind her, ducking his head to come through the opening. She stepped aside, saying:

"In case you don't know each other, Tom Peasley, Davie Stuart."

Peasley had an enormous energy, an enormous strength. Davie had seen him around the camp but oddly had not met him, and he offered his hand half-heartedly, trying to edge around him. The fireman's grip was so hard that Davie winced. The man laughed, a loud burst, and clapped him on the shoulder, knocking him off balance.

"Tom." Julia was sharp. "Take it easy, Davie's the boy who had the poisoned arrow."

"I know who he is." Peasley's grin was wide and appealing. "You're kind of famous, mister, the way you beat the venom."

Davie nodded absently and tried again to leave but Peasley kept his hand.

"Don't go. I want to talk to you. Bill Stewart told me you took a letter down to McLane. What did he say?"

Davie was hesitant to talk about that errand here, but Julia had declared herself, and if Stewart had already mentioned it he should probably answer. Also, through his personal turmoil, his professional mind pushed him to stay. He should know Peasley and this was a good chance to get acquainted.

Entirely on his own Tom Peasley had built a volunteer fire department on the mountain that now numbered six companies and sixty-nine men. He had talked money out of the mineowners and built a brick firehouse with a warning bell on top that had proved its value time and again. A natural political animal, he had surrounded himself with men from New York and gathered them into an organization loyal to the Union, intensely loyal to Peasley himself. Proud of his department, proud of the mountain and personally resentful of any threat to its security, he was its self-appointed watchdog.

"He's writing to Washington as Bill asked," Davie said, and turned back into the room.

Peasley followed him and dropped into a chair while Julia went to bring him a cup.

"How long do you think it's going to take?"

"I couldn't even guess at that. What I don't know about the ways of politics and armies would fill a library."

Peasley looked him over with a dour speculation and rumbled, "They'd better push it through fast if they want to hold this territory. Those Southerners are spoiling for trouble and as long as they've got those guns over our heads we've got to walk soft. We haven't a chance against them right now, and time's getting short."

They sat drinking and talking, Peasley doing most of the talking and Davie felt the pull of his magnetism. Almost intentionally, with a what-the-hell surrendering to the present insolubility of his private enigmas, Davie got drunk.

When he finally decided to leave he was unsteady getting up. Peasley was quick, coming to his feet, looming over him, taking his arm, saying:

"I'll walk along with you."

He kissed Julia and steered Davie out with easy solicitude.

The cool night wind helped and Peasley steadied him as they climbed the steep sidewalk to C Street. Davie would have gone on up to his rooms but Peasley stopped at the corner, holding his arm.

"I like you, Stuart. Bill says good things about you. I'll buy you a drink at the International and let's talk about you joining the department."

Davie did not want any more to drink but he liked Peasley and suddenly he dreaded the idea of being alone with his devils. They dodged through the string of moving ore wagons toward the hotel and walked single file along the narrow sidewalk, Davie in front, now without Peasley's support.

Just short of the saloon Davie saw Langford Peel in the middle of the walk and he stopped. Peel was one of those brawlers, killers like Sam Brown who called themselves Chiefs. He was drunk and swaying. Anyone wanting to pass had to step down into the street and go around him.

Behind Davie, Peasley said, "Go on, go on," and the big man's hand in his back shoved him ahead. Davie stumbled and bumped into the gunman.

Peel swore and reached for his gun, but Peasley's hand shot past Davie, caught Peel's shoulder and spun him against the stone entryway. Davie stumbled aside and before he could take the one step to catch his balance Peasley had lifted Peel off the sidewalk, shaken him in the air and thrown him into the road.

Peel lay on his back, stunned. Then he lurched up on one elbow, moved again for his gun, did not quite draw, and suddenly passed out.

Davie held his breath. Peasley was not armed, but stood balanced on his left foot, his right ready to swing. When Peel lay still he turned Davie in through the door, saying:

"I wish he'd touched that gun. I'd have broken his hand."

Davie stepped aside for Peasley to come even with him. "My God, Tom, why did you risk it?"

"Because I don't like that breed."

"He'll look for you now. He'll bushwhack you."

"No he won't." Peasley's grin was wide and easy. "He knows if he did the boys at the firehouse would skin him alive."

CHAPTER ELEVEN

Again Davie lay awake through what was left of the night, his mind worrying at his relationship with Aurelia, his rights and duties concerning her. Yes, he did love her. That had been at the back of his wanting to protect her from Mitchell, then from Boniface, and now had him agonizing over how to protect her from herself.

One possible avenue finally occurred to him. He thought of all the Californians she had gathered and sheltered at the ranch, all the people she had helped through Boniface's office. He had no doubt that she had enlisted them to follow Terry. Therefore it was not just she as an individual who was in danger. Hundreds of her beloved Californians could find themselves in a lot deeper trouble than the mere loss of land meant. He wondered if he could appeal to her on this score. He knew that she had no fear for herself. Time and again he had seen her courage. But if he could make her understand that her actions now might bring the final destruction down on her family and friends she might withdraw from the conspirators.

He wrote her a long, sober letter, harping on the grave danger she was courting. Then in a mood of gnawing frustration he went down to the brick tower and joined the fire department.

He went not because he could add appreciably to their ranks as a fire fighter, but because he needed companionship. He liked Peasley and found that he liked the other boys there. They were all young, a long way from home, themselves lonely in the nearly all male society, like those he had known in the early placer camps. Most of Davie's life had been spent in communities very short of women and he knew the value of Julia Bulette and her girls, but you could not spend your life in the D Street cribs. At the firehouse they drank, they played poker, they talked politics.

Davie had little background in the area of politics and before he had met Bill Stewart had had only a vague notion of the power fights in the East. Peasley's firemen had mostly grown up in New York under the wing of Tammany Hall. They had been raised Democrats but because of the split over slavery they were leaning toward the new Republican party. Davie learned from them and soon surprised even himself with a new, enthusiastic partisanship.

Then the news came that Wells Fargo had brought enough pressure on Washington to make them send help. Colonel Patrick Connor was being sent with the 3rd California Regiment to Nevada, to establish a military post on the Carson. The firehouse celebrated and Davie felt a swelling of pride in his first political act. It had been Mitchell's idea, Stewart had written the letter to initiate the action, but it was Davie Stuart who had convinced Louis McLane of the need of this protection.

Connor was a tough forty-year-old officer who had distinguished himself against the Mexicans at Buena Vista, and he moved fast. He established a camp, laid out a fort to be called Churchill, and with work under way he rode up the mountain and talked to Bill Stewart, Tom Peasley, and Davie Stuart, because Davie represented Wells Fargo, and sent a command to the Southerners to bring him the Federal property they held, the seven hundred guns left by Hays.

Terry had just come back from the Coast, made bolder by the progress he had found there. He felt that he had enough men to hold his fortified buildings, and ignored the order. Connor took his men up the hill, surrounded the Southerners and called on them to surrender.

It was one thing to terrorize the camp with his threats when there was no opposing force. It was another to defy trained soldiers while the Union was still intact. Terry and his lieutenants slipped away down through the mine workings and the rest of the Knights there opened the doors and brought out the guns.

Connor then demanded that they swear an oath of loyalty to the government, and when half of them refused he herded them down to the fort and put them to filling sandbags for the growing earthworks.

Davie Stuart wrote a long and gleeful account to Mitchell. *So we can now relax for a while and wait to see who is nominated for*

President, he finished, sealed it and added it to the packet being made up in the express office. He also wrote to Aurelia, although she had not answered his earlier letter.

Every day the date of the Republican convention drew closer the firehouse debate raged hotter. Some contended that Salmon P. Chase should be the man, some chose William H. Seward and some Simon Cameron. They made bets among themselves, and although Chase had been in the forefront of the abolitionist movement for years, Seward pulled ahead as their odds-on favorite.

On the day when the Pony Express was expected to bring the long-waited result of the voting at the convention held at the Wigwam in Chicago all of the firemen wanted to go down with Davie, to read the name as soon as it was pulled out of the mochila, but Tom Peasley roared his order forbidding them.

"Nobody but Davie goes, boys. Everybody leaves here, suppose there's a fire, and wouldn't that be great. And it's not fair for some to go and some stay. Just Davie, like he always does, and you set your minds to that. But"—he shook a big finger at Davie—"this one time you break your rule and come here first, before you stop at your office. I want us to be the first in Virginia City to know who we've got to work for."

When the Pony arrived Davie took off upcanyon as if he were one of the relay riders himself, breaking open the dispatch and reading it on the way. He threw himself off his horse at the firehouse and ran in, puzzled and discouraged by the news he brought.

The noise inside stopped, the poker chairs scraped back and Peasley shouted before he was through the door.

"Is it Seward?"

Davie shook his head, out of breath, and Peasley swore.

"Damn, don't tell me they picked Chase?"

Davie held out the slip of flimsy and managed between gasps, "Somebody I don't know about . . . named Lincoln . . . Abraham Lincoln."

There was a bewildered silence and then a hubbub.

"Who the hell is Abraham Lincoln?"

A disgusted voice said, "Some backwoods congressman or something from Illinois. All I heard was that he debated with Douglas on the Kansas question a couple of years ago."

The room was dismayed. Democrats in Nevada outnumbered Republicans two to one, and how could they hope to pull the necessary votes from the bigger party with such an unknown candidate?

The noise rose, angry and frustrated. What did the convention think it was doing? Was it trying to throw the election away on purpose? Who even knew anything about the man?

Peasley hammered a ham of a fist on the table and yelled for the floor.

"I don't know anything about him except he's for the Union and against slavery and that's enough for me. I can't do anything for him back there, but boys, it's our job to hold Washoe in the United States, and it's going to be some job now."

It turned out to be all of that, the fierce battle for the mountain and the silver that could finance an army for either North or South.

The divided Democratic party had nominated Stephen A. Douglas for the northern faction and John C. Breckinridge for the southern, and that split, Peasley felt, gave his people at least a fighting chance.

He drove the firemen to work on the mountain, to exhort every Republican, to raise his voice for the new man, to urge every northern Democrat not to waste his vote but to support Lincoln.

Parades and day by day speeches and the dispatches the Pony Express now brought regularly created a rising universal excitement, and as the campaign swept toward its November conclusion Peasley and Stewart wrote letters, sent wires appealing to the Republican leaders on the Pacific Coast for help.

They came, Thomas Fitch to harangue for the dark-horse lawyer who had beaten the elegant Douglas in debate. A huge crowd cheered his eloquence and cheered him louder when in the torchlight procession afterward he rode in the carriage with Tom Peasley and a radiant Julia Bulette.

The Southerners joined the mob that lined the street, to cat-call and boo, but the uniformed firemen with polished axes glinting, reflecting the bright flames, stalked them back into the buildings and the column passed in triumph.

Effective as it was, Fitch's appearance seemed dull compared to the shouting, stomping welcome roused by Thomas Starr King, not only in Virginia City but in the smaller meetings at Gold Hill, Silver City, and even that hotbed of southern activity, Carson City.

It was King who stumped every town in Oregon and California and whose thunderous oratory raised his audiences to a hysterical pitch, who was later credited with saving the Coast for Lincoln.

But the argument that moved Davie most was one he did not hear firsthand. Colonel Edward Baker delivered his Apostrophe to Liberty in a San Francisco theater, and left his audience weeping.

Tom Peasley read it aloud as it was reported in the *Alta,* with tears running down his broad cheeks, and the men in the firehouse wept with him, Davie included. Then the firemen had the speech printed as a poster and tacked to the front of every building along C Street.

Colonel Baker was the darling of the Coast, some said the leading citizen since Broderick's death. The two had been close friends, Baker as flamboyant a lawyer as Marion Boniface. He had been a congressman from Illinois, a colonel in the Mexican War, a friend of Lincoln. Then he had come to California and was now running for Senator of Oregon at the behest of the infant Republican party, covering every settlement in that state on horseback and campaigning for Lincoln as well as for himself.

In Washoe where Terry's policy had been making converts for months because of Washington's vacillations, sentiment began to shift. From all accounts this Lincoln, raised in the back country with little schooling but still giving an account of himself against the skilled and trained, began to sound like their kind of man.

The firehouse began counting noses, but the news the Pony Express brought was mixed, mostly bad. Douglas appeared to be gaining in the northeast, Lincoln had been booed in Kentucky, the East would go for Douglas and the South for Breckinridge. What then was left for Lincoln? Ohio perhaps, Michigan, Indiana, Illinois . . . it was not enough.

Tom Peasley increased his drive. Washoe had to go for Lincoln if no other territory in the nation did. Davie Stuart worked his days in the express office and his nights with the firemen. He had never believed that he could become so dedicated to a political proposition.

They drafted separate lists of miners, dividing those they thought were loyal, those wavering, and those in the southern camp. On the last they wasted no time. They concentrated on the doubtful men, cornering them in the saloons and boardinghouses and underground mine passages. They hammered at their doctrine. All men are equal. In a slave society a laboring man was at a disadvantage in competing with slaves. If the mountain was taken by the Southerners, they threatened, Negroes would be imported to work the mines and the prized four dollars a day that made the miners the highest paid workers in the West would be wiped away.

They did not have the field to themselves. Terry's organization was working just as hard, ignoring the loyalty oath Colonel Connor had imposed on them. Angrily Peasley appealed to the colonel to arrest the Copperheads, but Connor maintained a military neutrality, insisting that during a political campaign every voter was entitled to have his say as long as he did not commit an overt act against the government.

By Election Day the mountain was split into two savage camps. At every polling place the firemen stood armed guard . . . across the doorway from the armed Southerners. There were fights and squabbles and some shooting, but miraculously only two men were wounded and one of those by his own gun as he drew it. The vote was heavy. When it was counted Lincoln had carried the mountain, but by only a few votes.

There was no letup in the ferment of activity and the question hung like a pall, how had the rest of the country gone. The first results came over the bush telegraph from Placerville. Like Nevada, California went to Lincoln by a narrow margin. In Oregon, Baker won the Senate seat and carried Lincoln to victory with him.

Tom Peasley kept his firemen armed, gathered, and ready for violence, expecting Terry to try to take the mountain by force if the anti-slave candidate was elected.

The wait was tense and long. It would take nine days to bring the national result across the country. Then on the night of November 13, Pony Bob whirled past the gates of Fort Churchill shouting that Lincoln was President.

Davie read the dispatch and felt a chill foreboding. Although Lincoln received 180 votes in the Electoral College, he had won less than half of the popular vote against his combined opponents. The minority victory seemed to settle nothing, only to strengthen the promise of bitter times ahead.

Virginia City celebrated anyhow, a howling party at the firehouse, yelling crowds surging up and down C Street, torches and songs and congratulations that the mountain would stay in the Union, if it ever sobered up.

The Southerners had not moved. They kept out of sight. But Terry's threat still hung ominously over the camp . . . waiting.

CHAPTER TWELVE

Aurelia felt the thrill of anticipation as she talked over the election with Marion Boniface. The new President was strongly opposed to slavery. That fact brought the Republic of the Pacific one step closer to reality.

Boniface himself was glowing, crowing. "Lincoln," he laughed. "The luckiest surprise we could have. The best thing that could have happened for us. The crazy rail splitter really put himself out on a limb, harping that no state has the right to withdraw from the Union. Now when they do he's got only two choices, to eat his words and let them go peacefully or try to hold them by force. Force, honey, means war. Just hold your breath for that day, because if it's war in the East the Army will need all of its troops back there. They'll pull out of the coast and leave it undefended, and that's all I ask, that's all Terry asks."

She was nodding, agreeing. "I hate to sound bloodthirsty," she said, "but oh, I hope it comes soon . . . and where is Terry? Still in Virginia City?"

"I think he's already left, going to Texas to raise men there, to be ready for his drive up the coast."

"And then," she said in a triumphant tone, "California and Oregon will be ours and hooray for the Bear Flag."

Mitchell Randolph, too, was pleased with the election. His political interest was business-oriented and he came back from Oregon gratified that Baker would be the senator for the northern state. It meant the end of the hold Senator Joseph Lane had up there, and opened the way for the Union Transportation Company to extend its services to the new mines being developed in western Washington. But that was as far as his enthusiasm for the change in government went.

Being out of the state so much of the time he had paid no attention to his wife's activities except to follow the newspaper stories of her rise in the legal field, of which there were an increasing number.

Aurelia had indeed been busy through the last months. Besides her surreptitious recruiting for the Pacific Republic she had been attending the almost continuous hearings of the Land Commissioners. She had despised Senator Gwin for pretending to protect the original landowners while in effect he saw that the land laws were changed to nullify the treaty with Mexico, she felt the same about Edwin M. Stanton who said of the Californians in open court that he did not believe one word of the "lying thieves," and now she was facing another pair of lawyers representing the Federal Government against the Spanish claimants, Senators Judah Benjamin of Louisiana and Reverdy Johnson of Maryland. She was matching wits there with two of the best legal minds in the land, but to her surprise she and Marion Boniface had won more than half of the cases on the docket.

Her cup of professional joy ran over when after the last hearing Benjamin, who had known Boniface in New Orleans, came clear across the courtroom, tapped Boniface lightly on the chest and laughed ruefully.

"You did all right, Marion," he said, "but it was Mrs. Randolph who beat us."

It was too high praise for her to keep bottled up and in a rare breaking of their agreement to keep out of each other's business she took the story home to Mitchell. He was as pleased as she and proud of her, and told her so, and she laughed back at him, a mischievous giggle.

"You're doing mighty well yourself, from what I hear, Mitchell. Aren't the Randolphs becoming important though."

The next week the Randolphs were invited to a Sunday brunch in honor of the defeated visiting lawyers, Benjamin and Johnson, and Mitchell twitted her.

"Gwin will be there too, you know, a regular nest of enemies, and Boniface will be left out as usual. Do you want to go?"

"Indeed I do." She was emphatic. "Do you think I'd let those pompous crooks keep me away from a party, even one of Jack Talbert's dull 'little affairs'?"

Such "little affairs" were a regular part of life to South Park's self-conscious young society, formal, decorous, falsely hearty, the women separating themselves from the men to gossip and chatter over the problems of running their households, the men hovering over the punch bowl for their own business and political gossip. Aurelia had little affection for any Americans, but she had learned to disguise her boredom, and her reputation as a personality, her growing stature in the legal circle, set her apart, left her a little room to fend off intimacies and remain uninvolved.

The spacious halls were already filled, the laughter noisy when the Randolphs arrived. It was more than a nest of enemies, it was a nest of Southerners, trying to be gay in the face of the election defeat. Many of them Aurelia recognized as Knights and in them she felt a sober tension. She moved through the rooms, speaking to her hostess, accepting a cup of punch, then left Mitchell and went on, nodding and speaking briefly with the ladies as she passed them. With that chore finished she turned slowly, noting who stood in which small knot of men. She located Jack Talbert giving Benjamin a guided tour, found Gwin and Mitchell the center of a group, joking, and saw Talbert steer the visiting lawyer in to join them.

Then she saw Whitney Bedford come from the second room, obviously drunk, and stop in the archway. He glowered at Mitchell and began shouldering his way through the crowd toward him. Aurelia moved quickly, trying to intercept him and avert whatever trouble he would make. Bedford was a speculator who had started construction of an office building on Geary, had lost heavily in silver stocks and raised a loan on the property. Mitchell had bought the mortgage and was foreclosing. She had heard this not from Mitchell but from Boniface, who had told her the two men had had a fist fight in court and Bedford had threatened to kill Mitchell.

Mitchell had his back to the speculator and none of the laughing group noticed the approach of the angry man. A shift of bodies blocked Aurelia long enough that Bedford lurched forward, clamped a hand on Talbert's shoulder and said in a loud voice:

"Jack, I thought you were more choosy."

Talbert shook free, resenting the hand and the drunken words, saying curtly, "You're out of order, Whitney."

"I'm out of order? While you've got a damn turncoat Jew in your house? I'm just out of place. And I'm leaving."

Then Aurelia was there, slipping her hand under Mitchell's arm. He did not look down, did not take his eyes off Bedford who staggered away, bumping through the crowd that gave back, shocked and silent, but the arm felt as rigid as iron.

"I'm sorry this happened here, Jack." Mitchell took Aurelia's hand, bent his elbow and kept hold of her fingers. "We thank you for the punch. Good day."

They were the most comfortable-looking people in the room as they crossed it without hurry. No one else moved, not even lifted a cup to drink, until they had gone through the outside door.

On the street Mitchell seemed to forget Aurelia and his long stride was hard to keep up with. She was winded by the time he ushered her through their own door and she stopped in the hall, sinking into a chair to catch her breath. Mitchell went past without breaking his pace, to the cellaret in the dining room, and poured himself two stiff drinks of brandy. He was tossing down the second when she came in.

"Mitchell," she said, "the man's a fool. Don't let him upset you so."

Looking at her he showed her the dark anger in his eyes. "Damn him. That little act is going to be all over town by night. And everybody who hears it will take that crack at face value. How they all love to tear a man down."

For the first time Aurelia saw a human vulnerability in this man who held everyone at arm's length. She had never expected to be sorry for Mitchell Randolph but she was now and she wanted to make him talk, to get his hurt out into the open where it could be exorcised. She was as angry as he but she smiled at him.

"Which crack, Mitchell, that you are a Jew or that you are a turncoat? What kind of turncoat did he mean?"

He made an ugly mouth. "I don't fit his conception of a bowed-down caricature in a long black coat and a black skullcap, pulling on a long grizzled beard and wringing his hands and wailing like a Shakespearean Shylock. That's what a Jew is."

"So let him think it. He's mad because you took a pound of his flesh . . . his building . . . which wasn't really the kindest thing you've ever done. Why did you?"

"Because he refused to pay back a loan I made him last year. That is not the point . . ."

She interrupted him with a high caw of mockery aimed at Whitney Bedford. "How perfectly typical of the precious American business practice. Mitchell, for God's sake relax and be a Jew. Be proud of it."

His mouth was stiff, giving his words a harsh slur. "No. You don't know what you're talking about. The stigma is too ingrained, even in this country. It undermines and destroys a man. A Jew is despised all over the world, because of the spectacle they make of themselves in that getup, in that prison of tradition they hang onto."

"Mitchell," she pressed him. "Look at this . . . It appears to me that it is a very great achievement you have made here. You are recognized as one of the very best businessmen in California, you are certainly welcome in the most sacrosanct circles of this society. Shouldn't you be proud of that? As a Jew?"

Still he shook his head, lowering it like a tormented bull. "Aurelia, as a Jew I could not have done it. You are fighting prejudice yourself. You have gotten to be a very good lawyer. But you will not be admitted to the bar. Because you are a woman.

"I'll tell you a story. In Europe there was a man named Schonberg. An unusually brilliant man. And he was ostracized. He got on a boat and came to New York. His name loosely translated into French as Belmont, beautiful mountain, and when he landed he was August Belmont. He is now Mr. Society, enormously rich, representative of the Rothschilds and married to the daughter of Commodore Matthew C. Perry. He could not have begun to dream of that as Schonberg. And I, as Mitchell Randolph, am going to do the same thing here."

A sense of loss made her sick. With what difficulty they had come through the years, had beaten out a way of life from hostile truce to an easing of tension, into a period of growing amity. Now as if it were visible material she watched him tighten around himself a thickened armor of untouchability. She did not care that it would probably make him a harder man in the business world, hard practice was the order of the day. What she feared was an end of their accommodation, that she too would again be shut out of his fortress.

CHAPTER THIRTEEN

In December 1860—a month after the election of Lincoln—South Carolina passed an Ordinance of Secession in their state convention. In January 1861, Mississippi, Florida, Alabama, Georgia, and Louisiana followed. On February 1 Texas left the Union.

The government in Washington took no action when Federal property was seized.

On February 8 the southern delegates met in convention at Montgomery, Alabama, and formed a provisional government for the Confederate States of America and on the 18th of the same month Jefferson Davis was elected its provisional President.

President James Buchanan did nothing about any of these moves and from Sun Mountain it became clear that Lincoln, at his inaugural on March 4, would inherit only half a country.

The firehouse was draped in gloom. Terry was gone but that was no relief. He had ridden down the mountain with a few followers, heading for Texas to join the Army forming along the Rio Grande, but he had left John Newman and Dr. McMeans in Washoe to command the Southerners there.

Then the Pony Express rider brought Lincoln's Inaugural Address and Davie read the quotes from the dispatch to the assembled firemen. It proclaimed that the Federal Government would defend its authority and would hold the forts and places in its possession. Yet, said the new President, he had no intention to invade, subjugate, or oppress the seceding states. "You can have no conflict," he told them, "without being yourselves the aggressors."

"What the hell does that mean?" Tom Peasley pounded angrily on the poker table, and a wounded, howling argument broke out.

Was Lincoln not going to make any effort to hold the southern states in the Union? After all their work to elect him was this just another politician like Buchanan, simply out to feather his own nest? What were they supposed to do now?

Stalemated by uncertainty the firemen watched the Southerners take heart and move back into the open. The outcomes of two murders in the following weeks supported them in mocking the Union. One was committed by a woman. Laura Fair kept a hotel called the Tahoe House, catering to Southerners. When a Union man ran the Stars and Stripes up a pole over the hotel Laura first ordered him to take it down, and when he would not she brought out a revolver and shot him. She was arrested, but Crittenden, a leader of the Washoe bar and a Southerner, defended her and she was acquitted. Also acquitted was a gunman named Mayfield who had killed Marshal Blackburn, and whose only defense was that Blackburn was being unfair to the South.

Peasley's firemen raged helplessly and waited impotently while the Southerners strutted.

And then on April 20 the Pony Express brought to Stafford Hall station and Fort Churchill the news that precipitated the nation. Fort Sumter in Charleston Harbor had been fired upon and had fallen to the South. The long-awaited war was upon the country.

Jubilant, the Washoe Southerners prepared a manifesto announcing that the Knights of the Golden Circle were taking Nevada out of the Union to support the new Confederacy. It was held out of circulation while Newman and McMeans, pressured by the impatient Knights, made preparations for a hurried change of plans. They would not wait for Terry and his Texans. The South would need silver *now*, not in several months. They stepped up their drilling in the Gould and Curry. They distributed their arms and ammunition. They would gather their secret force and in a surprise move take Fort Churchill. With that in their possession they could seize the mountain and begin feeding its great wealth into the rebel treasury. Nevada's riches could win the war for the Confederate States.

It was a feasible plot. It would have succeeded but for one man.

Tom Peasley had one southern friend who did not believe in secession, who had come to Peasley asking to join the fire department, complaining that the Knights were trying to recruit him. Peasley had told him to join the Knights, to be his eyes and ears within the secret society, and that man sent a note of warning now, telling the fireman the new plan.

They have the strength to take the fort, and with the guns stored there they can arm a thousand more men and no one on the mountain can stand against them.

Tom Peasley set his firemen up as a committee of safety, and wired the Presidio, where General Sumner, a Union man, had replaced Johnson.

Send us arms to defend against large southern force here. Ship them in plain boxes to resemble shovels. Direct them to Taylor and Company Virginia City, and hurry.

Then he sent Davie riding downcanyon to alert the commander at Fort Churchill. With the outbreak of war Connor and half his regiment had been moved out, and the new officer did not believe the message.

"Stuart," he laughed, "there are scares like this all up and down the coast. Everybody sees a secesh behind every bush. If they do attack here we'll be ready for them, but I'm not going to ride up that mountain until I have to. If they try anything up there, let us know."

Davie rode back cursing such Union Army and government people as this. Were they all blind? Didn't any of them see what Terry saw? No. To them the mountain was no more than a bleak pile of sand and rock with a few thousand miners clinging to it. None of them comprehended that Virginia was the financial balance of the war. So far only Terry had realized that in southern hands the blue ore could offset the entire wealth of the northern states.

He sent a desperation wire of his own to General Sumner, pleading that he contact the War Department for immediate attention.

THERE IS NO GOVERNMENT IN WASHOE. THE DISTRICT IS FILLED WITH DISLOYAL, ARMED MEN. THE TIME HAS COME TO ORGANIZE THE TERRITORIAL GOVERNMENT IN NEVADA. IF WE HAD A GOVERNOR AND OTHER OFFICIALS WE COULD BETTER COPE WITH THE DANGER OF SECESSION. He signed it DAVID STUART, GENERAL AGENT, WELLS FARGO, NEVADA TERRITORY.

He did not know what McLane's attitude would be to his using the company name, and did not care. The mountain was going to be lost unless they could jar someone into action.

No help had come by the morning of July 5, when Virginia City awoke to find the new flag of the Confederacy flying wildly in the Washoe Zephyr from the flagstaff on top of John Newman's Saloon.

Newman himself was patrolling the sidewalk in front of the building, a rifle on his shoulder. Across the street two hundred armed

Knights of the Golden Circle were drawn up in skirmish line under the command of Dr. McMeans.

A crowd began to gather. Tom Peasley brought his Committee of Safety. Greatly outnumbered, they approached cautiously, Davie at Peasley's side, the big fireman turning his back on the skirmish line, facing Newman squarely and demanding that the rebels disperse and pull down the flag.

Newman laughed at him and called, "Turn around and listen to the doctor."

McMeans held up a paper, waving it over his head, and raised his voice to carry through the street:

"I have the pleasure to inform you that as representative of Jefferson Davis, President of the Confederate States of America, I have this day taken possession of the Territory of Nevada and hereby declare it now to be an integral part of the Confederacy. All mining claims are appropriated to the Confederate government."

There was a gasp from the crowd, but the two hundred men with their rifles presented, the many hurrahing Southerners gathering with them, commanded the moment.

Davie turned his head to the fireman behind him. "Collins, get word to Churchill. They'll have to come now."

Collins drifted back and the Committee of Safety retreated a hundred yards and stood their ground there. An explosive tension built up in the street, but no one moved.

Then a man named Waterhouse, climbing the rear of Newman's Saloon, appeared on the roof, planted the Stars and Stripes on the front corner, shook a pistol at the skirmish line and shouted down:

"I'll shoot the first bastard that dares touch this flag."

Rifles swung up and the Southerners, disciplined, waited for the order to fire. McMeans did not give it. A single shot would turn this block into a slaughterhouse. If there was to be such violence he did not want to initiate it.

The Union group shifted ominously, ready for the risk. A few had hunting rifles or short guns but most of the firemen had only their axes and the miners nothing but clubs.

Davie stood with his revolver drawn, holding his breath. This was surely a nightmare. He was not facing shrieking savage Indians here, nor saloon thugs, nor safe robbers, not anyone he could accept shooting. He was looking across at men who had led the camp, at merchants, at people he had served in the express office, men he had drunk with and played cards with and laughed with over a cock fight. This was Virginia City. These were his brother citizens. And unless something happened very soon to ease off this confrontation, the string of time would snap. They would be killing each other. A word. A laugh. A sudden movement would break it. And the awful tableau stretched out.

Into the silence the sound drifted, faint, then growing louder, a bugle blowing the charge. Gradually heads turned toward the divide, northern heads and southern heads. The Union flag appeared first, then the U. S. Army lieutenant, galloping over the crest leading a company of dragoons with drawn sabers flashing in the sun.

Davie barely glanced that way, then watched John Newman, wondering if he would fight. The saloonman gaped, hesitated, then ran in through his door. He ran out again, without his rifle and carrying a folded flag. Before the dragoons had pounded down the length of C Street he had pulled down the Stars and Bars and run up the Union colors.

The lieutenant pulled his horse in before McMeans and sat looking down grimly on the southern leader, his young face set in hard lines, shadowed by his helmet.

"By what right are you bearing arms? By what right did you fly that rebel flag?"

McMeans flushed and stood speechless and slowly his skirmishers lowered their rifles. They were ready enough, but cold steel is harder to face than the muzzle of a gun.

The officer did not give them time to muster their will. He ordered them to stack their arms and line up against the wall, and when they were laggard he raised a hand, ready to sweep the sabers forward. The Southerners surrendered.

Within an hour he turned his troop back down the hill, taking a wagon loaded with the southern guns with him. But he would make no arrests, saying that the Knights were civilians and he had no orders covering the situation.

The Southerners scattered, leaving the street, but Peasley kept his firemen in a tight knot.

"From now on," he told them, "none of you go anywhere alone, and never go unarmed. That lieutenant may not know it, but the war has come to Sun Mountain."

Virginia City simmered underneath a surface calm. Twice a week the Pony Express brought increasingly depressing news of what was happening east of the Rockies. Other states joined the Confederacy and were raising troops. The North was raising troops.

The fire companies in New York organized into a regiment they called the Fire Zouaves with Colonel Elmer E. Ellsworth in command. Most of Peasley's firemen, New Yorkers themselves, had known Ellsworth and many of the men with him, and with that personal interest they followed the dispatches as their old comrades were ordered first to Washington, then across the river to Alexandria in Virginia. There Ellsworth was killed. Peasley draped every firehouse on the mountain in black.

On top of that came Bull Run, with three thousand Federal troops cut to pieces, including most of the Zouaves. Not only three thousand dead, but thousands more wounded and the defeated Army reeled back on Washington.

The Virginia City Southerners, sullenly silent since being disarmed, came alive again, but this time they were met by Union opposition equal to their diminished strength.

President Lincoln issued his call for seventy-five thousand volunteers. The firemen wanted to answer. Davie Stuart wanted to answer. But Tom Peasley roared that they were more needed where they were, defending the mountain of silver. The best help they could give would be a recruiting drive.

They held a parade led by two drummers and a flag bearer, marching from the firehouse. Southerners tried to break it up, smashed one drum, but Peasley brought in another and they tramped on, down C Street, up the hillside to B and along to the city hall. They gathered a wake two miles long and in the meeting at the hall hundreds signed the roster.

They went into training immediately under Major Hungerford's skilled direction, drilling up and down the center of C Street. Davie could not stay out of it any longer, but he did not join Hungerford's company. He was too worried about Aurelia. All of his discreet urgings to her had gone unanswered. He had heard nothing from Mitchell, did not know whether he was in town or aware of his wife's danger. The time for a crackdown on the Knights of the Golden Circle in California was overdue, probably because Sumner must have been too busy reorganizing the Presidio thus far to move against them, but it would come.

Davie wrote to McLane, resigning from Wells Fargo, left his assistant in charge of the office and went to San Francisco. First he would somehow drag Aurelia out of the conspiracy, then he would enlist.

CHAPTER FOURTEEN

Events had been hectic in San Francisco too. As the war grew in scope, as the Federal Government was threatened by the news of Bull Run and the other defeats the Southerners grew bolder by the day. The Bear Flag appeared at a number of inland towns. It was flown at Santa Barbara, at San Diego. The Californians drilled openly and rumors flew that the governor and the legislature, still southern controlled, were on the eve of calling a convention to declare California independent. It was whispered that General Johnson was shifting the Presidio troops, putting into the strongest positions those companies made up of Southerners.

Johnson had resigned from the Union Army in April but until he could be replaced he remained in actual command.

To oppose him, stall for time, to try to hold the state in the Union, a group of businessmen organized, calling themselves the Thirty-four. They were not politicians. They were bankers, steamship executives, major merchants, very wealthy, very powerful, the most elite coterie of the city.

Three of them made a surprise call late one night on Mitchell Randolph. He had met them, done some fringe business with them, but he had not before been invited into their stratosphere. In his dressing robe he showed them into his parlor and was mystified when they insisted that he make certain the drapes were drawn tight before he lit the lamps.

He poured brandy for Sam Brannan, Henry Teschemaker, and William Ralston and waited to hear why they were there. Brannan, the one he knew best, from the early days and the frontier store at Sutter's Fort, was spokesman. He apologized for the hour, explaining that the Confederates had spies everywhere and they did not want to approach him openly because they did not know who they could or could not trust.

Mitchell said in a dry voice, "What makes you think you can trust me?"

Brannan said frankly, "We don't know. You see a lot of the 'chivalry' Democrats, yes, but you know a lot of Republicans too—your protégé in particular—and you've never shown any interest in politics. So we'll take the risk. If we don't take steps to keep this state in the Union it's going to secede, and that we think would be very bad."

"Bad for business, I agree."

"Bad all the way around." It was Ralston who cut in. "California is going to be a great state, San Francisco is going to be another New York, and I'm damned if I want them wasted. So we have to get hold of the Presidio. That's the key."

"I'd think so. Have you any practical idea how to do it?"

"We have. I wrote to the War Department and they're finally getting concerned. They're sending General Edwin Sumner out to relieve Johnson. Now we've just learned that some of the Copperheads intend to kidnap Sumner before he gets here, to keep control long enough to secede. That's why we've come to you. Somebody has to go to Monterey and meet his ship, and if any of us go the Copperheads will recognize us and switch their plan. But nobody will suspect you of mixing in, so we're asking if you will take this letter to the general to warn him. We have to have him here as soon as possible."

Mitchell Randolph laughed aloud. "I'll be happy to go, gentlemen. I don't want to see that gang of dreamers disrupt our development any more than you do."

He went to Monterey, waited a week until the ship dropped anchor, boarded her and delivered Ralston's letter into the general's hands. Sumner was a tough cavalry officer, contemptuous of civilian plots and not at all inclined to cooperate. Mitchell stayed aboard, sailed north with him and waged a campaign to convince him and by the time they reached the bay, Sumner had been moved to a different cabin, Mitchell occupied the one the general had used on the trip up from Panama, and Sumner had agreed to go ashore dressed as one of the crewmen.

When the steamer churned in through the Golden Gate it was met by the usual flotilla of small boats. Mitchell stood at the porthole watching as the boat made its slow way toward the Embarcadero. It was not long before the cabin door was shoved violently open and three men crowded in with guns in their hands. Mitchell turned and looked at them without expression.

"Who the hell are you?"

The first man inside had a deep drawl. "Just you be quiet, General. We don't want to hurt you."

Mitchell let his eyebrows climb. If they were mistaking him for Sumner so much the better, it would keep them from looking farther. He walked stiffly to the bunk and sat down on it, his eyes still flat on them.

The leader shook his head. "No, get on your feet. We'll go out through the cargo hatch . . . there's a boat waiting."

Playing out the part Mitchell blustered some, demanding, "What do you think you'll accomplish by this outrage?"

The man grinned. "Just want you out of circulation for a bit, long enough for Johnson to send the Union troops East. Say a week. Then we take California."

A voice from the passage outside called, "Hurry up, we're almost at the wharf," and a man stepped into sight.

Mitchell almost smiled at Marion Boniface. The lawyer recognized him immediately, then stared hastily around the cabin.

"Where is he?"

"Who?" The man holding the pistol on Mitchell looked as if he thought Boniface had lost his mind.

"The general, for Christ's sake."

The man waved the pistol to indicate that he had the general covered. Boniface grunted and swore at him.

"That's not Sumner, you fool, it's Mitchell Randolph and he isn't even in the Army." He swung viciously on Randolph. "What are you doing in this cabin?"

Mitchell drew himself up angrily. "Why shouldn't I be here? I paid for it at Monterey."

Boniface's usual poise deserted him and he said in confusion, "The purser's record shows that this cabin is General Sumner's . . ."

Mitchell shrugged. "It hasn't been since Monterey. Maybe the purser just forgot to change the listing."

"Then where the hell is the general?"

"I haven't the slightest idea." That was true enough. Sumner might already have gone ashore in one of the bummer boats or he could still be on the ship.

Boniface had not yet recovered but his lieutenant, still holding the gun on Mitchell, said:

"What do we do with him? He knows too much."

That appeared to bring the lawyer out of his lapse and he said, "Take him along. I know how to shut his mouth but let's get out of here."

They herded Mitchell out and toward the cargo hatch, and were intercepted there by police and members of the Thirty-four. The three kidnapers were arrested but somewhere during the walk Boniface had dropped out of the procession and escaped.

Sumner reached the Presidio and relieved General Johnson at once, and replaced all those officers who had leanings toward the South. Johnson fled to Los Angeles, gathered some two hundred Southerners and made a dash for Fort Yuma, but was cut off by a company of dragoons. Most of his followers turned back although he and a few men broke through, reached Texas and then the East.

But in the West the Copperhead cause was broken. Sumner settled in and began a quiet roundup of the leaders of the Knights of the Golden Circle. One by one they disappeared into prison or scattered.

Marion Boniface and Aurelia Randolph did not run. They decided that their tracks were safely covered and that although the dream of a Republic of the Pacific was postponed, if not dead, their office could go on as it had before.

Then Roper Duggan, running all the way from the courthouse, burst into Boniface's room out of breath and gasping his news.

"They're after you . . . on their way . . . got a warrant . . . Sheriff's deputy tipped me. You got to get out of here, fast."

Aurelia caught at her throat. "What will they do?"

Roper swore. "Shoot him, probably. Boss, move."

The ranch, Aurelia thought. If they could get Boniface there they could hide him, but how could they get him through the city? She looked at him and found his face untroubled, even amused.

"All right, Roper, if they shoot me you can have my watch."

"Damn it, be serious, will you? Sometimes I could bust your head."

"As you like. Now we are serious, and what, my ugly friend, would you suggest I do?"

"I got it figured. For now we stash you in the basement." Roper had a cot in a bare, dank room there that he called home.

Boniface grimaced. "I'd rather face a firing squad than be cooped up in that hole."

"We ain't going to leave you there," Roper pleaded. "Only 'til I get my lines strung. I've got a friend, Captain Bovary, I've done some favors for . . ."

"Like shanghaiing a crew?"

Duggan ignored him. "He's sailing for the Orient with the tide and he'll sign you aboard if I can get you to his ship."

Boniface groaned and Roper hurried on.

"Damn it, you won't have to work if you've got some gold in your pocket. Just believe me and let me run this show without always getting in my way. So maybe you won't like what we got to do to get you on board, but boss, please don't argue. They got a guard all along the Embarcadero and they're stopping every carriage and every hack. Now come on and get downstairs. The sheriff is trying to hold them but they'll be along any minute."

"And Aurelia, what about her?"

Dancing from one foot to the other Roper shook his head. "They ain't looking for her. They don't know about her. I'll get wind of it if they find out and take care of it. Boss . . ."

At last Boniface condescended to take the back stairs down and Duggan mopped his face with his sleeve and swung on Aurelia.

"You got any money?"

"I can get some."

"Get plenty, he's going to need it. Get it in gold and do it up in a fancy package like a woman carries. Go to the Maison and buy him a dress and shoes and bonnet . . . and a red wig, you got that? Take them all down to him, then come back here and see if they've been here. If they haven't, wait, then when they've gone get a hack—that driver you always use—take the boss down to North Beach. You can't miss the ship, she's square-rigged, the *Sea Queen*, only she ain't no queen, believe me. I'll meet you there. Now I got to go make the deal with Bovary."

He rushed out and she sat alone, gathering herself. This was like some theatrical melodrama on a stage, but it was no pretended act. Marion Boniface's life could depend on how good a performance she put on. He had coached her for the theater of the courtroom and now she must find how well she had learned.

She stood up, wanting to hurry, but pacing herself, and went out to the coat rack. She was just fastening her light wrap when feet came up the stairs and a young lieutenant followed by two soldiers and a sheriff's man walked in. She gave them an inquiring smile.

The lieutenant stopped, uncertain at finding a woman in the office, then said to the room in general, "We're looking for a Marion Boniface."

Horton coughed and would have answered but Aurelia beat him to it.

"He is not here today."

"Where is he?"

"I believe he went to Sacramento on the morning boat."

"You his wife?"

She smiled amusement. "No, Lieutenant. I work here."

He looked from her to the closed door of the inner office, then went past her and opened it, stepped into the empty room, then came out, disappointed and told one soldier:

"Plummer, you stay here. If he shows up arrest him. We'll search the rest of the building."

Aurelia felt a pulse pound in her throat, but she sat down quietly and watched them leave. She need not have worried. Duggan had fortified his nest with a pile of packing cases that hid the door in the dark corner of the cellar. There were times when the police looked for Roper.

Half an hour later the search party came back, disconcerted. The lieutenant looked at each of the clerks for a long, skeptical moment, but they kept their heads bent over their desks. Then he looked doubtfully at Aurelia. She met his eyes, seeming puzzled, and risked a question. Her voice sounded nervous but she thought that might be expected.

"May I ask why he is being arrested?"

He did not want to answer and to avoid it, since he was at a dead end here, he beckoned to Plummer and took his men away.

Neither of the clerks knew of either Boniface's or her involvement with the Knights and they turned around now, Horton saying:

"Now what in the devil is that all about?"

"I really can't say, Ezra, but whatever it is, stay with the story that he's out of town."

"Oh, sure. But supposing they come back and he's here?"

"I'd better go find him and warn him," she said, and at last got away from the office.

At the bottom of the stairs she had another fright. The soldier Plummer was on guard just inside the door well. She dipped her head to him and went on without a break in her step, then on the street she found the lieutenant and the sheriff's man posted on one corner, the second soldier at the other, all of them seeing her come out.

She stood on the sidewalk, pulling on her gloves and arranging her skirt, then walked to the cab rack and stepped into the chosen hack and was driven off. She found it hard not to look back, to see if any of them were following.

She went first to the Maison de Paris, bought the required costume and a decorative hatbox, then went to the bank. Finally she had the driver take her by the back streets to the alley at the rear of the office building. She left the hatbox, heavy with gold, in the hack and went down into the cellar, lifting her skirts away from the rats she knew were there.

She picked her way through the clutter and behind the pile of crates, whispering her name at the dark room. Boniface appeared out of the shadow.

"Bless Roper's devious soul. They missed finding me by a hair. What have you got there?"

"A woman's clothes and a wig. Get them on quickly and come along, I've got Herb Zeller and his hack outside, but you'll have to make a convincing female."

He chuckled. "My father broke me in as an actor playing a girl, so I come full circle. Can you trust Zeller?"

"Yes, I've bought things for his wife and children. Now hurry, then I'll drive you to the slip."

He was shucking out of his suit, stepping into the dress, talking while he changed.

"You're not going, I don't want to get you in trouble."

"Don't be silly," she said impatiently. "You may be a good actor but the wharf is guarded and if you have to talk to the soldiers your voice will give you away."

She went first up the stairs and down the alley to the side street with Boniface close behind her, making him wait until she was in the hack, watching the corner where the lieutenant still stood, with his back turned, before she motioned the lawyer across the sidewalk.

They drove off slowly, sitting close together, apparently deep in the chatter of two ladies out for a ride. But it was a long gauntlet down Market Street. At the wharf they were halted, but the soldier only looked into the hack to see if someone was hiding under the blanket on the floor, then waved them by.

They located the *Sea Queen* and the hack stopped close to the gangplank that ran up to the deck. They looked back and found no one interested in them. Marion Boniface put an arm around Aurelia and pulled her to him, his eyes laughing.

"Lady, I am glad I met you. It's been fun, hasn't it? All of it. Keep up the work, and I'll be back when I hear the Republic of the Pacific has passed a law admitting women attorneys."

He took the hatbox, left the hack and went jauntily up the gang-plank.

She watched him reach the deck, where a man came up and stopped him, watched them talk, then Boniface waved down at her and went into the ship.

Roper Duggan was not in sight. She waited for him a few minutes but was afraid to stay there long for fear of attracting attention. Roper could find his own way. Aurelia went back to the office, told the clerks that Boniface had gone away until his difficulty was straightened out and that she would try to find another lawyer who would take over their cases until he came back.

She found a young attorney who was glad to come into so well known a firm, glad enough to work with a woman. But it was not the same. And a mystery developed. Roper Duggan disappeared. She did not see him after he had left the office to make the sailing arrangement for Boniface, and she could not find out if he had been taken by the police.

She was worrying about Roper ten days later, in her dressing room at the house, changing for dinner, when Mitchell ran up the stairs, threw her door open and came in with a set, flushed face.

"In God's name, Aurelia. I thought you had better sense."

She had a sinking prescience but she said cautiously, "Better sense than what?"

"The Provost Marshal had me in his office all afternoon. They know you helped Boniface get out of the country."

Relief made her smile. "They may think so. They can't prove it."

"There speaks the lawyer." He shook a finger under her nose. "They can prove it. And if they couldn't, they don't have to. This is not a court game, Aurelia, this is war, the North is taking a beating . . . and you are an accessory in helping a traitor escape. The Army is not going to quibble much between suspicion and proof."

"You say they have proof. What is it?"

"They saw you in his office. They saw you take a hack, and ran the driver down. He told them he took you to the Maison. They went there and learned you bought a dress that couldn't possibly fit you, shoes you couldn't wear, and a red wig. Do you want more?"

She could argue that it was not proof enough, but she knew that he was right, the Army would not consider such legal niceties at this time. She would have to find another way out, and to do that she had to know more.

"What do they intend to do with me?"

He was pacing the room, made restless by the pressure of what must be done.

"If you weren't so well known, such a public character, they would have called you in and warned you to stop associating with Copperheads, but they can't let it go at that with your reputation. It would be bound to leak out."

"Then they mean to arrest me?"

"Unless you do as I tell you, yes they will. They gave me tonight to get you out of here. I've booked passage on a steamer leaving at dawn and you can get a boat for France from Chagres."

She had thought about that possibility but hearing it in his blunt words was like falling into ice water. The little ranchgirl she had been waked up in terror. She had never been out of California. France was half a world away. She choked that down and another objection appeared.

"Little David is at the ranch. I'd have to take him."

"You will not take him. You haven't even got time to see him. You can't do him any good if they stand you up against a wall and shoot you. Get some sense into your head for once. I've given you a free hand and you've done just as you wanted. You've gone too far. This is treason. They can't crack down on others and ignore you, and the only reason you're getting this chance is because Ralston and the Thirty-four sent me to warn Sumner he was going to be kidnaped. Now damn it, get packed."

She had started to turn to the wardrobe but she swung back and stood open-mouthed, betraying herself. "You?"

His eyes narrowed on her. "You knew about that? You were in with Boniface on that secession idiocy? You damned little fool. Pack . . . pack, I tell you. Get on that boat before the Provost finds out what all you have been doing and changes his mind about letting you go."

She did hurry then. Within an hour her trunks were loaded into a dray and she and Mitchell rode with them. The night was dark with a shrouding fog. The soldiers along the wharf were ghostly shadows, threatening, and she felt Mitchell's body tense when they were stopped. But the blockade passed them, then she was on the steamer's deck and Mitchell's big figure was the only familiar thing around, and a sense of the looming complete isolation from everyone she knew hit her hard. Boniface was gone, Roper Duggan had vanished, her son, her husband would soon be gone, and Davie Stuart.

"Davie," her voice was small, without its old confidence. "You'll tell him where I am . . . He tried very hard to make me quit the Knights."

"I'll tell him."

He was curt, then he gave her two envelopes and took her chin in one hand, holding it as if to command her full attention, as if he understood that her wits were scattered.

"One of these is a letter to the Duke of Morny, who is the Emperor's half brother and the most powerful man in France. I did him a favor a long time ago. Call on him and let him help you get established at court. This other is a draft on the Jecker brothers bank. It will establish your credit and take care of your bills."

When he left her go she curled her hand tightly around his wrist like a child.

"Mitchell . . . How can I thank you?"

"Thank me for what? Keeping you alive? What was I supposed to do, abandon you? You're my wife, aren't you?"

Hesitantly she said, "Not a very good one. Not as good as you deserved."

He put an arm around her, tipped her head up and kissed her. It was his first kiss in years.

"Little Aurelia . . . little Aurelia. I don't believe I'd want a different wife."

He stayed on through the night to be sure she was not taken off the ship and for the first time he talked about Europe, telling her about Paris as he remembered it, reassuring her. In the morning when the steamer wheels were turning in reverse, when the ship was backing into the bay, she saw his blocky figure standing on the wharf, watching the boat until he was finally enveloped in the drifting fog.

BOOK FOUR

CHAPTER ONE

David Randolph missed his mother terribly. He had believed her to be invincible and had always been much closer to her than to his father. Mitchell was away from home so much of the time that he seemed more like one of Aurelia's friends than a parent. Also, David shared her love of the ranch and her kinship with the Californians.

He had never liked the rough and tumble American boys of the city who called him Mexican. The first time it had happened he had run to his mother in outrage. She had explained to him that he was a Californian, not a Mexican, that he was descended from the blue-blooded stock. Those who made fun of him, she said, were lucky if they knew what their grandfather's name had been. Her contempt for most Americans was ingrained in him and while his English was good he spoke Spanish in preference and had even insisted that Nora learn the language.

And now his father was trying to explain to him how his mother's fantasies had caught up with her and forced her to run off in the middle of the night without even saying good-bye to him.

The ranch had been his security, his sanctuary away from the Americans. For over a year he had made regular visits there with Aurelia and had been caught up in the excitement of watching the Californians drill in preparation for the day when they would change the state into a member of the Republic of the Pacific. He had listened to his uncles argue the pros and cons of the rebellion and had sided with his mother and José in their dream of a new country. He had dismissed Duncan as a spoil-sport for the predictions that even if California did break away from the Union the

Americans would still be a heavy majority and would not live up to the promise of returning power to the Spanish families.

Then Mitchell had come down, raging at them all, calling them stupid and childish, and dropped the bomb that exploded David's world. Aurelia, he said, was on a ship, sailing into exile, he had only barely gotten her away, she would have been thrown into prison . . .

"For God knows how long, and she can't come back to this country until this damn fool war is over."

Before that shock was absorbed Mitchell took his son back to San Francisco and lectured him on the way on the reasons why California could not now secede, so that bubble shattered for David, and a week later a letter from Concepción told them that José, after days of talking about going south to join the Confederate Army, had ridden off to Mexico instead.

Knowing how Mitchell disliked the ranch and its people David thought that it would be a long time before he saw it again, and a loneliness overwhelmed him. He loved Nora and Joe, but they could not make up for everything he was losing, and he went to the South Park house confused and bitter.

Mitchell tried to help, took him everywhere he went, even on business appointments, but a bleak, empty unhappiness settled in him. Then Davie Stuart arrived from Sun Mountain and gave him another fright.

He came just before supper, while David and Mitchell were playing chess and David losing out of lack of interest. Everybody was glad to see him, Nora and Joe, and David in particular. He clung to his godfather as if this was one part of his family restored to him. But when Davie asked where Aurelia was Mitchell suddenly started shouting, telling what had happened.

"You knew she was in deep with that crowd. She told me so. Why didn't you tell me? Why didn't you warn me what she was doing?"

Davie got mad too and shouted back: "Why should I have to? She's your wife, why didn't you ever pay a little attention to her? Why didn't you know it yourself? And what good would it have done? What do you think you could have done about it?"

Mitchell sputtered and fumed and then shouted again, "So why didn't you yank her out of there? You've got more influence on her than anybody else. Why did you let her . . ."

"I did every damn thing I could. I wrote to her time after time. I argued myself blue in the face. And that's why I came here tonight . . . to tell her if she didn't get out and stay out I'd turn Boniface in myself."

For a moment Mitchell looked taken aback, then he growled: "And have that slippery ham drag her after him. Great. Anyhow, she's safe now. Well, let's not dwell on it. Nora's got supper ready, let's not keep her waiting."

They ate in an uneasy truce, both still ruffled, until near the end of the meal Davie said shortly:

"I've quit Wells Fargo. I'm enlisting in the Army tomorrow."

Mitchell's head had come up at the first words, but at the others he bellowed: "Enlist? You?"

To have had this godfather returned to him and now to hear him say that he was going to join the American Army . . . with his mother gone, José gone, the ranch and his grandmother beyond his reach . . . this was more than the little boy could handle. Choking to keep from crying aloud he ran, out of the dining room and up the stairs to his bedroom.

Davie Stuart looked at Mitchell, questioning, and started after David, but Mitchell waved him back.

"Let him go," he said in a low tone. "He's had a lot of jolts lately. Let him cry in private. Now let's talk about you enlisting."

"He needs help."

"He'll get it." Mitchell raised his eyes to the ceiling. "That register . . . it opens in his room. He'll be listening through it. He found out a long time ago that grown people talk more freely if they think young ears aren't listening, and I want him to hear, learn what people really are.

"So . . . Didn't that Piute trouble teach you you're no soldier?"

David Randolph, lying on the floor beside the register with his wet face in his hands, heard the question, heard glasses clink as Mitchell poured brandy, heard Davie's acid voice saying that a lot of men who weren't soldiers were going to have to fight to keep the Union together, then heard Mitchell again.

"Don't be a damned fool. You love the Union so much that you want to fight for it, stay here where you'll count for something. Join a militia company like the savvy businessmen are doing. There are a lot of hothead Copperheads still here and Lincoln has his hands full with the war in the East. We may still have to fight to hold California."

Davie brought up Lincoln's call for volunteers and argued that unless the eastern war was won there would be no Union. David listened as both men got drunk, battling over which way Davie would go, but he did not hear the end of the session. Emotionally worn out, he fell asleep on the floor.

In the morning he found that Davie had stayed overnight. And Mitchell had won him over. After breakfast they watched him leave to go tell Wells Fargo he had changed his mind and ask for reinstatement. David was only partly mollified, telling his father:

"He won't be in the Army, but he'll go back to Sun Mountain. He won't be around here."

Mitchell smiled down and rumpled the boy's hair. "He'll be around. Just keep your shirt on awhile."

Mitchell stayed at home that morning. It was not yet noon when Davie came storming back, choking on his words.

"McLane . . . the son of a bitch . . . you know what he said? He said that I'd let the company down by quitting . . . they couldn't afford to have somebody they couldn't trust in that important a spot . . . said he'd take me on as a mail clerk . . ."

Mitchell laughed at him. "He thinks I can't touch him any longer and he doesn't need to keep you away from me. How many times does this make that The Company has bloodied your nose?"

Shaking his head, Davie said emphatically, "No more. I'd wash dishes in a Chinese restaurant before I'd work for Wells Fargo again."

Mitchell's eyes had a dark, pleased brightness. "Better make that before you'd work for McLane again. Management, control of companies does change, you know."

"Oh, my God." Davie threw his hands into the air in his disgust. "Sure . . . sure . . . you're going to take them over. I know . . . I know . . ."

"One of these days," the voice was sleepy. "Don't write it off yet . . . But now you're out of a job again. Do you want to stay in the business? Will you come in with Ben Holladay and me now?"

Smoldering, Davie glowered at him. "Doing what? Pushing a freight line out of Salt Lake?"

"Oh, there'll be a little more to it than that." Mitchell was airy, roaming around the parlor, brushing the high backs of chairs lightly as though his touch would bring them to life, his voice lazy. "Coaches, mail, everything east of Washoe, when we pick off Russell, Majors, and Waddell."

David Randolph, watching his father and following the conversation with his bright curiosity, interrupted. "The Pony Express people? You mean you'll kill them?"

282

"No." Mitchell kept his face straight. "It's more like a poker game, son, but for higher stakes. You want to hear about it?"

At the boy's quick nod Mitchell set the stage for him. John Butterfield's transportation line through Texas and Fort Yuma, he said, had held the overland mail contract from the government, and Russell, Majors, and Waddell, with their route across the middle of the country, wanted the contract. They had gone deeply into debt trying to get it. Ben Holladay had been lending Russell money, and taking as security, vouchers signed by the then Secretary of War, John B. Floyd.

Signing those vouchers was dishonest, but Floyd did not care. He knew that as soon as Buchanan left the White House the South would secede, and furthermore Russell was kicking back some of Holladay's cash to Floyd and to Bailey, a law clerk in the Interior Department who was a cousin of Floyd's wife. His rationale was that he was southern, he wanted Butterfield to keep his mail contract, and was trying to drive the Russell firm under.

Floyd finally got nervous, so Bailey began stealing negotiable bonds from the Indian Bureau, money held in trust for the tribes. In all he stole eight hundred and seventy thousand dollars before they were caught. Floyd ran for sanctuary in the South and joined the Confederate Army when the war broke out, Bailey pleaded guilty, Russell pleaded innocent and was exonerated of complicity in the thefts and continued with R M & W.

But when the war did cut off the Butterfield line for use by the North, R M & W did not get the precious million-dollar mail contract which would have brought them back to solvency.

"And now," Mitchell told him, "Bill Russell owes Ben Holladay one million, eight hundred thousand dollars, and he hasn't any way to pay up. It can't be much longer before, as big as they are, R M & W falls in our laps. One thing I'll promise you, Davie, you'll never get bored working with Ben Holladay. Come on home. Come and help us build the biggest coach and freight line in the world."

"You can live here free," David said, but from the wistfulness in the tone the offer sounded more like a plea for someone else familiar to help fill the emptiness of the house than a favor to his godfather.

Davie spent the afternoon considering. Wells Fargo was not the only firm ruthless in its dealings and apparently the bigger they were the more piratical they became, even to the level of the national government. He did not approve of Holladay's tactics with R M & W, nor Mitchell's part in them, but he had to do something, and he finally moodily decided that probably nowhere else in the present business world would he find any less carnivorous venture.

Mitchell Randolph did not hide his pleasure the next day when he took Davie to meet Ben Holladay. David went with them and Holladay opened the door of the big house on the hill himself, took immediate and loud possession of the boy, tossed him on his shoulder, carted him inside and when he put him down clamped a gold coin in the small hand. David was instantly won over.

Davie Stuart, too, almost against his will, found that he liked the big, shaggy buccaneer. There was so much rambunctious vitality that seemed to vibrate from him. Like Mitchell, Holladay had many irons in many fires, and from the days when he had finally gotten a firm business footing, freighting for the Mormons, and his Benecia slaughterhouse, he had been expanding like a slow explosion. He was as well known in New York and Washington as he was on the coast. Some men called him scheming and unscrupulous, others swore that once he had given his word he never broke it. But whatever the reaction to him it was always emphatic.

"Come in, come in," he roared and his voice filled the big rooms as he towed them into his office, talking as he went. In spite of the early hour he poured brandy, sweeping a sharp, intense inspection over Davie when he handed him the glass and saying over his shoulder to Mitchell, "Who's this you're bringing to old Ben now?"

"Davie Stuart." Mitchell sounded casual. "He's been my partner since '49, ran my express companies. You'll need him for the R M & W reorganization."

"Oh?" Another quick inspection and a shrug. "I ain't got them yet. No rush is there? How are things shaping up in the North?"

"The new gold strike in that section of Washington that they're beginning to call Idaho looks promising. They only shipped about five thousand this year but new camps are starting up at Oro Fino, Salmon River, Owyhee, Walla Walla, Pierce City, Lewiston. They'll bear watching. But I want you to take Davie in now, give him some time to get used to you. Wells Fargo just dumped him."

"Wells Fargo? What's your partner doing with that outfit?"

"He's a good Christian boy, Ben, he had to turn the other cheek a couple of times, but he's had his bellyful now."

Ben Holladay's booming laugh filled the room. "All right, boy, you're on. I think Mitch just wants you minding the store while he flies around. He don't trust old Ben and that's a fact. So you just grab hold of my coattails and hang on for the ride."

CHAPTER TWO

The early weeks were a ride indeed. Trying to keep track of Ben Holladay was like trying to hold onto the whirlwind. Davie entered the San Francisco office and Holladay bombarded him with telegrams from all across the country, spawning new projects everywhere he went.

Mitchell was back and forth between San Francisco and Oregon with increasingly glowing reports of the progress of the new mines in the north. Then Holladay arrived, wanting to buy two steamships with which to cut in on the growing north coast traffic. He wanted the loan from the rising banker, William Ralston, rather than from Mitchell Randolph, to keep Mitchell, he told Davie, from thinking he owned him body and soul. Wells Fargo tried to block that loan to shut out the shipping competition to their affiliate, Pacific Steamship Company, but this time Holladay beat them off.

Davie stayed at the South Park house and with Mitchell gone most of the time he got to know his godson as he never had before, and began to understand Aurelia's concern for the boy. The bright young mind was already too adult, already making a loner of him. He would rather play cards with Davie or read the newspapers than play with the boys his age. With his partisanship for the Californians he seemed to Davie to be headed for trouble.

When in about two months Mitchell came home Davie talked to him about what he saw as an emerging problem. Mitchell listened as if at the back of his mind he had been half-aware himself of the imbalance in his son's life.

"I think," he said, "he had better be turned around. I think I'll take him up to the Columbia with me and let him see some Americans in action, let him get a wider perspective."

The little boy reacted with a whoop of excitement. He had never been anywhere except the ranch and San Francisco, and now they would go up the river by steamer, cross the portages, and climb the ladder of boats on the upper river system. He set off with his father with shining eyes, promising to write to Davie and Nora and Joe.

Write he did. First he was incensed that it cost eight dollars for the voyage from Portland to The Dalles, but sixty dollars on from The Dalles to Lewiston. He complained bitterly that they were charged seventy-five cents for meals and a dollar a night for their stateroom. Joe and Nora hooted at the letter.

"That little old tightwad," Joe laughed. "He's still got the first two bits he took me for, shooting craps. He's going to be richer than his daddy by the time he's twenty."

The letters continued, some of the information in them dictated by Mitchell, telling about property he was buying in Lewiston and in Pierce City, but mostly they were a record of David's own sharp observations of all he saw. The tone of them changed. He was meeting Very Important men, rich men, and he could beat most of them at either poker or chess. Davie had a picture of the consternation that must be following in the wake of Mitchell's nine-year-old son. And apparently those Very Important men were taking the trouble to court the boy, whether because he was Mitchell Randolph's son or because of his own oddity did not matter. David listened to their business talks with Mitchell and from what he wrote they appeared to be vying with each other in answering his questions to see how much of their financial dealings he could comprehend. Quickly he began to admire their world, the bustle, the business, and the romance of the mining camps entranced him. Davie thought he read between the lines signs of Mitchell's guidance, shepherding the boy into a new look at things American and fanning the spark of enthusiasm for the competitive life.

But when they returned to South Park, David was thin, too keyed up, his eyes almost feverish. Nora scolded Mitchell, told him he ought to have better sense, that he'd worn the boy plumb out, and put David to bed. He did not protest, but sank into an exhausted apathy that lasted for days, a puzzling remoteness.

Then the first letters from Aurelia arrived, one each for David and Mitchell. David closed himself in his room with his. It was written in Spanish and told about the wonders of the emperor's palace, the cathedrals, the sights of the city on the Seine. It said that she missed him every day and would come home to him as soon as she could. David cried himself to sleep with the paper hugged against his chest.

The letters came against a background in which all the war news was bad for the Union side. With each southern success the Copperheads grew bolder. General Sumner had been ordered to the East with most of his Regulars and the holding of California depended more and more on the militia companies. At Mitchell's urging Davie had joined the group of which Billy Ralston was a member and he was spending all the time he could at the Home Guard Armory.

Aurelia's picture of the French capital in Mitchell's letter reflected the confidence of the Southerners there, with some changes in her own point of view. She thanked him again for his help, said that the Jecker brothers had been more than kind. The Duke of Morny had arranged her presentation at court where most of the Southerners who had retreated from the war gathered and she was surprised to find herself feeling so at home.

You knew how frightened I was the night I sailed, she wrote. *All that huge world that I was going into, and knew so little about, terrified me. But it has turned into a great adventure and in spite of the reason I am here I am really enjoying it. Except for the eternal politics. And they are as sickening here as they are in California.*

Your friends the Jecker brothers having sold Mexican bonds in a vast amount and then maneuvered to have the French court impose the Austrian Archduke Maximilian as Emperor of Mexico to protect the money, the old pattern is repeating itself. As the Americans overran us, the French are overrunning our Mexican brothers, and worse, the infamous Dr. Gwin is here, scheming with the Duke of Morny. The whisper is that they have wangled a concession that will hand over to them all of Sonora. If that is true they will steal it like California was stolen. They will import miners from California and Nevada, who are southern sympathizers, and it will be the same rape over again.

When Marion Boniface and Terry talked about the Golden Circle it sounded beautiful . . . our way of life would be restored to us . . . but from here it looks very different. These Southerners are no different from the Yankees and we are being tricked again by Gwin and his kind. French troops are supporting a foreign court in Mexico, and all for the profit of the bankers and adventurers who don't care a fig for human rights.

At Napoleon III's court she was in the middle of the swirling winds of gossip and rumor, but knowing her as he did Davie made a bet with himself that she was already burrowing deeper into the intrigues. He had not thought about the Austrian in Mexico in the light that she presented it and he wondered aloud to Mitchell.

"I don't understand why Maximilian would sell out so much of that country to Gwin. What's it about?"

Mitchell Randolph chuckled. "Maximilian, Gwin, all of them, they're crazy. And I think the Jeckers have lost their minds too. Davie, they sold bonds that represent much more than Mexico could ever repay, and the cost of maintaining the French troops there is greater than the national income, by itself. Anyone who can add can see that the Imperial Court is going to fall of its own weight. And Maximilian is an ass who's spending his time making up a book of court etiquette instead of attending to consolidating his position, entrenching himself with the people he's supposed to be governing. He expects Gwin and his mining scheme to help pay off the debts."

Mitchell stayed on in town and Davie stayed with him. It was the longest period of time they had been together for years and with Nora and Joe there it should have been like old times. But it was not. Mitchell talked more freely about his business but there was a hardness in him that had not been apparent to Davie while they were so much apart. Now he relished the dog-eat-dog infighting of the growing business giants, laughing about the power battles as if they were some great game being played on a board with Comstock silver and California gold as counters.

Little David kept himself wrapped in the new remote shell, protecting himself from emotions too strong to handle, the loss of his mother and his father's seeming expectation that he could comprehend all of the grown man's devious financial world. Even the concentration required by his beloved poker and chess became too much pressure and he refused to join the games when Mitchell and Davie played.

Davie Stuart himself was fretful in the city. He missed the physical activity of Virginia City and working for Ben Holladay was like riding a grasshopper, with Davie knowing very little about what the man was really doing. Then Holladay arrived in San Francisco and with Mitchell spent the next weeks putting together a fresh deal, and this one Davie was able to follow.

Mitchell found the money and Holladay, starting with his two steamships, added four others to take part in the enormous traffic

288

between California and Panama. From there they expanded up the coast and cut deeply into the Oregon trade. If Wells Fargo controlled the land routes of the West Coast, Ben Holladay now had a large share of the water shipments. And with that operation functioning, he was gone again.

It was near the end of the year, Mitchell was in Oregon, when a wire from Holladay directed Davie to meet him in Atchison, Kansas. Davie took it upon himself to send his godson down to the ranch to stay with his grandmother, knowing that Mitchell would not approve but hoping that the atmosphere he had loved there, the leisurely company of the Californians, would again unlock the tense little boy. Then he started east. Atchison was headquarters for the R M & W freighting company and Davie thought he foresaw the culmination of Holladay's and Mitchell's long squeeze on them.

Holladay met him with a happy roar that told all the surrounding world what a fine humor he was in.

"Time's come, boy. Time's come to make a little move. Old Bill Russell is about to hit me for another loan and I want you in on this from the start. It's going to be your baby."

After the earlier scandal Davie thought that Russell was showing a lot of gall and when he said so Holladay guffawed.

"Gall's Bill's middle name, son. Now you're here on the face of it as Mitchell's partner, but you just sit mum and watch the fun, then you can tell Mitch about how slick it worked."

William Russell made them a courtly welcome, was flatteringly deferential to the partner of the source of money, and then showed Holladay a wry face.

"Ben," he said, "Congress ought to have given us that million-dollar mail contract, and they would have if it hadn't been for that unfortunate misunderstanding over those Indian bonds . . ."

"Misunderstanding, my ass," Holladay laughed.

Russell drew himself up in injured dignity, shaking his head. "Believe me, I had no idea Bailey had stolen them . . . but that's past, and I need new money to meet our payroll now."

"I ain't got it," Holladay said with happy bluntness. "Me and Mitch have been buying a mess of steamboats."

"Well, all right," Russell argued, "but you're holding more security than you need on your last loan to me. Give me back the six hundred thousand worth of government vouchers I put up then. I can borrow on them from somebody else."

"Man, what are you talking?" Holladay reared back in his chair, his eyes wide. "You never put up any such thing, Bill Russell."

Davie, suddenly alert, looked from the affronted Holladay to Russell and found the man's face draining of color. A half-strangled sound choked from Russell's throat and he shot to his feet, standing over Holladay, shaking a finger at him as though it were a gun.

"I handed those vouchers to you in this office and Majors was with us when I did it. Now, damn it, I want them back."

Ben Holladay arched his eyebrows, curled the fingers of his left hand lightly in front of him and blew on the nails.

"You got any kind of a receipt that says I got them?"

Russell gasped and went from blanched to livid, and shouted: "You damned cheap crook, what do you think you'll get by this trick? We can't stay in business unless we get money now and if we don't who's going to pay you what we owe you already?"

Holladay lifted and dropped his shoulders in a travesty of regret. "I'm sorry, Bill, but if that's the case I guess I'll have to take some action."

Russell backed away as Holladay stood up and his shout rose to a scream. "You can't take action, because then you'd never be able to recover a cent from us."

Holladay winked at Davie, nodded him to his feet and turned out of the room wearing a child's bright smile, leaving Russell rooted and raging.

Davie did not know which man to believe regarding the bonds. If Holladay had them it was the most blatant theft he had ever witnessed, or Russell could be lying, acting. He could not have played either part himself, but he had no real compassion for Russell.

On the street, keeping pace with Holladay's rolling, ambling walk, he said, "Now that you've pulled the rug out from under R M & W, what do you do?"

Holladay grinned at him. "Take them over. It's all set up. You see, last November we were given a bond of the company in payment of all the money we've advanced. Bill kind of forgot that. Also, Ted Warner and Bob Pease were given an in-trust deed so if the line defaulted they could take possession, conserve the assets until a forced sale could be arranged. They'll take over now as trustees and we'll buy the company in at the sale."

It did not go quite that smoothly. The sale was advertised on December first of '61, but other creditors of the line got an injunction that blocked it in the hope that continued operation might make profits enough to pay off the debts. A new upheaval of the war intervened however.

On January first of '62 the telegraph brought the cataclysm to the Coast. All of the eastern banks and the Federal Government had suspended specie payments. The vast purchases of war supplies had wiped out the Treasury's gold reserves and all payments would henceforth be made by greenbacks. Paper money. The western states were stunned. Their whole economy was built on metal. How could their citizens put their faith in a bit of paper that was nothing more than a very shaky government's promise to pay at some future time? If it survived.

Mitchell Randolph had just bought two shiploads of silks from China and paid for them in gold. If in reselling them he had to take paper and it depreciated he stood to face a sizable loss. So did William Ralston, who Mitchell said was always loaning to one business or another, was in a hundred different enterprises.

Ralston, in love with San Francisco, called a hurried meeting of the city's bankers and businessmen to resist the change. It was long and loud with argument. The proposal was made that the state legislature should pass an act making metal the only legal tender in California. A lawyer protested that the Supreme Court would rule such an act unconstitutional, that the Federal Government was now the only body with the power to coin or print money, but Ralston was defiant.

"We issued our own slugs before the mint was established out here," he insisted. "So did Oregon. We're in a different position than the eastern states, we produce the gold, and more than we can use. If every California banker will continue to issue gold to his customers, if the merchants will refuse to sell goods for greenbacks and if the employers will pay their people in metal we can stay on the gold standard even if we're the only state in the Union that does."

The room voted with Ralston. The greenbacks were duly issued throughout the country and promptly dropped in value, but California stood fast, trading only in metal.

Russell, Majors, and Waddell did not repay their creditors. In March the company was ordered sold. Holladay entered the winning bid, a hundred thousand dollars for the franchises, stock, wagons, coaches, and animals. There was a flurry of charges that Ben had stolen the company but the war, still going badly for the Union, absorbed all of the country's energies and attention. Holladay, however he had got it, had not only acquired a freight agency but had wiped out his only competition except for Wells Fargo.

Now, with the coastal steamships he had a pinchers empire around Wells Fargo itself. At least on paper. In the ensuing year Davie discovered that it was largely on paper.

R M & W had always been predominantly geared to freight haulage, as Holladay's Salt Lake line had been. Now Holladay wanted to expand the passenger side of the business, and Davie learned why Mitchell had originally planted him with Holladay. There was little difference between carting freight and passengers except in the scheduling of runs and the more elaborate accommodations required by travelers. Davie, the express man, was given the job of making the changes.

On a preliminary sweep through the territory he found what a large order it was. The line was at the point of complete breakdown for Russell had been too preoccupied with his stock gambling to supervise the system. The morale of the employees was low and the better men had joined the Army. The stations were wrecks. Most of the horses and mules had been stolen, some by the station keepers, others by Indians. It would take a dizzying amount of time and money to revitalize the line and integrate it with Holladay's Salt Lake string, but Mitchell and Holladay gave him a virtual carte blanche.

It was a great relief to be out of San Francisco, a pleasure to be traveling and working in the way he knew best. Davie Stuart ranged across the prairie, changing the route west of Atchison, following the Platte, the Sweetwater, cutting through South Pass and on to Salt Lake. From the Mormon city he wound down the Humboldt, around Sun Mountain, through Wells Fargo country to Placerville and on to the Pacific, although on that stretch the only passengers they would carry would be through travelers from the East.

The specter of Wells Fargo made Davie see the whole project as a perilous gamble. They were calling the new combination the Overland, which Davie privately corrupted to the Overboard. It was a tenuous, slender thread stretching between the Pacific Coast and Atchison where the westward pushing railroad terminated, but it did create a potential transcontinental mail route which the nation desperately needed since the southern line was closed.

Just as badly, the Overland needed that mail contract to stay alive and Wells Fargo was already in Washington bringing all the pressure it could bear on Congress to deny it to Holladay. Holladay was there too, fighting tooth and nail, while Davie rushed the reconstruction and new buildings.

By horseback and coach he traveled, leaving behind him crews to rebuild the stations and corrals and restock them. Every fifty miles he located a comfortable small hotel for those passengers who would choose to spend the night in a bed. He was well toward completion of the work before Holladay finally got his contract, but with that relief another problem rose.

The Southerners, afraid of the aid the Overland would give to the North, encouraged the Indians to attack the stations nearly as fast as they were built, to burn the Concord coaches and again run off the stock. There was no help from the Union Army that was staggering under the southern victories. The Overland kept going only by recruiting miners from the northern camps as drivers and station tenders, ordering them to protect company property first, to keep the wheels turning, to fight off Indians.

And Holladay with the mail contract safe had the bit in his teeth. He was insatiable, never content. He opened new offices in New York, in Washington, lobbying for more and more mail and freight contracts and when he got them pushing Davie to expand further and further.

By the closing days of '62 the Overland had spread a web anchored in Denver to serve the mining camps that were springing up through the Rockies and feeding their gold into the Union coffers, and another web out of Salt Lake to Montana and the Black Hills. It was a sprawling empire that covered the West more broadly than even Wells Fargo had been able to do.

Davie Stuart was working harder than he ever had before, but worrying too. He kept waiting for the giant of Montgomery Street to move against them. It was inconceivable to him that the express company that had successfully smothered all opposition for ten years would sit meekly by while Holladay became the dominant transportation figure east of Washoe.

Then another threat loomed above Davie's horizon. After years of wrangling the Congress, driven by wartime need, had finally passed a bill authorizing the building of a rail line from the Missouri River to the Pacific Coast, and Lincoln had signed it into law. Of course it would take much time to build it, but also it would take the Overland much time to come out on its investment, yet Mitchell and Holladay were acting as if the railroad would never be completed. Wells Fargo, too, was behaving as though the iron horse was a joke. Through '63 and '64 it began to seem that the big stage companies' assessment was right. It took the railroad men both years to lay a paltry twenty miles of track.

In mid-1864 a new bombshell diverted Davie's attention and

made Ben Holladay raging mad. A man named David Butterfield who was no relation to the Butterfield who had owned the southern stage route had the nerve to open a line between Salt Lake, Denver, and Leavenworth, Kansas, and the further audacity to call it the BUTTERFIELD OVERLAND DISPATCH.

Ben Holladay was vain of the name Overland. It was his brand, and he saw this upstart's appropriation of it as an outright steal. But '64 was not a year in which the freighter could do much about it. His empire might be the greatest transportation system yet under the administration of one man, with fifteen thousand employees, twenty thousand wagons and coaches and a hundred and fifty thousand animals, six thousand of them racing thoroughbreds, but he was spread very thin.

The Overland had mail contracts on seven different routes, paying them a million, nine hundred thousand dollars a year, but they had not been able to break Wells Fargo's hold on the rich traffic between Virginia City and the Pacific Coast. And Mitchell and Holladay were still pouring huge sums into their California, Oregon, and Mexico Steamship Company to keep their circle tight around Wells Fargo.

Wartime inflation with its resulting depreciation of the currency and the continuing large losses caused by Indian attacks had the vast system on the verge of bankruptcy. Davie doubled the passenger fares, making a ticket from Atchison west cost five hundred dollars.

Torrential floods in California had given way to a long-extended drought, particularly in the south, where three quarters of the cattle and sheep had died. The Californians around Santa Barbara were hardest hit, many of them selling off their land at a dollar an acre as it lay parching into desert. Mitchell Randolph was buying, urging Ben Holladay to invest in ranches, but Ben had no interest in real estate except for the mansions he was building across the country. There were four at the time.

Holladay called Davie and Mitchell in to San Francisco to talk about their tightening financial situation.

"We're doing all right in the Black Hills and Montana and Idaho," he said, "but Washoe is a bust. We've got to find a way to break loose some of the business with the Nevada mines. That damn Butterfield is going to cut into us right when we can't afford it."

Mitchell Randolph sounded sleepy in the way Davie had learned spelled trouble for him.

"Yes. It's time we moved onto Sun Mountain, opened an office there. We can send Davie over. He still ought to know a lot of people to scare up some business with."

Davie Stuart yelped in protest. "You're crazy for sure. Move in right on top of Wells Fargo? They've let us alone for a long time now only because we weren't crowding them, but do you think McLane would sit still for this?"

"Hell with them," Holladay snorted happily. "What can they do? We've got them surrounded now."

"You've got them surrounded, sure. With a net made out of spider web. They've got all the New York money there is to put you clear out of business with."

But he could not make an impression on the two promoters. In the end Davie went back to Sun Mountain, into the jaw of the old enemy.

He found himself a stranger in a strange town. Virginia City had grown enormously. The ugly wood buildings along C Street were gone, mowed down by the annual fires that had swept the town and replaced with brick structures, iron shutters over the windows to repel the blazes. There were many women and children, three schools, four churches. Davie tried to find old friends and it was a cold disappointment to scratch off the names. Bill Stewart was in Washington as senator for the state, writing mining laws patterned on those hammered out in the early camps. Tom Peasley was dead, killed in a stupid quarrel. Julia Bulette had been murdered by a thief for her jewels.

With foreboding Davie opened the Virginia City office and sent out his wagons and coaches. Most of the time they ran empty. There was precious little business for him with Wells Fargo so deeply entrenched. He was laughed at by McLane's drivers, jeered at by McLane's clerks as a little boy playing at express. Then one night while he sat having a lonely drink in the Oriental Saloon a Wells Fargo man, already drunk, weaved to his table, dropped into the opposite chair and pushed his face toward Davie with a wolfish grin.

"Mister," he said, "you're a dead man. You know that? You and Ben Holladay and the Overland, you're all dead. Right now. You just haven't fallen down yet."

It could be idle, unfounded teasing, but Davie had the feeling that it was not and his smile was a little stiff.

"Tell me about it. How are we dead?"

The man snickered behind his hand and winked broadly. "You're cut off at the shoelaces, boy. We're going to build a stage line from here to Salt Lake and on to Denver, and there we're contracting with Dave Butterfield to take us along to Leavenworth." He reached across to poke a finger at Davie's shoulder. "Mr. McLane's brother Charlie is in Washington right now, taking that old mail contract right out from under you."

Still poking at Davie the man leaned slowly forward until his face lay against the table top. He snickered again and went to sleep. If he had been a rattlesnake coiled there Davie could not have looked at him with a greater chill.

Davie did not dare put this news on the telegraph. He wired Holladay in New York, Mitchell in Portland, asked them to meet him in Salt Lake, using a code word that signaled *imperative*. Then he headed for the Mormon capital on an Overland stage.

It was true. All along the way he learned that Wells Fargo was indeed getting ready to open a competitive line. When he demanded of the station keepers why they had not reported the new activity to him he found that McLane had struck too fast. It was only three weeks since their first wagon train of workmen, tools, equipment had rolled out of Carson City heading east and a second train had left Salt Lake working west. Plainly Wells Fargo had decided that Ben Holladay had gone too far and was preparing to get rid of him just as they had rid themselves of other competitors throughout their history.

The mail contract worried him most. He felt that the Overland as the established system had the advantage in the field, but Wells Fargo had a lot of muscle in Washington and Ben Holladay had many enemies. Since the R M & W takeover the howls of fraud in that and other deals had dogged his name in the newspapers.

In Salt Lake while he waited for Holladay and Mitchell Davie talked to the Mormon leaders who had been so antagonistic to anyone except Holladay. He found a change of heart there. Louis McLane had been ahead of him, had personally made the trip to see Brigham Young. He had agreed to hire half of his labor force from the Mormon villages and staff the stations through the stretch between Fort Churchill to Denver with Mormon crews. Money in the right places, applied with expertise.

Ben Holladay was furious when he heard the story, and confirmed that there was pressure in Washington. Seward, he said, had warned him there might be trouble in renewing the mail contract. But he was very sure of himself.

"McLane is going to have to hustle to get into operation before winter sets in, and it will be brutal east of here over the mountains.

We'll just make it a little tougher for him where we can. What do you think, Mitch?"

"You get to Washington," Mitchell said, "and hang onto that contract. It's going to cost Wells Fargo a fortune to build that line. Let them spend it. Davie, don't be so panicky. Just do your job, keep the Overland running. It will work out."

Keeping the Overland running was easy to say, not so easy to accomplish. Their crews were already wild men, tested and hardened by fighting Indians, deserts, mountains, cruel weather, and they had a fierce loyalty to the big, loud, profane, colorful Ben Holladay, and when a Wells Fargo group either got orders or got drunk and decided to knock over an Overland station as a lark a war started that spread over the full twelve hundred miles from Carson City to Denver.

The original attack left three people dead, the station burned and fifty head of stock missing. The Overland crews reacted, wrecked half a dozen of McLane's new stations and stopped and burned a wagon train of supplies.

Davie raced over the route dropping off orders to stop the violence but found himself undercut. One crew laughed at him outright and the agent told him:

"Don't you know old Ben sent the word along? A Wells Fargo station gets burned, a supply train gets wrecked, twenty horses get run off, the boys that do it get a bonus. Hundred bucks a man."

Davie wired Mitchell, wired Holladay, got answers from neither but pushed on, trying to stop the fighting. He was caught in one raid himself at the station a hundred miles east of Salt Lake. He came in on the evening coach and was sitting down to supper when racing horsemen drummed out of the dusk, cut the corral fence, overturned wagons, and then turned gunfire on the log station building.

At the first high yell outside the swinging lamps were doused. The yell echoed up at Davie out of the Piute massacre. He jumped for a rifle and crowded against one of the narrow windows beside the station keeper, joining the firing at the shadowy horsemen racing around the building in a tightening circle.

"Indians." Unconsciously he said it aloud.

The man beside him spat. "Indians hell, that's what they want us to think, but them's Wells Fargo."

They beat off the attack before morning and in the new daylight found two white men dead in the yard, their faces painted Indian fashion even though it had been too dark the night before for them to have been seen. It was done, Davie decided, purely for the hell of it. It made him wonder again at what force made laborers fight for their employers. He had seen mine crews battle each other underground for no reward other than the standard four-dollars-a-day wage, and it occurred to him that sheer boredom with their work made any kind of a fight a welcome change.

Davie made no headway at all in stopping the outbreaks. He could only accept them, fight Wells Fargo on their own terms to keep the Overland afloat. It was questionable which side was being hurt worse. Then, at last, the government took a hand.

In May of '65 the civil strife that had been dragging to its weary, bloody close was over, and the Army could turn its attention to the stages. For months mail coaches had been raided, the pouches broken open and the contents scattered over the prairie. In July the warning went out to both companies: from then on troops would accompany the mail and anyone interfering with it would be shot.

The competition continued hot between the parallel routes and the wrangling over mail contracts kept Ben Holladay in an uproar. Wells Fargo and the Overland ran at a Mexican standoff until winter, when Mitchell Randolph called a conference in New York.

He was uncommonly pleased, his full lips smiling, the hoods dropped over his eyes as he told Holladay, "Ben, it's time now for you to buy out Dave Butterfield's Overland Dispatch."

A roar shook the big office as Holladay howled. "Buy him? Mitch Randolph, I wouldn't give that tinhorn the sweat off my balls. Why . . . why . . ."

Into his sputtering Mitchell said, "Not even to twist Wells Fargo's tail? Get them off your back? Don't disappoint me now, man."

The huge shaggy freighter stood glowering, huffing, but then thought changed his eyes and he shoved his chin forward.

"Randolph, you know something I don't. What the hell is it?"

Mitchell sat with a bland look on his face and his hands laced across his stomach, and winked at Davie Stuart.

"Butterfield fills a gap in Wells Fargo's route," he said mildly, "but they're only leasing transport over that stretch. They don't own it. Neither does Butterfield, really. He didn't put his own money into that company, because he didn't have any. He got it from Ed Bray, from the Park Bank. He's into them up over his ears and his operation is shaky, running in the red. Just like R M & W were. Bray doesn't like the look of it and he wants to get his investors out. Of course, you can sit back and let Wells Fargo buy it, but if you took it you could kick them out of that section and leave them high and dry with a hole in the middle of their line."

Holladay began to grin, then to laugh aloud. In the early spring of '66 he bought the Butterfield Overland Dispatch for half a million dollars. Stole it. And very quietly.

When that was securely in his hands Holladay and Mitchell made their next move.

In Wells Fargo's New York offices Danford Barney, a former banker, had been brought in to untangle the scrambled finances and had been made president. He and the men in command around him all had the point of view that the Western Division was of less importance than the Eastern. And with their Butterfield lease they were not worried. They had only to keep the pressure on Holladay until he must fall to them.

Then Davie Stuart had a surprise summons to meet Ben Holladay in New York. He was astounded when the freighter turned him toward the American Express Building where Wells Fargo had their headquarters, and told him casually that he had an appointment with Danford Barney.

Louis McLane was also in the meeting room. Davie had not seen him since their last unhappy interview in San Francisco, and when the introductions were made McLane's voice was chilly, saying:

"Mr. Stuart worked for us at one time."

"So he did, so he did." Ben Holladay sounded confused.

Davie had learned that Holladay was never confused. Everything he did had a purpose and often more than one. But for the life of him Davie could not figure what they were doing here. Apparently Danford Barney could not either. He opened the talk with a cautious, neutral question:

"Mr. Holladay, you wrote that you had an important proposal to make us? Well, we'll listen to it . . ." He left the impression that no proposal Holladay might make would interest him further than brief courtesy required.

Holladay did not see it that way. He sat down as if he owned the place, spread his legs and lit a cigar.

"I come over," he said, "to do you a favor, maybe save us both a little time and money. You still counting on that agreement with Butterfield to get you across that piece of ground, forget it. You ain't got it any more."

Danford Barney's banker's lips compressed and McLane reddened, anger slurred the crisp voice.

"Oh yes, we most certainly have. Even if your hoodlums try to burn down every station on that line."

"Nope." Holladay sounded as if his worst fear was realized. "I was afraid you was still counting on that route, but an agreement signed with Butterfield don't mean a thing to me."

Danford Barney spoke in a thin, cold voice. "What do you think you have to do with it?"

Holladay opened his eyes, wide and innocent. "Why, I own the Butterfield Overland Dispatch now. Ain't you heard?"

Barney leaned back in his chair and glanced at McLane, then said in a voice not quite controlled.

"When did this happen?"

Holladay was apologetic. "Why, couple of months ago. Didn't occur to me you wouldn't hear. Should have told you. Save you building all them new stations through there."

Louis McLane bent forward as if he would charge the man across from him. "Damn you, Holladay, we've had enough of your insolence. You block us out of Denver and we'll build on east to Atchison. Yes, damn it, if we have to we'll build clear to New York."

Behind the outburst Barney was patting at his lips, shuddering at the cost of such a venture, certain that his Eastern partners would never agree to it. Then he decided to do his own blustering from the side he understood, the money side. He said precisely:

"Yes, Mr. Holladay. We know how extended you and Randolph are. We can open the line to Atchison, and also cut our fares in half. How does that sound to you?"

To Davie Stuart it sounded like the death knell he had waited so long for. And from Holladay's face it was a shocking threat. The braggadocio washed out of him. His voice caught and even shook a little.

"Well, hell, fellows. That's going to cost you a pretty penny, and what for? I know you can afford to throw away millions fighting me, and if you do I can't lick you. I see it. Let's talk about another way. Why don't you buy me out?"

That was Holladay's second bomb and this one stunned Davie as much as it did the Wells Fargo men. But after the first dazed seconds McLane said incredulously:

"Are you serious?"

"If the price is right, it makes sense, doesn't it?"

McLane's tongue ran around his lips without his knowing it. All these years he had dreamed of a stagecoach system that would not only span the continent but whose feeder lines would reach into every town and mining camp in the West. And here it was, dangled in front of him.

Danford Barney recovered his poise more quickly. "We will consult our board of directors," he said, "and see what we can offer."

A second meeting was agreed on and Holladay and Davie left. Davie was still in shock. Ben Holladay who had fought Wells Fargo tooth and nail, selling to his bitter enemy?

On the street he said hopefully, "You don't mean it, do you? Isn't it just a maneuver to buy some time?"

"Mean it. We're selling."

"But Mitchell . . . what will he say?"

Holladay whistled a snatch of tune before he grinned at Davie. "Mitch's idea. A one-two punch. A little magic act." He wiggled the fingers of his left hand in the air. "Watch this hand, you don't see the other one picking your pocket. Ain't I a hell of an actor?"

"Mitchell Randolph giving in to Wells Fargo? Ben, I just don't believe you. He'll have your hide."

Holladay continued to beam, to prance. He fished a letter from his pocket, shook it out and passed it to Davie. It was in Mitchell's hand, eerie in the accuracy with which he wrote the script of the meeting they had just left.

Make them think they've forced you to the wall, it said. *Get them hungry. Keep them focused on stagecoaches, stagecoaches, stagecoaches. The railroad is coming but WF doesn't see that yet. We must get out while we have the time and can get a price. Take Davie along to see the fun.*

There was a clipping from the *Californian* enclosed. Work on the Central Pacific Railroad had begun again after the four years of doldrums during which only forty miles of track had been laid, but the newspaper took a sarcastic, jeering view of the new activity. Charles Crocker and Company, it reported, were importing thousands of Chinese laborers and claiming that now they would build up over the Sierra. It would be another spectacular swindle, the writer promised, and jibed at the promoters.

"The rails will never go over the mountains," he said flatly, "and Stanford and Crocker and their associates know it. Do they care? They do not. Their only interest is money. First they froze out Judah, the man with the dream, who has since died of a broken heart. Now they are at work wringing subsidies from the towns and counties with hollow promises to lay their tracks through those communities, and Huntington is camped like a vulture in Washington, hoodwinking Congress, grabbing more funds there with both hands . . ."

Mitchell had written across the clipping, *The days of the Concords are numbered.*

Davie accepted Mitchell's word. When had Mitchell been wrong in his foresight? But Wells Fargo did not take the threat seriously. In November they signed their sales contracts with Ben Holladay. For the Overland empire they paid Ben two million dollars, most of it in cash, plus three hundred thousand in Wells Fargo stock, plus a seat on the Wells Fargo board of directors.

Mitchell Randolph kept out of Wells Fargo's sight and let them go on thinking arrogantly that they had again pushed him out of the transportation business.

CHAPTER THREE

While the sale of the Overland to Wells Fargo was being negotiated Aurelia Randolph sailed into New York harbor. Forewarned that she was coming home now that the war was over and no retaliation was being taken on the West Coast against the conspiring Southerners, Mitchell sent Davie Stuart out to bring David East to meet his mother.

Now fourteen years old, David had grown into a moody, abrasive boy with a cockiness that his godfather thought was an armor to keep everyone from coming too close, to protect a too sensitive spirit and a too sharp mind. His curiosities on the trip betrayed him as new territories reeled past, the high mountains, the plains, as adventures excited him, but he hid them quickly behind a façade of boredom.

The week in New York before she arrived was no better. Mitchell was closeted daily with Ben Holladay and had little time to spend with his son. It fell to Davie Stuart to show the boy the sights, and this David openly resented, with a perception that brought his godfather up short.

"Do this. Do that. Go see this. Go look at that," the boy mimicked his father in a sulky tone. "He orders me around like I was a piece on a chessboard. You too. Do you always hop up and do everything he says, jump when he snaps his fingers?"

"Just now," Davie told him patiently, "your father is a very busy man. He wants you to get the most out of this trip and he doesn't have the time to take you around himself."

"He wants me out of his way." There was a scorn that came from hurt in the young voice. "He doesn't have time for anybody any more. I'll bet he doesn't even meet Aurelia's ship."

Mitchell did meet the ship with them, but the homecoming was a disaster for the boy. The woman who embraced him was nothing at all like the girlish mother in comfortable riding trousers and soft shirt that was his memory. Aurelia Randolph arrived decked in the latest of the Paris fashions, a silk skirt daringly short with a hoop that bobbed up in back as she hugged him to show a pair of bright-colored stockings and most of her legs. Her hair was ratted and piled in coils of curls, her face painted with rouge, her lips reddened and her perfume almost made him sneeze. He was embarrassed by her kisses in this public place, by her pattings and holding him out before her and squealing at how tall he had grown.

Davie Stuart too was uncomfortable at the apparition, as used as he was to the elegance of the ladies who paraded on Fifth Avenue, and Mitchell walked all the way around her for an inspection, shaking his head, silently laughing.

There were two more weeks in New York and Aurelia had a different costume in high style for every day, for every part of a day. The August Belmonts gave a ball to welcome Mitchell Randolph's wife back from Europe, and for this she had a gown dazzling in its glitter.

If she were a stranger to her wary son the boy was just as unfamiliar to Aurelia. They had lost touch. Neither knew what to make of the other. Davie Stuart saw the rift driven by the long separation and worried whether it could ever be closed. There would be their return west together and he hoped the two could reorient themselves in the confinement of the cars and coaches. For himself, Davie felt that he had lost altogether the long warm understanding they had shared. It was like something cut out of him, probably best since as Mitchell's wife she would always be out of his reach, but it was a painful wound nevertheless.

He and Mitchell saw them off and then Davie, empty and at loose ends all around, with nothing to do, roamed the town while he waited on Mitchell and Holladay. He was still technically working for Holladay but with the stage empire sold he had no enthusiasm for returning to San Francisco where Ben wanted him in the steamship operation.

Aurelia and David went west, first on the railroad and then in Ben Holladay's private coach, the last people to use it before it was given over to Wells Fargo. Mitchell had told her about the sale, but when she had showed her amazement that he would willingly let

Wells Fargo take anything he had had his hand in he had given her an enigmatic smile and said only to wait and watch. That something else was in the wind she understood, but Mitchell was unchanged, he would not talk about whatever it was until his own good time came around. She put speculation aside. She had her own life to pick up and reorganize, and her son to reacquaint herself with. That proved to be hard to do.

This was the first time she had crossed the continent and she was as curious as David had been, without his constraint. She began questioning him about the towns, the landmarks as they passed them, and he answered but there was none of the relish in him that she had expected. To her the trip was one of mounting wonder. The vastness of the land awed her. Across the wide western states she recognized the meaning of the armed guard who rode the top of the coach with the driver, felt the loneliness of the isolated stops where horses were changed and men watched through the nights with guns ready. The majesty of the mountains, higher than she had ever seen, thrilled her. The monumental job being done by the Americans she had despised, the taming of the wild country, forced her admiration. In France she had discovered that she felt more kinship with the Americans exiled there than with the Europeans, most of whom had been childishly puzzled that a woman of intelligence could come from the remote, "savage" West Coast of the United States. She came into San Francisco feeling for the first time that it was truly her home, and charged with a fresh eagerness to re-establish herself.

She had lost nothing of her position in the city. She was anything but forgotten. The New York society pages, covering the Belmont party, had noted without interest that Mrs. Mitchell Randolph was being feted before her return to California, but when she walked into the San Francisco courthouse judges, lawyers, attendants put on a spontaneous celebration. The newspapers dredged up the old antics and speculations of the Boniface days, sifted their files for the rumors that had filtered in from Europe. Now they could laugh in bold print at the day she had spirited the man who was her lawyer-mentor out from under the noses of the Provost Marshal, the night she herself had barely escaped to France.

There, they boasted, she had been the toast of the Imperial court, friend of the Empress Eugénie, companion of the half brother of Emperor Napoleon III. Only one story did she bother to deny, when an old reporter friend suggested that she had worked with Gwin to move into Sonora and establish a retreat for the California Copperheads. She challenged the man hotly, and learned from him that Gwin had been arrested trying to cross the border into Texas, had been held in Fort Jackson for two years, then returned to the Coast but was staying out of politics.

No one seemed to think it strange that a woman who had been an acknowledged agent for the Confederacy should be welcomed back as a heroine. The sentiment for the South that had so nearly taken the state out of the Union was as strong as ever, rebel yells echoed in the theaters whenever an orchestra played the stirring strains of *Dixie* and the Stars and Bars flew proudly in every celebration and parade.

California had not been overrun by troops as the South had been, was not impoverished as the rest of the country, where the greenbacks had dropped to a fraction of their face value. The West was still on the gold standard while Belmont and the other eastern financiers fought to bail out the faltering currency with loans from the big private bankers.

Business in the West was good. There was no time for bitterness. The conquered South was gasping under the heel of a military government but on the coast the men who had worn the Confederate gray were coming back, moving unchallenged into their former places. David Terry was again practicing law. Senator Gwin, his Mexican bubble burst, had turned from politics to recouping his fortunes. Of course there were missing personalities. Marion Boniface's office was closed, the clerks vanished and no one had seen or heard from the lawyer since Aurelia had put him aboard ship, nor had Roper Duggan reappeared.

The city was flourishing, growing again. Every ship, every coach brought returnees and new emigrants, men ruined by the war and looking for a new place to start again, veterans made too restless to settle back into the small towns they had come from, hunting adventure, excitement, easy riches.

The stock market was rampaging. Everybody from Billy Ralston down to the chambermaids and streetcleaners was trading in Comstock shares and wild fluctuations made fortunes and wiped them out overnight. Men and women working for small wages and knowing nothing about the power battles and manipulations that raged like lightning storms over Sun Mountain threw their pittances into the gambling and chronically lost them. For the first time a poor class was developing that was not the direct result of temporary depressions. The Bank of California was tightening its grip not only on the business structure of San Francisco but on the mines and mills of Nevada. Laborers and small storekeepers were gathering in protest, a new Workingman's Party was growing.

There were so many changes, there was so much for Aurelia to catch up with, particularly to learn where the subtle shifts in alliances were, who were the key people through whom a lawyer must now work, who held the legal and legislative power. To find out as much as she could in the shortest time she gave a series of parties, inviting writers, politicians, men from the legal scene, and listened closely to their talk.

To her astonishment David showed no interest when she tried to draw him into her activities. He spent most of his time away from the house and would not say where he had been when he came back. On the evenings of her parties he shut himself up in his room. She supposed that he listened at the register, uncomfortable among the grownups, and put his moodiness down to a stage of development that must be gotten through, unpleasant as it was.

But in the early morning hours as one party was breaking up a police captain Aurelia had known before the war brought the boy home. He had slipped out and been picked up with five older *Californio* youngsters for raising a ruckus in one of the fancy parlor houses.

Her guests thought it was hilarious. Aurelia did not. The boy was drunk, insolent, obnoxious, and he was taller than she, too big to spank. She bullied him up to bed and when she had closed the door after her last guest she hurried to the kitchen, anger in her voice.

"Has David done anything like this before, Nora?"

"I couldn't say." Nora was guarded, her arms deep in dishwater, not stopping her work. "He's been running loose quite some time now and I ain't been able to do a thing with him."

"But Mitchell. Doesn't he handle him? What does he do?"

Nora shook her head in helplessness. "That boy is plumb out of control. Mr. Randolph never would lay a hand on him. He used to threaten to cut off his allowance, and that child loves money. It worked for a while, then David learned his daddy had bought some land in his name and it was bringing in some rent, and that was the end of that. Next time Mr. Randolph tried it David up and told him he'd move down with his grandmother where he wasn't picked on, and you know how your husband feels about that place."

"I think," said Aurelia, "that would be a very good place for him just now."

In the morning she loaded David into a carriage, drove him down to the ranch and told Duncan to keep him on the property if he had to tie him. When Mitchell got back they would have to make a decision of some kind as to what to do about the boy.

While she waited for that day there was a happier diversion. Roper Duggan presented himself at the South Park house, his hard hat squarely on his head as always but the indoor pallor that had been his color covered by a deep tan. Aurelia squealed when Nora ushered him in, ran to him and planted a hard kiss on the startled man's mouth, then grabbed his shoulders and hugged him to her, laughing in delight.

"Roper. Roper . . . Where have you been? I couldn't find you anywhere."

He drew away, kicking at the rug, too intent on his mission for even a smile.

"I guess I just got back, Aurelia. Been out in the Pacific with Marion."

"He's all right then?" Her eagerness made her appear to pounce at him.

"Well . . . some ways yes. He's the reason I came to see you. I got to raise enough money to get a ship and go rescue him."

"Rescue him from what? Is he a prisoner?"

Roper bobbed his head. "Yeah. Sort of. He's on one of the Society Islands. I got shanghaied when we put Marion on that boat. We jumped it first chance we got and where we landed there was a queen. We been there ever since and she won't let him go."

"An island queen? What does she want with Marion?"

"Well, she took a shine to him right off. You know the boss, any woman catches his eye even if she is eight feet tall and three hundred pounds and kind of dusky. Besides, there wasn't much to do on that island. So she made him her prime minister, which was fine while the war lasted, but now she wants to keep him."

As hangdog as Roper looked, Aurelia had to laugh. When she could she said, "But she let you leave?"

"Not just exactly. A ship come in to trade and she shut us up in a storeroom. I dug a hole to get us out but the boss can't swim, so I swam out to get a boat. By the time I made the ship though she had her whole army out in their war canoe coming for me so I couldn't go back."

"A whole army in one canoe?" Aurelia's eyes narrowed. "Roper, you're pulling my leg."

"Oh no I ain't." Roper was indignant. "Her army is ten men as tall as she is and you never saw such long spears as they got. It gives me the shivers to think about it. Aurelia, you got to help me get him away from there."

"I'll make you a deal," she told him. "I'll help you if you will help me get the office open again. I'll have to find a couple of young attorneys who won't be above fronting for a woman lawyer until Marion comes back so we can have the place warm for him."

She had been putting off that task, not yet quite able to settle down, and Roper Duggan's reappearance acted as a charge to get her started. She was able to rent the old offices, which had been used by a series of lawyers through the war years and were vacant again, and she found two young men just going into practice and willing to work with her. By the time Davie Stuart and Mitchell returned West she was in business again.

It was late in November when they came, having been delayed by snow in the mountain passes. Over their first lunch in town Aurelia told them about David's escapade and what she had done with him.

"Imagine a child that age going to such a place," she said, and sounded shocked.

To Davie it was out of character for the Aurelia who had stood San Francisco on its ear, wearing pants, smoking cigars, playing poker, spurning conformity, and he looked toward Mitchell. Mitchell caught his glance and winked, saying:

"They've got to find out about sex sometime and there's no better place to learn than from the girls who know what they're doing."

She blustered a little, then stopped, seeming to recognize her inconsistency, and after a moment she giggled.

"Well . . . but isn't fourteen pretty young? Anyhow, the trouble is his attitude. What's the matter with him, do you know?"

Mitchell frowned, lifting his shoulders. "I imagine he's bored, come to think about it. He's so damned smart, so far ahead of his class in the school he's been going to. He's still a child in many ways but he's got a mind and a reasoning power that a lot of men would be proud of. And being very smart doesn't automatically give him an adult balance, there's so much that has to be learned by experience and no fourteen-year-old's experiences are very wide."

"I suppose so," Aurelia said slowly. "Maybe being with Duncan will help, like an older brother he can talk with."

"No." Mitchell's reaction was immediate. "There's no useful experience down there for him. I'll send him over to the college across the bay. He's pretty young but I think he can handle it, and the challenge ought to keep him occupied. I'll drive down this afternoon, have a talk with him and make the arrangements. Do you want to go?"

"Maybe you'd better go alone," she said reluctantly. "I think he resents me, that I was away so long. He may be more cooperative if it doesn't look as if we were ganging up on him."

When he had gone Davie started to leave but Aurelia said restlessly:

"Davie, do you really have to work this afternoon?"

His mouth quirked. "When Holladay sold the Overland he sold me out of a job."

"Oh," she sounded concerned. "I didn't realize . . ."

"Don't worry," he smiled. "I'll have some kind of place with Ben and Mitchell when they get ready to shove me into it."

"Good. Then can we take a ride and catch up on each other? Maybe drive out to the Cliff House and watch the sea lions . . . or, I know, take David's dog cart and go up through the sand hills. You don't know how homesick I got for the hills and the ocean, in Europe."

"Sounds like fun," he said, and meant it, wanting to learn how deep the changes in her went.

She headed for the stairs, running up them as she always had, calling back, "Go tell the barn man to harness Tartar to the cart while I change," and disappearing down the upper hall.

When she came down the short skirt that the Empress Eugénie had made the fashion in Paris was replaced by her old familiar black trousers and loose white shirt, and Davie saw that they fit her just as well as they had when he had first seen her wear them.

Aurelia was not a pretty woman, her face too thin, its bone structure too pronounced, but she was strongly interesting, and Davie felt the old stirring in him, seeing her now as he had always known her. She had affected him from their first meeting, first with resentment, then with pity and later with love. There was no question about it, Julia Bulette had spotted it at once. He had thought on the New York dock that the years had made a difference but he knew now that they had not. If she were any other man's wife he would have tried, would try now to take her away from him, but his relationship with Mitchell barred even the thought. Yet her touch when she swung to him and took his arm made him tense.

The barn man had the cart ready in front of the house, holding the horse's head. Tartar, David Randolph's favorite, was a big animal with a mean eye. Since he had turned ten the boy had spurned ponies and ridden or driven the meanest horses available. Tartar wanted to run and Davie gave him his head. The two-wheel cart spun along Geary like a runaway, the wicker body creaking and swaying as they jolted over the chuckholes.

Laughing, waving at the people on the wooden sidewalks, most of whom recognized the girl and waved back, Aurelia was more and more the gamine she had always been. The European experience seemed to be falling away from her before Davie's eyes.

The street climbed through steepening sand hills, the horse slowed to a trot and then to a walk, and they came over the top. Below them lay the water, sparkling under the sunlight, white breaker heads curling along the shore. They looked down on the Cliff House and the stretch of rocks where the sea lions roared and coughed. Davie tied Tartar and followed Aurelia along the cliff, enjoying the warm sun and the fresh breeze from the sea. There were still long stretches where no one was in sight. Aurelia stopped, looking at the horizon, drawing in a long breath.

"I missed you," she said aloud. "I missed you as I never thought I could miss anything."

For a second Davie thought she was talking to him, then he understood that she was talking to the sea and a crazy jealousy hit him. Not only Mitchell kept her from him, it was the elements themselves that she had thought of first, and there was no room in her for him. He tried to shake off the longing, the frustration, and then she made it harder for him, turning to him abruptly, saying solemnly:

"I missed you too, Davie."

Before he could pull himself together she was off, running along the edge to a path that went down the cliff side. She took the steep grade in little sidewise jumps to a small level place above the reach of the breaking surf and turned to watch him come after her.

"I rode a horse down here once," she laughed.

Glad of the change of subject, he was gruff, not sure of his voice control. "You could have broken your neck."

"Maybe I wanted to." She spoke with her head bent, sitting down on a rock, reaching for his hand to pull him to the ground beside her. She kept the hand, squeezing it, and went on, still not looking at him. "Davie, you'll never know how much your friendship has meant to me. Through all the troubles, you've always been there. Even when you were off around the country and I didn't see you for weeks or months I depended on you, I felt that you would come if I really needed you. But France . . . France is dreadfully far away. God, how I missed you there."

He drew a long breath and pulled his hand free, barely able to speak. "Aurelia, be careful."

She looked at the hand quickly. "Did I hurt you?"

"Not that way. Damn it, Aurelia, I love you. I think I've loved you since the day we met, even as I hated you."

"I know." The words were very low. "What made you hate me then?"

The corner of his mouth twitched with the irony. "I thought you were taking Mitchell away from me and Mitchell was all I had."

She nodded her understanding, and sighed. "It would have been better for you if you'd gone on hating me, found a girl of your own and married her. Haven't there really been any other women who interested you?"

He shrugged. Julia Bulette came into his mind, but you did not marry the Julia Bulettes. Or did you? A lot of the miners, the early tradesmen and bankers had married them, and he knew a few leaders of San Francisco society who had met their husbands in a parlor house.

"Mitchell shouldn't have married you in the first place. He never pretended to love you, all he wanted was your name, and a son."

She smiled at that. "But then I would never have met you at all. We wouldn't have anything. And now, Davie, I have something to say. In America a married man can take a mistress and no one looks down on him, but a wife is not supposed to take a lover. In Europe it's different. Most marriages there are arranged like Mitchell arranged ours, for financial, business, political, whatever reasons. Then both man and wife quietly find someone to love . . ."

He was sitting facing the water, his arms around his doubled legs. He came around as if he had been clubbed.

"You? Aurelia did you . . . ?"

His quick movement startled her into jerking back. She looked at him blankly for a moment, not believing he had misunderstood her, then bright color flamed in her face and she tossed her head.

"I don't believe I'll answer that question, Davie. I have never asked you what you've done and I claim the same right of privacy. Now let me be more explicit. I was offering myself to you, with all my heart."

He continued to stare at her and his own flush crept up into his scalp. Suddenly he clamped his hands around his head, holding it as if it were exploding, and yelled, a wordless cry that took all of his breath. When it was spent he filled his lungs again and the words spilled out in a rush.

312

"Aurelia, get a divorce. To hell with Mitchell. Marry me. Marry me."

She leaned forward, shouting back at him, "I can't do that. You know I can't do that. You don't want me to do that. And don't say to hell with Mitchell, you don't mean it. You love him too much. You don't want him hurt any more than I do."

"You don't want him hurt?" Davie was gasping. "You won't hurt him by divorcing him but you'll go behind his back and sleep with me? What kind of logic is that?"

"European logic. Mitchell is European. He wouldn't even care because he doesn't love me. If I divorced him, that would wound his pride and I won't do it, not after all he's done for me . . . for you . . . for everybody else he's taken care of. But Davie, I need you, I need you so much. Be my lover, Davie."

Davie scrambled to his feet and stood above her fighting his want of her, his hands hanging in tight fists.

"No. No. My God. I could never face him. I couldn't live with myself. I am not one of your Paris whoremen. Now get up, let's get the hell out of here."

She came to her feet slowly, droop shouldered, and her voice was small, thin. "All right, Davie. I suppose I've spoiled everything between us now, because you think I'm craven."

He started up the trail behind her, shaking. "God help me, no." It was more a groan than words. "Whatever Europe did to you, you were all alone. It's past. You're still Aurelia."

The drive back to town was silent. There was a wall between them. Not until she was safe in her room did Aurelia begin to cry.

CHAPTER FOUR

Davie Stuart ran. He could no longer see Aurelia without the fear that at some point his resolve would give way. He could never again be easy with Mitchell. The wedge was driven between them at last.

It was a week before he was missed, a week during which Mitchell and Aurelia were busy getting David into the college and talking to him until they were convinced he would stay there. It was another week before Mitchell learned where Davie had gone.

Randolph was having lunch at the Auction Bar when E. B. Crocker, office manager and head of the legal department of the Central Pacific Railroad Company, dropped into the chair across the table, a drink in his hand, and said:

"Mitch, I don't know why you let loose of that boy of yours, but I'm glad as hell to have him. Charley's got a mess on his hands trying to keep things moving."

Mitchell sat back, showing no surprise, nodding a greeting. "Which boy is that?"

"Stuart, the one who ran your express, ran Holladay's Overland. Who else?"

For a moment Mitchell said nothing, lifted an oyster from the shell and swallowed it, touched his mouth with his napkin.

"Glad to hear it." He sounded pleased. "When the Overland sold we didn't have a spot for him he liked and he's had the railroad bug a long while. He'll do a job for you. Where are you using him?"

"We hope he can straighten out our transportation snarl so we can move labor and equipment without falling over our own feet."

Mitchell took the information home to Aurelia, puzzlement and hurt in his voice.

"Do you know anything about it? Why he'd go over there without a word to me?"

They were in the parlor waiting for Nora's call to supper, having an *apéritif*, a custom she had learned in France. Aurelia's hand trembled and she put the glass down, stood up, walked the length of the room and back and stopped, facing him squarely. There were tears in her eyes.

"I do know, Mitchell. And it's my fault. I made a dreadful mistake, I've cut you two apart without meaning to. Baldly, I offered to take him to bed. He had a fit. He thought it would be a sin against you."

Mitchell sat without a muscle moving, without a change of expression even in his eyes. Slowly he lifted his glass and sipped from it and after a strained silence said in a quiet tone:

"It has occurred to me sometimes that a woman with your vitality would not live like a nun, on flagellation. I appreciate it that you've cared enough to keep the gossips here guessing, not knowing."

"Never mind me." She brushed a hand across the air between them. "It's Davie I've hurt, and your friendship."

He still looked at her. When he spoke she knew he had not heard her.

"But not Davie . . ."

"I thought he'd understand . . . the European way . . ."

Still he did not hear. "Not Davie. No. He's mine."

Her tears were thick now, falling. She put her hands over her face and her voice choked.

"He's gone. I've driven him away from you." Then in a loud cry, "Mitchell, I could cut out my stupid tongue. You have every right to hate me."

The tone reached through to him and he seemed to wake, to be aware of her again and hearing back through what she had said. In one of his quick shifts of mind he stood up, took her hands away from her cheeks and said briskly:

"Well, don't cry so. He'll cool down after a while. In the meantime he's in a good place. It will be very useful by-and-by."

When Nora came to call them they were composed, the subject closed, and they went in to the table together.

Unfolding her napkin in her lap Aurelia frowned. "I don't like it, him working for that railroad crowd."

"Oh?" Mitchell raised an eyebrow. "Why not?"

"They're the worst bunch of scalawags yet."

"And how do you figure that?"

315

"Mitchell, you know it's so. In case I have to remind you, clear back before I went away, when Theodore Judah was shouting himself hoarse to get a transcontinental railroad started and finally put that group together, Stanford as president, Huntington vice-president, Bailey for secretary, Hopkins for treasurer, what was almost the first thing they did? They froze Judah out. The engineer. It was his idea, his big dream. It killed him when they did that."

"He didn't have a patent on the idea. Carver, in the South, beat him to it by years, and Judah couldn't get to first base by himself, on his first survey. It took these men and the money they could raise to put it across."

"Yes, fine. And those men who could raise money have been raising it ever since, from the Federal Government, the counties, the cities, and it keeps disappearing into their own pockets. Judge Austin told me Charles Crocker did some fancy sleight of hand, resigned his directorship, started his own construction company to milk the railroad treasury and split the money with his partners. The judge says it wouldn't surprise him if they all decamped overnight with millions."

Mitchell smiled at her indignation. "Seems I remember that Austin was attorney for Wells Fargo and they've been fighting the railroad from the first. The name-calling isn't anything new. Sure the boys are creaming something off the top but that's common business practice. You used to recognize it. Railroad building takes a whale of a lot of money."

"Money," she said tartly, "they have. Grants from the government of a section of land on either side of the right-of-way for every mile they build, bonds, cash, what haven't they got? And Huntington sitting in Washington still grabbing. But what have they done to show for it all? Laid ten miles of track a year? At that rate the nation will go broke before they fulfill their contract . . . if they even intend to try."

"They've made a start. They were merchants, jewelers, hardware men, not railroaders, and they've made mistakes. But they're learning. Charley Crocker has now brought in several thousand Chinese for the labor force he otherwise couldn't find. That road will be built, Aurelia. Don't doubt it. There is an inevitable pressure behind it. That's why I keep on handling their bonds."

Davie Stuart on his preliminary survey trip had no such strong conviction, and his new job had started under a too familiar cloud. When he had introduced himself to E. B. Crocker and asked for a place the lawyer-manager had recognized his name, associated him with Mitchell Randolph even though he had used only Holladay as a reference, and once again Mitchell's magic name had made him welcome. He had almost walked out of the office, but what was the use? Where could he escape?

Once in the field he had the solace that they really needed him for what he himself could do. The office had been chaotic, Crocker harried. They were trying to drive a tunnel through the mountain under its crest and had a thousand men tied up on that section alone. They were trying to move work trains around on a shoofly. It was imperative to keep the existing track open through the winter. Crocker explained why.

"You know that the Railroad Act authorized two roads, one to build west from the Missouri, ours to build east. The way we've been held up, the Union is already coming across the Nebraska sand hills and bragging that they'll get clear to the California line before we can cross the Sierras. They're eating up the government land subsidies. If we stop for winter they'll have most of them, all the profit and land, and we'll be stuck with a railroad that climbs one side of the hill and that's all."

Davie thought of the snowdrifts thirty and forty feet high that he had seen on the summit in his days on the Comstock and shook his head.

"I don't see how you can do it," he said. "How can you move equipment in those conditions?"

"That will be your problem. You think you can figure a way for a thousand dollars a month?"

Davie tried to keep a straight face. He knew that many businessmen had piled up fortunes, but he had always worked for wages. This offer was twice what Ben Holladay had paid him. Then he let a grin come.

"For that kind of money maybe I can level off the mountain."

Crocker returned the grin. "You'll earn it. First you'll have to learn how to get around my pigheaded brother Charley and his superintendent, Strobridge. Strobridge is a driver but he's a troublemaker too. I've been trying to get them to use a steam drill to knock the blast holes in the tunnel but Strobridge is in love with single jacks and Charley backs him up. You have trouble with him, tell him you're working directly under President Stanford. And Stuart, anything you need, order through me. Just get the job moving."

In spite of the caustic laughter he had heard about the fumbling and blundering, the snail's pace of advance that had made many

317

people cry fraud, Davie was impressed by what had been accomplished. He rode the work train across the flats, through Junction, wound up through the old Mother Lode foothills to Clipper Gap and Illinoistown that had been renamed Colfax, all the laborious miles that he had walked so long ago. They turned up the mountainside around the sharp granite slopes of Cape Horn. There Crocker's Chinese army had chipped out a ledge barely wide enough for the right-of-way and a passenger looked straight down a stomach knotting two thousand feet. They passed through Dutch Flat where the engineer Judah had made the first breakthrough, sold the first forty-eight thousand dollars worth of stock to build his dream road. They inched on higher, up to Cisco that was only fourteen road miles below the summit. There Davie left the car, but the iron tracks kept climbing, all the way to that final pass which they had to drill through. To go over would be too steep a grade for the trains.

Cisco was the advance headquarters and there Davie met Charley Crocker. He was a big, florid man with a bull voice, an energy and an ego that reminded Davie of Ben Holladay. He had been a dry-goods merchant, but somewhere he had found an ability to get more labor out of a man than he thought was in him, and keep him loyal at the same time. He was Cholly Clocker to the coolies who swarmed like toadstools in their flat coned straw hats, and they worshiped him.

Montague was chief engineer and more than glad to have a man arrive whose specialty was moving goods and people.

Strobridge lived up to his reputation, a bully with ham-sized fists who could knock a man clear out of the right-of-way and was said to have killed a balky mule with a single blow between its ears. Jealous of his eminence with Crocker, he tried at first to obstruct Davie, but Davie used Stanford's name and the big man subsided.

Davie revamped the schedule of trains in and out on the single track to move with less interference, organized a plan for winter and sent for sleds, more horses and mules and skinners who might be able to keep supplies and crews moving after snow would close the line.

But winter came early. Before he could assemble all of his equipment and animals snow fell on snow. Men were put to shoveling to keep the track clear until more Chinese were throwing snow than working on the tunnel. Still they had to add locomotives to each work train to pull it up the hill. By January six chuffing engines were needed to shove through the rising drifts. Then above Cisco avalanches began to thunder down. Neither the trains nor Davie's sleds could get through and half-frozen crews were cut off in the fourteen-mile stretch. It was impossible to keep paths open between the work camps and roadbed. The coolies dug tunnels through the massive slides and walked back and forth, sometimes fifty feet beneath the crust. Supply dumps were swept away, trailing tangles of twisted rails and broken ties down the deep gorges. The white horror crashed down on bunkhouses and buried men whose bodies could not be recovered until the next summer.

Yet Charley Crocker said, *keep working*, and the crews worked on.

Beyond the unfinished tunnel other crews were rushing, grading down the Truckee Canyon and east across the Nevada Desert. On the east slope the forest was being cleared, pine trees eight feet in diameter cut into sections and rolled out of the way, the stumps blasted out, the roadbed was being leveled.

Supplies from California that were needed over there backed up at Cisco. Charley Crocker added thousands of fresh men and a road was tramped across the snow, packed hard enough to support Davie's sleds and his animals' hoofs. Thousands of tons of equipment began to wind over the divide. Three locomotives were taken apart and with rails enough for forty miles of track were hauled across.

Crocker was not an armchair boss. In a big fur coat and fur hat he rode the line back and forth looking like a great grizzly bear, urging more effort, more speed.

By the time the spring thaws began everyone was exhausted, and still there remained a seven mile gap above Donner Lake. The hardest seven miles Davie had ever seen.

Through the summer there were so many Chinese on the mountain that they fell over one another, but by the time the second winter closed down on them that gap was unfinished. Again Cisco became the end of rail and Davie's sleds hauled from snowline across and down to snowline on the Truckee side.

Word that the trains were stopped again brought a flood of renewed criticism from the scoffers. Even the Sacramento *Union*, a staunch defender of the Central from its inception, printed a series of letters from engineers in high places who said flatly that the railroad could never be anything except seasonal, that snow would force it to close at least five months of the year.

Cholly Clocker never doubted. Davie sat in the tiny construction office with him one day as he laughed over the letters.

"I may not be an engineer," Crocker said, "but I've got a surprise for these bonehead doom shouters. Davie, it took me a long time to figure it out and I got the idea too late for this winter, but come summer I'm going to build me a wooden tunnel clear over this hill. Make it good and strong so the avalanche can't bust it. Then let her snow, and we'll roll through there all winter as cozy as can be."

Davie Stuart laughed with him. "Sounds perfectly simple if you're willing to spend the money. Only, what about sparks from the smokestacks? What if they set the timbering afire?"

Crocker frowned over that for a while and then chuckled. "Why, I guess we'll have to carry extra water and some pails. Even an engineer ought to be able to see that . . . But Davie, you keep mum about this. I don't want anybody to know until it's done. I want that other railroad gang to think we're in deep trouble so they won't push any harder than they are."

In February Davie had an accident. He was riding a cutter on an inspection tour when the sound began above them. The ominous rattle of stones broken loose by sliding snow. His head jerked up and he saw it, the big mass coming down, separating around trees, bowling over them, uprooting them, tossing them through the air like kindling sticks, the boulders bounding down the mountainside ahead of the sickening white thing that looked alive.

It was ahead of the sled, not directly above, roaring over the road and on below. The wind it generated rushed past him, sweeping off his hat. He snatched at it and was off balance, leaning far out, when a big rock bounced against the sled and tipped it.

Davie went out headlong, with a yell. The road was narrow there, the drop steep, a hundred feet deep to the shallow canyon floor. His fall carried him over the edge and he hit and rolled. The snow was deep but hard-crusted and did not stop him. Rolling and sliding and spinning end for end he went down. He crashed into rocks and trees and slipped on past them, grabbing at branches, burning his hands as they whipped through them. He felt his spine crack against a tree trunk. Then he blacked out.

His driver, unable to turn the sled in so little room, ran back to the nearest work camp for help. They brought a flatbed sled, went down on ropes, found him alive and took him up in a sling and wrapped him in blankets. Then they headed for Cisco.

Charley Crocker was not there. Montague took charge, put him on a train, sent him down to the hospital in Sacramento and wired Charley's brother in San Francisco. E.B. took the wire immediately to Mitchell Randolph's office and Mitchell reached Sacramento almost as soon as Davie.

Lying so long unconscious in the snow Davie caught pneumonia.

One vertebra in his back was cracked, both legs were broken, and three ribs. His face and head were a mess of cuts, scratches, bruises.

Mitchell sounded awed, saying, "It's a plain wonder you're even alive."

Davie screwed his face up trying to smile through the bandages and wheezed, "You sure I am?"

He was in the hospital for weeks, then Mitchell and Aurelia came, to take him to the South Park house, they said. Davie refused to go there and Mitchell, knowing why, made no objection when Aurelia suggested the ranch. That was where they took him, flat on his back but past the pneumonia stage. It would be a year at least, the doctors said, before he could use his back normally, and the Crocker brothers sent word that they would have a job ready whenever he was able to go back. They continued to pay his salary and picked up his medical bills.

They arrived at Felicidad on the heels of another of David Randolph's increasingly frequent escapades. Even Duncan was unable to keep the boy in line. He was running with a group of boys from the old ranch families who spent their time thinking up ways to raise hell.

"This one," Duncan sputtered even while Davie was carried on his pallet into the bedroom and put to bed, "this one, they forced their way into an Oakland gambling club and took all the money on the tables. They said it was tribute for the King of Spain. Mitchell, the owner wants a thousand dollars to not have your son arrested."

In spite of himself Davie laughed. "The King's Fifth. Did they send it to Madrid?"

Duncan was too upset to see anything funny about it. "Indeed they did not. They threw a fandango at Emery Hall with all the college students. It was a riot."

"All right, I'll pay the freight." Mitchell was always short with Duncan. "Now clear out and let Davie rest."

The room emptied, Aurelia following the men who had carried the pallet, looking for Concepción, and Duncan trailing her, still muttering. Mitchell stayed, fussing over the bedcovers. When the door closed he said:

"That boy . . . he really worries Aurelia. She blames herself for getting into that Confederate rubbish, having to leave the country just when David needed her, and she blames me for not bundling him up and shipping him to her in Paris."

"And you?" Davie asked. "You keep on bailing him out of the troubles he gets himself into. Isn't that contributing to his wildness?"

"Possibly. But it's a battle of wills between us. He's trying to drive me into letting him go to Mexico and join José. José is down there with some kind of scheme to settle *Californios* below the line, and David is enough a romantic to think that's the answer." The corner of his mouth tightened. "He's very much like his mother in that."

Davie looked at the white plaster ceiling, thinking about the boys he had known in the mining camps, their urge for adventure that had brought them so far from homes, boys hardly older than David.

"Why don't you let him go for a while? He's so smart, he ought to get impatient with that kind of thing pretty quickly."

"Smart?" Mitchell was angry. "He's brilliant . . . but he's stubborn. He wouldn't admit he'd made a mistake when he saw it. No, I'm not going to chance his wasting his life chasing a bunch of half-starved cattle or raising bananas in a jungle. He'll grow up after a while and get interested in what I've been building for him. He likes mind games and there isn't any greater game than business.

"Well, let's change the subject. Are you too tired to talk awhile?"

Davie was tired, but Mitchell would not be staying over at the ranch, this would be their only opportunity, and something in his tone hinted something uneasy on his mind. He shook his head.

Mitchell blew out a sharp sigh. "About Aurelia. When you ran out and went with Crocker she told me why. She was damned upset, thought she'd broken you and me apart. Don't let it do that, Davie. She's been in a hard spot, even if it was of her own making. I don't say I like it, but I can live with it."

Davie could not look at him. He felt his face flaming and was glad when the other man turned his back. Neither spoke for a moment, then Mitchell switched again, to business.

"So tell me what's going on up on that mountain? Is Crocker going to make a year-round railroad or isn't he?"

"He is." Davie's voice was tight. "But don't publicize it."

"How?"

Davie's eyes came up and met Mitchell's then. "He asked me not to say. Do you want me to break my word?"

"I guess not. You've said enough for my purpose. I'm going back to town now, but I'll be down again. Get well."

After he was gone Davie lay thinking about the three of them. Aurelia, with the courage to tell Mitchell about her offer, and Mitchell, trying to clear the air with him. He felt that his body was not all that had to heal and knew that the common knowledge would always be there, between them all.

Through the months of his recovery he relaxed slowly, enjoying

Duncan and Concepción, trying with no success to break through to David on the boy's occasional whirlwind weekend visits. Aurelia did not come down again but Mitchell did, more or less regularly, bringing papers and news.

The seven mile gap on the mountain was closed.

The Union raced across Nebraska but then began having their troubles with mountains.

Louis McLane replaced Barney as president of Wells Fargo.

Ben Holladay involved himself with a railroad promotion in Oregon which Mitchell refused to take part in.

Word of Crocker's snow sheds leaked out. Mitchell came down laughing over that, saying, "The smart bastard. Now you're going to see some fur fly."

The Union and the Central were less than a thousand miles apart. It was obvious to everyone that they would soon join, that the lucrative mail contracts would then be switched from stagecoaches to the trains. But Louis McLane doggedly fought for the coaches against an increasingly hostile board of directors. The board at last decided to sell off the feeder lines. McLane resigned in protest and Barney's younger brother Ashbel became president.

"You're about ready to go back to work," Mitchell said. "And I've got a place waiting for you."

They were walking along the cliffs in front of the ranch. The bones were healed and only the vertebra still gave Davie a twinge when he wanted to use his back. But the other thing, the strain that he had thought was buried, flared with a strength that surprised him. He could not put himself under Mitchell's thumb again, do his bidding, be his boy, and he had a logical excuse.

"I'm sorry, Mitch, but I owe Charley Crocker. He's still holding my job, and I'll have to finish with him before I do anything else."

"No problem there," Mitchell was too bland. "You'll be working for him."

"Doing what?"

"Running the Pacific Union Express."

Davie turned so sharply that pain shot up into his head. "And what might the Pacific Union Express be?"

"A new company. Crocker, Tevis, Stanford, Huntington, Hopkins, myself, and a couple of others, insiders from the Central have incorporated it."

"What for? In the face of Wells Fargo? Nobody can start an express company in the West in competition with them."

"Sure we can. The Pacific Union will have the contract to carry express on the Central."

Davie grunted. "You—*are*—crazy . . . It takes more than a contract with a railroad to build up an express company. Wells Fargo may have sold their stage lines, but they retained the contracts to haul express on the whole network. That's where their strength is. They have agencies in every town west of the Missouri. You know that. And when they get ready to put their shipments on the Central they'll do just that. They're only holding off to force the Central to pay a high price for that contract. They'll just buy up your silly Pacific Union contract. You can't beat them. We've taken a licking every time we've tried, and I'm too tired to try again."

"But Davie . . ."

"Mitch . . . You and Ben Holladay were so proud of yourselves when you sold them the Overland . . ."

"We were. And if you think that wasn't smart take a look at what Wells Fargo is doing now. They're unloading at a loss."

". . . And retaining full control of all the agencies and express routes. Without those feeder lines you and Crocker and the rest haven't got a smell of a chance to get into express. To hell with it. Wells Fargo has whipped everybody who tried, and I for one have taken the last pounding I intend to."

Mitchell's temper slipped. "I never thought I'd see the day you'd quit."

"Only a fool mule goes on beating his head against a wall after he finds out it won't crack. I've done what you wanted me to for years, but I'm through. I'll help Crocker finish his railroad, then by God I'll buy my own ranch. I like it down here. I like this kind of living. And frankly, after the years with the Overland and fighting snow up by Donner Lake I'm ready for something different."

He turned and walked away abruptly. Mitchell hesitated, looking after him, then shrugged and did not follow.

Davie stayed disgusted. It did not help his mood when young David rode in at four o'clock in the morning, drunk and shouting to wake up the household, to show off a horse he had won in a poker game, fighting Duncan with his fists, screaming while his angry uncle wrestled him to his room and threw him fully dressed across the bed.

Davie had had enough of the whole mixed-up, involved mess. The idea of a ranch had burst out of him spontaneously. He had not thought of it consciously before, but why not? It would get him out from under Mitchell's domination. It would keep him away from Aurelia. And he had come to enjoy the quiet tempo. Further, he had always preferred open space.

A month later fifty acres bordering Felicidad on the south were offered for sale. Davie rode over to look at it but it was disappointing, rough, steep land shelving sharply off to the sea. There was though no one on the place and it felt good to be alone. He camped overnight and rode slowly back to the ranch in midmorning, resolved to keep looking for another property.

He came into the yard, dropped his horse at the corral and walked to where Duncan was repairing a broken buggy wheel, to report. Duncan was very much in favor of Davie buying a place but as Davie talked about what he had found he hardly listened. He kept working, angrily, taking his anger out in wrenching and pounding viciously at the wheel. Davie stopped talking about himself and said:

"What's wrong?"

"That damn kid." Duncan threw his hammer on the ground. "I'm going to bullwhip him, big as he is."

"David? What's he done now?"

"I don't know." Duncan straightened, wiping grease from his hands, glowering.

"What do you mean you don't know? What are you so mad about?"

"He rode in here last night . . . it's midweek . . . I jumped him for not being in school and he yelled at me that he was through there, that he wasn't going back."

"What did he say?"

"He wouldn't. Just kept ranting, cursing the school and everybody there, then he ran off to his room. Mother went to talk to him but he wouldn't open the door. I left him alone to sleep it off. I don't know . . . I used to be able to talk things out with him, he'd tell me some of his problems, but ever since Aurelia came back from Europe he's shut me out more and more. There's something very wrong. I've got to have it out with him when he comes back . . . he was gone when I got up this morning."

"Gone where?" Davie thought at once of José in Mexico.

"God knows. Not far I'd think. He didn't take anything with him."

"Have you sent word to Aurelia?"

"She's already worried enough about him. I want to find out more about whatever happened at school, try to cool him down and change his mind."

But Aurelia already knew. She and Mitchell came in that afternoon, calling before they got out of the buggy.

"Is David here?"

"Not now," Duncan said. "He came in last night but he rode out this morning and hasn't come back yet. What do you know about it?"

Davie helped her down as Mitchell got out on the other side, and a hand led the team away. Concepción hurried from the house. Aurelia did not answer her brother's question, saying anxiously:

"Was he all right? What did he say?"

"He was all steamed up about the school. He told me he wouldn't go back."

"No, I don't suppose he even could." She said it in an abstract way, as if her mind was not on her words.

Duncan asked again, "What do you know? How did you happen to come down?"

Mitchell's voice was heavy with trouble. "We didn't happen to. David attacked Judge Austin's son day before yesterday. He nearly killed him. They don't know yet whether the boy will live."

"Why?" Duncan's word was hard.

"We don't know yet. The sheriff came to Aurelia to ask her to have David give himself up."

Duncan's shoulders bunched as if to fight. "Give himself up hell. They'd hang him for murder if the Austin boy dies."

"Not if it was self-defense, and we have to locate him to learn that."

"We'll locate him. And I'll ship him to Mexico with José where they can't touch him."

The hostility crackled between Duncan and Mitchell. Mitchell said:

"That would be your way. Make him a fugitive for the rest of his life. No. We'll get him the best lawyers there are. If necessary I'll buy a judge. I'll buy a jury."

Duncan sneered. "Why didn't you buy the Provost instead of packing Aurelia off to France? I wouldn't trust any American to stay bought for a *Californio*, especially when the Austin boy's father is a famous judge himself. And what do you think standing trial for murder would do to a sixteen-year-old?"

Aurelia stepped between them, her hand against her forehead. "Stop it, both of you. First we must find him. Duncan, send riders to his friends' houses. We'll wait here."

She took Concepción's arm and went with her into the house as Duncan ran, calling up his crew. Mitchell stood stolid, looking after him.

"They never change. He's still living like his ancestors, like a hidalgo who made his own laws and got away with anything. Davie, what am I going to do with my kid? How do I reach him? How do I get him to grow up? For the first time in my life I'm helpless."

He did not really expect an answer and Davie had none. The only comfort he could offer was to stand by, to wait with him. They sat in the patio. They walked along the cliffs. They prowled the yard that was usually so serene and now was silent with tension. Aurelia did not come out again and Davie guessed that she was closeted with her mother. Duncan stayed out of sight, banging on the wheel in the work shed. The afternoon hours crawled as if the sun had slowed its descent. One by one the riders came back empty handed. Toward sunset Davie's suspicion was growing that David had on his own ridden south for Mexico, whether or not he had intended it when he left the ranch with no equipment.

He and Mitchell were just sitting down again for another restless pause in the patio when the hail came from the vineyard. They went out to the yard together. A fieldhand was pointing toward the crest of the hill where a single rider was putting a horse down the road at a fast run. By the time Aurelia and Concepción had come from the house and Duncan from the shed, still wearing the leather apron he used at the forge, the figure was recognizable as David.

They stood in a knot and watched him come. Like his mother and uncle he rode with a fluid grace. He saw them and drove at them, not slowing until he was nearly on them, then curbing the animal cruelly with the hard Spanish bit. With its head hauled back it danced to a stop and the boy sat loosely, looking down at them.

Mitchell said, "Get off that horse and explain yourself."

David backed the animal a step out of reach and curled his lip, his dark eyes black with hostility. "Why," he said, "here is my whole lovely family together at one time. It must be an occasion."

The words had a slur and Mitchell grunted. "You're drunk. Get down here and tell me why you attacked the Austin boy."

He did not dismount. An ugly grin twisted his face and he bent toward his father, perilously close to falling.

"To kill him. To shut his mouth. To stop the names he called me. I beat him in a card game and he started raising hell. First he yelled that I cheated. Then he said he should expect it from a stinking Spanish Jew." On the last word he jerked upright again.

327

Davie saw Mitchell's sharp wince, then the boy was talking again, getting louder, working himself into passion.

"That's what he called me, dear Father, and more. Oh, much more. He said my name isn't Randolph because that isn't yours. He said my mother was a trollop, wearing pants . . ." As Mitchell jumped for the rein David wheeled the horse away, dancing it around the group, shouting: ". . . all over town with a man every-body knew was her lover . . ."

Behind Davie, Concepción's whisper came, "Holy Mother, help him."

David faced Aurelia, his eyes so wild that they seemed not to focus. ". . . My famous mother who loves her little son so much . . ." He brandished his stiff crop at Davie then. "You, my fond godfather . . . he didn't know about you . . . are you sleeping with her too? . . . all of you . . . all of you . . . Duncan trying to tie me back to his rotting dead world . . . What have you done to me? How can I live?"

The terrible words stopped. The young face broke up. He screamed. And screaming he gored his spurs deep in the horse's flanks, fell forward on its neck as it leaped, and beating it with the short whip rode it straight for the cliff.

Whether he knew where he was headed or was blinded by the hurricane in him Davie did not know. He waited for the horse to veer. Beside him Mitchell shouted, "David, no . . . look out." The boy neither turned nor stopped. With a final goading rake of the spurs he jumped the horse over the edge.

There was utter silence in the yard. Then a rush to the cliff. Duncan was first at the head of the trail but Mitchell knocked him aside and ran headlong down the rock steps. Davie was close behind him. He could see the still body on the rocks of the beach and the horse beyond, its neck twisted half-around.

Mitchell reached the boy ahead of Davie, scuttling like a crab over the jagged footing, crouching down, laying his ear against the chest. Davie waited until Mitchell drew back and looked up with an empty face, then he bent to help lift his godson. Mitchell shoved him off roughly, picked up the broken body that was as long as his own and carried him alone back up the steps.

He climbed slowly. Not as if the weight in his big arms was too heavy, but as if the meaning of his burden would not become a fact until he reached the top. Until he joined the accused waiting there.

Aurelia had started down behind Duncan, had tripped and

pitched into him and he had taken her back and stood with her and Concepción there.

It had been too fast. Full comprehension of the finality had not come yet. They were all still empty vessels hanging in a void.

The only sounds were the wind, the dirge of the surf, and at the edge of the yard a hushed chatter as men drawn by the scream gathered, questioning the only one who had been witness to the plunge.

Then Mitchell came off the trail. He stopped in front of Aurelia. They looked at each other. And Mitchell walked on, carrying his child into the house.

Concepción reached for Duncan's arm, leaned heavily on it, and he led her after Mitchell.

Aurelia had not moved. Her eyes were dry, on the empty horizon at the far edge of the sea. Davie stopped beside her, numb. Slowly she turned to him and buried her face against him.

CHAPTER FIVE

Davie drove back to San Francisco with Mitchell, leaving Aurelia at the ranch. He did not want Mitchell to make the drive alone. He had never seen Randolph quite this way.

When he had gone up to David's bedroom he had heard a wailing inside and had waited until it stopped before he pushed the door open. Mitchell was on his knees beside the bed. As Davie came in he bent and kissed the boy's forehead, then stood up and turned, stumbling into a chair unseeing. Davie caught his arm and steadied him, and after a moment Mitchell pulled free and walked out of the room, his back squared and straight.

Davie stayed behind, giving him time to be alone, looking down at the young face that was quiet now, then he went down to the main hall.

Aurelia sat beside her mother, her still fingers interlaced on the table top. Duncan stood uncertainly beyond them. Davie sat down in the first chair he came to. Waiting for what? Mitchell turned around from the empty fireplace and spoke to Duncan.

"I'd like him buried in San Francisco. Will you send a rider to San José for the undertaker?"

Duncan went out, grasping at something to do. Mitchell crossed and put a hand gently on Aurelia's shoulder.

"You'd better stay here for a couple of days. I'll make the arrangements and let you know."

She raised her hand, laid it over his, then let it drop. Without another word Mitchell turned toward the door. Davie followed him without speaking, and Randolph did not object.

He drove as if the very action of controlling the horses could fill his mind and keep his thoughts off his son. He did not speak until they had passed the mission, then he said abruptly, without pre-amble:

"I tried to make a world where he could belong. He never hurt anyone. Why should anyone want to hurt him?"

There was no answer he could make and Davie did not even try. Mitchell was silent for several blocks, then he was fierce.

"At least he fought. He didn't take their insults lying down."

After that he was silent until they reached the South Park house. Here it fell to Davie to tell Nora and Joe, and it was Nora who let grief have its violent way with her. At first she rejected the news but when she did absorb it she threw her apron over her head and ran crying to the rooms she occupied with Joe.

Joe's eyes were wet, his ugly face twisted painfully as he went after her. Mitchell nodded vaguely when Davie suggested that they go out for food and they walked blindly up to Market, choosing a small restaurant where neither of them was known. Mitchell only pushed the food around his plate. Davie choked down a little. Mitchell began to talk, low and rambling, not looking up, not even speaking to Davie.

"Away back, I started out to climb a mountain . . . No, I started to build a mountain . . . and stand on top of it . . . to turn it over to my son when I was finished, to build it higher . . . He could have been the biggest man in this country." He brushed at his eyes and filled his lungs and let the air seep out slowly. "He's gone. Don't look back. Go forward."

As though a door closed behind him and a different man sat in front of it, Mitchell beckoned the waiter to clear away the dishes and when he had gone leaned forward, laid his arm across the table, the hand palm up as if beseeching.

"Davie, come back with me now."

Davie had never heard this man plead before. It shocked him. He knew what it meant. Mitchell Randolph had never hesitated to use any tool to get what he wanted, and that hand was reaching for Davie at this vulnerable moment. He backed away from it.

"Mitchell, don't . . ."

"Don't argue with me. Not tonight. Listen to me. I need you."

"Mitchell, I love you. I always have. You know that. But what is this, just to feel that you own me? To replace David?"

"No. No." Mitchell shook his big head savagely. "That's past. Put it by. I need you for a specific reason. To get at Wells Fargo."

Davie groaned aloud and again Mitchell shook his head.

"You have a stake in that too. Remember the Trinity shut-out. Remember how they tried to kill the Overland, how they have clubbed down everybody, how they have tried to smear the railroad out of existence."

Davie put his elbows on the table, wrapped his face in his hands and looked at Randolph as though he had never seen him. The big man's eyes were intent now, burning, compelling.

"I know you don't believe it can be done," he said, talking rapidly, "but it can be. It will be. Pacific Union Express is going to take over Wells Fargo."

Davie spoke in a barely audible voice, level, without emphasis. "Wells Fargo, with ten million dollars worth of stock outstanding, with assets even the directors don't know the value of, with agencies in every single town in the West, with rolling stock on every road. Pacific Union Express, a paper company, not a wagon, not an agency, not an asset except a contract with a railroad that isn't finished, is going to take them over.

"How?"

"That's better," said Mitchell. "Like this. The organizers of Pacific Union are also members of the Central Railroad directorship. They paid one dollar for that contract. It blocks Wells Fargo off of the Central except for through cars from the East, sealed. Billy Ralston's bank crowd controls the Comstock, mines and mills. They will want to switch their shipments from the Pioneer Stage Line to the railroad. The railroad men are local businessmen from away back, they have contacts, friends who have no reason to love Wells Fargo, who will ship Pacific Union. When Wells Fargo wakes up to how much business we are taking from them they'll come at us to buy us out. And we'll sell."

Davie closed his eyes and went on in his empty tone. "And Wells Fargo will own Pacific Union. What's different?"

"Quite a bit. Quite a bit. The selling price will be five million dollars."

Davie's eyes flew open. "You can't believe they'll pay that?"

"They will. Because we will show them how to buy us without it costing them a cent. They will increase their authorized capitalization from ten to fifteen million and pay us with the new stock. For a dollar and whatever it costs you to establish agencies and routes, maybe fifty thousand, we will receive one third of Wells Fargo's stock."

"Which is not control."

"Add in the three hundred thousand dollars' worth that Ben Holladay got for the Overland, which we bought, and what we've been buying quietly since the news that Wells Fargo was selling its feeder lines broke the market. All told it will put us in control . . . of a fifteen-million-dollar company, for an outlay of about three million."

Davie let the figures wash over him. He felt numb, floating in a nightmare. Only part of his mind followed what Mitchell was now saying.

"The reason I need you is to start Pacific Union operating, open offices here and in Sacramento and Virginia City."

"Why? Why go to that hocus-pocus? Why not just sell your little piece of paper?"

"We need a functioning company as bait. If Wells Fargo told its common-stock holders it was paying five million for a contract there'd be a scream you could hear in China, but if they're buying another express company they can get away with it."

Davie made a hard mouth. "May I submit that the stockholders of the Central Railroad will scream if a handful of their directors grab that five million instead of putting it into the company where it belongs."

"I know it sounds rough, but it's the only way to get anything done. Look at California twenty years ago and look at it today. It takes brains, vision, nerve for this kind of development and men like that won't take the risks unless they're going to be well paid."

Like it or not, Mitchell must be right. Railroads were needed, and ships and stage lines and banks. The Ben Holladays, the Billy Ralstons, the Mitchell Randolphs were building a country even though they stole the staggering fortunes.

"Davie . . . ?"

Davie bowed his head. He let it nod. And gave himself up to Mitchell again.

The Mass and interment were quiet, only the immediate family present. They stood in the windy cemetery, Aurelia between Mitchell and Davie, Duncan with his mother, Joe's thick arm around Nora's slight shoulders. After the service Duncan and Concepción drove back to the ranch, the others to the South Park house.

They were too quiet through dinner. Immediately afterward Mitchell left to attend a meeting, holding onto routine.

"Please don't leave, Davie," Aurelia said. "I can't sit here alone. Will you take a walk with me?"

Davie himself was restless with depression. On the dark street she almost ran the first two blocks, running away, he felt as he kept pace. Then she slowed until she barely moved and began the inevitable self-blame.

"Why didn't I realize what was happening? I had warnings, but I wouldn't understand. He was so bright, so sharp, so advanced for his age. I expected too much of him. It never occurred to me that his schoolmates would pick up the old gossip about Boniface and me, keep it alive so long.

"It was all an act. Mitchell knew it, you knew it . . . to attract attention, to publicize our land cases. I should have explained to David what we were doing."

"Stop it. All of us are to blame. We all thought about his mind and never considered what a child's perspective would see. He used to come to me with his questions, he'd listen to me, then after you came home he acted as though he hated me. I couldn't understand why. But I didn't try to find out."

She said in a low voice, "Nora told him you and I were in love, that I should divorce Mitchell and marry you."

"Oh Lord. How do you know?"

"He told me. He asked me point blank if it were true."

"What did you say?"

"That his father and I were married and would stay married. But I did not go further and make sure he knew I wasn't sleeping with you. He was too young to know about those things. And by the time he was old enough I had forgotten his asking."

They turned the corner and passed out of the cone of light from the street lamp and she stopped.

"What a mess I've made for all of us . . . going to France and making that hole in his life . . . I ruined your chance of a normal married life . . . I didn't give Mitchell honestly what he paid for . . ."

"Where did that business about the Randolph name come from?"

"My fault again. Mitchell would never talk about his origin and I didn't care. We just overlooked explaining to David. How blind. How stupid. How could we have ignored that all San Francisco was whispering about Mitchell like they whisper about anyone who becomes prominent? How could we have missed knowing that the children would pick up the whispers?

"Poor, sensitive, lonely little boy. We betrayed him."

Davie said roughly, "This isn't helping him, Aurelia, or you. Quit it."

"Nora . . . poor Nora. He was her baby. She gave him simple love." A whine on a rising note escaped her compressed lips.

334

Davie swung her in against him and held her while she sobbed. Then he kissed her and turned her toward the house. They had almost reached it before she spoke again, her voice laboriously matter of fact.

"Mitchell tells me he is in a new express company and that you will leave tomorrow to run it."

"Yes. And you, are you going to keep the law office open?"

"Until our current cases are closed. Then I'm going to help with a children's home Phoebe Hearst is founding. Mitchell and I will build a wing and name it for David."

They were on the porch. He opened the door for her, then took both her hands and held them tightly. He did not trust himself to speak. When he reached the sidewalk he turned and saw her framed in the lighted window, watching him.

CHAPTER SIX

To Davie, running the Pacific Union Express was running a ghost line.

He went through all the motions, trying to make the enterprise look genuine, but he could not bring himself to spend money on elaborate office equipment. His Scot blood rebelled, for it could not be long before Wells Fargo would take over his agencies.

He set up his San Francisco and Sacramento stations and then rode the Central over the mountain. The railroad was finished as far east as Reno, a mountain goat of a road, and from there he took the light stagecoach down the valley, up Sun Mountain to establish himself again in Virginia City.

The tenor of life in Washoe was no longer easygoing. The camp was tense, with ownership of the mines and mills further constricted. Under the coldly capable hand of William Sharon, Ralston's Bank of California had a stranglehold on the mountain.

One after another the mines, in debt to the bank, had run from bonanza into borrasca, and while they probed for fresh lodes the bank had bought them in at very depressed prices.

In those interludes the mills too were in trouble, with no ore to process. Wearing the hat of Virginia City agent for the California bank, Sharon had been loaning the mills money at one percent per month, half the interest charged by the local institutions. As the mills became unable to meet their payments the bank foreclosed. But the bank's general stockholders did not share in the profits to be expected from these acquisitions.

Sharon, Mills, Ralston and a few insiders of the bank crowd created the Union Mining and Milling Company and as such bought up the mortgages. As new ore bodies were found the group became the owners of the richest mining camp on earth.

Using the mines and mills as a lever they then took over the water company. And the lumber companies, cutting millions of feet of timber to feed the furnaces of the mills and build the enormous honeycombs of support within the mountain, the roofings and the floorings that became the roofings as level after level descended hundreds on hundreds of feet.

The one thing Sharon had not been able to capture was transportation. The Pioneer Stage line still controlled the toll roads for Wells Fargo.

Davie Stuart went to William Sharon to offer the Pacific Union Express with its tie-in to the Central Railroad as a faster, cheaper way to move the bullion out and bring in the materials needed by the insatiable town. Sharon, as cold and ruthless as they come, was quick to welcome him, but could not help him at once.

"We've got contracts with Wells Fargo," he said, "but some of them are running out soon and as they do we'll switch to you. In the meantime I'll throw what business I can to Pacific Union, but it will be slim pickings for a while."

It was very slim. Davie ran in the red week after week until in concern he went down to see Lloyd Tevis, to tell him how much the venture was costing.

"Never mind the cost." Tevis was emphatic. "The contract with the Central specifies that Pacific Union must maintain uninterrupted service, and we lose it if you default. Go ahead if you have to run empty all year. But make it look as impressive as you can."

Toward that end and to relieve his boredom while the new line slowly built a modest business, Davie initiated a race. Wells Fargo was picking mail off the Central at Reno and hauling it up the hill in a light wagon. Davie inaugurated riders like the old Pony Express and posted five relay horses along the route. Wells Fargo arched its brows and brought in some of the best riders from the Pony Express itself. Every day crowds gathered at the entrance of the International Hotel to cheer the winner in, and after the first week Wells Fargo consistently beat Pacific Union to Virginia City. Wells Fargo relaxed and remained the complacent giant.

Winter came. This year Cholly Clocker's snow sheds let the trains rumble over the divide and down the Truckee, and Davie met the trains, whatever the weather. The Central pushed on eastward, the westbound Union Railroad advanced across the flats, both grading

337

far ahead of the crews laying track. Toward spring the country was treated to the exceptional sight of the grading crews of both rival roads passing each other on parallel routes, Crocker's Chinese heading for the Mississippi while the Union Irish made for the Pacific Coast until Congress put a stop to that, passing a law that the two lines must join together at Promontory Point, six miles west of Ogden, Utah.

While Virginia City laughed or raged over this newest spectacle of the high-handed barons of finance, tragedy struck the mountain. On April 7, Davie was waked by Tom Peasley's fire bell. It rang and kept on ringing hysterically, signaling a major fire.

Davie had joined the department for somewhere to go, although the old political energy was gone out of it with Peasley dead and the Civil War over, and he ran, meeting up with the members of his company at the firehouse as they lined up on the sides of their engine, hauled on the straps and rushed down C Street.

Around the head of the Yellow Jacket mine a crowd was swelling and heavy red-black smoke rolled out of the entrance. At the adjoining Crown Point and Kentuck mines the elevators were hoisting up crews as fast as the cars could drop and lift. Father Manogue and John Jones, superintendent of the Crown Point, came rushing to direct the rescue work. Davie's team pushed through and began a rhythmic pumping while the nozzle men swept a stream of water over the building. One at a time every piece of apparatus in Virginia City, Gold Hill, and Silver City arrived. But all of them together made slow impression on the growing inferno.

Virginia City had had many fires but most had been above ground. This one was shaping up as the worst in the mountain's history. The mine shafts boring fourteen to sixteen hundred feet deep intersected at every hundred foot level with laterals that broke through from property to property, connected mine with mine.

The underground pumps held down the floods of boiling water that kept the temperatures below over a hundred degrees, but they were no help against gas and smoke. The roiling stuff spread and began belching from all three mine shafts.

Behind the furiously pumping fire crews and the off-shift miners scrambling to drag choking men off the hoists to safety a silent cordon of women, children, workmen, merchants, bankers, crowded, helpless, watching.

The smoke thickened, became so dense that no one could go below and live. They could only stand by their engines, pouring water in, hoping against reason that in the underground hell some of the men trapped there might have found air pockets sufficient to breathe.

By nine o'clock the cloud rolling from the Kentuck shaft thinned and two bodies were brought out. By noon the rescuers were able to get down the Yellow Jacket to the eight-hundred-foot level and four more dead were raised.

For three days they worked, probing as deep as diminishing gas and smoke would permit, but by the fourth morning it was undeniable that there was no further hope that anyone still in the workings could be alive.

The mines were sealed off. Steam from the boilers in the mine heads was forced through the air hoses into the depths. Two days later the shafts were opened and a few more bodies recovered. But after several of the men searching for others collapsed the shafts were closed again.

Davie dragged back to his room exhausted. For the past five days none of the firemen had had more than a short relief. He slept the clock around before he could go back to his agency.

It was days before all of the bodies were found. Forty-five had died, the worst single disaster since the beginning of the camp. No one knew what had started the blaze, perhaps an explosive mixture of gas had been triggered by a hot pipe, perhaps some miner had left his candle burning too close to a beam. It did not matter. Virginia City was shaken as it never had been.

Men gathered along C Street talking in hushed voices. A mass funeral was attended by everyone. John P. Jones who had been merely another mine superintendent was now a hero for his rescue work.

And the blame. There is always need to blame someone in such an accident and it was heaped in abundance on the heads of William Sharon, William Ralston, the others of the bank crowd, for not making the mines safer to work in. There were personal threats and a threat of a miners' strike until the underground was made gas free, until provisions were made for safety even against another fire.

Adolph Sutro thundered through the newspapers that if his tunnel had not been fought for so long it would have been built by now and the men who had died could have escaped downward. He insisted as he had been insisting that the four-mile bore was necessary not only as a passage for men and ore, but it would drain off the hot water and ventilate the gaseous chambers.

The obstructionists were again the Bank of California people, the Union Mining and Milling Company.

Sun Mountain was still obsessed with the Yellow Jacket fire in early May of this year of 1869 when the ceremonial spikes were driven at Promontory Point and the Central and the Union became a single transcontinental railroad line.

Davie Stuart figuratively held his breath, waiting for Wells Fargo to move. Through the summer of '69 the Pacific Union Express took more and more business from the giant company, shipping on the Central between Virginia City and the Coast. It was incomprehensible to him that they had not yet recognized that they must be able to use the trains, but still they stood aloof. Could it be, he wondered, that the eastern directors were still discounting the importance of the West Coast? But their stock continued to fall. As money men they must see that, and the glaring reason for it.

Or was there some flaw in Mitchell's plans? Was Wells Fargo sitting on a secret, letting Tevis and his people go on pouring funds into Pacific Union as they had with so many other competitors, until they were ready to reach out and pluck it off?

The more time that passed the more Davie worried. The races to Reno for the mail went on as if beating Pacific Union on that run was all-important to Wells Fargo. On the other hand Davie's business grew. By fall he had the accounts of half the mines and mills, those controlled by the Bank of California, which must be hurting Wells Fargo.

In October there was a cryptic wire from Mitchell. Davie was to meet a train in Reno prepared for a trip to Omaha. Mitchell was on the train and in a lighter mood than Davie had seen him since David's death, the old alchemy of energy radiating from him. When Davie asked him why they were going he dropped one eyelid in a long wink.

"It's a pleasure trip," he said. "For the biggest pleasure of my life. We are going to watch Lloyd Tevis make Wells Fargo swallow our bait, hook, line, and sinker."

"How can you be so sure?" Davie let his worry show. "How do you know they haven't got something up their sleeve?"

"Oh, I don't think so." Mitchell's laugh was easy. "It took them awhile but it finally got through their thick skulls that they have to have Pacific Union. They'll buy. Thanks to you."

Davie felt a chill of foreboding. For seventeen years Wells Fargo had beaten off all comers and his habit of expecting them to was strong.

"You mean they've approached you?"

"Not directly. That's not their way, if you recall. They went to Huntington in Washington, and then to Ralston, trying to get the bank to give them back the Virginia City business you took away from them. It was beautiful. Ralston said he'd talk it over with Mills, and D.O. suggested that we might sell out. Tevis and Mills and you and I are now going to meet with Barney and Bill Fargo in Omaha . . . neutral ground, if you like."

Davie was very surprised to be included. "I'm flattered and of course I'd love to watch," he said. "But why me?"

Mitchell Randolph was having fun. "Why, because you are general agent for Pacific Union Express. You'll be there to explain our projected expansion to Wells Fargo."

"Our what projected expansion? Something I haven't heard about?"

"You're hearing now," Mitchell said innocently. "Our plans are drawn to open agencies in every town in California, Oregon, Washington Territory . . . anywhere else we can find business to feed to the railroad."

"Oh now, Mitchell, they won't believe a come-on like that. They know it would cost a fortune and take years to do."

"But with the Bank of California behind us they can't take the chance. And they know you could do it. That makes you our ace, boy."

Davie coughed, feeling that something was caught in his throat, and shook his head. "Well, I can see it's going to be some poker game . . ."

The ride itself, over the Union rails, was interesting to Davie. It covered ground that he had crossed so many times when he had been running the Overland for Holladay and gave him his first chance to compare the grade, the cuts and tunnels with those Crocker had built over the Sierras, and he felt a loyal, almost personal pride at what Crocker and his Chinese had achieved. The Union had crossed mountains but the Central had had far the more difficult country to cope with.

Omaha was a dismal, raw railroad town with little other business. The streets were muddy from recent rain and the hotel was forlorn. Davie was very glad when Lloyd Tevis's and Mills's private car pulled in on the siding and he and Mitchell were moved into that.

It was Davie's first meeting with Mills, a quiet, reserved man, not easy to know. He was already acquainted with Tevis, through working for him and by reputation.

A Kentuckian by birth and a lawyer by training, Lloyd Tevis had proved to be a business genius in a society of business greats. He had been ruined by the St. Louis fire and landed in California broke and gone to mining. He had had no more luck at that than Mitchell and Davie. Then he found a post in the Sacramento recorder's office and was on his way, trading in real estate. He moved from Sacramento to San Francisco with his law partner, Haggin. Now he was said to be one of the richest men in California, with interests in the railroad, the California Navigation Company, mines, water companies as well as real estate. He had a courtliness, a charm, that never reached his eyes, and it would be he who would lead the maneuvering on their side of the bargaining with Wells Fargo.

Ashbel Barney and the Fargo brothers also came to Omaha in a private car and grandly summoned the Pacific Union people to it. Tevis smiled and took his party over to them without a quibble. They were greeted coolly. The New Yorkers who controlled the big company showed a dangerously low opinion of West Coast financiers and lack of knowledge of Lloyd Tevis. William Fargo recognized Davie and Mitchell with a bare nod and perfunctorily shook hands with Mills and Tevis, and opened the conversation with a condescension that said he considered the meeting little more than an annoying formality.

"I have it from Mr. Huntington in Washington that the Central Pacific is not happy with the performance of the Pacific Union Express, that he will be relieved when we buy it."

Davie Stuart's respect for Wells Fargo's astuteness took a sudden drop. It was true that neither Huntington nor his partners had any connection with Pacific Union as far as the records went. Tevis was president, Davie general agent, and a list of unknowns were named as directors. Nor was it public knowledge that Tevis was part of the railroad crowd. But had Wells Fargo really come here unaware of the interrelationship between the Westerners? For the first time he began to believe that the monolithic organization was indeed in trouble. He watched Tevis make a small bow that suggested acceptance of Fargo's charge and listened to the cool, even voice.

"I am sorry Mr. Huntington feels that way." Tevis's lips curved in a trace of a smile that might be an effort to cover embarrassment. "Still, our contract with the railroad is valid for ten years, unless we breach it in some way. There is not much Mr. Huntington can do about it."

Ashbel Barney returned the smile and cleared his throat. *"Unless you breach,"* he repeated. "That could happen, you know. You fail to meet your commitment once and Huntington can cancel the contract. We'd pick it up. You would be left with a worthless little express line from nowhere to nowhere. But instead of waiting for that we are willing to buy you out now."

"We appreciate that," said Tevis, "and we agree that everyone would be more comfortable if Wells Fargo owned Pacific Union Express. We are prepared to sell, at a reasonable sum."

The Fargo brothers exchanged glances of congratulations and Barney sounded offhand.

"I suppose you have an asking price?"

"We do, certainly. Five million dollars."

Shock froze the New Yorkers. Bill Fargo made a sound that could be a laugh of ridicule. There was a painful silence while they looked from Tevis to Mitchell to Mills for some sign that the figure was intended to be funny. They found none. Both men sat quietly, giving no sign that they had even heard the words. Then a flush colored Barney's face and he said stiffly:

"We didn't come fifteen hundred miles to listen to bad jokes."

"I do not make jokes about money, good or bad, Mr. Barney. You asked our price, I gave it to you." Tevis's tone was cold and he stood up, the image of an insulted man, and turned his head toward Mitchell and Mills. "If you are ready, gentlemen?"

Charley Fargo said quickly, placatingly, "Wait a minute, Mr. Tevis. I assure you no one meant to offend you, but you must admit that your figure is out of the question. Why, we have been in business nearly twenty years, we hold a monopoly on everything west of the Missouri, yet our capitalization is only twice what you're asking. You can't be serious."

Tevis looked stonily down his nose. "You people asked for this meeting, we did not. We do not have to sell."

William Fargo, fighting his temper, growled, "What's going on here?" He turned to appeal to Mills. "Mr. Mills, you have a reputation as a hard-headed, no-nonsense banker. Can't you explain to Mr. Tevis the absurdity of what he's saying?"

"I am only here as an observer," Mills said in a thin, unconcerned voice, "to see if the loans which Pacific Union Express have asked for are justified."

343

There was an almost audible sigh among the Wells Fargo team. If Pacific Union was looking for loans it could mean that the young express company was in financial straits. Tevis's outrageous quote would then be only an attempt to shock, to leave himself room for a generous come-down in the dickering while still hoping to get the highest dollar Wells Fargo could be conned into paying. It would follow then that they need only to keep talking until Tevis folded. Ashbel Barney dropped his eyes to hide their new brightness and said in his softest voice,

"Loans, Mr. Mills?"

"Why yes," Mills said without emphasis. "They have asked for three and a half million dollars. Mr. Stuart has shown us a prospectus for a large extension of their agencies up and down the coast. We are considering it."

The bright opportunity Barney had seen a moment before collapsed and shook his poise and he asked with more concern than he wanted to show:

"What kind of security are they offering for a loan like that?"

Mills sounded as if he expected more shrewdness from Barney. "Their contract to carry express on the railroad. I should think that would be obvious."

But Barney couldn't let it go, pressing. "You think it's worth that much?"

"The contract? How much did your company gross last year, Mr. Barney?"

Barney got the implication and did not like it and argued. "But it takes more than a single contract to make a property so valuable. Don't forget that we still hold our contracts with the feeder lines to handle their express . . ."

D. O. Mills shook his head teacher-fashion and spread his attention to cover the three men.

"As I said a few minutes ago, I am only an observer here, but we at the bank realize that it is only a matter of time until the whole coast is crisscrossed by rails. Already two companies are working to connect Portland with San Francisco. The Southern Pacific, of which Mr. Tevis here is president, is building down the valley toward Los Angeles. While I do not wish to presume to advise it would appear to me that the sooner Wells Fargo assures itself that its express cars will ride the railroads the more solid your position will be."

There was an awkward, thoughtful silence until Barney looked at his watch and said:

344

"Gentlemen, it has gotten quite late. Shall we say ten-thirty tomorrow morning?"

The Pacific Union Express group walked unhurried back to their Pullman. Mitchell hung a little behind with Davie, saying in an undertone:

"Now do you begin to see that they can be had?"

"I don't know, Mitchell," Davie said uneasily. "Nothing was said about their recapitalization. Supposing they're just scared off. Suppose they decide to wait and see if we do expand?"

"Then we'd start building agencies. But they won't. They asked for another meeting, didn't they? Don't undersell old man Mills, that was a beautiful job of harpooning he did."

"Well . . . talking about these kinds of figures makes me nervous . . . but what if they go you one better and recapitalize for twenty million, to make sure their control isn't jeopardized?"

"Good boy." Mitchell nodded in approval. "There is that chance. We've talked about it. But the way they've been letting things slide of late, letting both the Union and the Central contracts get away from them when they could have had them without question if they'd helped the railroad instead of fighting it, seems to indicate a failing judgment at the top there. We don't believe they are that venturesome any longer. We'll see pretty soon now. What we have to do is keep them thinking we are an immediate threat. Tomorrow morning when Tevis asks you to give him the number of agencies you can open in the coming year, you name every important place in the West."

But Davie was not called upon to go down the list of mythical agencies. Apparently the Wells Fargo men had been up much of the night wiring their directors for instructions, and only William Fargo met them, pleading that his brother and Barney were still consulting New York.

"New York agrees," he said, "that five million would be an unbearable burden on the company. How do you think we could meet such an expense?"

Lloyd Tevis smiled on the man fondly. "I don't really see a problem there, Mr. Fargo. If I were in your place I would increase your capitalization by five million and pay for Pacific Union with the new shares."

Fargo prowled around the coach. The possibility was obviously new to him and Davie held his breath, watching him think about it. Mitchell's, Tevis's whole premise for this raid was based on getting hold of one third of Wells Fargo stock. They did not want cash.

They could not go into the open market and buy control without kicking the price sky high and warning the big company what they were after. But if Wells Fargo bought this suggestion of issuing only a third more stock, giving it to Pacific Union, then with what the Tevis group already held the voting control would pass to them. They could elect their own directors. Those directors could choose a new set of officers. The reins of Wells Fargo would shift from the men on the East Coast to those on the West.

"It's an idea." William Fargo said it slowly, but there was relief in his voice.

"A workable idea." Mills was mild, as if this was the first he had heard of it. "The Central contract will add a third to your business. In effect you would be paying nothing for Pacific Union."

There could be no final agreement at this meeting and Davie agonized through the days while they waited on New York. Their success hinged on the imaginativeness back there. Their failure would mean a disastrous cost.

If Mitchell and Tevis and Mills were anxious it did not show. They played poker for stakes that made Davie sweat. He kept out of the game and driven by nervous restlessness went out to roam the raw town. There was not a thing in it to catch his interest. He stopped in a saloon, not so much for a drink as simply to hear human voices talking of simple things, the weather, wages, wives. A bar girl approached him, smelling of cheap perfume and clothes worn too long without washing, and he left, unreasonably annoyed.

And then Tevis brought back a piece of paper and tossed it on the poker table. An agreement signed by him and Ashbel Barney. Pacific Union Express was sold. Good will, equipment, agencies, and the contract with Central Pacific, for five million dollars worth of new stock issued by Wells Fargo. The company had not recapitalized to twenty million.

Davie expected the trip back to the Coast to be one continuous celebration. It was not. For the paltry expense of running the dummy Pacific Union Express these men had stolen one of the richest concerns in the United States so artfully that Wells Fargo did not yet comprehend what had happened, but there was no gloating on the train. Wells Fargo was hardly mentioned. The attention, the conversation, turned to other subjects, to a hydraulic mine Ralston and the bank were backing at North San Juan in the California hills, to a new railroad Sharon was planning up the side of Sun Mountain to connect Virginia City with Carson and Reno.

It was the first Davie had heard of that project and for a moment he thought it was a joke. Such a railroad would have to climb sixteen hundred feet in less than thirteen miles. But it was not a joke. It came to him that he was riding with a company of men so shrewd, so sharp-witted that he could only glimpse vaguely, after their accomplishments, the magnitude of their visions. It was such men as these who had in a short twenty years built San Francisco into one of the dominant financial capitals of the world.

Listening to their laughter, their talk, he began to realize what Mitchell had meant when he called business a game. It was not money of itself they were after, but power. Power to create, to make their dreams become reality. And still this was a car full of thieves. He thought of the way the silver nabobs manipulated the market in mining shares, jockeying prices to their own advantage and devil take the little man. He wondered what the rank and file of Wells Fargo stockholders would do when they discovered that their company had fallen to the railroad crowd. Would they try to fight, or meekly submit?

He had no advance notice of the bitter cries that later rose and echoed to the halls of Congress, of the special investigating committee that would grill the Tevis raiders and peter out in frustration under the smoke screen thrown up by the men here. After the changes in management Wells Fargo's capitalization was dropped clear back to five million. No one could prove how much the investment in Pacific Union Express was, or what it was really worth. The only thing that became clear was that Lloyd Tevis was top man.

At the moment Mitchell came back to sit alone with Davie and stretch himself in luxury.

"It's been a long time," he said, enjoying the words. "A lot of years, Davie, since I told you I would get that outfit. Does it feel as good to you as it does to me?"

Davie's smile was twisted. "To watch the old crowd being pushed out the way they pushed all the others? Yes. I wonder if they'll like it any better than we did."

Mitchell lifted a finger, cautioning. "They won't be out. They've got good connections in the East that we'll need, especially with America Express. They'll stay in, but Lloyd will be boss. And you'll have to start thinking a little broader, boy. You're going to be general agent on the West Coast."

Davie's head snapped around. "Me? In Louis McLane's old spot? Who says so?"

"It's on the reorganization chart. As soon as Tevis is president the place is yours."

His first reaction was to be dazzled. He was younger than any man who had held so high a rank. Then he was suspicious.

"Mitchell? All right that you've moved me around like a queen's pawn as long as I can remember. Now do I get this job on my own merit or are you still playing chess?"

"A little of both, maybe. Tevis is very impressed at the way you handled Pacific Union. You can cut it all right."

No more was said about it on the train. Davie dropped off at Reno to close the Virginia City office, turn papers, treasure and equipment over to the Wells Fargo agent there, a man he had fought through the short life of Pacific Union and who received the spoils with a smug, what-did-you-expect smirk.

Davie took two weeks about it, not because it took so long necessarily, but he delayed deliberately. The prospect of being general agent that had sounded so desirable on the train was becoming less and less attractive. First was his old dislike of being tied to the city, a desk in the Parrott Building, but now he had had an inside look at the ways of the top of the business world which he would move into. A man had to have a thick hide and eyes in the back of his head to survive in it. What personal satisfaction could he expect to take from such an ordeal?

When he went down to San Francisco he had made his decision. He came into Mitchell's office shortly before noon and was wrapped in a bear hug that squeezed the breath out of him. Mitchell picked up his high hat and cane and waved him toward the stairs.

"I was just on my way to look over some property on Columbus. Come along with me, then I'll buy you some lunch. We can talk on the way."

He was in a fine mood, talking as they went down the stairs and turned north up Montgomery, full of new plans now that the Wells Fargo fight was over.

"It will take maybe a year before everything is straightened out, and you've earned a rest. Take it, then come back and we'll build Wells Fargo bigger and better than ever."

"Mitchell." Mitchell was walking fast, his steps reflecting the pace at which his mind was running, and Davie with his longer stride had to stretch to keep abreast. "It's a big compliment, your thinking that I could run the coast, but I've been looking at it for two weeks. I know you won't agree, but I don't want it. You and I are different, we don't want the same things. You love business and the battle for power. That bothers me. I've lived in small communities all my life, places where I knew most of the customers by their first names and cared about them. If I sat up there under Tevis and those robbers I'd have to either hurt people or get hurt, and that kind of pressure would drive me crazy."

Mitchell twirled his cane happily. "It's the size of the job that scares you right now, Davie. By the time we're ready for you you'll be used to the idea."

"I don't think so. What sounds best to me is that little ranch I was going to start. That's all I want."

Mitchell was amused, he simply did not believe. "Don't get excited," he said. "You'll change your mind when the time comes. Here . . . we turn here."

They were at the corner of Montgomery and Pacific Streets. Pacific had led up from the original boat landing and during the first year of the gold rush had been the first road cut through the sand hills, but it had deteriorated rapidly. The Sidney Ducks had thrown their shacks up along it, and after them had come the cheap dance halls, the deadfall saloons, the Cheap John stores that advertised by flying all manner of clothes, like the signal flags of a ship, from long poles on the roofs. Trousers and shirts and coats filled out and flapped a frantic dance in the breeze off the bay, and were known locally as flags of Jerusalem.

Under one such banner part way down the block was a small huddle of half-grown hooligans jumping and jeering around the store front. Mitchell and Davie saw them as they made the turn onto Pacific and walked toward them.

Boisterous young packs of these Rangers were common in the section and Davie gave them scant attention. Then he saw what they were tormenting. A young Jew, tall and slender, with a black beard and heavy brows, black hair curling tightly over his head, crouched back against the wall, cringing away.

Davie heard the catcalls. "Ya, yid . . . dirty kike . . . stinking Christkiller . . ."

One hoodlum reached into the gutter for a handful of filth, dodged through and threw it into the frightened face, and they laughed like hyenas as the young man shrank farther back. Davie had a flash of pity for the victim.

Mitchell growled. The sound might have come from an animal's throat, a warning.

"The shame . . . the shame of him. Why doesn't he fight back."

Mitchell was running at them. Davie, taken by surprise, was a minute in starting, a few steps behind. Mitchell reached the rear of the crowd, lashing out with his heavy thornwood stick, grabbing and hurling bodies out of his way, a black grizzly bear storming in on them.

They fell back under the unexpected onslaught and did not immediately recover. Mitchell bulled through them, roaring.

"Get out of sight, you . . . Get out of my sight . . . You . . . you disgrace to your race."

He had his fingers in the young man's collar, twisting him away from the wall, turning him, throwing him bodily through the door of the store as he would throw something vile away from him. He swung on around to face the semicircle that was reacting now, snarling and crouching to attack. His cane struck, crashed across a face, and raised again, knocking his hat off.

Through the gap Mitchell had cut, that had not closed, Davie saw a quick figure duck under and in, saw the flash of a knife and yelled a warning. It was lost in the howls of the pack cheated of its prey. He saw the arm crook back, the hand drive forward, bury the long blade between the ribs on Mitchell's left side, turn and cut. Then he was in the middle of them, his hands around a neck, swinging the spidery body into the street, reaching for another.

Mitchell staggered back against the building sideways, hit it heavily, braced his legs and again flung about him with the cane. For an instant Davie thought the knife had missed. Then Mitchell collapsed.

Davie was berserk. A Ranger was lunging for him, swinging a slingshot around his head. Davie caught the arm and snapped the bone across his knee.

As Mitchell fell there was a short freezing of movement, then a rush as the Rangers scattered, running off, diving through nearby saloon doors. Davie did not look after them. Before they had gone he was at Mitchell's side, on his knees, watching the bright red pump out through the ripped shirt.

He tried to stop it, stuffing his handkerchief into the deep wound. Passers-by came running and he shouted for them to get a hack, to get Mitchell to a hospital.

A hospital would do no good. Mitchell Randolph was past help.

CHAPTER SEVEN

The funeral was not the largest San Francisco had seen. Senator David Broderick's ceremony was that some ten years ago in 1859, but Mitchell's was large. The church overflowed and the procession to the cemetery stretched back half a mile.

Davie and Aurelia were alone in the first carriage. Nora, Joe, and the captain rode the second. Mitchell's people. With the ill feeling against him among the McLeods, Aurelia had excluded them.

It was four days since the murder and Davie was still in some shock. It was incomprehensible that Mitchell Randolph was gone from the scene where he had played so large a part. On his last day alive he had been so vital, so victorious, so much involved with the future. In the decisions that Aurelia asked him to help with Davie's automatic impulse was to say:

"I'll ask Mitchell about that . . ."

"It's so senseless," he argued against the fact. "I never knew him to make a move without first thinking it out, weighing the possible results."

Aurelia took his hand, holding it. "Don't think about it now."

"But why? He didn't even know the man. He didn't rush in there to defend that storekeeper. He was furious at him."

"Pride of race," she said. "He wanted to be proud of the Jews."

"He had always denied them."

"He tried to." Her voice was soft. "I know how he felt. I felt the same when my people let themselves be browbeaten and swindled and scorned. I wanted them to stand up and fight back, for self-respect. You don't understand because you have always been an

American, you never belonged to a minority that was hammered down."

"But . . ."

She put a hand against his lips. "Never mind. Let's not question now."

The carriage turned in through the gate and wound up the curving drive toward the waiting grave. The service there was short as both of them wanted, but Davie's attention wandered as the priest's low voice droned the prayers.

The community leaders were there, Mitchell's business associates, Aurelia's friends. San Francisco boasted more millionaires than any city its size in the world. Mitchell would be proud to see this gathering of them. That had been the yardstick of his success. These were the men he had wanted to be accepted by. The lonely young man who had walked across Panama had come a long, long way in a short twenty years.

Aurelia sat beside Davie, silent behind her veil. On his other side Nora cried, trying to stifle the sounds. Joe's face was set in pain. Beyond him the captain blew his nose loudly and looking toward him Davie saw tears in his eyes. It was not the millionaire bankers and lawyers and real estate operators who were most important to Mitchell. It was this handful of people, each of whose lives had been influenced by him. He had directed them, and he would live on in them long after he had been forgotten by the rest.

The coffin was lowered. The priest threw on it the handful of dirt. The crowd began to break up, and he walked with Aurelia down the hill toward the carriage. Theirs had been the first in line and would be the last to leave.

They came abreast of the gatehouse and the monument maker stepped out, stopping the carriage, coming to the wheel.

"Just one moment, please. I'm sorry to bother you, but Mr. Stuart, I need some information for the stone. Can you tell me when and where he was born, and what inscription Mrs. Randolph will want?"

Davie hesitated, unwilling to say how little any of them knew about the man who had called himself Mitchell Randolph.

He looked back at the crowded cemetery, the rows of markers that climbed in even tiers up the hillside. This, it occurred to him, was a holdover, the last remnant of ancestor worship that had come down from earliest man. Mitchell had cut himself off from the past, done so determinedly. He had hoped to begin a new dynasty, free of the shackles and fears of the generations behind. What should be carved on his stone? He looked to Aurelia, but she shook her head, leaving it to him.

His first inclination was to say, "Just put The Man on the Mule." That was what Mitchell had been to thousands of men in the isolated foothills who had depended on him. That had been his contribution to the state. But it would mean nothing now. Those miners were scattered to the corners of the world. Few of them would ever visit this place, let alone see the stone.

Then his mind settled on what the inscription had to be and he said:

"Make it read, Major Mitchell Randolph, Californian, died November twelfth, eighteen sixty-nine."

The man looked at Aurelia, disapproving. Aurelia, facing ahead, did not see.

She said quietly, "Davie, let's go home."

Davie knew she was not speaking of the house in town. He leaned forward and told the driver to take the road south, down the peninsula, to the ranch.

Todhunter Ballard was born in Cleveland, Ohio. He graduated with a bachelor's degree from Wilmington College in Ohio, having majored in mechanical engineering. His early years were spent working as an engineer before he began writing fiction for the magazine market. As W.T. Ballard, he was one of the regular contributors to *Black Mask Magazine*, along with Dashiell Hammett and Erle Stanley Gardner. Although Ballard published his first Western story in *Cowboy Stories* in 1936, the same year he married Phoebe Dwiggins, it wasn't until *Two-Edged Vengeance* (1951) that he produced his first Western novel. Ballard later claimed that Phoebe, following their marriage, had cowritten most of his fiction with him and perhaps this explains, in part, his memorable female characters. Ballard's golden age as a Western author came in the 1950s and extended to the early 1970s. *Incident At Sun Mountain* (1952), *West Of Quarantine* (1953), and *High Iron* (1953) are among his finest early historical titles. After numerous traditional Westerns for various publishers, Ballard returned to the historical novel in *Gold In California!* (1965), which earned him a Golden Spur Award from the Western Writers of America. This story is set during the Gold Rush era of the 'Forty-Niners. However, an even more panoramic view of that same era is to be found in Ballard's magnum opus, *The Californian* (1971), which contrasts the *Californios* and the emigrant goldseekers while detailing the building of a freight line to compete with Wells Fargo. In his historical fiction, Ballard combined his background in engineering with exhaustive historical research. These novels are character driven, gripping a reader from first page to last with their inherent drama and the spirit of adventure so true of those times.

THE UNTAMED BREED — GORDON D. SHIRREFFS

**"Bristling with action...well done...exciting!
—Chicago *Tribune***

**AT THE DAWNING OF AMERICA'S GREAT
WESTWARD EXPANSION, ONE MAN STANDS
ABOVE ALL OTHERS IN THE RACE TO CONQUER
THE LAND—AND ONLY ONE WOMAN CAN EVER
HOPE TO CONQUER HIS HEART.**

The fearless trapper links his fate to the destiny of his
young country and to the three women who desire him.
Drawn to his arms, possessed by him even as they yearn to
possess him, they share their lives with the man called Quint
Kershaw.

In a land both breathtaking and brutal, a man's best hopes
for survival are slim, his chance at happiness nil. But Quint
Kershaw dares to challenge the untamed West, to claim any
woman he wants, and to carve out an enduring legacy that
will last forever.

_3696-7 $4.50 US/$5.50 CAN

BOLD LEGEND

"Written by the hand of a master!" —*New York Times*

GORDON D. SHIRREFFS

Bestselling Author Of *The Untamed Breed*

THE UNFORGETTABLE SAGA OF A MAN AS STRONG AS THE WILD FRONTIER—AND THE WOMAN WHO CLAIMS HIS HEART.

Master of two vast estates and one of the most important men in the territory, Quint Kershaw is a tough frontiersman at heart. When the U.S. Army invades New Mexico, Kershaw is the man they hire to assist them—despite his wife's protests.

Fiercely loyal to her Spanish ancestry, Lupita goes to any lengths to protect her land. First she denies her husband her body, then her love. When all else fails, she prepares to wage a battle that could destroy her home, her marriage, her very life.

Torn between the woman he desires and the nation he helped build, Quint has to make a choice that will forever change both their lives: He will fight for his country—and also to recapture his fiery beauty of a wife.

__3726-2 $4.50 US/$5.50 CAN

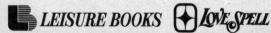